{CONTINUED PRAISE}

"Irreverent, outrageous, and fearless in his choice of material, Patrick Wensink has a true knack for absurdity."
— **JOEY GOEBEL**, author of *Torture the Artist*

"In his collection of stories *Sex Dungeon For Sale!*, Patrick Wensink demonstrates a gift for darkly absurdist humor that (just guessing here) surely derives from watching either too much or not enough television."
— **JAMES GREER**, author of *The Failure*

"Absurd, surreal, and funny."
— **LANCE CARBUNCLE**, author of *SMASHED, SQUASHED, SPLATTERED, CHEWED, CHUNKED AND SPEWED*

"Wensink has a sharp wit on display."
— **JORDAN KRALL**, author of *Tentacle Death Trip*

Broken Piano For President

Patrick Wensink

40% ALC. BY VOL. (A NOVEL)

A LAZY FASCIST ORIGINAL

LAZY FASCIST PRESS
AN IMPRINT OF ERASERHEAD PRESS
205 NE BRYANT STREET
PORTLAND, OR 97211

WWW.LAZYFASCISTPRESS.COM

ISBN: 978-1-62105-020-9

Printed in the USA.

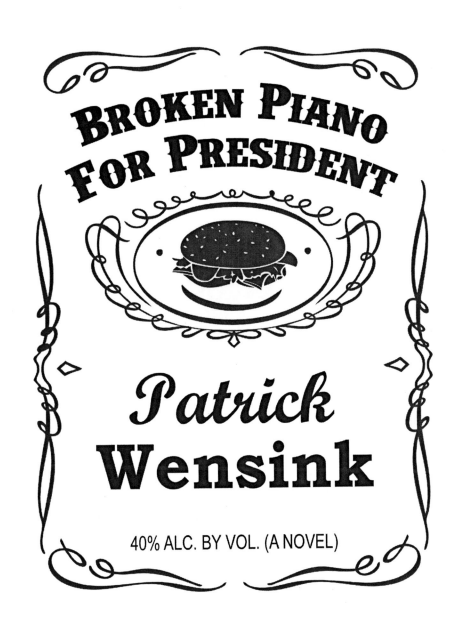

BROKEN PIANO FOR PRESIDENT

Patrick Wensink

40% ALC. BY VOL. (A NOVEL)

LAZY FASCIST PRESS
Portland, Oregon

Champagne for my real friends.
Real pain for my sham friends.
–Tom Waits

ONE

Hi, welcome to *Broken Piano for President*. Turn down the lights and fix yourself a stiff drink. Better yet, pour a couple cocktails and fix yourself a hangover.

Don't worry. Everything will be here when you wake up. Besides, our hero is sleeping off a bender of his own. Frankly, you'd be doing him a favor. He could use a few more hours of shuteye.

TWO

Boy, that was a doozey. How are you feeling this morning? There are some eggs on the stove. That always helps to get rid of a nasty headache.

Thanks, by the way.

Your dedication is appreciated. It's not every reader who bonds with a story by sharing the old, early morning flu. But now that you've put a few drinks in the tank and scratched another notch into the Hall of Fame, you'll have a deeper appreciation for what Deshler Dean is going through.

What? You don't have a Hall of Fame?

You really should. It keeps things in perspective. Drinking without curating a Hall of Fame is like raising kids without taking pictures.

Deshler doesn't have any kids, if you're curious, but you better believe he has a Hall of Fame. Hustle up and tack this morning down in your new Hall, because somebody special is waking.

THREE

Good morning, Hell, Deshler Dean thinks after waking.

Hangovers are nothing new for our iron-livered friend, but that doesn't mean they're not annoying. Hangovers are some black hair floating in life's martini. Worse yet, Dean would still be sleeping if not for this headache—a jagged rotation of skull-crushing bee stings and waves of calm.

Pain and peace.

Aches and angels.

The whole routine is so familiar. Familiar, except for this back seat.

Outside the car, birds start talking, morning sunshine grows full and windshield frost melts by the minute. That thin sheet of ice gets watery at the edges, white crystals evolving to something invisible.

Inside, he lifts from a leg-curled knot, yawns, rubs at stubble and glimpses around. The upholstery is white leather and smooth. The dash is wood-grained like antique tables. A golden hamburger swings from a thin chain around the rearview and captures Dean's attention. The perfectly carved medallion seems heavy, freckled by solid gold sesame seeds. It locks his eyes for a few moments. He's seen this thing before, but it's still so foreign.

The morning takes further shape like so many before it: with *Broken Piano for President* scratching around the tape deck in his head.

Dry lips mouthing the words to his favorite song, Dean is

maybe even a little proud for not sleeping outside again after such a boozy night. *This isn't Hell*, he thinks, frisking his zipper. *For one, I wouldn't have dry pants in Hell.* He smiles until both temples summon a lightning bolt of agony.

Even with heartburn sending lava up his chest, Dean's anxious to tell friends about this caper.

Waking up in an expensive car. Wow. This could be—he pauses until the swelling skull softens—*Hall of Fame material.* This hangover morning is fast turning fine and rosy, filling with comforting plans for bacon, eggs and coffee.

Pints of coffee. With a sprinkle of sugar. No cream. A hot gulp so bitter it'll shock away any headache for miles. Coffee sounds like magic as he admires his breath forming in the frigid air.

Dangling, that hamburger blinks golden Morse code. It's all so familiar. Maybe.

Concerns of automobile jewelry and familiarity flash away when Deshler makes a serious mistake. Dean commits an error that might just punch a one-way ticket to federal prison. It's a gaffe he doesn't even know he's committed until it's over: Deshler Dean simply looks at the front passenger seat.

There, he sees it.

Or her.

Dean's not sure how to classify this.

He rubs both eyes like a mirage, but this isn't the desert. First off, it's bone-breaking cold. Secondly, there's just no escaping this disaster in the car's white leather bucket seat. Period.

Good morning, Hell.

Dean coughs once.

He coughs louder.

He rips a long, fake cough. A bronchitis bark. Nothing moves but the burger around the mirror.

His throat drops to its normal Paul Bunyan growl, "Hello? Are-are you okay? Miss?" A hesitant hand shakes her shoulder with less-than-lifelike results. "Oh, shit."

That settles things. He is not alone. Or, technically, he is. Do dead women count?

Broken Piano crashes back through Dean's mind. The tune helps him focus and can't be unstuck. The drums are roadside bombs and the guitar squeals like 747 tires touching down. Most people say it's the worst song ever written.

Dean takes that as a compliment.

Sunshine warms a hole in the iced windshield. It highlights Dean's hands—fisted tight this whole time. His fingers sting and he is positive this morning isn't Hall of Fame worthy.

DESHLER DEAN'S HANGOVER HALL OF FAME

- **One year ago:** *Dunkin' Donuts.*

Normally, this wouldn't have been a problem. However, he woke up to a stunned morning manager kicking his feet. In a fit of drunken grace, apparently, Deshler broke into the locked shop without tripping an alarm and passed out on some sacks of flour. He escaped handcuffs by a cruller-width.

- **Four years ago:** *Marketing Theory 402.*

Deshler had no idea why he was standing in front of the class, but realized everyone was staring. His panic kicked in when Professor Adlaf spoke up, "That was an excellent presentation, Mister Dean, truly original. But now I'd like to ask you a few questions about Guerrilla Marketing if I may."

- **Two months ago:** *Mid-Fellatio.*

Quick tip: If you come to consciousness with a short

brunette between your legs, nothing kills the mood quicker than: "Have we met?"

Dean again glances at his problem. The corpse's blonde hair is a deep red stain, brown in the center. Her posture is stiff, wearing a thin black top. She's young and would be cute, if not for the whole dead-thing.

There is a stun in Dean's thinking, in his heartbeat, in his memory. *Focus,* he tells himself, but those old gag reflexes kick in. *Focus.* Whenever something serious happens, his brain changes channels—it thinks only of the band. *Focus.* Dean remembers the high school nurse saying something about needing Ritalin. He finally admits she might have been on to something.

Buying a minute or two to sort things out, edgy fingers snatch cheap cigarettes from a jacket pocket. "Easy, easy," Dean whispers, eyeing the blood-soaked girl. This stranger's car gets more uncomfortable each passing moment. "Retrace your steps, there's always a logical explanation," his voice turns spiky with panic, lighting the smoke. "For, you know, stabbing someone."

Our hero is a sliver of gristle and a mushroom cloud of hair. Exhaling smoke, Dean—ever the hungover mathematician—is fifty percent sure he didn't kill this woman.

But still, his skin develops a shiver and his jaw clutches like those fists. Without any notice, the most important thing in his life, the band, feels distant and hazy—a trick door in a dream.

"Okay, lady," he says, calm, like they chat on the phone every night. Or did, until her heart turned to meat. "I went to the bar with my bandmates, had a *few* beers…"

Thursday is Man's Night and Pabst Blue Ribbon is a dollar,

which is always a dangerous start. That's how arms grow mystery bruises. That's how wallets come up missing. Dollar beers are how people wake up next to dead girls.

The car's hood is red and laced with thin ice. Dean's flesh seems to be laced with the same frost. He whispers, head shaking, smoke trailing, "…and now, *this*."

This happens a lot when Deshler drinks. Not so much ending up next to dead people, but waking somewhere he never intended. Friends call Dean the Cliff Drinker. Meaning, when our hero goes out and has more than two, he falls off a boozy edge and forgets everything. Whole evenings are redacted from memory like confidential documents. Doesn't matter if it's white wine, whiskey or hefeweizen—Dean's recollections usually end up in the same state of disrepair. He cannot remember a time when he wasn't a Cliff Drinker. Shocking, right? Not since before he and his brother snuck a flask into a rock concert the night Dad went away in an ambulance.

Dreams of dark coffee completely dead now, Dean's parched mouth is flavored like nine-volt batteries. Smacking gritty gums and looking out the window, this part of town doesn't look like somewhere he'd normally hang out—the buildings are clean and new, there are sidewalks and all the stoplights work. The car is in a parking lot and hangs among the smell of wet grass and fryer grease.

Dean's teeth attack his fingernails. The gnawing begins, begging for a little clarity. There is an urge to push all this worry away, there's an urge for another dollar beer.

From that window, the backside of a giant blue and yellow dome looks familiar. It's impossible to miss Bust-A-Gut Hamburgers' blister-shape, even from its rear parking lot, even from the back seat of a strange car, even with a dead body blocking your view.

Dean knows he needs to move fast. It's only a matter of

time, he realizes, until some teen fry cook discovers this mess. Prison doors slam in his mind. Guards throw away keys and issue buckets for toilets. Denim uniforms and forced haircuts. The possibility of thick concrete walls separating him and the band races a spark across his brain.

The woman's butcher shop scalp reminds Dean of standing in front of an audience with the band's sound whipping through him. Some nights, pushing the group further, he imagines he's singing so hard—*making the crowd listen so hard*—his head bursts into a cherry pie mess like this. That sensation doesn't happen often, but when it does, it smolders like sex.

The bloody head does not smolder any sensations but panic in Dean.

Witnesses, he thinks, *there are no witnesses. It's the perfect crime…or non-crime, whatever.* Double checking for wandering eyes, his nose jams into the cold glass. He breathes smooth. The coast is clear. "I didn't do anything." He rubs throbbing eyes again and massages numb hands. "I'm not capable of this." With pressure easing off his skull, he says, "Okay, I don't know who did that to you, but I'm sorry. It's time to go. There's band practice tonight."

Deshler loves Lothario Speedwagon.

When not passing out in strange places, that band dominates the Cliff Drinker's attention. Dean knows he'll die if he doesn't hear Henry thump out the first notes of *Broken Piano* one more time. The Cliff Drinker's body will rust and rot if Pandemic's drums don't shatter vibrations up his spine.

Lothario Speedwagon is the lone good thing in life. Pretty much every day since childhood Dean would have gladly traded places with a gored stranger. But then he formed a band and started singing. He wrote lyrics. He did unmentionable things on stage. Dean refuses to lose that.

Shifting against the cold, stiff seats—inching toward the door and a continued, sweet life as a singer—something sharp jabs his ass. An icicle breath holds, slipping a hand into a back pocket, digging out a mangled screwdriver. The tool's been jammed and gouged until the fine silver point is a stump.

He inspects the shiny screwdriver. "A blunt object," newscasters and reporters could call it. He nearly forgot the scrambled pile of bloody hair riding shotgun and adds the two together.

I couldn't have, he thinks, picturing the amount of force necessary to stab someone. He can barely do a pushup. *Impossible.*

Our hungover mathematician is now about eighteen percent sure he didn't kill the blonde woman, which makes the gravel kick up that much harder when he pops open the door and sprints off.

Run, he thinks.

Do not stop.

Jaywalk if you have to.

Unused leg muscles cringe and catch fire. His cheeks and nose go numb cold. His eyes dry from the air. Dean's freedom sprint only gets halfway across the lot before he remembers the *blunt object* tattooed with prints and DNA. It's still in the back seat.

He turns and slowly, casually, wanders back to the bright red car housing a bright red girl up front.

Move-move-move. Witnesses will not think this is cool.

Witnesses will not listen to reasonable explanations.

Witnesses will call police.

At the car, that cigarette drops to the ground. Dean's eyes bloom wide, staring at the passenger seat. His aching brain has been working hard to catch up all morning, but now needs no explaining.

Good morning, Hell.

"Ow, my head," a voice from the gutter of a woman's throat says. Bold green eyes flip on and off. "I better not be late for work, Deshler."

He recalculates his percentages.

FOUR

Deshler's bass player and roommate, Henry Hamler, wishes America's most famous man was already dead.

Henry wishes this sour stomach would disappear.

More importantly, he wishes he could figure out where the candy is stashed.

An hour ago, Henry and his partner rolled up to Christopher Winters' estate: an enormous green and gray eyesore. Hanna-Barbera's idea of a Victorian mansion. The pair flashed credentials to a guard, walked into the home and set up shop.

Christopher Winters' biography bulges with success in politics, food service and even a dabble of oral hygiene. One financial magazine called him: "Ben Franklin arm wrestling Colonel Sanders with four-out-of-five dentists cheering them on."

Henry scratched nervous trails across his arms in preparation for this first face-to-face.

Now the young man stuffs a hand into suit pockets while wandering the halls, pretending to admire artwork painted before Ben Franklin flew his first kite. Henry rubs a thick beard and sighs. This dress shirt fits like spandex and these old slacks squeeze his junk. Henry pecks at M&Ms to hold off the shakes, but doesn't realize he's doing it until those sausage fingers scrape his lips. Shards of sugar coating stick to that mousy brown beard.

Winters' massive oak den reminds Henry of ornate cathedrals with its tall ceiling and odd stained glass shadows.

Books and dark wood wrap around the room. Across from a desk, Tony, the cameraman and producer for this mission, untangles the sound equipment. His scalp shines through thin hair. Those clothes are a decade out of style.

Watching Tony work, realizing there's no turning back, Henry's lungs mimic rusty mufflers. Tony, always a professional, ignores the noise pollution. A tall grandfather clock swings deep and its ticks reverberate among the rafters. Soft relaxation hums when a sweet smell reminds Henry of Grandpa Hamler: pipe smoke.

The clock clangs ten and Winters strolls into the office on cue, slipping a pipe into a pocket. Henry and Tony don't need introductions. You don't grow up in this country without knowing three faces by heart: George Washington, Babe Ruth, and Christopher Winters.

Winters is flimsy now, not the robust governor Hamler remembers. The man's skin is stained with liver spots and his entire body gives the impression it was scotch-taped together. That trademark red suit is as faded as grandma's drapes. In its prime, the three-piece was stunning like crushed tomatoes. For decades, Winters hasn't been seen in public without it.

Winters looks so small in this huge room. Henry thinks. *So helpless.*

The old man rattles around hollow and drags his body behind a desk, settling into a soft chair.

"Mister Winters, it's a pleasure to meet you," Henry says, jellybean cheeks glowing. The inexperienced interviewer tenses his stomach and smoothes coarse hair. Styling gel makes everything itchy.

"Hello, hello, good morning, hello," the wrinkled star says. Voice-over men make careers mimicking that folksy growl. "My, you're a big one."

"Sir?" Henry's confidence curls into a ball, sucks its thumb.

"Nothing. Nothing."

Tony dusts a little makeup on the millionaire's face before being swatted off. Henry scans the long mahogany hallway for witnesses and locks the door—the three are alone.

Fingers knot up and flex, knot up and flex. *If my life were a tasty Winters Hamburger,* Henry quizzes himself.

Hamler doesn't want this job. If we're being honest, he's scared to do this job. But before this opportunity fell into his lap, doing important company work was all he ever dreamed about.

"Enough of this bologna, son, let's get down to the ground beef. What makes you think…" Winters says as Tony clips a tiny microphone to the washed-out red lapel. The old man's signature mustard yellow dress shirt is wrinkled and the matching tie knotted crudely like a shoelace. "There needs to be *another* documentary made about me?" The old man lifts a half-empty bottle of bourbon from under the desk.

If my life were a tasty Winters Hamburger.

Dressed in the only suit he owns, Henry gulps just off camera. "Well sir, you're the most important American in the last…" Henry fiddles with a cufflink he's never worn and his beer keg stomach goes violent.

"Goodyear," the old man's throat chugs. "Ask yourself, if your life was a tasty Winters Hamburger, would you be the bun or the beef?"

"*Goodyear?*"

"It's a blimp. Maybe an uncle of yours." Winters takes a long sip, tired eyes locked on Henry's midsection. "Now, if your life was a hamburger…"

Hamler sputters: "That's a good question." He's always felt more like a bun. More like the bland foundation and less of the main attraction. Nothing like the guy people count on in these situations.

Henry scolds: *Get the guts to do a good job.*

"Hello? Hello? Earth-to-interviewer." Winters speaks up: "Son, I'm going to be dead soon. Wouldn't you feel bad…" His gummy throat clears. "If you wasted the last precious seconds of my life on something redundant?"

"I would never do that." Hamler tells himself this is a mistake. *Once a bun, always a bun.* He considers running down the hall, out the door and straight onto a beef patty.

Henry shuffles note cards for the right question, but it's all an act. A heat finds his chest and shoulders. *Forget it,* he thinks. *You need this job, you are locked in. You aren't going anywhere. Just ignore how ugly this is going to get.*

Tony fiddles with the camera. "Okay," he says. "We're ready to roll in five, four, three, two…"

Henry really doesn't have to ask any questions. The old man has done thousands of these interviews and yawns through his life story.

THE LIFE STORY OF A BURGER BARON

• Winters nearly captured Hitler in the final days of World War Two.

• His patriotic celebrity parlayed into a small fortune after inventing the electric toothbrush.

• He loved to barbecue for his friends and used that financial freedom to open a chain of hamburger stands.

Winters peppers his speech with slogans like, "A burger a day keeps the Nazis away," and constantly refers to something called *the Axis of Edible.*

In America, it's impossible to visit an airport, mall or interstate exit without a gray Victorian mansion outlined in green neon staring down your stomach. It's the unmistakable sign you've stumbled onto a Winters Olde-Tyme Hamburgers. Each restaurant is modeled after the founder's home, but with slightly more neon.

"Which," Winters says, running tongue over pale lips. "Led to my interest in politics. And as you probably know…" The man's deflated sigh fills the room.

"Please continue, sir," Henry does his best journalist imitation, sensing boredom. His legs fidget as blood tingles for more sugar.

"I was the governor." Winters waves a lazy hand, lets out a mile-long breath and stares dull into Henry's face. Babies are born, have families and die in that uncomfortable silence. It reminds Henry of when the band finishes playing a song—the audience never claps or cheers. Without fail, that familiar deep, dumb silence fills the room. It fills Henry, too. "And then I wasn't the governor."

This has to work out, Henry thinks as the old man slugs bourbon. The honey liquid glimmers against the morning sun. Through the enormous picture window, sculpted shrubbery waves on the lawn. *This is my last chance. I'm fired if I don't go through with this. God, I'm an unlucky bastard.*

"A few years ago, I retired and my son, Roland, took charge of the restaurants. He's a good boy and I love what he's done with the company. I'm told he's really given my Victorian mansions a modern image." Winters unloads a verbatim press release but stops after he empties the whiskey glass. "We're taking a break. I remember more as I run through things."

Winters takes actual minutes to stand, forcing the camera crew to look away and fidget. Eventually, he wanders off.

During the downtime Tony assures Hamler things are

going well, but he needs to start swinging for the fences. Henry needs to ask the question they came to ask. The same question that makes Henry's insides moldy with disgust.

"It's time to rise to the occasion, you know?" Tony says, giving his reporter a confident shoulder punch. The cameraman's voice echoes in the canyon of Winters' oak office.

Henry breathes deep and wraps two arms around his ballooning body. The last time Hamler felt this uncomfortable, a crowded rock club threw full beer cans at Lothario Speedwagon. *That wasn't all so bad*, he smirks. *Someone also hit me with a Baby Ruth.*

Winters returns slow and achy. His creased head wobbles from ear to ear. For the first time Henry realizes the American legend is a little drunk.

"My life," the burger baron grumbles, shaking the lone ice cube in the glass, *pling-pling-pling*. "Has been a complete and utter lie."

The old man looks pissed. His liver spots grow dark red and brown.

Scared to move this interview forward, Henry stammers. Hamler seriously doubts anyone will save the day and throw a Baby Ruth at his head this time.

Winters' voice stumbles. "Honestly, it starts before I was a toothbrush-whatever-you-call-it," he says, breath rushing through his nose like a bubbling teapot. The old man's voice is now wonderfully vibrant. "I *did* nearly capture Hitler. I was able to arrest many of his staff, people not mentioned in history books. Good God, I did things that made concentration camps look like summer camps. And," he says, looking daydreamy, "instead of being court-martialed, as I should have been, the Army tells me they appreciate my service. And they would like to help my bank account."

"My, that's quite a story." Henry keeps it skeptical, remembering his training. "Can you prove any of this?" Hamler tugs on that cufflink. He twists it. He runs fingers over every groove and dimple. It's silver with a black pearl inlay and on loan.

"Quite." Winters snuffs. "My men all took photos. There are documents, though I assume they are still classified."

The interviewer gathers a breath and wipes his forehead with a sleeve.

The old man's eyes shrink to oil stains. "I wish that was all," he says, vigor fading fast. That once-famous face soaks with tears.

Henry slowly digs a finger into his jacket pocket and pulls out the last M&M. He lets the sugar melt under his tongue until Winters' drunken vowels ooze and his voice-over purr crashes into a blubber. Winters claims the government reward for his World War Two service was a patent for the electric toothbrush.

"I was also given the recipe for the Winters Burger after a certain politician took a bullet in the sixties. I hired the gunman. I trained him myself. I didn't pull the trigger." He stops for nearly a minute to let bourbon touch those shaky lips. "But I may as well have. The CIA was very grateful. Don't make that face, that's how they pay under the table. Listen, son, the American people need to know. I'm a horrible person and they must learn." Winters' face begs for attention.

"Why are you telling us?" Henry asks.

"So it won't die with me. Everyone else who knows is gone now."

Winters claims his world famous hamburger concoction is little more than Grade-F beef and nicotine. A secret, Henry realizes, that will destroy Winters Olde-Tyme Hamburgers. Christopher Winters is no longer a harmless grandfather.

"I'm just an old man with a guilty conscience." His hands shake, jiggling a few ounces of bourbon into a glass.

"Uhm, we have to be on our way soon." Henry knows his moment to transition from bun to beef has arrived. His chest aches with the decision. "Is there anything else we should know, sir?"

"You don't believe me do you, Orca? Here I am, handing God's largest mammal history on a platter. I'm giving him a Pulitzer like I was *given* the governorship. And, instead, he just wags his tongue, hoping for another bucket of fish."

"Are...are you getting all this, Tony?" Hamler nervously chatters, hands moving wild.

Tony nods.

"Afraid of that." Henry drags his feet to the enormous window behind Mister Winters. The interviewer rests a palm on the cold glass. Lonely manicured shrubs are the only thing moving. Nobody is on the estate grounds to see what comes next.

"You don't care." Winters' lips are sloppy with whiskey. "Nobody listens to old men anymore."

Henry stands behind the aging governor. The nervous journalist tugs out a silver cufflink and reads Tony's eyes. The cufflink is the signal to end the interview. "You'd be surprised, Mister Winters," Henry says, fiddling with its black pearl as his guts drop down a roller coaster. "Your son, Roland, listens to everyone."

Standing over the corporate icon, Henry watches the old man's smooth scalp wrinkle in a shock of recognition. "Roland sent you?"

Hamler's round stomach brushes against Winters' spine. The skin under Henry's beard scorches, arm folds wobble.

He freezes.

"Oh dear," whispers the most famous man in America.

Tony takes a few steps toward them with a father's disappointed eyes. "Cut, cut. Just a second, sir, let me adjust the...lights."

With shaking fingers, Henry slips off the cufflink's casing, revealing a tiny syringe. "Wait, no, I've got it," Henry says, groaning deep and sad before slamming a needle into Winters' neck.

FIVE

Dean watches the green-eyed blonde dab her forehead and squint. His breath unravels through the cold air. He's holding the screwdriver, but doesn't remember fetching it.

In the shadow of Bust-A-Gut's dome, nearby traffic evaporates into silence. Luckily, it's early and the restaurant parking lot is still empty. Sun lifts above the blue and yellow hump, barely warming Dean's cheeks. He and the bloody woman are alone as she clicks open the door, never lifting her eyes off that whittled-down Phillips head.

The hangover king is having a tough time deciding whether his troubles are over or just getting started. He realizes it doesn't matter much—they both suck.

Dean's heart rate kicks gunpowder fast watching this ghost. Just a minute ago, she was dead. He is certain. His tongue gropes for just the right words to say: "I'm ninety-nine percent sure I didn't kill you." But they don't arrive, watching her rise on wobbly black heels.

This woman is tall. She could easily rest her chin on Deshler's skull if they were slow-dancing. But instead of the waltz, she leans against the car's frame, holding fingers to the deep wound. The pieces of blonde hair not globbed together with blood erupt off her head in fireworks. Her expensive clothes are bunched awkward. A floaty black top nudges the curves around shoulders. A black skirt ratchets tight to her hips. But all in a wrecked imitation of how everything probably looked the night before.

As usual, in times of panic, Dean's mind drifts toward music. This gory scene again reminds him of that long ago concert with his brother and a flask of schnapps. *Blood can be art*, he thinks, trying to settle down. *Guts and bile and violence can be art. What if this whole mess was a performance piece?*

Remember Gibby?

The night they took Deshler's father away, after Mom cried herself to sleep, Dean and his brother snuck out. They arrived just in time to hear the Butthole Surfers crush through a handful of heavy, druggy tunes with dangerous amounts of feedback. Dizzying layers of echo.

The concert was a punch in the face. A bloody nose of volcanic proportions. Everyone in the room *had* to listen. There was no choice. Nowhere to hide. Teenage Dean quickly realized that music was the only way anyone would listen to guys like him and Gibby.

The Butthole Surfers' lead singer, Gibby Haynes, stole the show. The image is still barbecued into Dean's memory: the lanky frontman crawling around the stage, half-naked, smearing fake blood across his body and face while the band pounded out an acid-soaked psychedelic mess. Strobe lights force-fed seizures. A cheap smoke machine burped white until the band was draped in fog.

Dean, like the rest of the crowd, couldn't stop watching. His heart jumped when Haynes pulled the microphone to his lips. The man was all stringy black hair and wide, serial killer eyes. Young Deshler listened to every twisted gurgle of words, hypnotized. Haynes spat fire and flung gooey red corn syrup all over the audience.

That blood.

After the show, Dean couldn't stop thinking about the red ooze. He couldn't stop thinking how a thousand people stood lobotomized, listening the way Dad never did. He couldn't stop thinking about the power a stage demands.

Later that night, when the flask was nothing but tin and fumes, Dean's older brother explained, between hiccups, that the concert was about expression. It all had meaning. It's all art.

Dean has been chasing that vision of art ever since. Looking to smear blood and breathe fire until they listen. The rumble it makes in his guts is enough to put up with parking all those cars, dealing with unenthusiastic bandmates, and the booing. God, all those boos. All that booze. It's enough to make a man optimistic after potentially stabbing a stranger.

The woman inspects her sticky red hand and flashes it to Deshler in disbelief. Blood streaks down the wrist as her eyes squeeze tight. "You know the odds of someone murdering you are something like three hundred twenty five-to-one."

"I think you have the wrong idea." Performance art fantasies blow into hazy smoke rings.

Less than a block away, morning traffic thickens with honks and raging stereo sounds. A naturally confused look plants itself on Deshler's face—mouth hanging down.

One of her green eyes pops open—a marble in the light. "But your odds of suicide are more like a hundred twenty one-to-one." Her lips and cheeks offer a vague outline of makeup. A face that took an hour to put on, flooded by a thin layer of mummified blood.

"I'm sorry, what?"

"Basically, we're a way bigger danger to ourselves than others are."

"I...I don't think I did." He points to the bloody hair tangle and his belly shrinks. "*That.*" Dean cringes, waiting for her scream.

That waiting kills.

She giggles and sighs. "I think I'm still a little drunk, Dean." Smiling wide, the girl shifts her weight forward and trips. She digs a bare knee into naked soil. "Owee," she laughs, "gimme the keys, please."

"I don't have any—" Deshler quickly checks pockets and stops, waiting for more words to come. "Keys."

"Shut up. Seriously, I don't feel very good. I think I hit my head on something." She stretches and yawns until cavity fillings shine amongst the blooming light. The woman steps close and gives Dean a faint, flirty look. Dean's muscles loosen. Fears of prison now completely vanished.

In the time it takes to stab a pretty girl in the head, this turns into one of the Cliff Drinker's finer hangover mornings.

DEAN'S NON-HALL OF FAME
HANGOVER MORNINGS

- **Dozens of Times** *Waking up in his own bed, alone.*

It happens much less than he'd like, but Deshler pushes out a boozy breath of relief when he sees the Listerine yellow walls of his apartment. He's never done the math, but its likelihood is somewhere around thirty-five percent.

- **Eleven Months Ago** *His Roommate Henry's Trunk.*

Neither he nor Henry knows how Deshler ended up in the locked trunk. However, Dean considers it a success, since after kicking the metal shell for twenty minutes to grab Henry's attention, Deshler found thirty dollars in his pocket that wasn't there before.

- **Countless Times** Any booth, barstool or bathroom floor, as long as it's attached to the bar he started drinking in.

"I don't want to be rude," Deshler says, slipping the screwdriver into his jacket pocket. "But we've never met before, have we?" He instantly regrets not playing cool, coaxing more faint, flirty looks.

"Jesus, you don't think *I*," she stabs a finger into her chest. "Know who you are?" The woman squints and shakes in disbelief.

What would Gibby do? he thinks and notices for the first time his cheeks are numb.

"Listen, nothing personal," one lonely step toward her. "Ehrm, I just don't remember a lot about last night. I had a little too much to drink."

"Think so, huh?" Her eyes roll, watching a dark bird swoop overhead.

Dean concentrates so hard on remembering this woman's face his vision whites out.

Nothing.

The only time Deshler's ever embarrassed is when someone recognizes him and he has no clue who they are. The Cliff Drinking style has almost no RECORD button. Rarely more than a sliver is ever recalled about the hours spent between sucking down cocktails and waking up with *Broken Piano for President* thumping between a headache. According to friends, he is incredibly productive in the Cliff Drinking state. During the last year alone, ten known women were swayed enough to make out, some even further. None of whom Dean remembers. Other times, witnesses claim to have seen Deshler escorting elderly women across the street, competing in spelling bees, winning Monopoly and, once, adopting a three-legged puppy.

Some sweet perfume, like vanilla, manages to find Deshler's nose across the icy air. Her smooth shoulders grow studded with goose pimples. "Does the Beef Club ring any bells?" the woman says.

Hangover bells in Deshler's ears ring a thousand decibels loud. However, none are connected to a Beef Club.

"Dod gammit," she hisses and inspects her feet for a long, long moment. "I've gotta get to work soon. Do you want a ride downtown?"

"Yes, please, that would be fantastic," he says, hoping that's the right answer.

She is speaking into a red cell before he finishes. "Hey, it's me," she waits a few seconds. "Yep, okay. Well, can you send someone to pick me up?" She waits another few breaths and makes a dramatic hand sweep. "Yep...well I'm here with the one and only Deshler Dean. Okay, see you then."

SIX

The cosmonaut swallows hard. Lungs and guts float up his throat. Television only shows astronauts spinning in circles, chomping on floating candies and loose droplets of water up in space. Nobody mentions the zero-gravity phobia of having all those important organs vomited up.

A few hundred miles above Moscow, he curses in thick Russian chunks. It's one thing to let millionaire thrill-seekers tag along on missions, he thinks, but this is too much.

The cosmonaut has dedicated his life to space exploration and practically abandoned a family back on Earth. *I am a scientist*, he reminds himself, *not a short-order cook.*

Knowing he is out of options, the cosmonaut stops and listens to the breathing apparatus hum. It's calming. Moscow agreed to another get-rich-quick scheme, which he'll never see a ruble of. But there is no other choice.

Stepping out of the airlock and into the depressing blackness of outer space, the cosmonaut tows a plump thermal suit—an exact copy of his own. A shiver works up the Russian's body.

Ten minutes into the spacewalk, the cosmonaut releases the tether connecting him to the limp suit. It twists and contorts like a bronze medal gymnast. He stares directly into the protective face shield and curses while it swims into orbit. Through the shield he sees the suit is stacked full with freeze dried hamburgers.

He wishes the suit good riddance and floats back to the

station to repair a solar panel.

A Winters Olde-Tyme Hamburger logo is sewn onto the drifting suit's chest.

SEVEN

"Insult to freaking injury," the formerly dead woman says, a wet towel pressed against her forehead. Deshler watches watery blood splash across the cushions of a very expensive car. "The Monte Cristo Burger. That piece of crap is the last thing I want to see today. I've said it about a billion times, but seriously, can't we come up with something better than a deep-fried hamburger? Honestly, I don't see what all the fuss is about. Did you know there was an article in the *New York Times*?"

Thirty minutes earlier, the car picked Deshler and the woman up on the sidewalk in front of the Bust-A-Gut dome. The driver didn't say a word. Now only a few miles into their ride, rush hour cars kiss each other's bumpers along the freeway.

"The *New York* F-ing *Times*," she sighs. "See," a smile forms and it startles Dean. "I told you I'd stop swearing."

Dean and the woman sit in traffic, studying the billboard that has her so upset. It features a giant crispy lump the size of a refrigerator, sweating grease. It looks like a rumpled paper bag but claims to be a sandwich. There's a blue and yellow logo at the bottom for Bust-A-Gut Hamburgers. Above this fried fist, it reads: "TRUST YOUR GUT—Catch Monte Cristo Mania!"

"Um, yes, you're doing a great job," Deshler says, happy to be off the subject of bloody wounds. "What exactly are we looking at?"

Twisting her neck, focusing on the billboard, the woman

says, "Yeah, like you don't know." She shoots another smile that must have been hell in dental bills. "I have no clue what Findlay is thinking. Whatever the new hush-hush secret is, supposedly, it's *killer*. You know?"

The billboard reminds Dean of the last meal he and his brother enjoyed with their parents so many years ago, the last time he ate Bust-A-Gut. It was a Teriyaki Beef Jerky Burger—the one you were supposed to eat with chopsticks.

The antique idea of hamburgers in Japanese style fades. His soupy stomach splashes unabsorbed beer. His mouth is as hot and dry as the smell coming from the car's heat vents. Outside, the sun is higher. Exhaust pipes blow steam.

"Come again?" he says. He is dizzy and wishes this woman would have stayed unconscious. Running away from that car with a head full of prison anxieties would be a vacation right about now.

"Clifford *Findlay*...my boss," the woman turns and stares. "CEO of Bust-A-Gut, second largest burger joint in this country. Dean, this isn't funny."

Findlay...he thinks about work and anyone he might have met there named Mister Findlay. *Have I dented this guy's fenders?*

"Deshler," she coos. "You're starting to hurt my feelings. Maybe you hit your head, too. Have you considered that? Matching concussions."

Her sweet voice rumbles his heart to life. That red-hot collection of arteries attempts to mule-kick his ribs. Life, for Deshler Dean, has been one long attempt to push everyone away. But this girl is someone he'd like to reel in.

"This is the part where you say, *sorry, Malinta*."

Dean's face goes lost. "Weird name."

"Oh, please. I've explained this a million times." The glassy curve of her cheeks and chin tightens, drawing in a thousand wiry lines. Her eyes are sharp, business eyes.

A million? Deshler wonders if it's possible to meet anyone a million times. *Have I met Malinta a million times? Have we kissed? Have we had sex?*

He admires her thin legs and green eyes and realizes the answer is "probably not." That overworked heart thumps double-time. Even with the open wound, she's a thousand times prettier than any other woman who has woken up in his bed.

"My name's Melinda. *Malinta* is a nickname. My little brother couldn't pronounce it as a kid. Sound…" she counts to five and takes a breath, "familiar?"

Screws tighten inside Dean's brain. *If you want to get through this, you've got to pull it together. You've got to be resourceful.* Then the answer races down nerve endings like electricity. *You've got to start lying.*

"Oh!" blasts open the silence. "God, yes! Wow, I can't believe I said that. I'm so hungover. I'm sorry, jeez."

The tight muscles in Malinta's face soften and that faint, flirty smile returns. A few bricks of confidence stack within Dean's chest, realizing he might be onto something with this lying routine.

"I had way too much to drink last night," he says with sorry eyes. "Plus, I think I might have done some drugs." He's pretty sure he didn't, but whatever.

"Deshler, we were gonna score together," she says. "Were you holding out on me?"

"No, no, somebody just gave me some at the bar last night." He trips on the words. "Some coke, I think."

"You *think* you did coke last night. Well, that explains why we drove all over town looking for more." The early sun hits her blonde strands and glows translucent. "I think."

"Yep," he says, leatherlipped, realizing he's balancing on a line as thin as that imaginary cocaine rail. "Sure does."

Malinta rolls her eyes once more, but stops midway through, caressing the window with her cheek. "Now that's what I'm talking about. God, what a great campaign. What *genius*." This is a sultry voice Dean wants more of. "I was serious back when I said I should send them my resume."

A billboard for Winters Olde-Tyme Hamburgers features a floating spacesuit. "SPACE BURGER has Landed!" it says. Its moon is actually a beef patty.

Malinta whips the towel off the bloody gash and saddles a hand on Deshler's knee. The hair around her wound is pink from water. "Now *that* is a campaign. Monte Cristo is just slapping a band-aid on a broken arm. But Space Burgers, that's, that's…" Her lower lip gets clamped by white teeth and her eyes close. "That's legendary. I hope we can do something *legendary*."

The driver doesn't seem to notice any of this happening. He crosses the bridge into downtown, swerving through lanes. Trees are planted along the sidewalks, but they are young and weak. The city will probably cut them down when their roots grow too large. All around are squat brick buildings, but two glass and steel skyscrapers tower much higher than the rest.

Malinta slides her hand further up Dean's leg. A numb excitement blazes along his body. His eyes droop. "What," Deshler says, "is a *Space Burger*?"

"Very funny." Malinta yanks the hand back into her lap.

He's suddenly lonely. Empty.

Little speechless huffs and puffs slip out like she can't understand what she just heard. "You know," Malinta says, slowly, inspecting her towel's strawberry stain. "You have a greater chance of being killed by a falling coconut than a shark attack?"

He waits, about to tell the driver to just pull over. Running away sounds reasonable once again. "Okay."

"I've done some research. One hundred twenty people die each year from falling coconuts. Your odds of eating it are three hundred million-to-one. Those suckers drop like bowling balls."

Deshler pops knuckles. The limo pulls in front of a skyscraper with a huge blue and yellow awning: "Bust-A-Gut World Headquarters."

"But only about forty people a year are killed by sharks. Those are like, six hundred fifty million-to-one odds."

"Why do you research this?" He scoots away, intimidated by the focus in her eyes.

"Point is, I don't know what the odds of dying from having your head up your ass are," she says, flipping hair, trying to hide the wound. "But I think you'll show us all." She opens the door and eases out. "I have to work. Bye."

EIGHT

"Dude, don't forget we have practice tonight," Henry says as Deshler struggles through the door. A slice of cold wedges in behind him.

Dean looks down at his jeans, splattered red from Malinta's towel. He needs to change, fast. "I'm fine, really," Deshler rumbles. "Don't ask how I am or anything." The greeting reminds Dean how little respect his bandmates pay. Jerks.

"Dean, if I got worried every time you magically disappeared from a bar," Henry blows smoke through his nose, lying on the couch. "And wander back home at noon, I'd have an ulcer."

"Nothing says, '*I care*,' like an ulcer."

"Please," Henry laughs. Dean notices an ant hill of white dust on the coffee table. A snowdrift, really. "You're a big boy. Not much of one, but you are, technically, an adult."

Dean tiptoes around the room's few open gaps. Their apartment is so tight Deshler regularly gets leg cramps. Each room is so rotten with beer stains and old newspapers that Hamler's allergies fight constant wars. They've shared this place for over a year, but neither has bothered to decorate much beyond plugging in the television.

"Well, I care. See," Dean says, feet kicking away microwave dinner boxes. "I got you your favorite." He tosses a candy bar.

Inspecting the bright wrapper, Henry perks: "Awesome. You're not such an abortion after all." His voice lacks its usual enthusiasm for comparing Dean to terminated pregnancies. Henry's mind seems to be chewing on bigger things.

Dean knows he should ask what's up, but doesn't. Henry is one of maybe two people Dean hasn't pushed completely away. Friendly little moments like this only exist with his best friend. Dean knows he's lucky because of that, but would never admit to the fact.

"You're a real sweetheart. Why so dressed up?" Deshler yells from his bedroom. He digs through a clothes pile for his uniform. The bedroom isn't much larger than the living room. It's stacked to the knees with clothes and records and empties. Some days it's more like a birdcage with ashtrays.

Henry watches his belly stretch the dress shirt buttons, teeth ripping through chocolate and nougat. He notices a dribble of Christopher Winters on the breast pocket. Just a splash where syringe and neck became one. "Job interview," Henry mumbles, massaging stomach muscles that have been cramping since removing the cufflink from the old man's flesh.

"Didn't go well, huh?" Deshler says, walking out in wrinkled black pants and a red crested white blazer. Hair designed by Tornado Alley.

"Eh, who can tell?"

"You'll land one, don't sweat it. You're a smart guy. It'll happen."

"I don't know if I even want what I'm going after." Henry lights up another cigarette and dips a finger through the powder. He sticks it in his mouth, closes eyes and melts back into the couch with ecstasy.

"Dude," Deshler says, slipping on a tie.

"Drop it."

"Are you eating sugar?"

"Lay off. I just needed something sweet, you know?"

"Beyond that candy bar you just wolfed down?" Dean regrets saying that, judging by his roommate's eyes.

"Eat shit."

"Don't start snorting it or anything."

"It helps me relax." He frowns. "I need this stuff." Hamler rolls over. A ghost of cigarette smoke hovers above his body like Christopher Winters haunting him.

"Okay. So, practice tonight. Seven?" Dean wildly checks pockets for keys until he spots them on the coffee table.

"No, man, nine-thirty, same time we always rehearse," Hamler says, questioning Deshler's dedication to the band. "Don't miss it. Pandemic was pissed last time."

"Right, right, right, sorry, man. I'll be there. I gotta run to work." He twirls the keys through the air in a jangly cartwheel. "Apparently rich assholes still can't park their own cars. Take it easy."

"*Nine*-thirty. We've actually got a gig this week!"

The door slams and Henry listens to the cigarette burn away in the silence. His stomach is a bucket of snakes. He is always sick with guilt after a job. *Why do I get stuck with all the dirty work?*

These greasy heaves are different than the ones after breaking no-name executives' fingers and extorting trouble-making branch managers. There's a powerful urge to apologize.

Henry feels like Lee Harvey Oswald. He has destroyed an icon.

Leaving the estate in their fake news van, that kick of sickness worked up Hamler's chest. "Henry," Tony said, patting his protégé's shoulder. "You did an awesome job. You're getting so good at this. I think soon you'll be ready to go out on your own. We really trust you. You're the best junior agent Olde-Tyme Hamburgers has."

"Tony," Hamler's face faded into gray. "I don't know if this is for me. I feel like shit. Do you know who that guy is?"

"*Was*, do I know who he *was*. The answer is yes, of course I did. But today he was just another job, all that terrible horseshit he'd done before, you heard him. Concentration camps like summer camps. *Gross.* The boss is right, Christopher Winters was a loose cannon. He was a security threat."

"I can't think like that."

"You will."

Hamler loses focus when the neighbors start having sex. The thin apartment walls thump and crackle. It makes Henry's stomach flip completely over, calculating the months since he last slept with anyone. *I need to get out of here. Go buy some new strings.*

Slipping on shoes, he reconsiders. *God, our band is stupid. I don't want to practice tonight.*

The guilt from the Christopher Winters job embroiders his every thought. For a second, Henry considers jumping through the apartment window and breaking his neck. He dreams about taking off his other cufflink and stabbing himself. He thinks about going to the store for more candy.

He chooses candy.

NINE

Dean stands in front of a hotel forty hours a week.

The hotel is a tall cube of white brick. Carved beasties spout water from the rooftop during storms. When politicians or Hollywood stars swing through town, they stay here. Both hamburger companies treat foreign dignitaries in its mosaic of meeting halls. Dean parks all their cars.

"Come on, just answer the question. Which way would you want to die?" Dean says.

"Can you really die from a falling coconut?" Napoleon asks.

Standing straight on his little legs, Napoleon's a sawed-off shotgun in a white dinner jacket. A block of mushy flesh and tattoos hidden underneath. He's worked this shift several years longer than Dean. It was the first job he took after deciding high school was a dead end.

"Yeah, man. Those bastards are heavy, all that coconut milk. I heard they fall at something like two hundred miles an hour. That'd crush your skull, buddy." Dean rubs Napoleon's buzzcut.

A slim silver car pulls up. A woman in sunglasses floats past without looking either in the face. Napoleon jumps behind the driver's seat. He returns to the awning a few minutes later. "Well, I mean, I guess coconut."

"Really? I saw you as a shark man."

A black car worth several years of Deshler's salary rolls slow and gropes the curb.

"The shark would be drawn out and bloody…I'd be helpless. Way too much biting and chewing for me. Plus, salt water in an open wound…no thanks. I guess if a coconut killed me, it'd be over in a snap."

"I'm disappointed," Deshler says, straightening his jacket. "I'd give you a fighting chance against a shark."

"Thanks," he says with pep. Napoleon eyes their next customer. "Hey, man, you know that video camera I bought?"

The man in the car is a blob. He oozes out like the seat is waxed. He flips a few stray French fries from shirtfront to his mouth. A bulldozer chest fills out his ketchup-colored suit to the point of demolition. Each stitch is pulled rigid as a violin string. He looks like Christopher Winters twenty years ago, if Christopher Winters had swallowed a tugboat.

"Uh, no I don't…" Dean says, fading. His headache almost completely gone.

"It's cool, really cool, just picked it up a couple days ago. Some old Sony, it actually uses VHS tapes. *VHS tapes!* I'm getting pretty handy with it. There's some stuff you need to check out."

"Yeah, buddy, sure."

"Twenty bucks at the Goodwill. Shot some crazy footage last night. You should see it. You're the star of the show, if you know what I mean."

"*What?* Yeah right. Whatever."

Dean marvels at how the man's suit wraps his skin like a red ink stain. Extra chins waggle under a plump brown mustache. He stands tall and adjusts the mustard yellow tie around a mustard yellow shirt.

"Good afternoon, sir," Deshler growls, helping the thick man with the door. "Welcome to the—"

"Hey there, Mystery Boy." The man flashes a set of teeth like crumbling cement. "Long time no see."

A familiar, confused sensation weighs Dean's body down. The same feeling when that Malinta girl woke up and started talking. Dean is perfectly comfortable blacking out, but he's not so wild about this sudden trend of forgetting Cliff Drinking acquaintances.

Some things, he decides, are better left ignored. "Thank you, sir. Will you be staying with us long?"

"Seriously, Deshler, you need to drop this gig. What are you trying to accomplish by parking cars? It's like you're on one of those religious missions, like self-punishment. Ask yourself, if life were a tasty hamburger would you be the onions or the ketchup. Wait no, let me start over."

"Sir?"

"Would you rather be the relish or the *something-something*?"

"I'm not following."

The man smiles and undoes a jacket button. "Good one, buddy, never mind. You do what you gotta do. You know where I'll be." The man wobbles a line to the door. Napoleon holds it open as the man turns back: "See you at the Beef Club tonight, Dean?"

Deshler's successful morning of lying rears back. "You... bet," passes from his throat and through the chilly air in gray gas. He stands for a few seconds and lets the breeze scratch his cheeks, failing to recall any time they might have met.

Blank.

Finally, Deshler slips behind the wheel. Other than how to barely work a stick, Deshler knows nothing about cars. He grinds the gears and pulls off. Dean does, however, know a cool car when he drives one, and this isn't the coolest by a long shot.

DESHLER DEAN'S COOLEST RIDES

- **The Batmobile**

No shit, *the* Batmobile. Not the space shuttle-looking piece of crap Michael Keaton drove. The original from the sixties. The owner was in town for a comic book convention and decided to stay at Deshler's hotel. No fenders were dented.

- **The Pope Mobile**

A few years ago the Pope was in town speaking to 50,000 people at the arena. This was actually the backup Pope Mobile. It was little more than a bulletproof pickup truck with a Kevlar phone booth in the back. No doors were scratched, amen.

- **The Oscar Mayer Wiener Mobile**

There is a giant hotdog that drives around the country spreading goodwill and news about franks. The driver said he wanted to eat at the hotel's restaurant but couldn't find adequate street parking. It was amazing the giant dog was allowed in the city limits, this being such a hamburger town. By some miracle Deshler convinced the wiener man to let him find a spot. It was a lot like driving an eighteen-wheeler, which Deshler has also done. No buns were burned.

- **A Giant Slice of Tofu**

Not nearly as exciting as the hotdog, but slightly more memorable. Some woman named Wilhelmina was in town, trying to promote healthy eating. She wouldn't stop talking to Dean about the protein benefits of tofu as opposed to meat. No beans were curded.

Out of habit, Dean reaches in his breast pocket for a burned

Lothario Speedwagon CD. Slipping a copy into everyone's player is his form of guerrilla marketing. Though, he's pretty sure it never converts any fans.

Deshler zones out and wishes his band had a more artistic name, like the Butthole Surfers. He wishes people would take them seriously. He wishes people would listen. He kind of wishes audiences would stop throwing things, but kind of doesn't. Shaking up listeners' anger and confusion is the price an artist pays, he is reminded.

Dean parallels the car and the passenger door lets out a painful squeal, grinding against a parking lot guardrail. The opening bass notes of *Broken Piano for President* fill the stereo so Deshler doesn't hear the impact. It's too bad, too, because Deshler likes to keep a tally of all the fancy rides he ruins.

Jogging through the lot back to his post under the hotel awning, Dean snaps out of that band-focused haze. There she is again, across the street with a white bandage wrapped around her head like a World War One casualty. The girl doesn't see Deshler. Words bubble up to the surface of his throat, but hold back. He's not sure if this Malinta's the kind of woman he should ever talk to again. Maybe he's not the kind of guy she'd like to talk to again, for that matter.

"Dude, do you know who that guy was?" Napoleon says, jealous.

"Possibly?"

"Roland Winters." Napoleon's fingers make a ridiculous *ta-da* move.

"What? The hamburger guy? Christopher Winters' kid?"

Napoleon slowly nods as if Deshler just came back from the dead and asked for a cigarette. "What was that shit he said to you?"

"I wish I knew." He realizes this isn't a lie. *What was that slob babbling about?*

"Dude, I can't believe I let you drive his car," Napoleon says with kid brother awe. "That guy is *Mister Hamburger*. What did it smell like?"

"Oh, you know," Dean tries to remember, but goes back to lying. "Space Burgers."

"Ahhh, I knew it. No wonder he looks like that, it's gotta be impossible to stay in shape eating junk all day. Though, I hear that new Space Burger only weighs about a third as much as a regular Winters Burger. Crazy huh? *Healthy* burgers."

Napoleon parks an elderly woman's Lincoln. She walks syrup slow to the door Deshler holds.

Napoleon wanders back to the awning jingling keys, tossing them from hand to hand. "God, man," his hefty partner says. "You look like shit. Do you have any clue what you did last night?"

TEN

Lothario Speedwagon has played together for half a year and is banned from all but one bar around town. The electricity has been switched off the stage fourteen times. The band has only finished its set five times. Five that Deshler remembers, at least.

Shows usually end early when the singer throws things, which include, but are not limited to:

- Chairs.

- Ziploc bags of water.

- Microphone stands.

- Hamburgers.

- Ziploc bags of ketchup.

- Other bands' equipment.

- Beer bottles.

- Punches.

- Ziploc bags of urine.

The band self-released a cassette, *Broken Piano for President*, a few months ago. Tapes, being insanely outdated, are cheaper than CDs and seven-inch records, while being a million times cooler than MP3s—at least to the band. The lowest deal they could get was for five hundred copies pressed without artwork. In lieu of professional cover art, the band slapped on a Lothario Speedwagon sticker and randomly glued pieces of junk to the plastic tape cases. Dean's favorite copy features fingernail clippings and bloody band-aids. At the time of this publication, three hundred and five copies have been sold. Two hundred and sixty went through the band's website to Japan.

The band is confused, since Lothario Speedwagon has never played in Japan and none of its songs feature Japanese lyrics.

Practice is held in the drummer's basement. His house is seemingly kept standing by thumb tacks. There's a stiff breeze even when the windows are closed and what chunks of paint still hang to the slats are, at best, colored primer.

Downstairs, mismatched scraps of carpet are nailed along the basement walls to dampen noise. For decoration, Pandemic hung a couple thousand Christmas bulbs. Every string is set to a different blinker schedule. The effect is close to LSD sequences in sixties movies.

Behind Hamler's amp is a garbage heap of bright painted masks. Dean came up with the band's image one hungover morning after waking up in a costume shop/arts and crafts store: Day-glo papier-mâché masks and a lot of black lights around the stage.

The mysterious look also keeps their identity a secret, which has come in handy more than a few times after rocky performances.

At nine-thirty, Pandemic and Deshler lie around the practice space floor sharing a bottle of Night Train wine. The taste isn't unlike kerosene cut with Kool-Aid.

"What is wrong with your roommate?" Pandemic says. "I don't have time for his slow-ass screwing around."

"Beats me," Deshler says, bum wine burning a pool in his stomach. "He was crying about being on time this afternoon. Here we are." Dean recognizes a familiar germ growing inside him thanks to the wine. Some call it creativity, others call it trouble.

Dean's heard rumors that Juan Pandemic is rich. He and Henry's friends, who have played in bands with Pandemic before, back this theory up. Trust fund baby, they say. But from every angle Dean doubts that nametag applies to his methamphetamine-smoking drummer.

Juan Pandemic's skinny face and shaved head are scattered in welts from uncontrollable scratching. His everyday wardrobe consists of stained sweatpants and no shirt. He's thin as a coat of paint and, occasionally, when he stays up for five nights in a row, carries a vinegar cat piss stink soaked into his skin. This aroma, Dean learned, is a signpost of brewing a batch of crystal meth. Hardly the calling card of a man who gets a check from daddy every month, Deshler thinks.

With all this raggedness, though, one can't spend more than a minute with Pandemic without getting the impression he thinks he's better than you. As far as vain meth addicts go, he tops the leader board.

All flaws aside, Pandemic is a madman drummer. He beats a fairly standard drum kit, plus his homemade Konkers, with brutal power. Pandemic's Konkers include a metal trashcan— sometimes ignited with lighter fluid—cookie sheets, an oil drum, hubcaps, industrial springs and a mutilated car hood. His hands are scarred and enormous and bash away like sledgehammers. When the band is at full-tilt, Pandemic's a junkyard in an earthquake. He's the perfect backbeat for a group like Lothario Speedwagon.

"You want more of this shit. I can tell," the drummer says, picking something hard and yellow from his eye.

"Well."

"You haven't started talking weird yet. That's not right. I have a couple more in the fridge."

"Yeah, dude, it's not so bad after a few sips." Deshler swallows a breath, scaring away building heartburn. "Hey, wait, talking weird?"

Pandemic runs upstairs and Dean loses himself, thinking about Malinta. *God, what a woman. But then again, I did nearly kill her.*

Didn't I?

I should stay away.

"I don't normally drink this shit, but I'm slumming it tonight." The drummer stomps back down. "One for each of us. You can thank me later," Pandemic says, holding two bottles of electric green Night Train.

With each sip Dean senses that little germ graduating into a plague of creativity. There is no talking, just wet gurgles between the men. It's satisfying, Dean thinks, to wait and just build up this magic pressure.

That steam pushes against Dean's temples, tight, right as his roommate thunders down the rotting wooden stairs.

"About time, Henry."

"Don't start, man, just don't." Henry's stomach still feels oily and evil. "Can we just jam a while? I don't want to practice our old shit today. I want something new. Something slow and dark."

Nobody argues and the band slithers through some riffs. Lothario Speedwagon is Pandemic on percussion, Henry on bass and Dean on vocals with occasional urine-tossing. They have a reputation among a tiny percentage of fans as a revolutionary live act. However, the vast majority of crowds around town think they are, at best, art school masturbation. Or, as the local alternative weekly said: "A kick in the shin to anyone with functional hearing." Deshler taped that article to the refrigerator.

Henry plucks some strings. His bass is detuned and hot-rodded to sound like a table saw through a stop sign.

Deshler's mile-long vocal chords come across somewhere between southern gospel preacher and Navy foghorn. That deep voice rattles his guts when hitting low notes. He never sang for school or for choirs or suppers. One day he just tried out the microphone and fell in love.

An hour into practice, the magic pressure builds a bomb from countless sips. The singer is frustrated because his creative plague didn't explode. It's close, but he can't light the wick. Dean snarls lyrics he hates, but can't stop repeating:

She drinks all the Night Train
Riding on the bus
You know you're getting old
When your momma hates your guts

Words rattle off in different cadences, trying to find a fit for the musical chaos.

And when the aerialist
Begins to blow you a kiss
You better slit your wrists
'Cause that's when the credits roll

Nothing works, but Dean knows art takes time. His art takes a little more than most. After their first few months together, the band only has five complete songs—the ones recorded for the *Broken Piano for President* tape.

Dean digs for that *click* when the drums and the bass and his voice snap together to form some fire-lunged monster. They'd probably write more tunes, but Dean has a hard time remembering lyrics.

Today I found my brother
lyin' in the gutter
Said, "your suit is full of holes
and it's tearin'"

He wiped the dust from his pants
Looked me straight in the face
and said:
"If you were a carpenter would you be Jesus or Karen?"

That one strikes the target.

To Dean, Lothario Speedwagon just pushed the detonator on a stack of TNT. The explosion is narcotic. It's the only time the world is all ears, nobody ignores him. How could they? In Dean's mind, his parents—probably both sealed in boxes since last they spoke—finally sit up and take notice.

Dean smiles between swigs of wine, still coherent enough to catch that thrill. Far too often he's blacked-out during these little victories and only catches a glimpse from boom box practice recordings.

Deshler's tried a million different methods, but can't write an ounce of a song without several pints of booze shaking his liver to death. While this is good for creativity, it cuts productivity out of the picture. Every band practice is walking a fine line even smaller than the one this morning with Malinta.

The band works up a thin layer of sweat and finishes more bottles. In the middle of a collective noise-demolition, Pandemic holds a metal sheet over his scuffed head, yelling:

"Stop, stop, wait, hold on." The band spins out of control with feedback and drunk muttering through the PA until the insect buzz of thousands of Christmas lights fills the room. "What time is it?"

Henry looks at his phone. "Only ten forty five, why?"

"Oh, man," Pandemic pouts like a child with melted ice cream. "Why didn't any of you tell me?"

They look confused.

"We're done. Now I'm missing the webcast."

"Webcast of what?" Deshler asks, again questioning everyone's commitment. He slumps against a wall, his loose skull bobbing side-to-side.

"Jesus, dude. Come on. The Space Burger webcast." Pandemic fetches a laptop and starts typing.

"Oh, shit, right," Henry says. "You better hurry, Comrade."

"Huh?" Pandemic looks at Henry.

"That sorta means, 'dude,' in Russian. I took some classes in college."

"Some?"

"Minored."

"Hey, we're practicing," Dean's voice is like a nasty shove. "Don't you guys care about this?"

"Man, we can listen to my fine-ass drumming later. This shit's important." Juan looks down at his screen, face glowing blue.

Through a haze of turpentine wine, Deshler thinks it is kind of odd that Pandemic has a laptop and even more unthinkable that this dump has Wi-Fi. "What are you guys so worried about?" Deshler says, annoyed.

"I swear, man, you are totally out of it. Do you know what year it is, who the president is?" Pandemic says.

"Cute," Dean says.

"What did they teach you in orphan school?"

"I went to regular school," Dean gets red. "Quit being a dick and tell me what's up."

"Okay, Oliver Twist. There is a spacesuit floating around in orbit. If you have the right burger wrapper number sequence, you can control the jetpack from Earth."

"Why would you want to do that?"

"Duh, so you can feed the starving cosmonauts with all the hamburgers in the suit and become famous," Pandemic says.

"And win four hundred and sixty thousand dollars," Henry adds.

Pandemic says, "Yeah, I forgot." He tugs hamburger wrappers from deep inside his sweatpants and smoothes them out. Each has a sticker with a different bar code. "It's a real life video game. This is pretty much the most important thing in the world. Don't blow it for me."

"The further the suit floats away from the space station, the harder it gets to guide it back, obviously," Hamler says.

"Big deal. What if nobody does?"

"That's totally unlikely," Pandemic says. "There are four hundred and sixty thousand winning numbers. You can enter your number at any time to control the suit, but anyone else with numbers can override you and steal the controls. The last person in command when the suit floats home is the winner. The whole country is a team. Get some patriotism, asshole."

"Isn't that kind of like *Cannonball Run*?" Deshler says.

"No," Pandemic sounds blunt and mean. "Plus, the cosmonauts don't have any other food. Not even freeze dried ice cream. Their lives are in our hands. So, stop being a total douche, and give a shit about all this."

"So…what? Practice is over because of a hamburger?"

"Sorry, man. I guess I'll have to save somebody's life instead. I feel real bad about it."

ELEVEN

"Welcome back to *Cosmonaut Watch*," our anchorman says, raising his voice, slowing his English to a crawl. "Dimitri... how-do-you-feel-up-there?" His jaw and hair are carved from the same rock.

The picture quality is bleak, hazed.

The screen fills with a floating head, covered in a scrubby beard and lonely eyes. "We are now fine, has only been one day," the man says with a Moscow diplomat's tongue. "The Russian Space Program has trained us to sustain such tragedies."

"Do-you-miss-eating?"

"Yes, of course."

"Do-you-miss-gravity?"

"Not too much, no."

"How-long-can-you-and-your-fellow-cosmonauts-survive..."

The picture dissolves into black and white fuzz.

"Dimitri, *hello?*" The camera flashes from the scramble back to our anchor. "I apologize for the technical difficulties. I'm told we are having some satellite issues."

"We are needing the America's help," the dark Russian accent says behind a wall of television quicksand, eloquent enough for a cocktail party. "It is up to you to eat hamburgers and save our lives. We cannot survive much longer."

"Thank you, Dimitri. Godspeed," our anchor says. "Chilling, truly chilling. Let's take a look at the suit on the monitor, can we, Hank?"

The screen fills with a globe orbited by a cartoon space station. The animated suit floats further away. It has traveled one hundred miles and gives a countdown until the suit enters the atmosphere and burns up, essentially starving five Russian astronauts to death.

America has six days and fourteen hours to guide the suit back to the station.

TWELVE

A few sassy notes of *Broken Piano* crush through the Cliff Drinker's ears. All is good until a Night Train headache jabs knitting needles where a brain used to be.

"C'mon, wonder boy," some acidic voice calls. "We're almost home."

Deshler's vision flickers. His bloodstream is still around fifteen percent booze. An opportunistic vampire would call Dean a cocktail party.

He smells leather or new car from a can. His body bounces, which is not a friend to headaches.

"You busted your ass tonight, kid. Just get some rest," the voice snorts. "In your own bed, you know?"

Deshler sits up from a pretzel curl. Periodically his vision wipes the fog from its window. That confused look returns like it was tattooed across his face—mouth hanging open deep. Deshler is fifty percent sure this is a limo. The other fifty percent says it's a hearse.

"Sorry, I must have dozed off," he growls like someone is standing on his throat.

"Dozed my eye," the man says. He's at the opposite end with his back to the driver. An orange glow kisses the roof from dim lights, though not enough to lift the veil of darkness around the man's face. He wears a black brimmed hat. "This song and dance is getting real old, young mister Dean."

The mystery friend trend twists Deshler's patience into stiff knots. *Gibby*, Dean decides, *would play along*. "Is this…is this a real limo?"

"Yep."

Words slip from Dean's mouth like they're skating down soapy hallways—he can't control them. "And I'm guessing we didn't just get married."

"It's the boss's limo, big shot," he says, as if Deshler should know already. "I'm taking your ass home."

"What time is it?" Dean hates asking that question. It's always later than it should be. He—without fail—blacks out more hours than previously thought possible.

"Who knows? Wristwatches are for assholes. Sun's not up yet, if that's what you're worried about." His snorty words trip into a laugh. "Let me guess, you have to get to that stupid valet job."

Deshler's vision comes into full clarity. "So if this isn't our honeymoon, what've we been doing?"

That voice turns red and sharp: "You drunk bag of shit, you're a piece of work you know that?" A chasm of silence holds. "Burning the midnight oil on the new campaign, maybe? I swear, some nights you don't know when to stop drinking and start thinking."

Deshler's clarity floats away like a sneeze. He manages to mumble, "Sounds like we're old pals," before a wave of cheap wine swallows all clarity.

"You're a real case study, Dean."

Deshler's eyes don't crack apart until the thin stranger drags him from the limo. As the Night Train swims away, Dean recognizes the red brick of home.

"If you weren't the best I've seen since," the man laughs.

His long gray hair scrapes his shoulders, capped off with that black bowler. "Well, since *myself*." One hand grips Deshler's collar and one hand locks the back of his belt, holding a Cliff Drinker puppet. "If the boss didn't have his head buried so deep in your lap."

Deshler's toes drag lines into the sidewalk frost as his apartment door comes into focus. "Who's *the boss?*"

"Tony Danza, you prick," the man says and spins Deshler around swift. His ass hits cement stairs. The dense cold swallows his flesh. The man's face is a garbage bag of wrinkles. He's probably somebody's grandpa. Some unfortunate, twisted kid.

The gray-haired guy crouches down to Dean's level with a creamy look of concern. "Sorry for busting your balls. I'm gonna do you a favor. Listen, the next few weeks are crucial. You've shown us a spark in that empty head of yours." He rises and begins walking away. "You prove there's a bonfire inside and you'll be in a good situation. Trust me." The man slips back into the limo and a steamy breath of exhaust floats into arctic morning air.

THIRTEEN

In addition to selling their tape online and at gigs, Lothario Speedwagon mailed out free copies of *Broken Piano for President* to magazines and websites they thought would review it. Though, the band is still not sure how Japanese reporters got a hold of the cassette. Here's what the press has to say:

- "There's a guy yelling about pianos…maybe…it's hard to tell because it sounds like he's underwater. And I think there are a couple other guys destroying a Chevy with hammers. My speakers are bleeding." **–Le Bombsquad.org**

- "Thirteen minutes of uncomfortable hell." **–Standard Times Review**

- "The deepest voice this side of the Grinch." **–Tucson Weekly**

- (Translated from Japanese) "Lothario bad bad bad noise feels good good good to young ears!!!!" **–Nagano Weekly Gazette**

- "Who wasted money on this thing getting printed?" **–Squeege Blog.com**

- "I don't get it." **–Broken Mirror**

- "A tape? Seriously? Who makes tapes anymore? I had to go to my grandma's house just to listen to this stupid thing."
  –Imperfect Scrawl

- "In a world where so many bands try very hard to seem insane, you get the vibe Lothario Speedwagon just rolled out of bed that way." **–Clap Amp Quarterly**

- "My first thought was, 'Eewww, are these fingernails and band aids?'" **–Static Magic Monthly**

- "I didn't hear a guitarist in the mix. However, that doesn't mean Lothario Speedwagon isn't torturing one in a dark shed somewhere." **–Weekly Observer**

- "Until now, no band has properly captured the sound of tossing bags of urine at you. Enter Lothario Speedwagon."
  –Impact Weekly

- "I want to think these guys are just that cool for making a tape, but my best guess is that they're just that dumb."
  –[YELLOW] Journalism

- (Translated from Japanese) "Ear holes make yummy buzz, melt bubble gum to trashcans. Babies dance! Babies dance!" **–Tokyo City Blues.com**

- (Translated from Japanese) "Burn Lothario like nuclear missile of love. Hail, hail, hail, The Anti-Beatles."
  –Osaka Daily News

FOURTEEN

The blankets are tight over Henry's face when the phone rings. Christopher Winters' liver spotted skull disappears from behind dream-soaked eyelids. Henry was reliving that sudden head jerk of recognition as poison mixed with the old man's blood. He relives it five times a day.

"Hello," he croaks.

"Hey, how's it going?"

"I feel like crap, Tony," Hamler tells his mentor.

"Henry, last time I'm saying this. You did the right thing. Plus, Winters was ancient, he might have died of old age a split second before you got him. BANG! His heart turns to cement. You probably didn't have anything to do with it."

"Nice try." Hamler coughs. "You know, the only thing that makes a person feel guiltier is having someone say they shouldn't feel guilty at all."

"Wow. I'll write that down."

Maybe, Henry thinks, I wouldn't feel so guilty if there was someone to tell these problems to. Not a shrink or anything. Just someone to hold in bed. Someone who doesn't make him feel like shit for crying so much. Loneliness and guilt, Hamler's observed many times, fit together like some awful sandwich.

Hamler untucks the sheet from around his ears and checks the clock. Lunch was an hour ago.

"I'm just saying it's possible. Hearts are weird like that. Anyway, put on that nice blue suit of yours, there's more work today."

"I called in sick, Tony. There's…I can't…I'm not doing shit today. Maybe ever."

"Oh, good. Drama Club."

"Don't, Tony."

"Look, I told you I understand. That's why you won't have to get your hands dirty. You might even enjoy yourself." A few crackles of dead air fill their talk. "You might even get *laid*."

Henry sighs against the phone. It swirls into distortion as defenses collapse. "What're you thinking, exactly?"

"You'll dig this. It'll take your mind off things."

Henry is nearly out of butane and it takes a fair amount of voodoo for a spark. His first cigarette of the day melts both arms to gelatin. *This*, he assumes, *is probably what junkies feel when they shoot up after years on the wagon.* He breathes smoke slow into the receiver. *That feeling of peace.* "I don't think this is a good idea."

"Just some simple recon work. Get to know a person and pump them for info on their next project," Tony says. "Nothing sticky or dangerous."

"I don't know how to pump people for information." Deep inside, Henry admits this doesn't sound so horrible.

"Get 'em drunk, get 'em high, give 'em a foot rub. Who cares? The important thing is, I want you to work alone. No more Junior Agent garbage."

"You really think I'm ready?" Henry can't tell whether the bacon sizzle in his chest is excitement or nicotine.

"When I watched you pin-prick that old man I could see it in your eyes. It was love."

"Love?"

"You love this job, don't you?"

"Um, let's not go that far."

At the start of the next work day, there is a temp named Henry Holgate at America's second-largest hamburger chain: Bust-A-Gut. He makes copies and fetches cappuccinos like a textbook admin. He makes three trips a day to the candy machine. Once in a while, the young spy plays lost and pokes his head around the office. He briefly catches a glimpse of the target coming out of a meeting and scurries away. *She looks different than the surveillance photo*, Hamler thinks.

"Getting the lay of the land, Henry?" his new boss says. The man's skin is so smooth Hamler counts the pores. The boss has an obscure title like Assistant Vice Manager of Dairy Acquisitions. It takes Henry until lunch to realize his boss, Martin, is a cheese buyer.

"Totally," he says with a laugh. "Copy room, coffee maker, mail room—the Big Three." Secretly, Henry dances with the excitement of actual espionage work.

"You're a hard worker, Henry. You'll fit in great here at Bust-A-Gut." His boss is dressed expensive—black shoes glowing.

"Thanks, it's really exciting to be somewhere that's such a big part of my life."

Martin, deep-skinned and Latino with a tiny black goatee, looks Hamler's chub up and down. Generously, he ignores the slick gel job hair. "I don't buy that, Henry. You're in too good of shape to eat burgers." The boss's eyes are a forcefully confident brown. He exudes a damn-near perfect presence except for those uncontrolled nasal snorts every few sentences.

"Monte Cristo is practically my middle name," he says, rubbing a Santa belly, impressed with how good he is at lying. "Honestly!"

"Whatever you say, Henry."

"So, I have a weird question," Hamler says. He's trying to organize a chain of command for his report to Tony. He doesn't know what size fish Martin is yet. "How does cheese factor into what goes on here?"

Martin's brown eyes bulge, wet and offended. "Eh, well, cheese is pretty important to our success. *Frankly,*" his voice lowers as coworkers buzz in all directions. The office is a puzzle of moveable cubicle walls. Daylight is nonexistent in Bust-A-Gut's home office—replaced overhead by long fluorescent bulbs. "There's big talk of a Mozzarella Stick Burger. Revolutionary."

"How is that revolutionary?"

Martin stuffs his tongue deep in his cheek until it pops out like a gumball. He leans in whisper close. "The bread," his nose snorts, "will be fried mozzarella shaped like a hamburger bun. Ground beef, bacon, cheddar and….well, pickles and shit, all book-ended by fried *cheese.*"

"Wow, that'll knock people out." Henry holds for a second, exactly as he learned to lie in spy school. "I'm speechless."

"Needless to say, it'll make the competition look like crapped pants."

"What?"

"Forget it." Martin spins on his heel and his purple striped tie whips Henry. "Oooooh, here's a high-roller you've got to meet. Kiss her ass, Henry, and you'll go straight to the top!"

That familiar first-cigarette feeling of peace sinks in deep when Hamler turns and sees the woman he was sent to spy on.

"Not bleeping likely, Martin," says an insanely tall blonde woman with a bandage wrapped above her ears. "Malinta Redding. Nice to meet you."

FIFTEEN

"Dimitri," our *Cosmonaut Watch* anchor says. "I'm sure you are weak and malnourished, but can you say a few words to the folks here on Earth?"

There is static clatter when the cosmonaut's blurry mouth moves—pictures beaming down faster than sound. Dimitri's beard is a patch of overgrown weeds. Now his once lonely eyes just look empty. Embarrassed. Halfway through his speech, the delayed words reach American ears, totally out of sync like black market film dubbing.

"Please, America, we are at your mercy," he wrestles with English. "You must eat Space Burger and play game to save us. We have not eaten in many days. We will die soon—" A thunderstorm of static crackling cuts him off.

"Di…Dimitri?" our beautifully tanned anchor asks. "Well, it appears we've lost feed with the space station again." He pauses, reading a report on the desk. The newscaster rubs his face like aluminum tears are leaking from those steel eyes. "Folks, this is life or death here and only you can help. So far, two hundred and twelve thousand lucky numbers have been used to guide the Burger Suit back toward the space station. It will take a lot of your help to get it home. Winters Olde-Tyme Hamburgers is the only place to get those lucky numbers and save our starving Russians. And it's the only way for you to become a thousandaire in the process. But that is not the issue, folks. Innocent people are *dying* up there. Only we can change it. Together, as a team."

The graphic shows the suit and the space station inching closer, but still hundreds of miles apart in real life.

Our anchor stuffs a finger in his shirt collar and tugs a tie loose. "America, the fate of five cosmonauts is in your hands." Hands fold like prayer. A salty glaze of sweat covers his forehead. "Please buy an extra Space Burger tonight."

SIXTEEN

"Dude," Napoleon says, mist and frost whipping past their cheeks. "Did you read the paper today?" Downtown's old brick buildings are merely a squint in the skyline.

"Nope, why?" Deshler says. He inhales cool air through a sober head. Dean wishes the valet awning was better protection from the elements as the clock-stopping hum of boredom creeps in. It's like sitting in the corner as a boy, in trouble with Mom again. Morning is always this slow, things never pick up until happy hour when all the executive autos need parked.

It has been five days since Dean's touched a drop of alcohol. Five days since he woke up in that limo. It has also been five days since he's shown up to work late. And at least as many since he's wet himself. Dean's banter with millionaires, which used to consist of grunts and nods, has improved to the point where a good stock market joke lands the former Cliff Drinker a twenty dollar tip. He's only scratched and dented four cars. Less than one per day—easily a record.

"There's a blurb about your band and a preview of tonight's show."

"No shit?" he says, with an *Oh, golly* kind of face. "Let's have a look." Dean is a little skeptical, knowing Napoleon's track record of saying practically anything for attention.

"I forgot it at home." Napoleon's breath evolves into steam. "But, basically, it said Lothario is gaining some cult status in town. Something about being an unpredictable live act."

A little sad, wanting to believe his parking partner, Dean says: "Get out of here."

Yawning, Napoleon stretches short, soft arms. "It said something like you're Iggy Pop with a bright orange mask and Ziploc baggies."

This makes Deshler blush, since the four singers he's always modeled himself after are:

- **Iggy Pop** "Stooges era, of course, before he sucked."

- **David Yow** "From the Jesus Lizard, before they left Touch and Go and sucked."

- **Nick Cave** "But only when he was in the Birthday Party. He never really sucked, but you get the picture."

- **Gibby Haynes** "Strictly the Butthole Surfers' eighties work." Dean will never admit it, but he can't stand their nineties stuff when the band sucked.

His heroes not only used their voices to express themselves, but their bodies and actions, as well. Part performers, part performance artists. When drunk, Deshler's voice gets dreamy and he says things like: "They stitch together these Frankenstein monsters of guerrilla art and punk rock." This talk sends his friends from zero to eye-rolling in no time flat.

Those eyeball spasms are nothing compared to his near-biblical quoting of Haynes. "One time, this foster home my brother and I were crashing at had a rad magazine collection. I read this interview where the journalist was talking about touring and asked Gibby, 'Where do people usually get the most pissed off?' And Gibby, wow that guy's a genius. Do you know what he said? His answer was, 'Between the ears.'"

Lately, thankfully, Dean's kept these proclamations to himself.

A wind tunnel-tested yellow sedan pulls up to the awning. "Man, that's heavy," Deshler says, rubbing fingers together until they regain feeling. "Maybe some people will show up tonight and buy some tapes."

"Yeah, tapes are a hot commodity. People love 'em," the little valet says, doing his usual attention grab. "Speaking of which, I told you about my video camera, right?"

"Uh, it doesn't ring a bell."

"I got it at the thrift store…VHS tapes…*seriously*? You don't remember?"

"Hmm. Wish I could say I did."

"Let's hang out after work. There's this cool car wreck I shot. It's right up your alley," he says, searching Deshler's eyes for any spark.

A sturdy, sailor-looking guy steps out of the car. His posture mirrors the city's dueling skyscrapers. His gray suit looks like it's never been worn.

Napoleon hustles up to the car door with a smile. "Welcome back, sir. Don't worry about a thing. I'll take care of your baby."

"Back off, tubby," the man growls. "Look at this beautiful machine. They'd have to peel you out with a shoehorn." The man dangles keys in front of the valet's bubble cheeks. "I've told you a million times, son, you'll never get to drive this car. I need my man Deshler Dean to park it."

This harpoons Dean's attention. He doesn't recognize the yellow car and an all-too-familiar confusion nestles in tight.

"Yes, sir," Napoleon says.

The man stops and turns around. "Here, go buy yourself a burger." He dunks a five in Napoleon's breast pocket.

This guy reminds Deshler of a football coach when he steps

up and gives a nod. "All systems are a go, buddy." The man is quiet enough to keep Napoleon out of the loop. Dean stares hard into that face. It's intense and focused and has probably made people pee themselves.

Deshler returns a stiff nod. This unfamiliar kind of talk boils a pot of spaghetti where his stomach used to be.

"I mean, this is gonna blow up big *time*," the sturdy guy says, showing off a white marble slab of teeth. "R and D is having trouble actually converting fried mozzarella into the shape of a bun. Some shit about structural integrity. Looks like we might have to use provolone. But seriously, who knows the difference?"

"I'm glad," Deshler clears his throat. "To hear the mozzarella is going well." He hopes this lie is enough to pass. Dean wishes he was humble enough to simply say he doesn't know, but dark pride won't allow it.

"You better be!" the man says, slapping Deshler's white jacket shoulder. The coach's skin is tanned. He could be on posters for California tourism. "It's the best damn idea you've ever come up with."

If you guessed this news jerked our hero back a step, you'd be right.

The man continues, "Hell, it's the best thing Bust-A-Gut's had in fifteen years. Better than the Monte Cristo, I truly mean that."

"I do what I do," Deshler says, wondering if he actually heard the word "idea" or not.

"Absolutely," the man says, searching for credibility in Deshler's eyes. Digging deep. The guy's fingers pinch a sorry white lapel. "Anyhow, we've gotta get you out of this getup. You should be wearing pinstripes, Dean. Anyone ever tell you that?"

"You'd be surprised. But you know me." Deshler smiles,

the gap in his teeth forms a goalpost. "I like to make an *honest* living."

"Oh, you *got* me," he says, covering an imaginary gun blast to the chest. "See you tonight, buddy. It is Friday after all." The man laughs and passes the keys to Dean.

Deshler slips behind the wheel and hollers, "Tonight it is."

The accelerator needs only a tap to roar the engine. Dean can't look at the RPMs, his mind is off so far. Deep in that mind, it's like a streetlamp over a dark road. Warm peach light fills a space for the Cliff Drinker's memory, but just out of reach. He's pushed people past the light. It's dark outside the lamp glow and it's getting crowded. Whoever's out there, they're close, he can almost touch them, recognize them. But he can't. It frustrates the hell out of Dean.

When the car is safely parked and Deshler is out of sight, he opens the glove box and searches through paperwork. "Thurman Lepsic," he says, holding the car's registration. "I bet I know who knows this guy."

Deshler is too dazed to even pop in a CD for Mister Lepsic.

Napoleon has a strange twist in his lips when Deshler returns. "What did I just see, man?"

"Nothing, don't sweat it."

"That asshole talked to you for like an hour." Napoleon gives his partner a prize fight jab. "I suppose you're going to tell me you don't know who Thurman Lepsic is either?"

That nasty pride builds a dam over his mouth and stops Dean from honesty. "He was just babbling about the gas pedal sticking and not to take it over fifteen. The usual bullshit, Napoleon. Lighten up. I'm sorry he was a prick."

"He can say whatever he wants to me. That dude is like, second in command at Bust-A-Gut. Lepsic is right below Clifford Findlay. His tie tack is worth more than your life."

"Then he should have tipped better."

SEVENTEEN

So right now, you're probably saying something to the effect of: "Jeez, there is a lot of burger talk flying around. This book is one coldcut away from being a butcher shop menu."

This is the point I'd say: "Yeah, maybe you're right. Is this a little overkill?" You'd shrug and I'd feel kind of guilty.

So maybe it's time you were brought up to speed about the Burger Wars, the Beef Club, the Winters Family, Globo-Goodness Inc. and Burger Town, USA.

Let's start at the top. Last fiscal year, Bust-A-Gut's three hundred and fifty worldwide domes had a stronger income than many small Asian nations. However, Winters Olde-Tyme Hamburgers, with its six hundred and twenty Victorian mansions worldwide—including the recently opened *Winters Antarctica*—pulled in about as much money as a certain *huge* Asian nation we will not mention.

It wasn't always this way, however. Hamburgers, in general, weren't multi-national corporations. In the beginning, burger stands were regional and as unique as the cities themselves. Their buildings weren't designed by focus groups and dropped out of assembly lines. You'd better believe the food wasn't either.

Hamburgers, at one time, didn't come deep-fried or even *freeze dried*. Hard to swallow, I know. You've gotta trust me here. Many years ago a hamburger was simply ground beef and a bun.

Naive days.

It's wildly disputed who first chopped a cow into tiny bits, cooked those bits in a flat circle and slid it between bread. Frankly, it doesn't matter. That guy's not in this story.

The first serious hamburger restaurants in America opened during the 1920s and 1930s. The patties were tiny, quickly made and each cost about a nickel. Almost overnight, lunch counters across America sprung up producing similar sandwiches, known as sliders. Most popular were the White Tower stands in the Midwest. In a trend as infectious as measles, dozens of other entrepreneurs sprouted copycat stands to cash in. Some memorable shacks included: White House, White Cabin, Super Tower, White Burger and the doomed Detroit establishments: White Boy and White Devil.

However, these businesses faded in a cloud of griddle steam during the 1940s and 1950s with the popularity of drive-ins and the malt shop. Gradually, what burger stands remained branched into thinly linked regional chains.

Even at this infant stage of meaty lust, America knew an itty-bitty burger didn't satisfy. The Cold War was hot and it was un-American to fill your hunger with an armload of puny sliders. May as well grab a bowl of borscht on the side.

Much like American waistlines, burger sizes inflated during this time. In 1952, truckers, linebackers and hungry tummies near Dayton, OH nearly fainted when regional burger powerhouse Beef Boy introduced the Fat Boy. Two quarter pound patties shuffled between three pieces of bun and a pile of onions, pickles, ketchup and mustard. The young chef and owner, Harold Dobbs—barely old enough to shave—became the first superstar of fast food.

The Fat Boy's popularity allowed the Beef Boy chain to ooze across borders to Indiana, Kentucky, Michigan, Pennsylvania and West Virginia. At his peak, the 1954 fiscal year, Dobbs— now lovingly called "Double Harry" by customers and peers alike—operated ninety-two restaurants, the largest chain in the country, and served nearly a million Fat Boys.

Parody proved to be Double Harry's downfall. Much like White Tower a few decades before, Beef Boy's competitors adopted the double hamburger ethic and the *Boy*-craze sizzled like raw meat over flames. Notable copycats included: Chunk Boy, Double Boy, Buff Boy, Man Boy, Boy Boy, Coy Boy, Nature Boy and Well-Mannered Boy.

Beef Boy was swallowed by this expanding sea of imitation Boys. Unable to adapt and properly expand the empire, Double Harry and his franchise filed for bankruptcy and closed shop on all restaurants during the winter of 1956.

Once a staple of the Dayton culinary scene, Double Harry quickly vanished and was soon rumored dead.

While Double Harry's greasy presence fell into America's drip pan, its favorite Almost-Hitler-Catcher and top Electric Toothbrush inventor was just firing up his stovetop.

EIGHTEEN

There's an envelope in the mail addressed to Deshler. He opens it and finds an Arbor Day card. He doesn't know when Arbor Day is, but it doesn't come at the start of winter, he knows that.

Missing: One Screwdriver. One Red Car. One Pint of Malinta's Blood.

There is no return address. The postmark is from Deshler's zip code. He throws the card away and spends the rest of the day trying to forget ever seeing it.

NINETEEN

Okay, so back to the burger story. Sorry, I had to look over some notes.

A Winters Olde-Tyme Hamburger publicist tells us its beefy empire was founded by Christopher Winters in 1955 with money saved from his various fortunes. Today, the company spreads a message of "Good old-fashioned American fun and values through ground beef." This is reiterated by every restaurant being modeled after Winters' green and gray Victorian mansion: a place Winters claimed was as happy and well-rounded as a sesame seed bun. All employees dress like nineteenth century bankers and bankers' wives to truly illustrate the old-fashioned goodness of its product.

Prior to the first set of Victorian gables poking a hole in the skyline, most burger restaurants, including Beef Boy, didn't have enough fuel in their engine to expand beyond a couple states. Thanks to Winters' nationwide popularity and bottomless wealth, there was a neon-lined Victorian mansion in every American state, most of Canada and Guatemala by the time the 1960s rolled around. The company's founder was never seen in public without his trademark outfit: A ketchup red suit with mustard yellow shirt and tie. He often said in interviews: "I'm so serious about hamburgers, I wear the colors on my back."

Until his death, Winters' suit, traffic-jamming smile and hamburger philosophy (capitalizing on both dining propaganda and World War Two rhetoric) were staples of American hearts and stomachs.

HAMBURGER PHILOSOPHY CLIFF NOTES

- "If your life were a tasty Winters Burger, would you be the bun or the beef?"

- "I may have let Hitler slip through my fingers, but mark my words, that'll never happen with these Stay-Crisp Winters Fries."

- "Only a communist would limit himself to a single Winters Burger for dinner."

- "Burgers, fries and a milkshake—now that's what I call the Axis of Edible."

- "Enough of this bologna, let's get down to ground beef."

- "A burger a day keeps the Nazis away."

On the flip side of the bun, Bust-A-Gut rocketed to *overnight sensation* status during the early eighties. There is no corporate information regarding the chain's founder. In cataract-inducing type at the bottom of its press releases, it reads: "A member of the Globo-Goodness Corporation Family of Corporations." In 1977, weeks before a marketing blitz declared Bust-A-Gut was "the same Bust-A-Gut flavor you've always loved, just new," two mildly popular American burger chains, Ground Beef Grotto and You Want Pickles on That?, were purchased for undisclosed sums and remodeled into domes. Suddenly, the fast food landscape was crowded with yellow and blue. The restaurant's image was far more subdued than Winters'. It basically said: "This restaurant is blue, yellow, and clean. Enjoy." In a matter of weeks Americans began asking themselves how they'd ignored this restaurant that, apparently, had always been around the corner. After all, it was shaped like a bubble and that's pretty hard to miss.

The domes proved impossible to ignore in the decades to come. But Winters and his kingdom of mansions wouldn't give up the skyline easily.

TWENTY

It's been over a week since Christopher Winters passed away. "Peacefully," a press release reads, "in his sleep from heart failure." All Winters Olde-Tyme Hamburgers employees wear black armbands with turn-of-the-century uniforms.

Hamler crunches through a Space Burger while talking on his phone. Styrofoamy cheddar just lacerated a cheek. This is the fifth lunch break in a row he's spent car-bound. Spending so much time alone, without someone to come home to after a day of lying and spying, has worked his confidence down to a pile of sawdust. Possibly lower than after the Christopher Winters mess.

"So, like I said," the young spy mutters between snapping bites of Olde-Tyme space-age beef. "This fried cheese thing is owning everyone. I heard some dude in the shitter talking about how they've adjusted the composition to forty-five percent mozzarella, twenty percent provolone, *thirty* percent something called Gluten Solvent and five percent *other.*"

Outside, the sky is a gray mash of dense clouds. The first snow of the year drops across Hamler's windshield and melts watery upon landing. The crisscrossing power lines above the parking lot shiver with the breeze.

"Other," Tony says like a professor.

"That's all I have, man. I had to pick my legs up in the stall just to get that." His cheek tastes like copper. Bloody cheese.

"Okay, that's helpful, really." Tony sounds disappointed. "Really, Henry. Great work."

The car is so cold, steam rises from the bag the way Indians believe souls escape the body. The soul of a freeze dried cow vaporizes into a pine air freshener.

"Have you interrogated Malinta Redding yet?"

"I don't see much of her, Tony. I mean, the least you could have done is get me a job in her department."

"Hey."

"Sorry. Sorry." Henry slouches low. Recognizable faces from the office return from lunch, hustling across the frosty parking lot.

"There weren't any. Just focus on Malinta Redding, she's the key. I don't really care about mozzarella sticks, the boss certainly doesn't. She's the gatekeeper. Redding is your primary objective."

"I'm sorry, I'll try harder."

"Anything else?" Tony says, desperate. "Before I let you go."

Henry holds his wrapper. The lucky Space Burger number is 12171979.

"Uhm, oh yeah," Henry's voice picks up. "They are running a hush-hush thing called *Salute to Genius*. Some commercials about Christopher Winters and what a great guy he was. It makes me sick to my stomach."

Tony whispers, "*Shit.*"

"No, I can handle things, don't sweat it. I just don't think this job makes anything easier. He *is* dead because of me." Henry's tongue runs a back-and-forth line across the cheek.

"I'm not talking about you." He is violently quiet. "I'm talking about this horseshit ad campaign. Our memorials won't be ready for another few weeks. The competition can't beat us. Winters was *our* founder. Next thing you know they'll be blasting Russians into space."

"Oh, sorry...I don't know much—"

"Just." Tony huffs through his nose. "Just pump Malinta.

Force booze down her throat. She's got a weak spot. Get info from her, okay?"

"Sure thing, sir."

The phone dies. A quiet wraps Henry. It's just him and a bag of steam. The car smells like a griddle. His heart sags further with aching dead weight.

Some guy from accounting walks by and squints into Henry's windshield. The undercover agent slinks below the dashboard line.

He crunches through a few more bites, trying to recall the last time he didn't suffer such loneliness. Cuts kill with the chewing.

A bang on the window explodes Henry's silence.

"Hey, what are you doing?" Malinta says.

"Oh, Jesus," Hamler peeps, bucking in his seat. He grabs the familiar gray bag with old-fashioned green lettering, crumbles and stows it under his seat.

He opens the door.

"Hey, Malinta, you scared me." He steps out.

"Sorry, I just caught you out of the corner of my eye." Her lips click *tisk-tisk-tisk*. "And I saw what you were eating."

Embarrassment washes over his face and fog pours from his nose in the chilly air. "Busted, huh?" He debates the next move. *My cover*, he realizes, *is officially blown.*

Malinta wears a red and white hat, obstructing her wound. For the first time, Henry focuses on the rest of her. Eyes, even trained spy eyes, are always drawn to gauze and blood spots. The cold pinches her lips into a pink so deep, daughters want their bedrooms this color. *She's cute for a girl*, he thinks.

"Don't sweat it, Hol*date*," she says. "I kind of prefer Winters myself."

"It's Holgate," Henry Hamler says, relieved. "And, can I just say, *whew!*"

"But that's a bleeping secret."

"No problem."

"I'll tell you something else. I also really like healthy stuff. Tofu, veggies, soymilk. All that. I love it. Is that weird?"

"Wow, I'll have to..." Henry's pulse slows with the lies. "Try some."

They share a silence, but Hamler doesn't recognize it. This quiet isn't the icy lonesome that normally crowds his time. It's something whole. Something welcomed.

"Wanna hear a big secret?"

They look at one another as their breath knits together. Hamler holds off speaking for a long while. "Um...sure."

"I even play the Cosmonaut Game." Her words are tense and whispered as the breeze. "A couple nights back, I got to fly the suit for sixteen minutes until some punk stole the controls from me."

"Really, how was it?"

"It was the warmest feeling I've ever had. Knowing I was helping save those poor, stranded astronauts. It was..." Her eyes glide up toward the sky.

Hamler counts the hairs in her nose. "What?"

"I think it was the most rewarding feeling of my life." Her face turns cutesy and childlike. "That's not sad, right?"

"I don't think so—"

"It made me realize I don't get that feeling a lot. Being a good person. It's so much easier in our business to manipulate and cheat and be self-centered."

"Don't get carried away, you're not—"

"It makes me want to be a better person. I'm trying, obviously."

"You are?"

"The curse words. Hello?"

"I think we should talk about something else," he says,

hoping to get a speck of top-secret info.

"Okay, okay, but wait…can I tell you one last secret? I'm trying to be more honest, too."

"Just one more, okay?" he says, proud of what a great spy he is.

"My odds of dying by falling off a ladder are six times higher than dying from a terrorist attack. Twelve-thousand people worldwide broke their stupid necks falling off ladders last year. Only two-thousand died from terrorists. Doesn't that seem wild?"

"That's…" He bites his lower lip. "Comforting?"

Henry watches her nod the same way his mom does when letting an expensive chocolate melt in her mouth. "I'll say. I've been researching that kind of stuff for a special project. It's amazing. Life is really precious. Too precious to spend being an awful person."

Henry takes a silent balloon of breath and holds it. He touches cold fingers to the arm of Malinta's wool coat. "You are an odd woman," he says, letting the breath seep out in ghostly ribbons. "You want to get a drink after work?"

TWENTY-ONE

Okay, you've been very patient for the thrilling conclusion to Burger History 101. This is where the Monte Cristo batter hits the fan.

Prior to Bust-A-Gut's immaculate conception, Winters enjoyed dictatorial dominance in the fast food market. Having an American hero for a founder proved as popular as Mickey Mouse peddling your amusement park. Winters' burgers spread with epidemic speed throughout post-war America. History being the repetitious bastard it is, the competition developed its own Axis of Edible.

This all changed in 1979.

A rivalry was inevitable since both beef giants were headquartered in the same city. No one is sure why Bust-A-Gut opened its main operations down the road from Christopher Winters' office, since its parent corporation was located wherever it was located. Much like Winston-Salem mothering cigarette giants, the city became the capital for all things fried and bovine, quickly earning the nickname: Burger Town, USA.

Bust-A-Gut consistently finished third place during its first few years of operation. That is, until Globo-Goodness Corporation purchased second-place Ka-Pow! Drive Thru and converted each of its one hundred and eighty eight restaurants like Hollywood actors to Scientology.

Still, Bust-A-Gut was never taken seriously until it slipped under the 1980s' hot neon spotlight. The restaurant unveiled a new menu featuring fried chicken, BBQ pork sandwiches, roast beef, doughnuts and "The Shot Heard 'Round the World" in the hamburger industry: The Double *Cheeseburger*. Apparently, nobody thought of mixing a couple slices of cheddar with Beef Boy's *Fat Boy* recipe until this point.

You know how an avalanche can start by someone yelling really loud? Consider the double cheeseburger the full-throated yodel that sent Burger Mountain rolling.

Bust-A-Gut's broad menu catapulted the mysterious wunderkind into first place in sales. Since then, the gastronomic arms race between the two giants has heated up like clockwork. One adds bacon while the other adds another layer of beef and cheese. One tops its burger with three-alarm jalapeño poppers while the other slides in a layer of onion rings. This cold war hit full-force with Bust-A-Gut's "Bonzo Breakfast Burger." The Bonzo consisted of three alternating layers of beef, cheese, fried egg and country sausage stacked Dagwood-style between two waffles. Syrup came fifty-cents extra.

Health Watch International, a consumer advocacy group, chastised both companies for going so far as to produce sandwiches with four times the recommended daily amount of calories and saturated fat. Health Watch referred to the Bonzo as "a Cardiac Grenade."

Health Watch also initiated an investigation with the help of the popular television news program *Nightbeat*, claiming Winters Olde-Tyme actually invented trans-fats and MSG. The results were inconclusive.

A few years ago, the burger landscape shook to its knees when Roland Winters jumped behind the CEO desk. The young Winters imitated his famous father as much as possible, even wearing matching clothes. But the boy was never taken seriously and several top executives resigned upon his promotion. Soon, the plump offspring of America's hero ushered in the era of extreme dining. Winters Olde-Tyme Hamburgers switched its focus to habañero chicken sandwiches, pork rind spinach salads, monster fries, and all-you-can-eat BBQ ribs. The beef patty was left for dead on their doorsteps.

Bust-A-Gut quickly returned this serve.

The word "cheeseburger" basically fell out of favor in the American dining dictionary. For a while it was the neglected orphan of fast food.

However, several years ago, without fanfare, Bust-A-Gut introduced its Retro Burger line of ground beef. The return of sizzle-fried patties and melted cheddar was a throwback for American stomachs. With even less flair, Roland Winters changed its name from the short-lived *Winters Olde-Tyme Extreme Eatz* back to the original Olde-Tyme Hamburgers.

Immediately, the burger behemoths started slugging away in the bout's twelfth round. As opposed to the "More beef and cheese…and country sausage" mentality of years past, Roland Winters and Bust-A-Gut CEO Clifford Findlay are currently in the midst of revolutionizing cholesterol counts as America knows it.

Winters' Reuben Sandwich Burger birthed Bust-A-Gut's Teriyaki Jerky Burger. (Two all-beef patties, special sauce, lettuce, cheese and a quarter pound of teriyaki beef jerky on a sesame seed bun. "Don't forget the chopsticks!" the commercials claimed.) Olde-Tyme responded with the Lunch-on-a-Bun (a submarine hoagie roll with three beef patties, cheese, onion rings, French fries and, at the tail end: a slice of hot apple pie). Sales blimped for both corporations as the general public anticipated each side's response like summer blockbusters. Despite outcry from Health Watch International and several subsequent *Nightbeat* specials, the war continues. Rumors of rampant spying and sabotage buzz through online blogs.

Recently, Bust-A-Gut threw the blue and yellow gauntlet

with its Monte Cristo Burger, a double bacon cheeseburger with onions, tomato, lettuce and Baco-naise© all dipped in a thick batter and deep-fried until golden. The dome-obsessed restaurant bragged about the process locking in the flavor and American stomachs agreed. It soon ground all sales records into powder and snuffed them up its nose.

In a publicity stunt, the Bust-A-Gut's mascot—Bonzo the Burger Clown—died from a heart attack after eating a Monte Cristo. The commercial coroner determined his passing had nothing to do with calories and arteries, rather his taste buds overloaded from the sandwich's freshness. "Talk about dying with a smile on your face," the television doctor proclaimed.

Monte-Mania swept the continent for several months. The deep-fried lump even appeared on the cover of *Time*.

Winters counteracted with an even larger strike, a blow so deep many consider it the final word in the Burger Wars. Just prior to the death of its founder, Olde-Tyme Hamburgers unveiled the revolutionary Space Burger. Modeled after astronaut food, it is the world's only freeze dried burger. Customers marveled that it weighed less than a pack of gum, but tasted like Styrofoamy meat.

NASA was approached as a marketing partner, but proved too expensive. Soon a new ad campaign, in conjunction with the budget-priced Russian Space Program, was launched.

TWENTY-TWO

"Yes," a broken Russian voice says. "Hamburgers do taste better in zero gravity, comrade." The screen fills with a press photo of the four-man, one-woman space team. According to our *Cosmonaut Watch* anchorman, video feed is still unavailable with the space travelers.

"Luckily," the man with perfect teeth and a non-regional American dialect tells us, "we can still communicate with the cosmonauts via radio."

"We did not think we would ever eat again," says a voice the viewer is told belongs to Dimitri. He sounds squeakier—less diplomatic than before. Something has changed in this man and not for the good. "Thankfully, many brave Americans guided our Space Burgers home."

"Now, Dimitri," our anchor says smoothly. "Just who is that lucky person? I'm told you are the only ones with equipment to determine the winner."

"Ah, yes, yes," the squeaky voice says, like stepping on a canary. "But our Russian space equipment is much slower and weaker than your state-of-the-art American computers. We will not have answer until eight PM, Eastern Standard Time tomorrow."

"Well, Mister Cosmonaut," our anchor says. "We'll all be tuned in with baited breath for the results. Any final words before we sign off tonight?"

"Yes," Dimitri says. "Thank you America, but thanks also to Winters Olde-Tyme Space Burgers for saving our lives. It is truly the finest hamburger in the galaxy."

"Ha, well gosh," our anchor says. "There you have it folks, we did it. We saved the cosmonauts and it's all thanks to you and Space Burgers. Don't forget, tomorrow at eight PM, five Western, we'll announce the results. Please stay tuned for another thrilling edition of *Nightbeat*."

TWENTY-THREE

The bar Malinta picks looks wet. The floor and seats and tables have a greasy black vinyl glow. Henry runs palms along the booth to check that it's dry before sliding in. The light fixtures sweat a delicate blue light below.

"I'm thinking gin for you," Malinta says, rummaging through her purse. "Gin and tonic. Rocks maybe."

Henry has a sweet tooth for dessert wine, but spy training has taught him to adjust. "Wow, you got me nailed. Gin and tonic has been my drink since I was eleven."

"You should try and branch out. Have you had a good scotch? That's my top dod gamn choice. Gin, well, people should only drink clear liquor at the beach."

"I'm up for anything."

The scotch is old enough for middle school and boils down his throat. "It's good." Henry exhales nuclear breath. "I've been missing out my whole life." He slips fingers into his shoulder bag and rubs a Peppermint Pattie between his fingers, knowing it would cool his stomach the way it did after the Christopher Winters job. *Unlike love*, he thinks, *candy never disappoints*.

"Yeah," she purrs.

Oddly, Henry Hamler isn't nearly as frustrated with this job as he imagined. In fact, the last few days have been fun. He enjoys being someone else. When he's Henry Holgate, he's not the guy who murdered Winters. He's not the romantic equivalent of bowel cancer. Not to mention, he hasn't even thought about Lothario Speedwagon.

Instead, Henry's a stealthy Serengeti predator. Something soundless creeping through the brush. A mouth filled with dagger teeth. He's an obsessed animal, getting closer and closer to Malinta. Wooing her into the jaws of espionage.

Or so he tells himself.

"How's it been going," Henry says, "being a better person?"

"Hard."

"Really? You seem pretty good to me."

"Maybe I am. I don't know. I think everyone is toughest on themselves. I just sometimes look at the mirror and think, *this girl isn't very nice. This girl would be a terrible mother*." Outside of the office, Malinta slows down a gear or two. Where normally she spoke in a long string of sentences, she now breathes and pauses and closes her eyes in between.

"Kids?"

"Yeah, I think I want to be a mom. I mean, not like today, but someday soon. I never used to think that. I used to only want the fanciest title possible at work. But, I think a little kid would be cool. That's not scary, is it?"

"Yes."

She laughs and nods. "Tell me about yourself, Henry. Why are you working here?"

He holds back a cough just like the first time he smoked grass. The sting of scotch turns Henry's mind surprisingly fast. Instantly, Henry invents an interest in working for a good American product that makes people happy. He is really into global logistics. His family grew up surrounded by memories of burgers…plus, he's a spy.

"Aren't we all," she says. "I just killed a KGB operative in my bedroom last night."

"They're tough," Henry says, kicking himself for letting the booze break down his honesty. "That cold Russian blood pours out like honey, I hear."

"Among other things."

"So…" Henry takes an airy pause for drama, gracefully changing the subject. "Tell me something I don't know. Tell me how this place works."

"Runs itself really," she says, blowing blonde hair from her eyes. "I just collect a paycheck."

"That's not what I hear." He leans across the table, eye contact the whole way.

"Well, temps hear a lot of stuff," she sucks an ice cube from the empty glass. "Mostly the hum of copy machines." She laughs at her joke. A little, tight burst.

The after-work crowd fills the tiny room. Men in shiny shoes and women with haircuts the price of jewelry compare martinis. Gradually, Henry and Malinta have to raise their voices. Six empty scotch tumblers spread across the table by the time Henry's boss slips in the booth.

"Well, look at this group," Martin says. In the low blue light his Puerto Rican skin is espresso dark. The boss gives Hamler a once-over before his thin hips scoot the spy against the booth wall. "I didn't expect either of you here."

"I'm just getting to know our new employee, Marty."

"You've already forgotten my name, Ms. Redding?"

She grins and crushes a cube between her teeth.

"Well, Henry, catch me up to speed about yourself," his boss says. "Tell me the dirty secrets."

"Actually," Henry says, wagging a half-full glass over the table. "Malinta here was going to spill the beans about Bust-A-Gut." His jaw grinds, feeling this interrogation get complicated.

"There are a lot of beans, eh, Malinta?"

"More than you can count." She orders another scotch with fingers in the air. "What's new in gouda?"

"See, Henry, Malinta and I started together. Has it been two years? Some of us gave blowjobs for promotions and others plan cheese now."

"It's not like you don't have skills to offer."

Henry dives in and practically screams over the increasingly sharp chit-chat. "Let's not get off the subject here. I was promised dirt. You know, blackmail material."

"Okay…"

"Like real dirt."

Her eye hooks upward, thinking. "Well, my odds of dying from a snakebite are three and a half million-to-one," she says, raising an eyebrow. "But your chances of dying from a heart attack are two-point-five-to-one. That's forty percent of this entire room. How's that for blackmail, Henry?"

"Way to blow the safe open." Martin supplies a golf clap.

"That wasn't exactly what I had in mind," Hamler says, not sure whether that was sarcasm or not.

"Seriously, someone in this country dies from heart failure every two minutes," her left eye staggers closed. "Every third is a son-of-a-bitching." She cringes. "Son-of-a-*bleep*ing *Winters* customer."

Martin and Henry take a drink and cautiously eye one another.

"What about Bust-A-Gut customers?" Henry says.

"Who cares? Especially when we green-light my next campaign. Instead of thirty-second commercials, think thirty-minute news magazines blabbering about the deadly effects of Space Burgers." Her whiskey-soaked eyes squint and see two confused faces staring back. "Let me dumb it down for you boys. What if someone said Pepsi and Coke give you hemorrhoids? Instantly everyone will buy Dr. Pepper. Nobody asks if Dr. Pepper does too."

"If Winters is Pepsi, who's Coke?"

"More important," Martin says. "Who's Dr. Pepper?"

Henry kicks back the rest of the drink. His body is overcome once again with that first-cigarette feeling. He makes a mental note and lets Malinta ramble. He pulls out his cell and checks the clock. Lothario Speedwagon has a show in three hours. *When Malinta is done*, he thinks, *I'll bail out of here.*

The strong grip of his boss's right hand locks on Henry's thigh, tight enough to count the veins in that baby fat leg. Henry slowly glances toward Martin and blows smoke over his face.

In twenty minutes Malinta is sleeping in the booth while boss and temp kiss.

TWENTY-FOUR*

Excerpt from an eye-rolling conversation between Deshler and a friend.

DEAN: The longest I ever waited? I once had to wait three months for a video to arrive.

FRIEND: That's ridiculous. Was it something kinky from Thailand? Ping-pong balls or orangutans and stuff?

DEAN: No, better than that. It was this rare Butthole Surfers tape.

FRIEND: Oh, dude, don't start...

DEAN: Gibby was wild as shit at this concert, Milwaukee or something. There was smoke, a small pile of burning trash on the stage, an old medical school film of a penile transplant playing behind the drummers—

FRIEND: *Drummers?* As in plural?

DEAN: Yes, they had two. I've told you this. Anyway, he was singing real nasty. Gibby just ripped apart this mannequin and there were chunky plastic limbs everywhere. He took out this wiffleball bat...

FRIEND: Dude, come on, this was only interesting the first hundred times you told me.

DEAN: Gibby'd pissed in the bat's tiny opening earlier, and was swinging it around. Called it his Piss Wand. It splattered the audience. He was singing "The Shah Sleeps in Lee Harvey's Grave."

FRIEND: And this guy's your hero? That's kind of messed up.

DEAN: No, not at all. Look, I needed that. When I bought that video my brother and I were staying at, at, at this relative's place. My folks were...you know.

FRIEND: Gone?

DEAN: In several senses. Anyhow, Gibby burned into my skin like a fog lamp. He was up there doing it, bringing people to their knees like a puke-stained preacher.

FRIEND: You're sick. I need to go home. Can you grab my coat? You should really try watching some of that Thai porno. Sounds like you need a little culture.

DEAN: Gibby broke the rules. He did everything, so now anything is possible. His art was so over the top that he clear-cut a forest for the rest of us to march through. I can do anything I want. My art is free, thanks to him.

FRIEND: I'll be sure to send him a card.

TWENTY-FIVE

The rabbit ears of the Cliff Drinker's senses twist and dip until they pull in a decent signal. Dean's eyes are closed. Blood beats through his head like cymbal crashes and he's out of air. Someone is jumping on him. A rib starts cracking. Feminine breaths huff like pumping weights.

Dean can't remember the lyrics to *Broken Piano for President* at this exact moment, but the music is there, wandering his skull.

A voice moans: "*Ohhh.*"

There's a twenty-five percent chance this involves bench pressing.

Deshler's eyes open. A nude woman bounces into his groin—blonde hair scurries over her face and stops at a bare chest. She is thin enough to count ribs.

"*R-R-R-RRR*, yeah," she says.

There is a zero percent chance she is pumping iron. Squat thrusts are another story.

He's seventy-five percent sure they are having sex.

The woman has a white bandage around her head.

"Ahhhh, whuuuuuh?" Deshler moans. He's one hundred percent sure this is sex. With Malinta, no less. A wave of amazement floods over his body. Like most of his previous hookups, Dean had no idea he is smooth enough to reach this point, but he's not arguing.

"There you are...I thought—" She slows to breathe deep a few times. "I thought you died on me."

"Wha...huh? Oh, yes! No, I'm alive," he hoots, wondering if this is an accident. *Maybe she tripped and fell?* he thinks.

"Don't stop, I'm close, I'm—" she gasps. For a split second, looking into her green eyes, Deshler's crushing skull ache disappears.

Do not forget this moment, he thinks. *Don't forget her skin. Don't push her away.* He stops to take in a sober glance. *Don't do anything stupid.*

Yellow bangs flop back over her face and Deshler goes cross-eyed again.

Dean returns to consciousness with gravity bullying him around. He can't lift an arm or wiggle a toe, but his eyes crack a flinch.

"Wake up, softie," Malinta nursery rhyme sings. She is curled into his body. "Wake up, softie. I won't tell anyone."

"Tell *what?*" he says, waterlogged.

"I won't tell anyone that you went soft on me. Lucky I finished or I'd tell your little buddies at Beef Club," she smiles. Her fingers dance through Dean's chest hair. "You feel okay?"

"I'm fine. Just tired," he says, smelling Malinta's hair, the shampoo sweetness planting fresh flowers in his lungs. "I played a show last night, I'm beat."

"You played a *what?*"

Thanks to the newspaper article, Lothario Speedwagon sold more than a few tapes at last night's gig. They actually offloaded the remaining stock of *Broken Piano for President* due to the overwhelming attendance. The article's picture didn't hurt either. In it, Deshler hung from his knees on a drainpipe in a dingy basement club. His bright orange mask was stained down the middle from a bloody nose, he howled into a microphone and yanked a frightened woman by the hair like a caveman.

For some reason, he wore this same getup walking around before last night's show. The blood was now crusty and browned. Mask recognition meant half the packed club bought our neon-faced hero a shot of bourbon.

Lothario was headlining a three-band bill at The Purple Bottle. The club is the musty basement of a downtown carpet cleaning service which hosts rock shows and a bar. Lavender paint snowed from the walls when Lothario cranked amps to max. The cigarette smoke near the stage was so thick it acted as a makeshift fog machine. Add that to their dozen black lights and fluorescent face gear and the Lothario's heads floated through dark haze like atomic particles.

Besides house parties, The Purple Bottle is the only place in town Dean, Hamler, and Pandemic can still get a gig. But even when the Bottle is packed, it's no great feat. The crowd couldn't fill a bus.

Deshler doesn't remember ever touching the stage. Lying next to Malinta on cool, clean sheets, he hopes it went well, especially with the big performance piece planned for the show.

Morning light slashes through window blinds and burns on Deshler's bare stomach. The bedroom is a foreign country. The walls are empty and cheddar yellow, trimmed in blue. It's so clean he doesn't even see any clothes on the floor.

"Hello," she snaps her fingers. "You played a show, Deshler?"

"Nuh, nothing, forget it."

She sighs and rolls off the bed with a squeak. "Come on, get up Mister Secret, I'll make some coffee."

His performance art piece was supposed to mimic the meat grinder of society. Gibby cleared the forest, now Dean had to make a statement amongst the leftover wreckage.

Nobody listens unless you force them, he thought before the show, complimenting himself on being such an artistic genius. *This isn't pissing into a baseball bat, but it'll do.*

Deshler bought ten pounds of stale hamburger buns, three heads of lettuce, seventeen tomatoes and value-sized containers of mustard and ketchup. He planned to cover the audience with these ingredients, making one large human hamburger while the band did its thing. The ketchup and mustard would be tossed out in Ziploc baggies.

The French press whiffs through the bathroom while Dean unrolls a condom into the toilet. His piss lasts exhaustingly long. From the mirror reflection, Deshler thinks about checking into a hospital—his hair is another night's sleep from knotting into a single dreadlock, his arms and legs are covered in blue-purple bruises and his chest stinks like condiments. Every step is like stumbling around on stilts.

Dean's mouth, however, hangs unchanged, still confused as ever. His lip is plump and split open.

He flushes and pauses for a second, wishing he could remember what convinced Malinta to jump into the sack. It's starting to get on his nerves, this Cliff Drinker's memory. He's amazed at his ability to pull Malinta close and gets anxiety knowing he'll eventually push her away like all the others.

The kitchen's electric yellow walls and blue trim are exactly like a Bust-A-Gut dome, too. Deshler worries about Malinta's psychological state and overzealous job loyalty when the plates and mugs match this paintjob.

"Un, deux, trois, quatre..." Dean discovers her pulling cups from a cabinet—speaking quietly, privately, and with an accent. "Quatre...q...q—"

"Cinq," he says.

"How'd you know that?" She turns, eyes surprised.

"Three years of French in high school."

"Me too. I used to be able to read whole French novels, but I just let it go. Isn't that sad?"

"I don't know."

"I think so."

"Are you going to Paris or something?"

"No. I just think I should relearn it. It's a shame to let talent go to waste. A good person wouldn't just waste all these valuable bleeping skills to sell hamburgers. She'd be well-rounded."

"I've never had one thought about cinq until today."

"Drink your coffee."

"Café." He grins and sips.

Her eyes don't say *funny*, but they don't disagree, either. She passes him a full, hot mug.

Sitting at the table, the black coffee cuts Deshler's tongue like a branding iron. "Do you have any crème?"

She squints.

"Cream."

"Oh. I doubt it."

"Any milk?"

"Uhm..."

"Sugar?"

She smiles, head shaking. "Darned if I know."

Deshler sips and winces. Nude, his legs are crossed in an attempt to be casual. Malinta, in a blue and yellow robe, laughs through her nose.

"Why do you talk like that? Are you born-again or something?"

"Stop. Don't be mean."

"Seriously," Dean says.

"You know."

"Remind me."

"Because, stupid, I'm a lady. I'm a good person. Or, at least, I'm supposed to be."

"And swearing's not—"

"Yes, yes, yes. Don't rub it in, I know I sound dumb. Eventually, I'll cut it out all together." Her finger begins twisting a lock of hair. "Someday you'll thank me when our kids don't speak like truckers."

"Our?"

"Don't F-ing start."

"Start what?"

"We've talked about this. Don't act like you don't know I want a family."

"Right, right. It's…ah…too early. Can we please just discuss something else?"

That giggle returns. "Okay, wise guy. I can't believe you tracked me down last night," she says through a smile.

"Me neither," he says truthfully.

"I got *so* drunk with my coworkers at a happy hour. Where did we even run into one another?"

Deshler looks around the room, pretending not to hear. "You have," he forces down another sip. "A great place."

"It's not mine," she says, squinting one eye. "It's *Clifford's*."

Deshler leans forward and rubs a stubbly chin. Another massive headache isn't far off.

"Clifford Findlay, right?" Dean says, amazed he remembered the name. Still not sure if he's ever parked the Bust-A-Gut chief's car. "Why aren't we at your place or mine?"

"Take a wild guess."

"He's a nice guy?"

"Uh, yeah, Bust-A-Gut's president, the most powerful man in hamburgers, is just doing this because he's a nice guy. He's not kissing your ass or anything." Her shoulders tighten. "Er, butt…rear."

"Derrière?"

"Cut it out."

Dean can't stop watching the blinding yellow walls. "I'm serious. Just tell me. Your paint isn't *that* bad."

"You've seen my place enough to know the answer." She grows red and picks an arm scab. Malinta's attitude jumps the rails and her face gets dark. "Fine, you want to screw around this morning, here's an answer. I'm sick of playing this game," she says, fishing a cell phone from her purse. "Talk to someone who enjoys your little stunts."

The phone is ringing when Deshler presses it to a throbbing ear. He swears it's an hour between buzzes.

"Lepsic here."

Deshler's confused morning growl says, "Thurman Lepsic?"

"You got him, who is this?"

"Deshler Dean…" The sensation of swimming and sinking pulls inside him.

A shotgun blast of recognition rattles the phone. "Ahhhhhh! My man! I *thought* that was Malinta's phone number. Things must've worked out last night."

The Cliff Drinker is paddling with a wrecking ball tied around his waist. Water sloshing at the neck, filtering salty into his mouth. "Errrrrr," Deshler says.

Malinta's head cocks, half-listening, half-burning a hole through his forehead.

"Well, I'm on my way to Miami for mozzarella testing. Help yourself to Old Man Findlay's wine cellar. Just don't touch the Dom Pérignon eighty-three."

"Wouldn't," he says, faintly, "dream of it."

"Perfect. Enjoy yourself. You've earned it. And I'll see you in a couple days."

"Thanks for the hospitality, Thurman."

"Hey, what Mister Findlay doesn't know won't hurt him. Now seriously, you've earned it."

"Stop."

The phone vibrates with Lepsic's chuckle. "One last thing," his voice slinks into a whisper. "Squeeze Malinta's ass when she's on top. Drives her wild."

Dry air hisses through the phone. Malinta pours another coffee. She has a wrinkled, confused forehead. "That wasn't Findlay, was it?"

"Thurman Lepsic."

The space between her lips splits wider. "I dialed Findlay's phone number. God, it's weird that he'd answer. What do you think that means?"

"He seemed pretty friendly...again."

She stands and tucks hair behind an ear. Bare feet pace from the sink, across the room, to the refrigerator. "He should be friendly, being your *other* boss and all."

"You bet." Dean swallows scratchy, selling himself hard on this lie, forgetting he doesn't know what Malinta's talking about. Playing along, nodding. *This is still more fun than parking cars,* he thinks.

"How can you sit there and not be a little freaked out by this? We're talking about the same man who practically puts a tongue in your throat every time he sees you. The guy who pays the Beef Club waiters to keep your whiskey glass full, no matter what. First, he tells you to crash at the CEO's penthouse. And now he's answering that same CEO's phone?"

"Are you thinking what I'm thinking?"

She waits, sips, and waits more.

"They're *doing* it," Dean says.

"You have no idea what's going on, do you?"

Deshler's body shrinks, his knees pull together and arms wrap around his chest. Familiar chills arrive. The same lonely confusion from that first night he and his brother spent in separate foster homes.

Malinta's face is upset, changing shades of color. She speaks with whip-snap arms and hands. "Sometimes you don't act like a rising star. I mean, you *created* the Monte Cristo Burger, for God's sake. It'd be nice if you at least pretended to be Bust-A-Gut's golden boy once in a while."

"Ohhh," he holds this noise for a breath. Her last words punt away lonely sensations like a boot in the abdomen. "Oh, you'll believe anything you read on the bathroom wall."

"Look, I've never told you this before. I didn't want to give you a big head." She tops off his coffee. "But I'd never seen anything like it when you staggered into the Beef Club six months ago."

Deshler looks at her in a twist of confusion.

"I mean, yeah, you were just some dipshit valet from downstairs and the place was packed with execs."

"Why didn't they just kick me out?"

"Remember what you said to Christopher Winters? I hadn't seen the old retired bastard—*gentleman*—look so pleased in years. You walked around like you owned the place. Kind of sexy."

"*The* Christopher Winters? The governor and the hamburger guy? The dude who invented the electric toothbrush?"

"God, he loved you. You're such an idiot. I mean, how would you *not* think Clifford Findlay would get goo-goo eyes, too?"

Playing along, nodding. "That was so long ago. I don't even feel like the same person. I hardly remember it."

"Yeah, no wonder. You're always drunk. Lucky for you nobody notices. The others are just as hammered."

"I don't—" he gives up in embarrassment.

"Remember that night you got in an argument with our accounting chief about the world's most delicious sandwich?"

"Of...course."

"I can't believe he claimed the club sandwich was perfect. And, hah," a fast hand covers her mouth to stop laughing. "And your response, I never told you, but it's kind of a catchphrase around work now."

Deshler's fingernails ruffle his scalp, wishing this morning was over. He anticipates a cringe. Forgotten Cliff Drinking stories always get embarrassing fast.

"You told Greenie Bowling, the head accountant guy, that 'compared to a Monte Cristo sandwich, the club tastes like crapped pants.'"

A breath of relief sneaks in. This story isn't so bad. "Does that even make sense?"

"You tell me. In less than a month we were deep frying Monte Cristo burgers in fifteen test markets. And then, well, *boom!*"

She smiles in a way that makes the room a few shades clearer. Her face graduates from faintly flirty to plain flirty. Deshler's heart smacks. An ashy thought of kissing her reshuffles the information about Beef Clubs and executives and fried sandwiches.

"Oh, that old thing," Dean mumbles. He suddenly cools down with the need to sleep. Lying, he quickly learns, is exhausting. "That was just an accident, you know? Anybody could have done...what it is I do."

"Don't be modest." Before Deshler takes another hot black sip, her fingers are massaging his shoulders. "Lots of stuff comes about on accident. Bubble gum, thousand island dressing..."

"Thanks, that's a big help."

Malinta stops rubbing, leans over his shoulder and kisses his forehead. "Wow, you really are an idiot."

He steadies himself and stands. "I'd rather not talk about it." Fingers go shaky touching her hips through the robe.

Before Dean finishes speaking, Malinta pulls back, arms and hands darting again. "Oh, this again? Not so fast. I still haven't forgiven you for letting Winters sink in his claws. What a jerk."

"Easy, have some respect, that guy just died."

"Duh, Roland. What did he say to get you on their side?"

"Side? Like a fight?"

"It's bigger than a fight, dummy," she says. Dean loses concentration when her robe unties a bit and showcases some thigh. "Don't act like the slut of the hamburger world doesn't know it's a fight."

"Slut?"

"Slut's not a bad word."

"Me?"

"Yes, you. Playing both sides of the Beef Club. Mister double agent."

"Oh, crap," he catches these words as they slip out. He turns the lie crank in his head and, "Sometimes I forget that stuff," plops out.

"It works. You really saved your own ass coming up with the Space Burger and that whole cosmonaut thing." Noticing Dean's wandering thigh eyes, she cinches the robe in a yank. "You are shattering what used to be a friendly rivalry."

"How me? Don't blame me."

"When you swung *back* to Bust-A-Gut's side, I saw a change in management. Like, joy or something. That fried mozzarella burger is going to destroy Winters. It's the next logical step. Plus, I've been working on projects of my own, you know?"

Gulping, head dizzy, he sits back down. "I need something to eat. I need aspirin. Or cyanide."

"Do me a huge favor, Deshler. Come with me to the club tonight. Don't drink, just hang out sober. I want to try an experiment."

"I think it'd be best if I stayed away for a while."

"Oh, mister responsibility, now? Just do it, come for me. Sober."

"I'll try. What time is it?"

"Like, three."

"Shit, I'm late."

TWENTY-SIX

Our tightly manicured anchor seduces the business-end of a camera.

"Welcome to *Cosmonaut Watch*. Big day for these heroes, so let's just get down to the action, shall we?

"After safely splashing down near the Black Sea, the five stranded cosmonauts were welcomed home. A tickertape parade stretching the length of Moscow was held yesterday. In a ceremony that night, Russian Premiere Michael Medvedev gave the space travelers the nation's highest honor, the Order of St. Andrew.

"The cosmonauts' ordeal, which played out right here on national television and internet broadcasts, became the number-one program in America during Sweeps Week.

"According to Winters Olde-Tyme Hamburgers, the final contestant to guide the suit home, and winner of the contest, will be announced as soon as he or she is located. The company is having more difficulty than previously anticipated tracking down this hero.

"We sincerely apologize for the delay.

"A Winters representative assured me that even though they are rescheduling the broadcast, it will be quite worth the wait. This is an exclusive here, the winner will be revealed in a prime-time special reuniting the wayward spacemen and the lucky hero whose love of hamburgers saved the Russians. A once-in-a-lifetime television event. If you miss this you might as well turn in your citizenship. You may not love freedom as much as you think. Please tune in, folks.

"And next, a preview of tonight's *can't miss* edition of *Nightbeat*."

TWENTY-SEVEN

"So they're hitting below the belt?" Tony says. The hot water in his mug swallows a green teabag and turns morbid colors.

"I guess, I mean." Hamler fishes through a leather shoulder bag for a cigarette. "If what Malinta Redding says is for real, they're only doing research on heart attacks. Big deal." There's a casualness in his voice, a softening of once-jagged edges.

The coffee shop Tony chose is silent during this weekday lull. It's dark for the afternoon and full of hanging plants. The barista reads a book, jawing some gum.

"Tell me the truth here." Tony sips from the cup and puckers his face. "Are they in production on this heart disease piece? Do they have families of dead guys spilling their guts? Doctors, scientists, whoever else producers get for this shit?"

"Can't say."

"Did you ask her?"

He thinks about Martin's five o'clock shadow sandpapering his lips. "No, Tony. She was shitty drunk. Like, five scotches."

"That's the *perfect* time."

Martin's hands were strong, felt dangerous. "Yeah right, I was lucky *that* slipped. I'd like to see you do your job as tanked as we were." That strength and danger transferred to Hamler like an anti-anxiety mainline. His lips were ready to fall off. They'd been so lonely until Martin.

But now it's that beating, kicking, uppercutting muscle in his chest that threatens to skip town.

"Look." The calm coffee date snaps and falls to Henry's

feet. The bare anger of a man trying to do his job stares back at the young spy. "I've done my duties bouncing off the walls on angel dust because *that's* what the situation called for," Tony says through grinding teeth. "I do not miss Bonzo the Burger Clown."

"Jesus. You did that? *You* killed him?"

"Not important. My point is, I did my job. And I did it well."

A steamy snake from Henry's coffee charms up between the men. Hamler's shoulders drop soft. "You're right, I've got a lot to learn I guess," Henry says, hoping to cool his boss down a few hundred degrees.

"There is no room for sentimentality in the workplace." Tony's finger darts to his mouth, working a nail between teeth. He closes his jaw and sucks on nothing.

"You're right. I can't let obstacles stand between me and—"

La Cucaracha plinks from Tony's cell phone. He fetches it from a coat pocket and answers without a flinch.

Henry jerks back to the Purple Bottle's stage last night. He remembers fumbling through a few notes of *La Cucaracha* on his bass while Pandemic lit his cymbals on fire with rubbing alcohol. The crowd went into mob-mode, half stomping up the exit stairs and half launching buns and vegetables at the band. Henry called it a night after a tomato exploded off his chest. Being in a band didn't feel like a lot of fun at that moment.

Hamler's boss stands and walks into the restroom, whispering to the phone.

The Lothario show was packed. Hamler was incredibly late, but when he stepped on the short stage a sweaty fog rose to the ceiling from the bodies. They only finished a few songs, though. Before turning off the bass amp, there was a lot of pushing near the front—someone pissed about mustard in a girlfriend's hair.

Dean was face-down at the lip of the stage, unconscious, sweat glossed across bare shoulder blades. Day-Glo mask nothing but shreds around his ears. The black lights amplified papier-mâché scraps into nuclear chunks. The blood from Dean's mouth was a growing dark pool of motor oil under the purple gleam.

Hamler sparks a cigarette and listens to his ears squeal in the silent coffee shop. He probably isn't supposed to smoke here, but it's not his first worry.

Henry's ears began ringing when he set the guitar against a giant speaker cabinet and clicked on the distortion pedal. The gutter symphony of feedback was enough to rattle Dean to limp consciousness.

In a move as traditional as the band's psychedelic tribal masks, Hamler lugged the vocalist over his shoulders and carried him offstage. Roll credits.

Maybe I should have missed that whole gig, he thinks. Flashbacks of Martin's scruffy face remind Henry why he nearly missed it, originally. The scent of the cheese buyer's hair stays fresh in Henry's mind.

Hamler sips coffee and asks, *Is it worth it? I mean, when we walked off the stage nobody clapped. Were they entertained? It was art, but they didn't cheer. I guess it was art.* He realizes it would feel nice to make art *and* have people enjoy themselves. *There has to be a mixture. But is that art? Are people supposed to cheer for art?*

Maybe I'm not a band guy.

Maybe I'm not an art guy. Deshler's an art guy.

I don't even like playing bass. Whose idea was that?

Lothario Speedwagon's a dumb name. God, I've been wasting the last six months. I could have been working overtime or something.

I'm pretending to be someone I'm not.

Tony returns and speaks like a coach offering to buy the little league team a pizza, "Okay, guy, you need a ride." He slices a fingernail back between teeth.

"My bus ticket is still good, thanks." Henry is unusually feisty today.

"No, you misunderstood. You-Need-A-Ride. As in, you and I are going to ride in my car together." He picks up a coat and briefcase, tonguing something toothy. "Now."

Tony's car is disappointing. Hamler assumed it would be a sleek spy cruiser. Something incognito and fast. Henry always figured if he stuck with this gig long enough, the big payday would arrive. Instead, his boss drives a heavily dented Japanese sedan. Tony picks up a fistful of Bust-A-Gut drive-through bags from the passenger side. "Research," he says. Everything smells like French fries. It smells like good fries, like grease.

They pull around the block. "God," he says, picking a tooth, blood on the fingertip. "I hate steak."

"I can't afford it."

"That's gonna change," Tony says.

"I doubt that," Henry says, noticing the glove box doesn't latch. It hangs open like Dean's stupid mouth.

"I'm sitting on a lotto ticket with your name on it."

"What?"

"The boss says kill Malinta."

Tense, Henry's feet lock against the floorboard, back shoving into the seat. "Not me."

"You're the only one. You're close. Our inside man. Look, he wanted you to torture her first. Pull out fingernails, burn her with a lighter, play your band's stupid tape."

"Hey."

"But I said no way. I went to bat for you."

"I said I'm through." Henry realizes his confidence has taken a leap. He wonders if his new romance might be a bit of the answer. Making out, it seems, is better than therapy. "You promised nothing dirty on this job. No *final* solutions."

"I don't remember that precise conversation. We never said *never*." He pulls that wet red finger out of his mouth with a sigh, marveling at a fleshy chunk.

"Do not make me do this."

Tony's voice shifts to calm now: "Henry, it's done. Tomorrow's your last day at the office. You found a full-time gig delivering pizzas, so you're quitting. And then killing that vice president of marketing."

"No."

"Or the other way around, I don't really care."

Hamler's head shakes, snorting through his nose like a hay fevered pig.

"Yes." Tony rubs something gooey on a pantleg and lets the

sound of the city and the car's heater fill the silence for a few blocks. "This isn't a negotiation. It's your job."

"What good will this do? We'll lose any chance at more info."

"The boss, Roland Winters himself, says this heart attack program can't air. We're banking that it's only in the development stage and that Redding trumped up its importance. This is top priority shit."

"I just can't make myself do that again. It felt all…" Guilty memories claw for air and paint a fresh layer in his mind.

"I told you, Henry." He looks ahead at old women crossing the street. "This is not a negotiation."

TWENTY-EIGHT

"Dude, I'll grab it. Just sit tight," Napoleon says, out of breath. "I love the German ones."

Deshler didn't have time to fix his clothes after leaving Findlay's condo. The Cliff Drinker's white jacket arm is torn and his lapel mysteriously stained with cabernet. He's in jeans instead of black slacks.

I would rather work as a chemical toilet than park another car, he thinks, shaking off the dents and scratches he's already embedded on some cars today. *This is not what an artist should be doing. I should be writing a song, not paralleling some asshole's Beamer. Gibby wouldn't be caught dead parking cars.*

The afternoon brings a charcoal sketch of darkness and aching wind over downtown. Office windows above the street pop white light onto the busy motorway below. There is stillness, loaded thick with chill.

A family pours from the green German SUV. They are a wholesome catalog spread of glossy photos, fixing one another's jacket collars and adjusting each other's knitted caps.

"Hey, I brought the paper today," Napoleon says walking toward the family, then turning. "You can check out the music reviews if you do me a favor."

Deshler grunts as tired eyelids seal together. He stands and flings the hotel entrance open, nearly knocking the youngest boy to his ass. He apologizes in some raw pirate dialect. "What favor?"

"Here, I transferred some of my films to DVD. Just for

you. You really need to check them out." He gets no reaction from Deshler. "You're in one."

"I don't remember that."

"You were kind of drunk."

Dean grunts.

"But I think it came out pretty sweet. You won't be disappointed." Napoleon passes the silver disc in a plastic sleeve along with the newspaper. Next, he trades a valet tag for German keys.

Alone under the awning, Deshler flips open the daily paper. The entertainment section has a sidebar about the band.

Dean sets the DVD on his wooden stool. "Ghrmmmm," he growls, blindly finding vocal chords. "Interesting."

He flips the print toward a streetlight. The band's article is strong-armed to the edge of the paper by a piece about John Cougar Mellencamp coming to town.

LOTHARIO SPEEDWAGON CRASHES

The Purple Bottle was packed in anticipation of cult hotshots Lothario Speedwagon. Fans I spoke with were there more to see what happens, rather than hear what happens. This turned out to be the smartest reason to pay the door fee, since there was little to be heard, but plenty to watch.

The band's pipecleaner-thin drummer sat down first as their homemade light kit flickered (think twenty Black lights on the fritz) and he hammered a tribal riff on his kick drum and the hood of a Chevy Lumina. He was alone, save for the empty bass rig to his left and the flash and pop of lights. His paper mask was a splash of hot lava.

In a heatwave of crowd pushing, Lotharios's singer emerged from behind a curtain to a scatter of howling fans. He appeared to be victim of some horrible kitchen accident. The equally anorexic frontman stumbled out naked to the waist, swinging a flood lamp like a lasso around his head. It gave his body a strobe light effect, which flashed a culinary disaster: Hamburger buns, lettuce, cheese and tomatoes stuck to his flesh, greased in ketchup and mustard.

"Thank you, I love your haircut as well. This is Broken Piano for President," he said with an Australian accent and face-planted into a song. His Satan-deep voice rattled loose more than a few kidney stones.

At the precise moment the singer flopped into the front row, covering everyone in condiment goo, a stocky guy in a shirt, tie and toxic green mask strapped on the bass. He looked like my psychedelic accountant and created torturous noise fit for ending hostage standoffs.

What happened during the next song was disputed from different fans. As Lotharios's rhythm section stumbled into a sonic mess that's best described as "car crash rock," the show was over.

The bass gurgled tuneless notes and drums clunked like garbage cans in a trash compactor. Finally, someone took a swing at the singer. Apparently, one fan didn't appreciate the mustard-hair treatment given to his date. The vocalist was unconscious for ten minutes as the band rolled on. Finally, the drummer lit his kit on fire, the bassist's amp blew feedback and someone tossed the singer over a shoulder fireman-style.

It's safe to say the wheels have fallen off the ol' Speedwagon. Question is, "Were they ever meant to stick in the first place?" And "Would we want them to?" This

is art, kids. Take it or leave it.
Me, personally, I'll leave it.

"Holy crap," Deshler says as Napoleon walks back. A popcorn bag of excitement bursts in his chest. "Did you read that thing?"

"Uh, yeah," Napoleon says, hesitant. "Sorry."

"Wow, they wrote a lot of stuff about us."

"But it wasn't good stuff."

"No such thing as bad publicity, dude."

"I don't know. This seems close."

A black car pulls in quiet as a dishwasher. A familiar man in a ketchup red coat sloshes out and stares at the pair.

"I think it's great. It sounds like people were entertained."

"Dude, seriously?"

Before either looks up from the paper, Roland Winters' voice dives in: "Hey, there's my slugger. How goes it, Dean?" He is a walrus with his mustache and heavy coat. "Let's grab a drink. Take off that ridiculous outfit, buddy."

Napoleon stumbles to Dean's side like a first mate. "Oh-um, sorry, Mister Winters, sir," the plump valet says, fixing his tie. "I'll be more than happy to put your car in its usual spot."

Deshler nods and points a finger at the walrus. "Right." His open mouth converts to a smile, recalling this morning's naked chat with Malinta. "Roland Winters…yeah."

"Terrific, Greg," Winters tells Napoleon.

"It's Napol—" He quivers before realizing the man is long gone.

The executive's coat flaps open and his burger belly stretches like a latex glove. "C'mon, Deshler." A walrus flipper wraps around Dean's shoulder. "The guys've been asking about you lately. We don't want to lose *The King*."

Napoleon's cheeks ripple as if he's three-fourths swallowed

his tongue. Little dragon shots of haze puff through his nose into the freezing air as pink fingers rub Winters' keychain.

"You know." Deshler's eyes drop to the ground. His mouth hangs momentarily confused. *I might as well see what this is all about,* he thinks. "God, yeah, I'd…" He eyes Napoleon. The small valet seems so pathetic. "Alright, forget it, yeah! Napoleon, tell the boss, tell her…you know."

A yellow SUV and a tiny Italian sedan are behind Winters' car. Napoleon can't hear them speak, but the drivers' lips practice unhappy patterns.

"Dean…whuh?" his partner says, eyes squinting with hurt.

As the glass doors close with Dean and the CEO of Olde-Tyme on the other side, Napoleon hears the executive say something that sounds like, "I think you'd look good in red."

Napoleon spots the special DVD still atop the wooden stool.

TWENTY-NINE

"Thanks for joining us here on *Cosmonaut Recap*," our titanium-chinned anchorman says. "I'd like to welcome the men and lady everyone has been waiting for. We've had a ball watching the highlights of their space oddity: the starvation, the psychosis, the laughs. But now it's time to hear from those brave souls who fought zero gravity and zero dinner to be here tonight." Our anchor stands and extends an arm to the side of the stage. "Please welcome the Moscow Five."

The television audience shakes the recording studio with applause. The Hollywood version of a space station—flashing lights and white padded walls—serves as the backdrop for five futuristic egg chairs. The entire set still smells of wet paint. The flimsy wall shimmies like aluminum siding in a tornado.

Four men and a woman in identical powder blue jumpsuits walk out smiling and waving. The men's hair is trimmed short, three have hefty chins and thick waists, jumpsuits wrapping their bodies like wetsuits. The woman's black bangs hang in front of a skinny face, her smile busy with destroyed teeth. The fourth man doesn't look anything like the three other male cosmonauts. He's so tiny he nearly disappears in profile. Unlike his commanding officer, this spaceman looks like he nearly starved to death up in the station.

"Wow, welcome," our anchor says, shaking each member's hand. "Glad you could be here."

The cosmonauts sit and our anchor takes a stool to the far

left. "Just so everyone at home can get it straight, introduce yourselves, please."

The astronaut closest to the host chatters to the others in choppy, harsh Russian. The cosmonauts nod and smile and murmur to one another.

"I am Dimitri, captain of the team," the first man says in a thick accent. His eyes don't look as empty as they did beaming down from the space station. They seem rather lively. "I will do interpreting for my comrades."

"Yuri, I Yuri am," the second says, looking much like his interpreter.

"Pavel," says the third, bulky and healthy.

"Sonja."

"Keith," the skeletally thin man says, hardly audible through his Russian tongue.

The audience giggles politely. "I'm sorry, *Keith*, did you say?" our anchor asks.

Keith is a broomstick with cheeks, nothing like his hearty comrades. He glares confused at the host while the audience continues.

Dimitri hammers out some casual Russian and Keith mumbles back.

"His parents," Dimitri says through a deep accent. "Are big fans of Rolling Stones and Keeeth Reechards."

"Ha, huh, wonderful," the host chuckles. "So are we."

The next five minutes revolve around Dimitri interpreting the team's sentiments. Keith and Sonja never smile. Their words grind past sore tongues, like speaking is exhausting. Their voices have seen hell and it's a Russian space station.

Dimitri explains for the television audience: everyone is glad to be home. Everyone missed their families very much. Yes, Space Burgers are delicious. No, the crew never thought they'd die, they had faith in the American people.

"So, I've got to ask," our anchor says with no accent. The guy's a total pro. "It's on everyone's mind. You folks have been back on Earth for about a week now. Still no *big* announcement. No contest winner."

"Yes, yes," Dimitri says with a blush. "We understand America demands to know. And we all want to tell." He breaks to say something in Russian. The muscular cosmonauts smile and nod. "As I mention earlier, sir, we are on tour of Winters Olde-Tyme Hamburger restaurants throughout country. And Sunday night, on national teevee, we will finally announce winner."

"Wow, that sounds spectacular."

"You-will-not-want-to-miss-it."

THIRTY

The Beef Club, as it's unofficially titled, is the entire eighteenth floor of the hotel. When Deshler and Napoleon have slow nights they discuss the Club. Or what they assume the Beef Club is like.

Napoleon guesses it's a cigar lounge, a nook from turn-of-the-century England. Everything in dark wood and brass. The chairs would be, as Napoleon put it, Creampuff Leather. Seats so huge and soft your rich ass gets a hug. He guesses visitors drink brandy and scotch and not much else. Members debate with stogies between their teeth, looking out over the city, planning the next Space Burger takeover.

Deshler's view is vague. He's never had a decent answer to stack against Napoleon's dream. Frankly, Dean's sober imagination is nothing to write home about.

Inside the elevator, Roland Winters and Dean small talk about the weather and basketball. The CEO swipes a keycard through a slot, a bulb lights green. He presses the eighteen button. "What's today, Friday?" Winters says as the box lifts.

"Uhm, no, it's Thursday."

"Thank God. This place will be a veterinary office full of table scraps tomorrow. Just like every Friday. I don't need that now."

Dean lets out an uncomfortable cough to fill the silent pressure building in the elevator.

"God, I hope those Bust-A-Gut assholes aren't here. Not today." Winters straightens red pant legs. "I'm not in the mood for that shit, you know?"

"I hear you," Dean says, almost too assured. He makes a note to play it down, be neutral.

"Scum suckers," Roland hisses. "Oh, I'm sorry, no offense, buddy. Not everyone who works with Bust-A-Gut. You, for example."

The elevator pings and the doors open right into the Beef Club. It isn't what Napoleon dreamed.

There is no oak. No bowtie-wearing bartender. No Creampuff Leather. It looks the same as the employee break room in the basement, but six-times larger and with a killer view of downtown.

Long fluorescent bulbs pop and sizzle overhead, soaking a yellow stain into the room. The couches are mismatched—some blue, some floral, some plaid. All are worn, stained, and hemorrhaging stuffing. The walls hang cheap photo prints fading orange. The room clutches a frat house quality Dean hasn't seen since visiting a buddy at college.

The Beef Club décor, you see, has a lot to do with its founder.

A few decades back, Christopher Winters and the owner of the hotel started the Beef Club. The American hero wanted somewhere his executives could unwind. In fact, several years after its inception, the benevolent burger boss even allowed Bust-A-Gut's people to join as a goodwill gesture. However, Winters was heavily bottom-line oriented and asked the hotel owner to decorate the club as inexpensively as possible, which turned out to be left-over hotel furniture from storage. Over the years a few people mutinied by hanging out in classier spots, but it never caught on. Winters dropped by the club every night, and wherever the man-who-nearly-caught-Hitler went, a crowd of followers remained. Heavy drinking on Fridays at the club is an institution. Rumor has it if you miss a Friday, you might come back to work without a job on Monday.

The bartender is the same kid Deshler's seen working at the lobby lounge. Dean laughs at how wrong Napoleon's theory is. This bartender's not the kind of guy who serves millionaires, he's the kind who huffs clear glue at break time. He has big, dumb eyes and a mouth that drops open when nobody is looking.

"Beer for me," Winters tells the kid. "And Deshler, you want your regular?"

A thousand drink orders rubber-ball-bounce around his skull. He's never had a regular drink at any phase in his life. At least not that he remembers.

"Right on, sir," the kid says. "One PBR and a Rusty Knife."

A Rusty Knife, Deshler learns, has something to do with whiskey, muddled cherries and sugar. Crushed maraschinos float like bits of flesh cleaned from an old blade.

The sun has nearly disappeared and the room crowds with men and women dressed to kill in the boardroom. Most drink cheap beer or wine from screw-top bottles—two drinks Winters Sr. and his tight wallet always enjoyed.

Deshler and the CEO sit at a wobble-legged table by the window. "Enough of this bologna, let's carve the turkey," Winters says, edging close. Dean looks at the CEO's skin—heavy wrinkles raccoon around the eyes and across the forehead.

"Let's do that," Deshler says, shaking his hollow skull, dreading the next words.

"My father loved you. He had a lot of faith in Deshler Dean. And if my dad had that vision, well, by golly, so do I. Christopher Winters was a genius. A genius I have a hard time living up to, as you can imagine." He straightens his imitation ketchup blazer.

"Consider yourself lucky." Deshler sips the drink. It tastes like Night Train and kicks at the head, leaving traces of buzz. "My Father was sort of sent off when I was young, but even when he was around he wasn't that fantastic. Good dads are a rare commodity." Dean's eyes feel inflated, his throat clears.

"Yes," Winters says, drawing it out uneasy. "I don't think anyone wants to hear that story twice, thanks."

Dean tries to push away all memories of Dad and Mom's blame. He attempts to pull in Winters. Dean's curious where this is going.

"Let's get to it. Have you thought about my offer? I hope you have."

"Sorry. Remind me, Roland, what's, ah, you know, the offer again?" Dean smiles at how easy honesty is. *Maybe this trend will catch on*, he thinks.

The walrus sighs and rubs at his temples. He grabs the mustard yellow knot around his neck and loosens it. "Christopher Winters is spinning in his grave, God rest his soul. I take it the answer is no?"

"Easy, easy," Deshler's flustered mouth guns out. "Let's just, you know, talk. *You* should talk."

"You're either in or out, Dean. Quit dusting my cock." Winters hails a waitress. Deshler looks down. His Rusty Knife is a stack of loose ice cubes. He doesn't remember finishing. "You've got a knack for this business. The Space Burger, that entire campaign is genius. Our profits have gone up two percent since it kicked off." Winters grows tense in the arms, crushing the beer can slightly. "I'll even give you credit, Bust-A-Gut's Monte Cristo...people eat that shit by the shovelful. You played ball for the other guys and really got us on that one."

A waitress brings a beer and a tumbler of Rusty Knife. Dean gulps down half, trying to stop his shaky arms from going completely haywire.

"And...and I know you're working with Findlay's people on another project." The CEO's bulky fingers fidget with the can tab, decapitating it. "Intelligence says it's something to do with cheese sticks. That's fine. I don't blame you for working with Bust-A-Gut again. You're a free agent."

Deshler silently agrees, keeping eye contact. The room rumbles with voices. One overhead light is switching on-to-off every few seconds.

"The Winters family knows…I know, that you could make a great VP of Development. Harry, the Chief of Development, knows it, too. He's excited to have you aboard. I mean, your reputation looks like the Fort Knox vault around here."

Deshler takes this in. Whiskey torpedoes around his brain, sinking tiny battleships of logic. He says the first thing on that evaporating mind. "Did the governor really say all that?"

"Absolutely." Roland's cheeks blush into cuts of salmon under a creeping layer of stubble. The bags below his eyes sag. "It keeps me up at night, trying to maintain Dad's legacy, walking in his shadow. I mean look at me, I'm the B-movie version of Christopher Winters. Getting you onboard was a dying wish from my father. He told me on his death bed to get that Dean kid at all costs. I just want to see that come true." Winters takes a gulp of beer and nearly chokes. "God…God rest his soul."

"That's flattering, Roland," Dean says, with a shallow pool of confidence filling. Dean recognizes this sensation—it's happiness. His entire life, when this feeling arrives he pushes it away. It's wrecked many friendships, loves, jobs and bands.

Most people on the receiving end of this push just stare at our hero like he doesn't know what he's doing. But Dean knows why he does it. It doesn't mean he hates himself any less, though.

Winters checks over his shoulder. A dark-skinned guy with a soul patch talks about the difference between sharp cheddar and extra sharp cheddar to a group. They ball fists behind their backs.

"So…?"

Magically, Deshler's second cocktail is gone. Skin hangs like it could dribble off his bones and into a puddle. A gentle hum starts in the chest and vibrates through his body the way several drinks inspire him before band practice.

Winters' sad eyes hold the stare. Dean fights off fidgets under their pressure.

The Cliff Drinker reminds himself that the alternative is parking cars eight hours a day and, apparently, Malinta thinks it's sexy when he struts around the Club like he knows something. Deshler is one tongue click from uttering: "Yeah, Roland, I'm in," and embracing happiness for once in his life, when a man with a salt and pepper beard clears his throat.

"Sir, we've made some progress on the contest winner," the man hisses into Winters' ear.

"Great. Talk to marketing about it."

"It's *you-know-who*. Harry is picking *you-know-who* up right now. The CEO should come by the office and say…" the man strains from behind that salty, peppery beard. "Hi, perhaps."

Winters eyes this man with shock. He's beaming hot and his posture is tight. "Oh, well, oh. Yes, I should. Deshler, let's sew this puppy up tomorrow over lunch." The CEO is up and practically out the door. "Are you free?"

"Completely," he says, thankful to have more time to think.

"Call Deb, she'll schedule something."

The waitress brings a third drink without a word. Deshler's brain unhinges and he stares at the lights across the city. It's relaxing, the warm buzz and the headlights going up and down the street. Fragments of Winters' talk enter Dean's consciousness, but fade to the skyline going to bed, getting dark, outlined in gentle orange streetlamps.

It doesn't even bother him that the room is thick with that musty cellar scent.

The revolving door of Dean's life swings and when he looks

up, Malinta is sitting in Winters' warm seat.

"What are you doing here? Drinking?"

"I'm…yes. It's called a Rusty Knife, apparently." His pool of confidence dries up, getting caught in the act.

"I know that."

"Right."

"You said you'd come with *me*, sober. And my coworkers said you were talking to *Roland Winters*."

"Yeah, we were discussing work."

"Deshler," she says with a shocked frown. "What about Clifford Findlay? What about Bust-A-Gut? Where's your allegiance this week?"

"I'm trying to figure that one out myself." He glances down. The whiskey and cherry are gone. His chest sparks with sour mash heartburn.

"You're gonna blow it. I just know it." She leans back, shoulders and confidence slackening. "Forget Bust-A-Gut, what about *us?*"

The waitress delivers another drink. Deshler looks at his hands and the tumbler, they shake in and out of focus. A tiny earthquake.

"It's like every time I start to trust you, I get shoved away. Like you want to hurt my feelings."

"That's not it."

"Well then?"

"Um…um…" it's there now—the why. Dean never quite saw the why all these years until now. He sees it, but is too embarrassed to explain that he pushes in hopes that someone, anyone, will return. "Um…" It hasn't worked with his parents, or his brother, or countless friends and girlfriends. Why would it take off now?

"It's always *um, um, um*," she snaps and stands. "Close your mouth."

THIRTY-ONE

Pandemic thrashes under the covers. It's the bull's-eye of frosty early winter weather, but his air conditioner is cranked up to eight. He is sweating through boxer shorts. The bedroom window is painted black with a layer of aluminum foil taped to the glass, blocking out this evening's fading daylight. The drummer has been up for nearly three days straight.

Pandemic can't purge the angry amphetamine juices from his body. Growing up, experimenting with drugs provided a clean perspective. One his father didn't understand or condone. Now, he smokes it and doesn't remember why. His jaw clenches enough to grind chicken bones to sand. His teeth are grains of rice. His muscles ache. His temper is spring-loaded and sensitive most days.

Juan is not who he used to be.

This thought, mixed among a dozen others cycling through his mind at once, causes him to pause. Pandemic knows his old self, but draws a dark curtain in his mind around that man. *You are better now than before*, he thinks. *You are the best drummer on earth. You are the handsomest dude in town. You are smarter than, like, Einstein and—* This pause escapes when the quiet bedroom explodes in metallic hammering. Pandemic's doorbell is a retired school alarm he wired in order to hear during drum practices. An icy silence fills the drafty house for a few moments. His eyes are wide open in the dark room now. Cool air touches his cheeks. There's soft knocking at the door, then the bell rings another carpet bomb across Pandemic's head.

"I'm busy here," he yells.

A few minutes later, those massive, scarred hands pull the front door open. Two people in matching green shirts tense at the sight of a skeleton in its underwear. They twist up noses and jerk back from the rotten odor floating from the living room.

The porch floorboards bend down hard. The paint is chipped and mildewed over. Shimmering webbing hangs overhead.

"I said I was busy," he sniffles. Pandemic's face is vanilla pudding skin.

The short black guy cranes up his neck. "Sir, sorry to bother you so late, is this the, uh—" He snaps a fast glance to his left. His partner is old and bored. The guy clears his throat. "Is this the home of Timothy Winters?"

Frigid evening air washes over Pandemic's body, balls slink upward and chest pigments burst into a light, rosy Rorschach.

"Are *you* Timothy Winters?" the older woman demands.

"Wrong house, fellas. Get off my porch before I buy a gun and learn to use it," the malnourished drummer says, knees shivering. He wraps blade-of-grass arms around that chest.

The man and woman bite lips and wait. Two cars pass the porch.

"Then," the man says with a fake smile. "Is this the home of *Juan Pandemic*?"

Pandemic flashes veiny eyes, dropped far back in his skull, between the two strangers. The older lady shifts a fist in her jacket pocket, the coat's breast slips open revealing a gray patch stitched into her green polo.

Pandemic knows what the shirt says and dreads the idea of continuing this conversation. "Shoo." That shirt gives him a jolt of a scare. It's one of the few things on this planet that can. "Shoo."

"Is that your name?"

"Vamos."

"Is. It?" The woman's voice is big now.

"Possibly."

"Well, sir, we've got some news," the woman says, not offering a fake smile. "May we come in?"

The living room is dark and smells like old refrigerators and rotting vegetables and untrained cats. Metal folding chairs are scattered, some on their feet, some flipped over. A stack of newspapers as tall as a toddler sits under the window, spoiling into yellow parchment.

"Mister Pandemic," the short man says. He sits nearest the door and rests a briefcase on his lap. "We have to get some things out of the way before we can tell you *exactly* why we're here."

Pandemic grumbles and wraps a blanket, freckled with cigarette-burns, around his shoulders.

"You need to tell us the truth." The lady sits next to the newspapers, absently scanning for a publication date.

"You guys aren't the cops, I'm not stupid." His neck cocks, "Or intimidated."

"No, we are not, sir."

"I'm not scared." He mumbles lower, with less pep. "I see your shirts."

The black man pops the case open and sifts through papers. "Good, this will be a lot easier then."

"Timothy, we need you to verify that that's your name," the gray-haired woman says, scooting her chair in Pandemic's direction.

"It's Juan. Why don't you come back tomorrow?"

"Now it's Juan. It used to be Timothy, right?"

"I'm calling my lawyer."

"Come on, kid. Look at this nest you call home," the lady says, switching her voice to motherly and caring. "You know you deserve better than this. Don't you, Tim?"

Pandemic bites his tongue and scratches a shoulder deep. It leaves red map lines from untrimmed fingernails. He can't make eye contact—can't even come up with an insult.

"What you tell us is confidential. There are only a few people who know about this. One being your father, of course."

His dry mouth swallows. It tastes like two rice-kernel teeth slid down with it. Juan can't fight who he is, so he gives up. "Yeah, I used to be Tim," he says, staring at the naked floorboards. "I changed it legally. So what? I'm better than Tim now."

"Yes, clearly." The man is calm, watching a mouse sniff its way across the floor. "That's Timothy James Winters, right?"

"Your dad is Roland," the woman says. "Your grandpa is Christopher, correct?"

"Uhm, yer, yes, I suppose. Yes." He jitters under the blanket, shifting his head from corner to corner of the room in a meth-twitch. A nervousness he hasn't shown in years.

"Son, we're from Olde-Tyme Hamburgers," the wrinkled woman says. "I'm Delia and this is Pierre."

Pandemic claws at raw scalp scabs. He notices for the first time the woman's left coat sleeve is empty. Delia is missing an arm.

"Son, your father wants to see you."

Wrapping the blanket tighter, Pandemic sneezes and lets the globby mess simply hang. "No way, I don't need that. I…I'm cool."

"It's—" Delia begins.

Pierre flicks one finger to stop. "Tim, it's complicated. It's not just for a family reunion, you see. Your dad tells me he is really excited to spend time with you and wishes that he did more often. But, you see, there's more to it than just that."

"What? The old man needs a kidney or some bone marrow? That'd be just about perfect." His voice gets unvarnished and nasty. "You tell him my kidney isn't for sale and I hope he dies—"

"Settle down," Pierre's voice is louder, more commanding. "It's nothing like kidneys."

"Son," Delia tweets. "You won the Space Burger contest. You're an international hero."

THIRTY-TWO

Since *Cosmonaut Recap* aired, Winters' Space Burger gets all the attention. Bust-A-Gut is combating with a media blitz praising rival burger magnate Christopher Winters. Three different ads air hourly on the major networks during primetime.

Commercial one involves a montage of Winters photos from his days in the Army (nothing summer camp-like, thankfully), his rise to fame as benevolent hamburger baron and his stint as governor.

Commercial two and three are basically the same thing. A woman walks through a gallery of photos of the dead man and says some witty, caring words about each stage of his life. All the commercials end with a touching portrait of Christopher Winters with his wife, son, Roland, daughter-in-law and grandson, Timothy.

Immediately following these ads in every American market, another commercial appears. This one begins with a heart monitor's bouncing blue-green spike—bleep…bleep…bleep…bleep.

The monitor suddenly stops and an intense electric death wails for an uncomfortable ten seconds.

A male voiceover, deep and carved from authority, breaks open the ad: "Winters Olde-Tyme Hamburgers and Bust-A-Gut want you dead."

The voice pauses for a breath. The strong *skree* holds steady throughout. "Find out more about their plot to kill you at www.healthwatchinternational.com. Sign up for the newsletter and receive a free tote bag."

Another sitcom begins.

THIRTY-THREE

"Big surprise, you look like the black plague," Roland Winters says, stomping into his office, ripping off a coat.

"We're not black," his son says.

Pandemic—born Timothy James Winters—sits in a heavy leather chair. He picks at the moon-surface of fleshy sores on his scalp. He wears a pair of clean slacks and a blue button-up shirt three sizes too large. A bony sternum pops through the gap in the collar. A man with long gray hair and a black hat forced Pandemic to slip into this outfit before setting foot in the corporate headquarters.

The CEO's office is an oven. It's huge and dark and constantly kept at body temperature. Pandemic doesn't know whether to curl up and go to bed or sprinkle garlic powder on his ribs and keep baking.

"I couldn't have made this up if I wanted to," the walrusian CEO says, summoning the same frightening, near-Hitler-capturing intensity Christopher used back when Roland was in trouble. "My father dies and Bust-A-Gut beats us to the punch in honoring him with a commercial. Then my drug addict son wins the big contest for everyone to see. And to top it off, he's about as thin as his crackpipe."

"Dad, I don't want to be the winner," he says, pinching eyes shut. "And I don't smoke crack."

"I'm sure fame and fortune is killing you, Tim," the father says, sitting across the desk, pulling a mustard tie completely loose. "That's why you played the game. That's why you are sabotaging Grandpa's—" He frowns and lowers the finger pointed toward heaven. "My company." He pulls the tie completely out from the collar.

"Look, it was an accident. I was just trying to do something nice. I was trying to help someone. You wouldn't know anything about that kind of shit."

"Well, it doesn't matter what I know, now. You've got a television date with some cosmonauts. Let's make the best of this."

"Cross me off that list," he says, scanning for the exit. All the doors look the same and there's about five of them. "Find someone else. Some other clown."

"Your uncle Jimmy was a clown. Elephant killed him, you know that. Have a heart."

The man with long gray hair and a black hat stands to the side, motionless. Winters shoots him a look, but that garbage bag wrinkled face doesn't budge.

"Tim, I've let you suck your thumb long enough. Your mother and I let you play in this rock group and we…I…turn the other cheek with the drugs. God, it would kill her. *I* look the other way, son."

"I'd classify Beth as a step-mother." Pandemic smacks gums and runs his tongue along the mouth's border, daydreaming about going home and smoking. "Speaking of elephants, how is Beth?"

"Damn it, Tim," he says, counting the ceiling beams and wheezing a tired breath until his blood pressure mellows. Roland's mustache flutters when the eruption begins again. "Pay attention to me. You either do this or you never come home again. I'm asking a favor here. I need you now, son. This is important." Roland Winters' imitation of his father crumbles and his mind scurries into a corner labeled: **Public Relations**. That fatherly growl softens to something smooth. "You won fair and square and you're gonna go through with this. Maybe not *you*, exactly."

Pandemic picks some rocky yellow crust from an eye. He slouches deeper into the chair. "No."

"You're in or you're out of the family. No more trust fund. Got it?"

The hands of an ancient grandfather clock chop away. Its gears fill the room with mechanical chunks.

Pandemic looks older, maybe more so than his father. A face beaten with too much of everything. "I suppose, I mean...I..." He has never been able to stand up to Dad and feels weak remembering past battles.

"Good enough," Roland snaps, rising and moving to the opposite side of the desk. "No drugs, got it? You'll say what we tell you to. You'll be the perfect spokesman, because you have to be. When this fiasco is over, you can run away to Timbuktu and I'll keep you afloat. I don't give a damn what you do, then. But I need you this time, kiddo. The company is at war."

"Uhm...wait...um..."

"Jesus, you're falling apart. Look at your head. Double Harry is going to get on the phone right now and find someone to patch you up." He rests a hand on his son's shoulder. "And find someone to keep an eye on you."

The father's hand pinches Pandemic's flesh. The son slouches deeper.

"Isn't that right, Harry?"

THIRTY-FOUR

Deshler opens the mail. There's a letter from his zip code. It's a Halloween card with Snoopy doing something cute. It's too late for Halloween. Plus, who sends a card for Halloween in the first place?

I've got the time. You've got the trouble. We should talk. Malinta's skull would agree, don't you think?

THIRTY-FIVE

The morning sun cracks through blinds as the apartment whistles from steam heat registers. Henry washes his face at the bathroom sink. The cool water burns like Aqua Velva. He takes time shaving and makes sure nothing dribbles on his shirt or tie. *It's important to look perfect on your last day*, he thinks, dreaming of Martin and that thing he does with his tongue.

Henry carefully twists on cufflinks and adjusts the holster around his ankle. "By the end of the day," his boss, Tony, told him, "Malinta Redding—Bust-A-Gut's vice president of marketing—must be dead. Period."

The cufflinks uncoil into metal wire strong enough to choke a yeti.

"I know what her job title is. You don't have to be so dramatic."

"I don't have time for smart asses."

"At least tell me, does our budget go beyond cufflinks?" Henry, still feisty with love, snapped at headquarters.

Tony, scalp glimmering beneath a sad lattice of hair, sneered, "Here, smart ass." He passed the young spy a small green water pistol. "Get her with this and the autopsy will look like a poisonous spider bit her. No joke."

The gun is heavier than Hamler anticipated. The holster slips around his sock and pokes its grassy colored snout below the pant leg.

An all-too-familiar seasickness swirls Henry's stomach. The same weightless paranoia that preceded the Christopher

Winters interview pounds on his conscience's entrance. He doesn't know how he'll kill another human being. Henry prays, in the back of his brain, that Malinta's odds of dying from a ladder fall finally pay off.

When the apartment door shakes and bangs, Henry's peaceful despair blasts away. Hamler nicks his chin with the razor. Instantly, a spittle of blood rivers down the porcelain. The door gives a wooden cough and squeaks open.

Henry's so tense his blood pressure could power a windmill. He inches toward the living room and estimates the seconds it will take to remove the spider-bite gun and stop this burglar.

There is a rustling near the couch, empty cereal bowls clattering, newspapers tossing against the wall. Tony warned his protégé about the *other company's* spies, how they are blood-thirsty thugs and, yes, it's not impossible Henry could be an assassination target.

Hamler is convinced just such evil is flipping through the magazines, making a mess.

Before poking a head around the corner, he wonders how he'll explain to the police that a complete stranger died from a black widow attack in the living room. There is no chapter in the Olde-Tyme Espionage Handbook about that.

Wounded goat moans rumble from the room. Henry is a flash-second from storming in and filling this monster with venom. The newspapers stir again and the assassin roars as if a devil's pitchfork digs into its back.

Henry bounces around the corner in a police takedown stance, ready for anything.

"Oh, shit, there you are," Deshler says, sounding like Louis Armstrong with strep throat. "You getting ready for wrestling practice or something?"

Hamler's teeth tense, fists tight. They hurt a little. "I almost killed you, Dean."

Deshler wobbles, holding a clump of business section over his face. "Sure, dude," Dean slurs with a laugh, voice muffled by newspaper. "Kill me with kindness." The paper soaks up a wet red stain around his mouth.

"No, I was." Hamler loosens the fingernails from his palms and flattens his fists out. "Never mind. What happened to you? It's like seven o'clock, are you aware of this?"

"Well, Henry, yes and no," he says peeling sticky newsprint from his face, revealing a bulging right eye and a smear of blood across his chin. The white work uniform speckled dry brown. "I assume, since the sun is out, that it's early. But no, I didn't catch the time when I woke up to three people *beating the shit out of me* in an alley."

"Dude," Hamler says with a cardiologist's seriousness, "I'm so sorry." Hamler assumes Bust-A-Gut's thugs have targeted his best friend.

Deshler has a gash in the shape of a seven on his chin. It is carved typewriter-perfect.

"Yeah, me too. Shit, the last thing I remember was having a drink with this girl at a club. Gorgeous, tall girl." He holds out hands in measurement. A sharp whistle jets through the gap in his teeth. "She kind of got pissed at me, so I think I had some more drinks."

"You think?"

"Real funny. Next thing I know, I'm waking up in the alley behind the hotel getting my ribs and face worked over."

"Who? I mean, what did they look like?"

"One was this skinny-ass son-of-a-bitch with long gray hair and a black bowler. I think I've seen him before." Dean decides to leave out the part about sharing a limo. "One guy was this Mexican dude with a soul patch, I think. I mean, look, time flies when you're getting beaten."

A cluster of Henry's belly muscles clench. Shock? Love?

Anger? More like disappointment. "What did you do to him?"

"What did I do?"

"Sorry. Why were they doing this?"

"Man, I don't know. I don't remember. I didn't even get a look at the third one. I managed to kick one guy in the face, though. I mean I landed my foot square, heard his nose crunch and everything. Then they all just walked away. Left me to die."

"To die?"

"Well, to suffer. Ground's cold, man."

"You don't look that bad, really," Henry says, hoping to make up for the beating he secretly takes responsibility for. "I mean if we wash the blood off, you can hardly tell your eye is doing that thing. You'll be cool."

Dean grunts and lies on the couch. "Forget it. Not the first time, not the last, right?" He grabs Hamler's pack of smokes and lights up. "Why are you so dressed up? Are you still working that temp job?"

Hamler sucks in a freezing cold breath. It stings the teeth. "Yeah, but it's my last day." His shattered insides reform and sour at the thought of using the poison gun and never seeing Martin again. He unwraps melty Hershey's Miniatures from a pocket and turns toward the door. "Gotta run."

Morning holds an ancient quiet at Bust-A-Gut. The World Headquarters is a haunted library at the bottom of the ocean—nobody is home.

Hamler needs to throw up. He also craves a Snickers, but needs to throw up worse. The old ghost of Christopher Winters' bald, dying head blows raspberries on his stomach. A record-setting queasiness burrows deep. Henry thinks about having to give Martin a resignation letter. Add a murder to the To-Do list and it all shades that gut an ugly green.

Hamler weaves around a maze of cubicle walls looking for a bathroom. Each partition painted company colors—blue and yellow, blue and yellow, blue and yellow. The men's and women's rooms are down a long hallway directly next to one another.

A meteor shower falls in Henry's belly. The reality of unrolling that cufflink and wrapping it around Malinta's neck is repetitive and punishing. Hamler's knee joints go Jell-O.

Ten paces from the restroom and vomit freedom, he rounds the final corner and a stick of dysentery TNT explodes within.

"Henry, I've got some stuff to talk to you about today. There might be an opening in our department…full time! If you're interested, I mean," Malinta says. She has a small band-aid over that old head wound. She stares down at Hamler from white high heels and a matching dress. His throat ties into a knot and his bowels go granite. She flies toward the women's room and turns around at the door. "Oh, and good morning. You look really handsome today."

His cufflinks burn holes at the wrists. The spider-bite contraption is a ball and chain. Hamler's heart rate punches while the white noise of the office explodes through his ears.

The innocent liver spots on Christopher Winters' scalp come back. He pictures tiny white kitten whiskers sprouting from America's hero's head. It reminds Hamler of the pink scar soon to be around Malinta's neck.

He stops thinking about death and his breathing returns. A fresh memory buzzes loud in Hamler's head. Sensations of accomplishment are dusted off and spit-shined. His stomachache is gone, recalling that brief electric zap of success after they moved Christopher Winters' body to the couch. The look of approval on Tony's face leaving Winters' estate was a thrill that, until now, Henry pushed into the dark. *It wasn't that bad*, he thinks. *Actually, it was kind of cool. Easy, in fact.*

Stop being such a chicken and do this. Just like the other night with Martin, he swallows dry, *just jump into the fun.*

By the time Henry starts paying attention, his feet are floating across the women's room tiles. Malinta quietly pisses. He sees bone white heels under the stall. Hamler's training has conditioned him to mentally simulate several angles at once.

POSSIBLE ANGLES

• He can quickly slide beneath the toilet wall and spider bite her ankle. Though, Tony harped on the importance of plunging the tiny gun near the heart.

• He can jump over the stall and wrap the wire around her head while she sits. This, too, requires some gymnastics.

• Hamler can play possum and walk into the stall nearest her and wait. When Malinta finishes, he can exit behind her and choose the cufflinks or the little pistol.

Option three sounds best and he walks slowly to the toilet, trying not to make a sound. The door is cold against the pumping blood in Hamler's fingers. Before he twists the knob, Malinta's toilet flushes and her door swings open. Close enough to smell each other's breakfast, those green marble eyes lock onto Hamler's face.

Oh, shit. Henry's courage fizzles, now his stomach is full of Pop Rocks and Pepsi—throwing up sounds like a great idea again.

Malinta slowly shakes her head with a hint of a grin. Hamler's training manual taught him to assess this situation, as well. It is possible one of three things can happen:

- She thinks you are a pervert and will scream.

- She knows you are a murderer and will scream.

- She thinks you are a perverted murderer and will scream.

Her warm breath and the sting of perfume floods Henry's face as her mouth opens in slow motion, teeth shine in the dull light. "*In*-appropriate," she purrs. "Mister Holgate."

Henry fumbles with the cufflink. It won't slip through its hole. He gently pulls so as not to frighten his prey. But those fingers are stiff.

"What the bleep would your boyfriend say?" she asks. Henry's mouth cracks open, lips dry. Malinta swoops down, dive bombing Henry's face. The kiss stops all wrist fidgeting. Malinta's mouth is odd. It reminds Hamler of kissing Grandma.

"I want a baby, but not this bad," Malinta grins.

"N-nnn," the dictionary in Henry's head is filled with blank sheets. "No-ooooo."

"I won't tell," she says with a wink.

Henry watches Malinta and her tight white dress walk out the door. The cufflink pops impotently from his wrist in a dental floss dangle.

He gathers it up, stuffs the metal thread in a pocket and

walks into the men's room. Henry's throat is wrung tight and scratchy. He's disappointed and relieved about the failed execution. More disappointed than relieved, he realizes. That scares him cold.

Henry turns on the faucet and watches shiny water disappear. *What is wrong with you?* *What is wrong with you?* *What is wrong with you?*

Hamler's cell phone rings before water splashes his face. "Have you taken care of our problem yet?" Tony says. There is a pause as Hamler debates taking a drink. "Hello? Did you hear me, Henry?"

"I didn't get a chance yet, sorry." He palms water to his mouth.

"Perfect."

Embarrassed, he repeats, "I'm sorry."

"No, really, it's perfect. Your mission objectives have changed. Drastically. Get the hell out of there. Don't kill *anyone,* don't swat a bug…don't even clean up your desk. Hear me?"

"Y-yeah, sure. But—"

"Just move. We obtained some files last night. That bitch, Malinta, lied to you. Bust-A-Gut isn't planning a smear campaign. I don't know where she got off telling you that," Tony chirps out a laugh. "God, we need some drug addicts. Drunks are unreliable informants. Never thought I'd miss cokeheads."

Henry walks toward the door, phone between shoulder and ear. "So what's going on, then?" All disappointment has vanished. Henry realizes he was lying to himself. Being a murderer is not who he is.

"Okay, I'll fill you in more when you get here. But Mister Winters personally asked me to set this up. It's big."

"What?"

"Have you ever babysat before?"

"No."

"Do you want to travel?"

He thinks about Martin's scruffy chin and the chance of rescuing their infant relationship from the fire: "No."

"You speak Russian, right?"

"Tony, seriously."

"I'll see you in an hour. You're doing great work, Henry. People are paying attention."

"Tony," he whines.

"Bring your translation dictionary." Tony hangs up.

The office remains silent. His feet against thin carpet are the loudest thing imaginable. Henry hits the elevator down arrow and waits. Adrenaline and bile pedal through his body, mute compared to a few minutes ago, but constantly rearranging themselves.

The bell plings and metal doors slide apart. A crush of young executives squeeze out. When it clears, Martin stands across from Henry. His brown skin has a tanning lotion sheen and his perfect black hair gives off a dry warmth. Oddly, he has a huge bandage across his nose.

"Just the guy I wanted to see."

"Hey."

"What's up, Henry? You feeling okay?"

"What happened to your face?"

Martin smiles. His teeth are distractingly straight. Henry's seasickness sloshes back with love. "You aren't leaving me, are you?" Martin says with a laugh.

THIRTY-SIX

"Hello," a woman's voice says on the other end. "Is this Mister Dean?"

The phone's hard plastic is an icicle against the Cliff Drinker's ear. Buried under a quilt, he's just drifted to sleep after three cigarettes and a few specks of Vicodin. His face throbs raw and sore.

"Yep, yeah, who's this?"

"Hi, sir, this is Deb, Mister Winters' assistant. Roland wants to confirm that you two are still on for lunch today."

"Oh, shit, um." He releases a lungful of air and feels the swollen eye bulge. "Okay, sure, where?"

"Twelve-thirty at the Club."

"Should've guessed. What time is it now?"

"It's eleven-fifty-two, sir. Sorry I didn't confirm earlier."

Deshler hangs up and digs through a pile of shirts. The room is stale with unwashed clothes and dead circulation. He pulls out a pair of wrinkled jeans and a stained sweater.

Dean daydreams about Malinta while brushing his teeth. He wants to kiss her with these clean lips. He wants to nibble her ear. He can't remember entirely, but is kind of sure they didn't part on the best terms last night.

Henry is right, Dean thinks after washing blood from his face. *I don't look horrible*. The eye is a balloon and his chin is stenciled like a quarterback's jersey.

Cleaning up, he mentally ties together the previous night. Rusty knives and Malinta's face juggle in and out of the darkness. His shoe kicks someone's nose with a crack felt all the way back to his teeth. Staring deep into the sink, looking at the blood mix with stains from Henry's shaving accident, Dean remembers a woman.

The sun wasn't totally up and orange streetlamps still flooded the alley. The men focused on pounding him in the stomach and ribs. A long-haired lady floated in the darkness and leapt forward in a panther bounce. She swung and connected with Deshler's eye. Before impact he saw her other sleeve flop like empty hosing. No arm.

Downtown, Deshler parks around the corner and out of Napoleon's sight. He kept the hotel's backdoor key and slips through the employee entrance. He avoids stepping on the dried stains of his blood in the alley.

Upstairs, the Club is completely empty of its usual guests and clean from whatever mess happened the previous evening. Noon sun gives everything a glow. Winters' long table is packed near the back. Roland is dressed casual: his red suit and yellow shirt, but no tie. No matter how casual, it still fits poorly. The CEO introduces the Vice President of this and the Director of that. Everyone seems familiar with Deshler.

"Dean, this is Olde-Tyme's core. These are the people you'll be working with," Roland says with some authority. "These are the smartest folks in the business."

"So I hear," Deshler says. A self-conscious surge drowns him. Everyone wears a suit, though none as flamboyant as the boss's. Dean can sharpen a knife on the women's skirts. The men's ties are centered with elaborate, perfect knots. Deshler shifts in a chair, realizing something smells mildly like the zoo's monkey house.

He is that something.

"We want you *exclusively*, son."

"No more freelancing," a guy says.

"We want those ideas," a middle-aged woman says. Deshler forgets her name and title. A late-stage hangover settles between the Cliff Drinker's ears. It makes concentration impossible. His chest and stomach puff with gas and swelling.

"I'll say," a spectacled man with chins agrees. "We need to keep him away from those Bust-A-Gut pricks. That mozzarella stick thing is gonna kill us."

A maternal-looking woman drops a wet cough into the air.

"My dad, God rest his soul, once said something about the hamburger being the heart of this country…and maybe the fries being the fingers. I don't know what all that meant, I was really going somewhere with this. Anyhow, I have to apologize, Deshler. This isn't my normal style," Winters says with a heavy grin. His mustache is glazed wet. "But we all agreed an intervention is our best bet. I'm not gonna twist your balls here, but we want you on our side." He slowly rotates his thick head around at the other execs. "We need you here."

There is a quiet lull. The room seems empty except for this table—those shabby couches pushed to the walls. Winters sneezes into a napkin. A foreign emotion breathes lightly in Dean's ear. Flattery has been almost non-existent in his life since that time he won a spelling bee as a kid. He realizes, just a little, it feels good to be wanted.

"You'd better take care of that," a young waitress says. "Flu's going around. Can I get everyone's drink orders?"

Beginning with the CEO, the table orders either beer or wine. Sitting next to the boss, Deshler is last in the rotation. The hangover takes hammer-swings at his brain's mushy gray space. That head is Hamler's pumping bass speaker. *One more drink,* he thinks, *and I'll collapse.*

"I'll, uh…" Dean swallows hard, everyone watches. His stomach shrivels to a fiery lump. "Just have a Dr. Pepper."

Ten pairs of eyes glare in confusion. "Dean," the CEO says very publicly. "Are you feeling well?"

"Maybe he means a Flaming Dr. Pepper?" a man whispers across the table.

Deshler's shoulders tense into a thick rope of muscle. "I'm fighting…a cold myself. I'm trying to go easy."

"Oh, God, you scared us for a second, Dean." The table clucks with laughs.

"No worries."

The woman returns with drinks remarkably quick. Winters waits for her to leave before speaking again. "Okay, let's get down to business. Name your price. Company car? You bet. Stock options are all there. Free range of the executive condo in Turks and Caicos. I'll even let you borrow my jet." Winters halts for drama's sake. "We're that serious, Dean."

Deshler sips soda and waits for all the eyes to stop burning through him. He wonders how he got to this point. *God, I hope Malinta isn't pissed. Signing on with Winters pretty much ruins any other shot of sex.* He wonders how he ever came up with those original burger ideas…or *if* he came up with the original ideas.

This table seems convinced he did.

"Oh Christ, sorry we're late, team," a familiar voice at the entrance says. Everyone at the table, including Dean and Winters, turns around to see who's so apologetic. "We…oh, gosh, there's no excuse. My apologies," says the skinny man from the limo with gray hair to his shoulders and a black bowler. Dean bangs knees together and a spritz of sweat builds under his arms. That swollen eye somehow stings worse.

An older woman trails. Her long hair also gray. She is dressed in a saggy, frumpy suit with one arm swinging full and the other sleeve empty.

For the first time in a long while, things are starting to look familiar to the Cliff Drinker. He doesn't like that. *Don't panic,* he thinks. *Maybe this isn't what it looks like. There are other reasonable possibilities.*

OTHER POSSIBILITIES RUNNING THROUGH DESHLER'S HEAD

• This is a reality TV gag. This is the final episode and somehow Dean just won a million dollars.

• Well, that's really it. Dean can't focus on other possibilities for fear of unloading his bowels.

"No problem, guys," Roland says with warmth. "We're just getting to the good part." He stands and nudges Dean, "Deshler, this man is royalty. Meet Harold 'Double Harry' Dobbs. He's a legend. He invented the double hamburger back in the fifties. What was your place called, *Lard Boy?*"

"*Beef Boy,* boss. Quit pulling Dean's leg. You know as well as anyone."

"Well, my father scooped Harry up, just like I am with you, and he's run our Development Department ever since. Also created the Lunch on a Bun way back when. God, we sold a million of those pieces of trash. You're good, kid, but you can learn a lot from this fella."

"We've actually met, chief," Double Harry says with a grin. "Haven't we, guy?"

Deshler's hand trembles and extends. "Yep, sure h-have."

"Ha, I should have known. Wonderful," Winters says.

"Nice chin," Harry whispers. "Sorry, we got a little rough with initiation. All in fun, okay?"

"And this little lady is managing the entire Cosmonaut campaign. She's really taken your baby and run with it, Dean."

Her crow's feet blossom and she wipes a gray flash of hair from an eye. "Delia Ellery, pleased to meet you," she says, extending the good arm and focusing in on Dean's swollen face and gashed chin.

Dean gives her the wrong hand and uncomfortably shakes a backward greeting.

There is more chatter over drinks and business plans.

After a few sips of soda, Dean agrees to work exclusively for Winters Olde-Tyme Burgers.

"Well, mister Vice President of Development," Winters says with an intimidating seriousness, pretending he is a former governor. "What do you have for us? This Cosmonaut thing is only gonna last so long. We'll move into our Christopher Winters Memorial campaign and then…" He looks at Double Harry.

"It's your pageant kid," Harry says, dead enough to win an Oscar.

Another executive crashes out a coughing jag and excuses herself. The table gapes at its newest member—wrinkled, pungent clothes and all—waiting for an answer. In the silence, half the room sniffles and sucks back the mucus of an early cold and flu season. One man looks like a baseball bat named *influenza* smashed him across the eyes. He sweats and breathes hard. He winces while swallowing.

Deshler suddenly gets hungry. "Flu…" his eyes close and this new job feels like it is falling through the slats in the floor. A miserable lifetime of valeting jams between his ears. A lifetime without Malinta. But, he reminds himself, there's still the band.

So it's over before it really started, he thinks. *Big deal, right?*

"Um, Flu Burgers."

Winters squeezes his eyes together and kicks back a white wine. The sweaty CEO then softly blows his nose.

Double Harry rubs rugged cheeks. "What, Deshler?"

"Look, everyone is getting sick right now, right? What if we…what if there was a delicious hamburger that made your cold and flu symptoms go away? Medicine and meat, together." All his recent lying habits start paying off. These words rip through the room like forest fires. This is how he writes song lyrics, just stream of consciousness. This, he assumes, is the Deshler Dean they know. The smooth, drunk Deshler. The guy who embraces a challenge. "Nobody's ever fought hunger and sickness in one stroke. This will revolutionize the industry."

Dean has no clue where this came from. Never in his life has he considered putting beef and medicine together. He's never thought about grinding Tums into tacos or Halls in a hotdog, but here it is, rushing out of him like it's printed on cue cards.

"What will revolutionize the industry?"

"We're a little late in the game to get these out on time, cold weather's already here, but if these hit during the dead of winter, we'll destroy the competition for the rest of the fiscal year." Deshler gulps soda, he's never mentioned the words *fiscal* and *year* together, either. He's pretty positive he's never even said the word *fiscal* in any context. But, again, there it is, feeling kind of comfortable. "We're the only restaurant that cares about serving great food and making our customers feel better. It can't fail. Our clientele will go bananas."

The group takes a sip from their drinks and focuses on Dean's stained jeans. Winters and Double Harry give each other a glance and a nod that doesn't say yes or no. The rest of the table stares at the two leaders, waiting for a sign.

In the lull, Dean notices he's out of breath. His muscles are tensed from top to bottom. It's a strange moment when he admits that he really wants this to work.

The CEO and Double Harry stand.

There's a moment of tense nothing.

The leaders give a hearty clap. The rest of the table erupts like a homerun is hit. Someone actually shouts, "Go team."

THIRTY-SEVEN*

Another excerpt from an eye-rolling conversation between Deshler and a friend.

Friend: This is the worst music I've ever heard.

Dean: Lighten up, it's just expression.

Friend: That dude just sang a song about seeing an X-ray of a girl passing gas.

Dean: Well, sure, that's rough...but it's kind of like Wilson Pickett and Otis Redding, right?

Friend: Yeah, they always sang about farts.

Dean: Right, okay, probably not. But when they started screaming and hollering soul music, most listeners thought it was just noise because Sinatra didn't sound like that.

Friend: So?

Dean: So, I'm saying, sometimes the population doesn't start listening when you're right underneath them. Sometimes it takes a long while to get the message across. But you have to keep plugging, they'll catch up. Pickett and Redding just found a new way to express themselves. Just like Gibby.

Friend: *I saw an X-ray of a girl passing gas?*

Dean: Check it out, my dad—back when he acknowledged my brother and I were alive, before his problems started—told me his parents grounded him once just for saying Elvis' name at the dinner table. The King was obscene to most of America. Now he's on a postage stamp.

Friend: I saw an X-ray of a girl passing gas.

Dean: Give it a decade. It'll be the new *Heartbreak Hotel.*

THIRTY-EIGHT

For once, the band practices on time. Ceremonies begin as Pandemic sits on his stool pounding a pickup truck suspension spring. There's a wiggly *doink* each time he smashes the coil.

The overhead lights zip and pop Christmas colors at staggered moments. The wet air and stale beer aroma reminds Henry of his dorm. He sits on top of the amplifier cabinet—eight ten-inch speakers stacked tall—a mini-fridge of low-end bass. Plucked strings stir a seismic rumble up his body.

Deshler is splattered across the cement on his back, those sore ribs and chest sting less this way. He runs his tongue over gap teeth. One is cracked from Delia's left hook.

Deshler's microphone weaves through a dozen effects pedals until he sounds like an underwater drive-through window. The PA speakers are polka-dotted with gouges. Once, he is told, the Cliff Drinker drunkenly jabbed tiny holes in the tight fibers with a screwdriver. The amplifier blasts like CB radio traffic on Neptune. Deshler loves it.

Busted my tooth
On the twenty-eight rail
Picked up my pantleg
And stumbled back to jail
I go—bang, bang, bang, bang, bang, bang, bang
Like a creepin' kitten
Doin' the midnight stalkin'
Why don't you kiss my hands

And let my fingers do the talkin'?
Bang-bang-bang-bang-bang-hey-hey-hey

Practice started an hour ago, but nobody's actually played a song or jammed on an idea. The three sit around warming up, ignoring one another, each too wrapped up in his own crisis.

Doink Doink, go the drums. *Blump, Blump, Blump* goes the bass. *Doink, donnng, blump blum.*

Deshler rolls onto his stomach and chokes down the microphone, "Sscrrshttt, Krrrrath, chk, chk, chraaaah," comes through the twisted amplifier system.

"Huh?" Pandemic screams, noticing the singer's eyes are wild and focused in his direction.

Blump, ba-blump, blump, blump.

Deshler drops the microphone. The thump echoes like a gunshot down a well. "I said, what's with your face? It looks... clean."

"Man, give me some room. I'm not a bottle of vodka," Pandemic's voice lifts over the bass, finishing his sentence with an explosive snare shot.

Deshler reaches for a warm forty of malt liquor. "I hate vodka."

"Vodka hates you, too."

Blump, blump, blump, blump, blump, blump.

Henry watches his shoes hang a few feet off the ground. Most of a cigarette is a pile of ash in his lap. He can't stop thinking about work or Martin's goatee and shattered nose.

"How did you get *that?*" Hamler asked Martin back at the office, pointing to the spot where Dean busted the man's face. Hamler wanted to rub Martin's cheeks, sweetly kiss that nose.

Henry wanted to whisper, "There, there, there," in his ear.

Martin shrugged and mumbled. "Some asshole, this hotshot *everybody* hates, was talking shit at the Beef Club last night. This rookie spouting off about Bust-A-Gutters *and* Winters people. We shut him down. Sometimes little jerks like that have to be taught a lesson, kind of an initiation."

Hamler pictured his roommate. This wasn't a surprise, but it made him mad. Drunk Deshler ruining another part of his life. *Son of a bitch*, Henry thought.

"Anyway, it's not important. You aren't leaving me, are you?" Martin said.

"Oh, well, here's the thing…" Henry said. He was sorry, but something better came along—something about delivering pizza. He was really sorry. He held the elevator until it impatiently pinged.

"Oh, okay, gee that doesn't sound like you, Henry."

"We should…" Henry managed to say until Martin's eyes fell to the floor. "We could…" the doors slowly brought themselves together and sliced his heart in two. "Bye, Martin."

Henry threw up twice in the ground floor bathroom. Waiting for the bus, cigarettes and a peanut butter cup didn't make anything better.

Deshler rises from the floor and thumps his head on a low-hanging pipe wrapped in lights. "Dude, Juan, what are you talking about?" His walk jiggles a little, balance slightly lost. "Your scabs are all gone, you look…" Dean swoops close and squints through the green and red and blue flashes of light. Pandemic's skin shines where crusty flesh used to welt. "Do you have a suntan?"

"Dude, I'm warning you," the secret Timothy Winters says.

He points a drumstick at the wobbly singer. "Drop it. It's none of your business. Just lie back down and beat the shit out of your liver some more."

Blump-blump-blump-bl-blummmmm. Low notes drown out their voices in Henry's head. He syncs their lip movements with thick bass plucks. He dreams of kicking Dean in the nose.

This new job doesn't sound as easy as Tony says, Hamler thinks. His mind wanders away from Deshler and Pandemic's argument into a feathery dream. *Killing Malinta sounds like hitting golf balls off the moon by comparison.*

"Just tell me if you're a cross-dresser," Deshler says. "I'm okay with it. Everybody needs secrets. It's what keeps people alive. Everybody feels important and special with them. Who wants to be themselves?"

"Then why would I tell you if I had a secret?"

"Because you didn't keep it secret *enough*." Deshler is close to his drummer's face. He counts beige makeup spots covering meth-fueled scratches. Pandemic's teeth are still a destroyed picket fence. "I know there is a secret, now you have to tell."

"Lay off, man. I will break your stupid orphan neck."

Dean's face goes a little childlike. Its sharpness softens, like his eyes are preparing for tears. But tears don't factor in. "Dick."

"Leave me alone."

"No," he sneers, sick of being the only one ever expressing himself. "Tell me."

Blump-blump-blump-blump-blump.

Pandemic's movements go edgy, like he wants something proper to hit Deshler with. *Dean might be bigger than me,* he thinks. *But still a skinny jerk.* Pandemic hasn't smoked in two days. He feels weak and empty. His bones stutter like the marrow is drained.

An icy clarity hits Hamler—a solution to his problems.

The answer's always been there, he realizes, but didn't shine obvious until now.

Pandemic and Dean bicker on. Dean licks his thumb and leans toward the drummer's head, like a parent rubbing at a kid's sticky jelly cheeks. "Hold still. Hold still."

Henry cuts in, determined to start living life on his own terms. "You know, I've been thinking." *There'll be other Martins. There'll be other jobs. This starts right here.* "The band needs a change."

The other two shoot stares as he blows smoke into the lights.

"What fun is art if people don't enjoy it? I want to make music people will clap about. Something I won't be embarrassed to let my mom hear. Something at least on CD."

Deshler slugs down the rest of that warm bottle. Pandemic digs a rut into his cheek, centimeter by centimeter. A speck of purplish red scab shines through flaky makeup.

"Check it out," Deshler smiles at the drummer. "Cat Stevens is playing bass now. Yeah, you buy an acoustic guitar and I'll write some songs about my grandma and getting to bed on time. It'll be a hit."

This conversation reminds Henry of trying to tell Tony to stop giving him unwanted assignments. *Nobody listens,* he thinks. *Take control.* "Look at us, bro. We're not going any-where. This band is an *enormous* waste of time. People threw vegetables. What are we ever going to get out of this? It's not supposed to be this way. This isn't why I joined."

"It's art," Deshler says, voice rising in defense. "Art isn't supposed to be fun. It's supposed to be challenging. It's *fun* to shock people and make them think and express something."

"Well, I don't...agree. This just isn't me." He withers, but stops short, reminded of the confidence Martin's affection brought.

"This band isn't supposed to be who we are. It's about those moments when you *aren't* yourself." A comfort arrives in Dean's mind—reminiscent of the Winters lunch meeting. Here, like improvising the flu fighting hamburger, he's winging it. The idea of not being yourself has never crossed his mind. But damned if it doesn't sound right. "You aren't really living until you are someone else. Don't you," he takes a deep, drama club breath. "Don't you see? I thought we were on the same page with this stuff." The singer's head shakes, shocked that in all these months his best friend didn't even learn that much.

"Um…I'm not saying I don't want the band. Just maybe we could do things different."

"Nobody listens to *fun*, Henry." Deshler shoots Pandemic a *can you believe this* look and swings back toward the bassist. "You can't have art and fun, that's when things start to suck. That's always when a good band goes wrong. That's how you got the first couple Genesis albums."

"We can be the first ones to do it right. That's what I want, man. Take it or leave it."

Deshler throws the bottle behind him. It *plonks* against the wall but doesn't shatter. It rolls to a glassy, hollow stop at his feet. "Because that's just…it's…dude, people are finally coming to our shows and you want to change? We were in the newspaper!"

"I'd like to try something different, too," Pandemic says over Deshler's shoulder. Pandemic's never thought about it before, but change sounds good now. Plus, he wants a way to dig claws a little deeper into Dean's snotty orphan ass. "Yeah, something *really* different. You know, grow artistically. Make pop music."

"Forget this shit," Deshler huffs, shooting back-and-forth looks at the others. "Just forget it."

The singer stumbles into the corner and grabs his coat. He

turns around shaking his head, muttering.

"Oh, dude, also," Hamler says, squishing into a sour face. Tony ordered him to cover up this new duty. His mission for the next seven days is top secret. "I can't practice for about a week, I've...I've, uh, got to go home for a funeral. I'll be out of town."

"Oh, whoa, strange coincidence," Pandemic says. "I can't practice either, I forgot. Ahhh, yes-yes-yeah. I've also got a family funeral."

The two eye each other, unaware of the real coincidence.

"I give up," Deshler says as he climbs the stairs with a stagger in his steps. "Maybe we shouldn't have any more practices ever."

"Maybe."

"Well, I...Maybe."

THIRTY-NINE

The next morning, Henry drags a suitcase up Olde-Tyme's skyscraper and stops at the floor marked *Lettuce Acquisitions*. Technically, *Winters Olde-Tyme Covert Operations* doesn't exist. Corporate smoke and mirrors, you see.

"Big man wants to chat, wants to give you a handshake or something before you leave," Tony says in a hurry—sweat hanging from sideburns. "C'mon, we've got to move if you want to be on time for tonight."

The office doesn't look like a spying nerve center. With its *blah* name, eggshell walls and beige carpet, it *looks* like Lettuce Acquisitions. Just another boring department in an office building.

"Jesus, okay. Let me at least take my coat off."

"I'm not joking around here. This is top priority, hustle up."

Waiting for the elevator to the Executive Suite, a crowd of suits stuffs into another elevator. One voice buried in the mob snags Hamler with fish hook violence. "I'm thinking we can make it a sauce," the familiar voice says. It growls deep and nervous—Isaac Hayes on a first date. "Like ketchup and Nyquil." It sounds like the lead singer of Lothario Speedwagon. Or the former lead singer of Lothario Speedwagon. Hamler decides it's just some stress hallucination. If it was actually Deshler Dean, he'd break that little shit's nose—amongst other things.

Hamler and his boss ease into an elevator alone. "Why me?

There have to be a dozen guys who can babysit."

"Because, we think you need a new challenge. Okay?"

"This sounds like a load of bullshit." Six dozen floors flush past them. Henry breathes and waits for the right moment. "Look me in the eye and tell me what's the deal. Why do a bunch of Russians need me, of all people?" The doors wishbone apart. Hamler's question is chopped off by a man he's only seen in company promotional materials.

The CEO looks like governor Christopher Winters, but with a greasy mustache, an extra chin and a stain on his yellow tie.

"Ah, Tony, thanks for coming so quickly. This must be agent Hamler, perfect. You look like a man I can trust. Come in, come in."

"It's a pleasure to meet you, sir," Hamler says, shaking the CEO's surprisingly limp hand.

Down an oak hallway lined with photos of Henry's first kill, Roland Winters hacks and dices his arms while speaking. "Okay, so you've been briefed, yes? We have some nuggets. Apparently Bust-A-Gut's intelligence corps is going to try something funny. We don't have any concrete info, but with those heartless savages, anything's possible. We need someone to be a bodyguard of sorts."

"I'm your man, sir."

"Henry is really showing lots of promise, chief. He was, uh," Tony searches for the politically correct way to say *boss murderer.* "The main man with the *C.W. thing,* you know?"

Holding the doorknob to his office, Winters drops a solemn church nod. A brief memory of okaying his father's assassination. "Nasty work, but important. I thank you, son."

When Henry enters, he is swamped by heat—a thermostat stuck on broil. Four men and one woman lounge around in blue jumpsuits. They each nibble doughnuts. Black coffee is in the air. Another guy, standing at the window with a huge pompadour and thick glasses turns and stares. The man's skin is colored like circus peanuts. Hamler suddenly craves a handful of the mushy orange candies.

"I trust you know who these gentlemen and lady are," Winters says as the cosmonauts line up to shake hands, wiping powdered sugar from fingers. Compared to television, their faces are weird. Three have chin waddles and muscles and real tans. The other guy and a girl are pale and thin with horrible teeth. "This is Dimitri, Yuri, Pavel, Sonja and Keith. The, huh," he laughs, "Moscow Five, I think we are promoting them as."

Hamler shakes hands and says hello.

"Okay, so you'll be around this crew all day, every day. You don't let them get into any trouble. Anyone suspicious walks within an acre, you *solve* the *problem* with a gun if you have to. Got it? There are millions of dollars riding on this tour's success. We'll start tonight with the big television shindig, then nail both coasts for promotion. Be back in a week, you hear?"

"Absolutely."

Delia Ellery, leaning against the wall with her stump to the bookcase, clears her throat. The CEO turns around and rolls his eyes.

"And this," Roland says, faking forgetfulness. "This is the *big* winner of the contest. Henry Hamler, please meet…" Winters eases a heavy sigh, "Mister *Juan* Pandemic."

America's newest hero steps up. His black hair is a horrible wig, his tan is fake, his glasses have no glass. It takes the young spy three blinks to figure everything out. "You've *got* to be kidding me," he says, shaking his drummer's hand.

FORTY

The Cliff Drinker wakes, shocked to be in his bed, neatly tucked and warm. He looks around the room: no pools, trails or specks of blood. *So far, so successful,* Dean thinks, kind of proud. He gropes the soft skin around his face—a night's rest without being beaten by one-armed marketing execs works wonders for swelling.

Deshler gets up and dresses. After wrestling a comb through wild hair, he slips off to Winters headquarters. His first real day at work hums by without incident. People claw at each other to get near the new hotshot. Dean is shocked to see everyone stop and listen whenever his mouth opens.

Early in the morning, leaving Winters' dark wood office after a meeting, Deshler has a breakthrough. "Mister Dean," the head of the test kitchen says. "You can't just mix cough syrup and raw ground beef. There is no amount of breadcrumbs we could add to keep this from cooking into sludge."

"Damn," Deshler says. "Well, hmm, what if we marinated the onions in cold medicine?"

"I don't think that would mask the eucalyptus flavor well enough. That is our goal, sir, to make this healthful and edible."

Getting into the elevator, another sober idea cartwheels through Dean's head: "I'm thinking we can make it a sauce," he growls deep and nervous—Isaac Hayes on a first date. "Like ketchup and Nyquil."

"Well, gosh, sir." This takes Dean by surprise, the man

calling him *sir* is fifteen years older, easily. "*That* seems feasible, we could have a prototype ready by the end of the day tomorrow."

A cheek-burning smile plants itself across Dean's face. People are listening for once and he doesn't have to cover them in mustard or bellow into a microphone. The foreign whip of satisfaction zings through his nervous system. He draws it in close.

What would Gibby do? he thinks.

Nothing.

Come on, this always works. What would he do next?

Nada.

You know, that's a load of horseshit, he thinks. *What would Deshler do? Now that's a question.* This new perspective toughens Dean's posture. It doesn't actually make him stand straighter, but it certainly feels like it.

Eager to keep this good luck and not wanting to run into Napoleon near the Beef Club, Dean chooses to eat dinner down the street from the Olde-Tyme office. He walks through the snowy dark, whistling something upbeat and unknown before slipping into a cramped Italian restaurant. Alive with garlic and fresh bread air, his stomach calls for the entire menu.

A glass of wine and a table for one, he stops to appreciate today. Did he feel this good turning eighteen, leaving foster care behind? No. Did he feel this alive when that box of *Broken Piano for President* tapes arrived from the printer, smelling new and full of promise? Close, very close. But, still, no. Was turning twenty-one this rewarding, tossing his fake ID and buying that first legal case of beer? He doesn't remember.

There, gnawing on a buttery breadstick, Dean sees this could be the first entry into a new Hall of Fame.

THE BEST DAYS OF DESHLER DEAN'S LIFE

- Today.
- Today.
- Today.
- Today.
- Today.

Sunning himself in the warm tones of satisfaction, Deshler's solid gold streak crashes just after the shrimp fettuccine arrives.

"Well, there you are," a woman hisses, sing-songy.

Dean's chin lifts with a noodle swinging from his lips. Malinta—tall as a basketball pro—and Thurman Lepsic—in a three-button suit tight enough to cut off circulation—hover over the table.

"Malinta, your head looks great."

She tucks a blonde bundle behind her ear. "You're a popular man today. Your name is on everyone's lips—*everyone's*."

Lepsic checks his hair in the window. Bust-A-Gut's intimidating VP next plants himself across the table and Deshler determines his skin soaks under ultraviolet heat lamps most of the day.

"Didn't see you parking cars," Lepsic says. "Your nitwit friend seems to have some theories, though."

A subterranean guilt stiffens inside him. The feeling of being on someone's shit list without even knowing. It feels not unlike the day paramedics wheeled Dad off, leaving a wet red trail from the dining room to the front door to the driveway. Deshler never knew so much blood could come out the ears. But young Dean's guilt didn't start pushing until Mom began pointing fingers. Fortunately, on the first night of that lifetime grounding, Deshler's brother snuck him and a flask of schnapps into a Butthole Surfers show. His posture felt tougher that night, too.

Dean drops his fork. He's hot and itchy, like being caught in a lie. His mouth is leather. "Oh, you don't say," is all he manages. *Wait, I didn't do anything wrong.*

"You and I had an understanding, Dean," Lepsic says. His five o'clock shadow spreads across his face like an action star. "If you think this is a bargaining chip, guess again. You're lucky I don't hang you from your ankles over the bridge."

Malinta's red wool coat goes to her bare knees. Her arms are crossed and it's obvious they will not end up in bed tonight. Lepsic clears his throat, deep and ugly.

"Can I order anyone a drink?" Deshler says, hoping to defuse this bomb and buy some time.

"Mister Findlay gives you such opportunities. Such a life," Lepsic says and flashes a menu open. "You stay at the Bust-A-Gut penthouse for a weekend, we give you massive freedom and this is how you repay us? Jumping ship. Come on, the Globo-Goodness Corporation Family of Corporations deserves better than this. Wouldn't you agree?"

"They deserve only the finest," Dean says, not totally knowing where this comes from. He's riffing again, the same way *Broken Piano for President* was written.

"Just tell me, just whisper in my ear," Lepsic says, cupping a hand to the side of his head. "Just say this horseshit isn't true and I'll leave you alone. Malinta will probably stick around and order a drink, too. Just promise me that I've been lied to by..." He looks at the ceiling and licks pink collagen lips. "Let's see, by my coworkers, by my assistant, Jesus, even my acupuncturist."

The restaurant spins to life. Lepsic moves slow as the entire room chases its tail. Dean grows nauseous sorting a big idea out between his ears. This lie folds into a beautiful origami swan, so neat and perfect Dean is positive it won't work.

Malinta stamps her foot but still manages to look calm. "Well, Dean?" She locks hands on hips, "*Well?*"

"What exactly have you heard, Mister Lepsic?"

"Oh, jeez, *Mister Lepsic*," he wipes his forehead with a napkin and pokes a fork in the air toward our hero. "It's me, Thurman. I'm your friend. Haven't we built a trust? Oh God, when people start talking like this I get really nervous. And then, once in a while, when those nerves start to chew on my brain, I hang people from their ankles over the bridge."

"Yeah, I've heard," Dean says. He's unfolded and refolded his big plan, he likes the shape. "Okay, *Thurman*, what have you heard?"

Lepsic rolls his shoulders and neck until they crackle. "Heard you're the VP of Development at Winters. Heard you took Bust-A-Gut's job offer and crapped all over it. Heard Clifford Findlay, your rightful boss might I remind you, the CEO of this company, isn't too happy either."

"*Furious* is a better way to F-ing put it," Malinta adds.

"What?" Lepsic turns sharp to his sidekick. "Stop that. You sound like a little kid. You used to swear like a prison guard."

"Sorry."

"I liked that."

"I'm sorry."

Returning focus to Dean: "Let's just say he's pissed."

"*Ticked.*"

"He is not a man you want to tick off—" Lepsic shoots Malinta another look. "Piss off."

Deshler nods. The whirlwind room draws tighter, waitresses make a breeze as they blur past. Steam pipes of customer noise wail louder than before. Malinta leans forward so she doesn't miss a vowel.

"Would either of you like something to eat?" Dean says.

"Supposedly they have a New York strip that will make you cum."

"Get serious," Lepsic says, running a palm over his cake frosting hair. "You know I don't eat that garbage."

"Shrimp fettuccine is a knockout, too."

"C'mon, quit clowning around."

"Meatballs?"

"You know I'm vegan. Haven't eaten anything born with eyes…hell, anything *born* period, in fifteen years."

The room washes in silence again. There is a tickle in Dean's throat. That confused face reappears—jaw swinging open. He restocks that origami genius plan for a moment. "Wait, so the vice president of the second biggest *hamburger* restaurant in America doesn't eat meat?"

Lepsic's eyes roll until they are blank white bulbs.

"Seriously?"

"I think you said it best once, 'Doesn't matter if I'm selling beef or balance beams: it's just a job.' You know me, Dean, I'm into the logistics, into the challenge." The man softens a little in the face and shoulders. "I'm certainly not here because my daddy gave me a title like that idiot, Winters." Lepsic's bare fingers pinch out the candle between them. "Which brings me back to my point, we hear you're lead-off hitter on Olde-Tyme's development team."

All the noise, all the rattling plates, all the servers babbling out tonight's special are swallowed by a wall of quiet in Dean's head. The only sound he picks up are ears ringing and a growing heartbeat.

A couple guys have gotten tough and macho like this at Lothario Speedwagon shows. Dean has defended himself with mixed results.

MIXED RESULTS

- **Q:** "Why don't you assholes stop making all that noise and play some Zeppelin?"

  A: Dean stopped the band to belch through an a cappella version of *Dancin' Days*. He reached the second line of the song before the man broke the singer's rib with a fist.

- **Q:** "Hey fag, why don't you come over here so I can kick you in that stupid pink mask?"

  A: Dean walked to the edge of the stage in between songs—during the usual confused silence—lifted that pink mask and vomited back a cheap bottle of cabernet atop the heckler.

- **Q:** "Hey, why did you get all this mustard in my wife's hair?"

  A: Dean didn't have time to answer because the man's fist immediately followed the word "hair" and smashed his teeth.

"Well, Dean," Lepsic says, his face growing distant. "Are you on Winters' team?"

Without the distinct height advantage of a stage or a vomit-cannon full of red wine, Dean decides this is a time for peace, not war. He unrolls his plan, studies it one last time and decides to give it a try. *What would Deshler do?* He thinks.

Here is the answer.

"You bet your ass I'm on their team," Deshler says and pops the shrimp in his mouth. Dean hears dishes rattle and orders taken again. The pair across the table grows redder with anger every second he spends chewing. Dean pushes one last shrimp around the plate and lets the fork squeal across cloud white china. "That's exactly how I hoped it would look." The room's tension begins to deflate.

Lepsic clears his throat. Malinta straightens her skirt with a tug. Deshler swallows and their eyes laser on him again. "Go on," the muscle bulged vice president growls, unsure.

"How better to stay ahead of the competition than having one of *us* in the development department?" Despite what Malinta told him, Deshler is still about thirty percent sure he's never worked for Bust-A-Gut. But judging from Lepsic's face bending into a grin, this is the right answer.

The space between his shirt buttons spreads as his chest takes dramatic breaths. Dean begins to wonder if he can survive a drop off the bridge. Hopes the water isn't too cold, because it's a long swim. "Then what do we have Corporate Intelligence for?" Lepsic says.

"Good question. Why do you?"

"Cut the cutie pie business."

"How deep are your agents? What do you have, some janitors and some mailroom clerks? I guarantee I'm the only VP at Winters who is a…" Deshler grins. "What's the title you offered me at Bust-A-Gut?" He lets that one sink in, stunned that it actually fell from his mouth. Dean wishes he had a beer. "At any rate, I'm the only Bust-A-Gut employee who's a VP at Winters, I'll bet your sister's virginity on that one, *Mister* Lepsic."

Dean doesn't look, but it seems like every customer and waiter in the room pauses. The puddling sweat on his body senses it.

Lepsic rocket launches a laugh, it rattles icicles loose above the entrance. "Look at this guy," he says to Malinta. "When does he sleep? When does he turn off?"

"I'm a natural, what can I say?" That one also slips out unannounced. *Jesus, I'm really good at this bullshit,* he thinks. *Being a singer or an artist or whatever isn't my calling. For sure.*

"He certainly," Malinta carefully mouths the words. "Is one-of-a-kind."

"I'll have HR whip up a contract outlining all this, of course. I mean, how do I know you're not pulling the same stunt on us? Mister Findlay is never pleased with deception. Unless, of course, he's the one doing the deceiving."

Deshler twists some pasta around the fork. "You know I'm not pulling the old switcheroo because Winters is a fool, Thurman. Plus, you'll kick my ass if I do anything like that, am I right?"

"My man," Lepsic says and sniffles.

The room's tension is totally out of air and Dean relaxes. He starts wondering how much cash he can get if he sells all those Butthole Surfers records and bootleg videos. *Who needs Gibby?* he thinks.

"So where is Mister Findlay anyway? I haven't seen him in…"

FORTY-ONE

"You need a mustache or a beard. Sideburns. Something to fatten your face," the CEO of Olde-Tyme Hamburgers tells his son through chubby cheeks and push broom mustache. "That wig and those glasses aren't cutting the ketchup."

They are alone in Roland's oak cave office. Pandemic plucks a brandy bottle off a shelf, sniffs and glugs it like soda. He flushed his meth down the toilet days ago and it's rearranging his brain cells. He's actually been thinking a lot about what Dad had to say during that original late-night meeting. Most days, Juan Pandemic or Timothy Winters or whatever name he's going by, is so filled with anger his shoulders ache from stress. Most days only a sweet pipe to his lips can cure it. But lately, he's been upbeat and it feels great.

"People don't want a junkie for a contest winner. A skinny, ungrateful drug addict. They want the all-American hero. They want your grandpa. Everyone wants Christopher Winters."

"Look, Dad," he says. A sudden snake of nostalgia twists between Pandemic's lungs, wrapping around the heart, laying eggs of fond memories and family pride. His mouth soaks in the familiar juices of Grandpa Winters' backyard barbecues. Juan remembers the warm fuzz of superiority when kids at school made a big deal every time he brought *the governor* for career day. He'd never felt so good or so superior to others. "I've been thinking. And, you know, I'm sorry. I'll help, I'll go around and say whatever you want me to say. I'll kiss babies and shake hands with Russians. I'll help."

With the ink drying on Lothario Speedwagon's death certificate, Timothy realizes being a Winters is all that's left. This is the last chance to do something right and get back some of that old pride. Not many people can be part of a legacy, let alone an American legend, he decides. He tells himself art is for losers. When was the last time an artist bought a new car? When was the last time an artist was elected governor?

The sloppy CEO waits for his son to bust into a laugh. He doesn't, so Roland coughs. "Son, this is the smartest shit you've ever told me. I'm glad your head is finally out of your ass."

"I want to be a part of this company, Dad. It's my legacy, you know? Maybe when this is done—"

"Keep your trap shut about being my kid, though. If there's *another* thing Joe America can't stand, it's nepotism. If there's something Joanne Customer hates even more," he says, waistline stretching tight across his stomach. "It's nepotism in a *contest*. Jesus, that would ruin me." He pauses and rubs that mustache, "*Us*. Take a second, Tim, and ask yourself, if your life was a tasty Winters Burger, would you be the tomato or the lettuce?"

Juan removes the phony glasses and squints. "I don't think you're using that right. Anyhow, I can do that, Dad. But like I was saying, maybe when this is over in a few weeks I can come back and work with you. Learn the business. Be part of the family."

"Maybe, Tim."

This is how most of Pandemic's debates with Dad end. But for the first time, maybe thanks to sobriety, it gurgles through his brain who has the advantage. "No, Dad, not maybe. I'll do this, but you have to cut me in. I know a lot of things about this company. Grandpa told me a lot of stories. Things after the war, murders for recipes, you know?"

"Your granddad was bat-shit crazy, I'm sorry to say. He

made all sorts of stuff up. He earned everything in life through hard work and being an ax-murderer of a business man. When his mind started slipping he jazzed his resume up. It'll happen to you someday, just wait. Dementia's genetic."

"Well, I know what I know," Pandemic says. Fingers lift to his face and scratch once, then the hand gently pulls into his jacket. He sucks in breath until his chest stings and the snake wiggles its rattle. This pride blocks his brain's begging for crystal meth, but pride's growing weaker. "And I know a lot of people want to hear."

"Mmmm-hmmmm," his father says.

"I can forget shit real easy, pop. I just want to be involved," he waits a breath and quotes a brochure he read in the lobby an hour ago. "I just want to be part of America's largest family-owned company."

"Son, I've been waiting to hear you say that for years. You meathead, I might just love you yet."

FORTY-TWO

A few blocks from Winters headquarters, a giant stage was hammered together on a production lot. It's a replica of an Olde-Tyme Hamburger restaurant, Victorian neon and all. The only difference is a missing fourth wall and the addition of studio seating for a few hundred.

Henry and Timothy Winters/Juan Pandemic haven't been in the same room since shaking hands several days back at Olde-Tyme Headquarters. Hamler spent most of the morning with Tony, learning to aim a gun and obtaining a last minute concealed weapon license. The bandmates find one another in a dressing room behind the fake restaurant.

Cameras roll in a few minutes.

Hamler isn't fooled by the new disguise. He recognizes his drummer even with the addition of facial hair. He spots those huge hands and dynamite-blasted teeth under a fresh *Magnum P.I.* mustache.

"Dude, what the?"

Behind a black bushy lip and under a stack of imitation hair, Pandemic's jaw tenses. "It's nothing, man."

The two dance a tight circle around each other like stray alley animals. Pandemic in his getup looks as phony as pudgy Hamler in his fresh off the rack two-piece gray suit.

"Nothing?"

"Just, please, forget it's me. I'm just some dude. I just want to get all this over with. Besides, what the hell are you doing here?"

"I just landed this temp job, I had no clue I'd get to travel, much less, you know..." Hamler smiles, but is annoyed, having to conceal his real job as a spy. The new take-charge guy buttons up that anger and cracks a jawbreaker between teeth. "Be...your ...*bodyguard*."

"Uh, yeah," Pandemic says, stretching a rubbery *yeah*.

"Juan, man, what's going on?"

Henry looks so pitiful Pandemic can't hold back. "Well, okay, I won the big contest. I'm the guy. I guess you know that, though."

"Why didn't you tell me, why did..." he trails off.

"Sorry?"

"What's up with all this business?" Hamler says, scanning the drummer up and down.

"Everyone does this. Everyone who gets famous." Pandemic scratches his scalp, the toupee droops to one side. "I don't want people stalking me and shit. Now that I'm a thousandaire."

Henry's face twists into a skeptical mash. "Dude, please. Come on, give me something better than that."

The cosmonauts, wearing signature blue jumpsuits, are spread in a constellation throughout the room. The beefy ones flirt with young production assistants in broken English. Keith and Sonja, desert-island skinny, watch each other from opposite couches, not speaking. Sour faces saying: *I need an appendectomy, quick.*

"Well," Pandemic says and rubs a hand across his eyes. "Okay, well, you wouldn't believe me anyhow."

"Dude, look at us. Look where we are. There is a short list of shit I wouldn't believe about you right now."

A SHORT LIST OF SHIT HAMLER WOULDN'T BELIEVE RIGHT NOW

- Pandemic is a magician.

- This is a Candid Camera-type reality show, and Hamler just won a million bucks.

- The drummer from Lothario Speedwagon has a skull made of melted silver dollars.

- Candy bars give you genital rickets.

- Pandemic is the grandson of the guy who invented the electric toothbrush and heir to a hamburger fortune.

"Alright, man, but you've got to promise to keep this under wraps. I can probably get in trouble or something. I'm trying to play shit cool, and let people know I'm a responsible dude."

"Responsible dude?"

"Do you want this story or not?"

"Well, I am your bodyguard. I should know everything, wouldn't you say? For safety's sake."

Pandemic nods. "So you know the Winters Hamburger place?"

"The restaurant you won the contest for? The one paying my salary? *Yeah*, I'm familiar."

Juan Pandemic spreads apart the leaves of the Winters family tree and shows the branches that lead to: "Son of Roland."

"Get out of here. Bull*shit*, get outta..." Hamler's fingers tense at odd angles while digesting this. Henry recalls stuffing a cufflink in the governor's skin. Now Christopher Winters has a whole new identity and his ghost ties a fresh set of guilty weights around Hamler's neck.

"It's true. I'm sorry I never told you, but, you know, there's a lot of stuff that went down between my old man and me. There are about a million reasons why I do what I do."

"So you're really going to get a job with your dad after this? You'll be, like, a hamburger guy?"

"Yeah, totally."

"I've never known one of those before."

"Me neither. Well, I mean, besides my dad…and my grandpa…and my uncle and some cousins. Aunt Pam, too, I think—"

"Right, gotcha."

"That's why I'm trying to play it cool. I know it sounds kind of lame. But I figure I can't be drummer for crummy bands the rest of my life. This is a chance to do something with myself. It gives me butterflies thinking about it."

"Are you sure that's not, you know."

"Man, I haven't smoked in forever. I'm serious about this shit. Quit trying to bring me down to your level."

"That's really cool. Good for you. I've kind of been thinking something similar."

"Meth? When did you start smoking anything stronger than dicks?"

"Funny."

"Man, I'm just kidding."

"I'm talking about bands. I'm too old for a band, you know?"

"Yeah."

"I need to take charge of my life. Be an adult."

"You do, I agree."

Hamler doesn't know if he should laugh. "I don't want to be thirty and making shit money and have my hearing go out and smell like mustard. I think *this*," he waves an arm, "is the life for me. Not exactly cool, either. But it feels safe. I don't get to feel safe often."

An older guy in headphones swings the door open and announces curtain is in one minute. Timothy Winters is ushered away by assistant directors and makeup women. Hamler shuffles behind the crowd.

The show opens inside the fake restaurant with the Moscow Five chit-chatting about the dramatic changes in their life since coming to America. Dimitri—captain and interpreter—answers rehearsed questions.

Yes, they still eat hamburgers once a day.

Oh, he's not one to say, but yes, American girls are much prettier than Russian ones. No offense, Sonja.

No, none of them are married.

They love outer space for different reasons, but feel it is their duty to help all of mankind with their work.

Yes, their parents are very proud back in the Mother Country.

There's a one minute commercial break, which includes a Bust-A-Gut spot honoring Christopher Winters, followed by another thirty-second spot on the same topic from Winters Olde-Tyme.

The show returns. "If not for our next guest, ladies and gentlemen," our wax dummy anchor says. "These five cosmonauts would still be in space. Starving, lonely, cold, drinking their urine."

Chatter buzzes among the crowd.

"Moscow Five, are you ready to meet," our anchor says, spreading a smile across the audience like jam on toast. "The

American hero who saved your lives?"

On cue, the five space travelers nod their heads in rehearsed awe, as if Gandhi were fixing his sarong on the other side of the door.

Our host's question, "What do you say, ladies and gentlemen?" is met with a roar. "Here he is, the Winters Olde-Tyme Hamburgers Space Burger Contest winner, Mister Juan Pandemic."

Pandemic trips over his feet under the brutally hot stage lights. The final ten minutes are spent discussing different reasons why the man with a bad haircut and worse mustache loves America and hamburgers. The climax comes when he says he hopes the Russians will take their second opportunity at life as a blessing.

Backstage, Delia mumbles, "Damn it."

In rehearsal, Pandemic was ordered by the tour manager to say, "Blessing from God," at this point in the interview. Marketing finds Winters burgers are not selling well in the southern United States. Religion, however, flies off the shelf in Dixie. So, Olde-Tyme Marketing assumes, tying a God-fearing Christian hero to their chain will bolster market share.

During the interview, Henry stands stage left with Delia and her lonely arm. She checks a watch and flips through script pages. Henry peeks under his jacket every few minutes to make sure his gun hasn't sprouted wings and flown away. It tugs heavy on his shoulder, it carries with it a dangerous sort of tingle—a gravity of purpose. He plugs two fingers into the opposite jacket pocket occasionally and slips a few Milk Duds behind his teeth. It slows that hammering chest and settles his vision.

The two don't talk. Besides the time Juan failed to give the thumbs up to God, Delia's lips are silent the entire program.

During the final minutes, Pandemic is presented with a

cardboard check as tall as a basketball hoop for $460,000. The astronauts hug him, the music plays, the crowd claps, and they invent smiling small talk during the credits.

Spotlights go cold and the group walks offstage.

The cramped hallway is a jungle gym of old props and extra lighting equipment. Pandemic struggles to carry the check. In an open space where the backstage area shatters into a thousand dim alleys, two teenage girls with faces painted green and gray begin squealing. The knobby one with braces has a t-shirt that says, **SPACE**. The other girl, plump and pimply, wears a shirt that reads, **BURGERS**.

"Oh my God," they scream, parting a sea of angry cosmonauts like some guy in the Bible. "Juan, Juan! We love you, Juan."

Pandemic jerks backward and nearly falls out of the toupee. He holds the check over his head with two hands like a spear.

"I want your baby, Juan," the one with braces snarls, shoving Keith to the ground. "Get me pregnant!"

Henry jumps from behind the contest winner and clotheslines both girls before their greasy fingers touch Pandemic.

Flat on their backs, the young ladies take a communal gasp and stare at the babyfat bodyguard. "I'm sorry girls," Henry rehearses the words Tony fed him earlier. There's a growl in his voice—the kind Henry imagines a take-charge man would have. "Being an American Hero is quite exhausting. Mister Pandemic would love to impregnate both of you, but is terribly tired." His new suit jacket flaps open as neurons plunge hot rivets into his brain. *Holy cow, I just stopped two psychopaths*, he thinks.

Henry's exposed jacket provides a top-notch view of that gun from the girls' angle. The Pandemic fans scramble, say sorry, and run down the hall.

This is what I was born to do. Nothing's felt this dead-on *since...*Henry thinks of making out with Martin at that bar, but quickly extinguishes the urge.

"Wow, Henry," Pandemic says. "You're the best bodyguard ever. You totally smashed those chicks. And they were ugly. Good eye. I will only be impregnating the cute ones!"

Keith watches the girls scurry off, sitting on his ass. His face is a bonfire. He rattles off a clipped Russian burst directed at the Pandemic fanatics. The cosmonaut lifts up and punches the cardboard check, splitting it in two novelty chunks. The angry spaceman starts sprinting after them.

"No, no, no," Hamler says, grabbing Keith by the shoulders as the skin and bones cosmonaut flies past. He breathes into the space adventurer's face and speaks slowly, lumbering through the Cyrillic alphabet. (Keith,) he says in Russian with a thick American accent. (Relax, those stupid horses have now moved.)

Hamler's mangled Russian delivers Keith a smile. He holds a hand up to say truce. The spaceman's face drops back into seriousness and grapples Henry Hamler's arm. (I did not know you spoke the mother tongue,) Keith says in the mother tongue.

"Dude," Pandemic says, fixing his fake mustache. "When did you pick that up?"

"I told you, man, I needed a minor in college."

Keith yanks Henry close, the sweaty heat of anger steams through his jumpsuit collar. The spaceman says, (We will be good friends soon. There is a need for men like you.)

"Best bodyguard ever." Pandemic smiles and slaps Henry's back.

FORTY-THREE

Commercials roll after the Cosmonaut show. Two spots declare Monday night the new Thursday night. These comedies are wholesome enough for families, but raunchy enough for fraternity brothers. Here's what *TV Guide* has to say…

One car ad boasts a bigger gas tank and the same square footage as a motel room. The next claims to be the only automobile J.D. Power and Associates rated as "Indestructible."

It's ten and America's favorite news source begins. "Tonight on *Nightbeat* Live," our female announcer says. "Is your mechanic ripping you off? Benjamin Lambers goes undercover to find the hidden truth beneath your hood." Televisions across the country feature men in grease-smeared overalls shielding faces from the camera. "And later…a cannibal in the White House? We may be closer than you think." A shot of 1600 Pennsylvania Avenue flies in. "But first," the woman's voice lowers dramatically. "Are your hamburgers really safe? *Could* America's passion for fast food have a connection to its mysterious rise in obesity? Find out next on," synthesized newsy music swoops in, "*Nightbeat…Live.*"

More commercials—brown soda, sitcoms, extreme green soda, prescription anxiety drugs.

"Welcome back," the voice from the opening says. It's attached to a light-skinned black woman with short hair named Sharon Smalley. Her blazer is red, her glasses are tortoiseshell. "It's no secret Americans are gaining weight," she looks into the camera. A graphic appears over her shoulder. It reads, "*Death*

Burger?" in bloody scrawl that compliments her suit. "But who's to blame? Some say it's fewer physical activities due to technology. Some say it's simply genetics. But recently there has been some discussion in the medical community claiming our waistlines are directly tied to fast food consumption. *Nightbeat's* Leah Pullem takes a closer look."

A silent fade to black washes over the screen. "Studies say your chances of dying from a falling coconut are greater than a shark attack," an over-rehearsed, less professional voice says during split images of palm trees and great whites. "Almost six times greater. Find that hard to swallow? Well, your chances of dropping off a ladder and breaking your neck are higher than dying in a terrorist attack, too."

The camera shifts to a short female reporter with spunky reddish-brown hair in front of a Winters Olde-Tyme Hamburgers. "However, hardest to swallow are your chances of dying from heart failure. Studies suggest one in every two-and-a-half Americans die from coronary disease. Of that group, over half of those heart sufferers dine here." The camera pans to include the familiar green and gray Winters sign in front of a Victorian drive-through window.

Leah cuts to the artery of this problem. Studies reveal a single Space Burger, while only one-eighth the weight of a bacon double cheeseburger, contains nearly four times the daily fat and calories required by a human body. The list of preservatives sounds like a Swahili lesson.

She asks unsuspecting customers if they are aware of these statistics. An elderly woman is shocked and asks if they make a Salad Burger. A skate punk says, good, he wants to die young anyhow, and orders two more. A young mother and father drop their jaws, pluck space-age beef from their children's thick fingers and toss the discs in the trash.

Leah speaks with one Winters employee who wishes to

remain anonymous: "Sure, we know," he says. "But Leah, it's not what we *know* or what we *think*. It's what our damn customers want." The camera shows the man, but blacks out his eyes. The viewer can plainly see gap teeth and a fresh scar on his chin the shape of a seven. The man slurs words and frequently stops to hiccup. "People *want* more meat. They *want* cheese. They want their bacon strips batter dipped and fried in shortening. Jesus, don't be an asshole, it's supply and demand." In the dim light the man slugs back a can of beer and burps.

Stock footage rolls as he finishes speaking: assembly lines of Winters employees slap together freeze dried ingredients so fast their foreheads sweat.

"No, no I don't think Winters Olde-Tyme Hamburgers is directly tied to the obesity crisis, that's *horseshit,*" the man's voice grinds deep: Fat Albert impersonating a semi-truck. "People can easily choose not to have a tender all-beef patty with natural Wisconsin cheddar for dinner. But they do. Are you calling our customers stupid?"

Leah shuffles some papers and clears her throat. She asks if the mystery informant has any final statements.

The man drunkenly smears his words. "Well, Lisa, clear your calendars and your colons because it's not Olde-Tyme Hamburgers' fault America has great taste. And we're here to stay." He concludes by flashing a wide smile, his teeth a seven-ten split. The man's head wobbles and he pops open one last hiccup before the scene cuts out.

"But what can be done to stop this madness?" says our anchorwoman back in the studio.

Leah sits behind the desk now, too. "Well, Sharon, when we return I'll speak to a gentleman who says the hamburger is the Hitler of our generation. He also says Christopher Winters won't come close to capturing this ruthless dictator. I sat down one-on-one to learn how this man plans to wage a D-Day of his own."

More commercials: Import beer. Fast cars. Funny sitcoms. Nightly news preview. Slacks sale. Anxiety drugs. And, oddly, hamburgers.

"People," the show returns with a sunshine voice. He is a short dark-skinned gentleman behind a podium. He addresses a yawning crowd, crossing vocal styles between congressional filibuster and Muppet. "We need to fight these oppressors. We are shackled by Big Beef and its propaganda." The man wipes his forehead with a handkerchief. His eyes bulge into a pair of globes. "This is the first day of the rest of your lives. Folks are addicted to everything from cigarettes, to shopping, to sex…even food. It's not just drugs, ladies and gentlemen. Food addiction is *real*. And it is *really* killing us. Health Watch International is really going to put a stop to it."

The screen cuts to a shot of Leah and this man sitting on a patio near the eighteenth hole of a golf course. "Dexter Toledo is the spokesman for Health Watch International, a health and wellness advocacy group taking on the impossible task of breaking America's obsession with all things greasy and beefy."

"Leah, these are wonderful times we live in," Toledo says happily. He wears a white and red polo shirt and a straw golf hat.

"That's not what I expected you to say, sir. Not with thousands of Americans dying from heart failure each year. Not with more children growing morbidly obese by the hour. Not with the restaurants one-upping each other with increasingly outrageous gastronomic stunts every day."

Toledo closes his eyes and shakes his head the way people do when Jesus enters their hearts on late night church shows. "It's a wonderful time, young lady, because we have the power to change all that. *All* of it. I'm not happy saving one person from heart disease and kidney failure. I want to save a million. I want to see cancer move ahead of heart disease as America's big murderer."

"You *want* people to die of cancer?"

His eyes widen a twitch. "Let me rephrase that. I want to live in a world where we have to worry about real threats like shark attacks, falling from ladders, and coconuts—not what's for dinner." His voice is peppy as Santa Claus after a pot of espresso. "Health Watch informs America of its options and how to fight Big Beef where it hurts."

"Where is that?"

"In its wallet and its image. I want to show America how people are happier and healthier when they eat an apple off the tree, not a hot apple pie from a tiny cardboard box."

The show concludes with Toledo providing stunning scientific connections between heart attacks and deep-fried bacon cheeseburgers. He calls for all Americans to break their addiction. "America, Health Watch is setting up a center near you. Health Watch challenges Big Beef to come up with more evil foods. In fact we dare them. It's just going to give us more ammunition."

"Wow, that's a powerful message. Any final words, sir?"

Dexter Toledo stares deep into the camera with his first serious face of the interview: "Have no fear, *Healthy Wally* is on the way."

FORTY-FOUR

What would Deshler do?

Dean strolls into work well-rested. Birds chirp new songs, colors reinvent themselves. *The band didn't work out for a reason*, he thinks. *I can be an artist,* this pauses his walk down the hallway, mouth unhinged a little, *just a hamburger artist. Lothario would waste my time and creativity.*

His Gibby-centric orbit is misaligned—maybe permanently. He's been reading Christopher Winters' biography and brushing up on Hamburger Philosophy. "I Saw an X-Ray of a Girl Passing Gas" has been pushed into the darkness in favor of "Axis of Edible."

Dean has a stack of notes under his arm. Ideas for new burgers, more writing than he's penned during Lothario Speedwagon's entire lifecycle. His feet skitter across the office floor, excited to speak. Anxious to be heard.

Winters' Olde-Tyme Development Office is roomy and sterile. People smile when they see Dean. Exotic new burger smells pipe out from under closed office doors.

After pouring coffee and reading email, he decides to check on the new recipe. He sits behind his desk and phones the Olde-Tyme Test Kitchen. "So how does the secret sauce look?"

"Oh, well, sir," the scientist's voice cracks. "See, we…see we're making progress, but I was told you were off the project. Something about, well, the *Nightbeat* show last night."

"Wait, what? Slow down."

"Sir, Mister Double Harry asked that we keep a lid on this

situation." The scientist's voice is antsy to get off the line. "If you have questions, I'd go to him. I'm sorry. I really am."

Deshler slams the receiver and dials with a swoop of finger punches. Harry answers. "Yep?"

"I just spoke with R and D." Dean is out of breath, lungs can't catch up to his confused brain.

"I'm sure you did, kid. Don't twist yourself up about it. Let the project go. We've got lots more to worry over."

"Ridiculous. Have you talked to Roland about your little move? Harry, this project is my baby."

"Dean," the double hamburger inventor says with a sigh. "Do you watch much television these days?"

Harry recaps last night's *Nightbeat*, saying things like: "Well, now, we can't prove that it's anyone we *know*. But it's pretty easy to narrow down all the gap-toothed employees with a damned scar like that on their chin."

"Harry, I think I would remember something like that, don't you?" Deshler rubs the puffy scar tissue below his lips. He regrets going to bed early. He regrets not answering the phone when Malinta's name came up on the caller ID around eleven last night.

Or did I go to bed early? he wonders. *Has the Cliff Drinker been out?*

Harry isn't listening and starts speaking before Dean's lips close. "Now sure," he says. Deshler can picture the smile on that wrinkled face. "It was most likely an actor, an imposter. But we've got to take all the precautions we can. This is top-secret stuff we're working on. All you have to know is that the sauce prototype is about ready. It'll be in test markets next week. Now, unless you have a confession to make, I need to go."

"It couldn't have been me, Harry. I was home all night. I went to bed early," he protests, all the while wondering if anyone's ever gone to therapy for *sleep-drinking*. Our booze werewolf knows he didn't go on *Nightbeat* last night. But can't shake the thought that this does sound an awful lot like something a Cliff Drinker would do.

"Do you think I'm stupid? The show is live, but those segments are taped in advance. It could have been yesterday, it could have been shot two weeks ago. Can you account for all that time?"

"Uh, well…"

"Like I said, relax. All you have to know is we'll be hitting the test markets soon."

"That seems quick."

"No, not really. You'd be shocked how promptly we can get things from research to marketplace. It's being fast-tracked."

After he hangs up, the rest of the day melts in the palm of Dean's hand.

At a secret lunch with Thurman Lepsic, Dean's head sinks into his neck even deeper. "Listen, Deshler, I don't give a shit what you did on television. Hell yes I saw it," his second boss says, voice bursting in brutal Molotov tones. "It stuck a firecracker in all our asses, but we're moving forward."

Lepsic sucks in his lunch: a springy lump of tofu and steamed asparagus. Dean doesn't touch his club sandwich during the forty minute ass chewing.

"You smooth out whatever wrinkles you've caused. Just drop this whole *I'm innocent* shtick. It'll only trip you up. You track down more information about this *Hypothermia* burger. Which reminds me, Findlay and I were discussing your services—"

"Where is Mister Findlay? I haven't seen him in…" Deshler slows to a hush. He doesn't remember ever meeting the CEO of Bust-A-Gut. Can't even picture the boss's face.

"Yeah, yeah, yeah, we should hold a family reunion. Never mind. What I need to know is what have you done for us lately?"

"Mister Lepsic…Thurman," he says, reading a eulogy. "I've been spreading myself pretty thin. I haven't had an—"

Lepsic, with wood-stained tan, flips the last nub of bean curd in his mouth. "Right now, gimme something. Gimme an idea, hotshot." He wipes large lips and rests behind an empty plate, working a string of asparagus out from his teeth. "I'm not paying you to be a spy. I'm paying you for ideas."

"Well, sir. We've got the Mozzarella Stick Burger. I haven't read any reports yet, though I'm sure it'll knock people out. But…"

Lepsic glances at his watch, pulls out a long cigar and lights up. The smell of smoke and the gluey thrill of tobacco squeeze sweat from Deshler's hands. He hasn't smoked a cigarette all day—something buried within his genetic code aches for nicotine.

He tries to summon the Drunk Deshler that wowed the Winters management a few days back. "But what if we made the burger even *more* irresistible."

"Now we're getting somewhere. Let's hear it. Let's hear it," Lepsic says, listening, eyebrows dancing.

"We've got a big battle to fight with Winters. So what if," Deshler's voice curls to a whisper. *Cigarettes…cigarettes… cigarettes.* "What if we put nicotine in the meat? I'm sure there's some way we can get around the FDA. Restaurants duck those guys all the time. Winters is stroking them right now. If nothing else, just for test markets and maybe the first few weeks of launch. Give people an itch for this product. It's like subliminal advertising, only *subliminaler.*"

Lepsic counts his fingers and adjusts several shining rings. He rolls the Havana Regulár between thumb and index, letting gray smoke glide to the lights. He gives a corner-of-the-eye glance toward the waiter.

Dean stares for so long that Lepsic takes a second, more

concerned, glance. Deshler fills the gap with a low, invisible groan. The VP shifts eyes upward without moving his head. He licks his lips and locks back on Deshler. "Do you read any of our reports?"

"Yeah, of course," Dean lies, guilty for dipping back into those Gibby-centric ways.

"I find that hard to believe, buddy."

Deshler can't get cigarettes off his mind. "It's a great idea. I can take it to Winters if you don't like it." He awards himself a medal. He is a double agent of the highest degree.

A burst of smog flows out Lepsic's mouth during a laugh: "Yeah, go ahead. Be my guest."

Deshler stares and waits for the punch line.

"Dean, we already put nicotine in our burgers. Been doing it for years. Go right ahead, let your pal Roland Winters know. Christ, his dad *invented* that idea. We even put that stuff in our milkshakes."

"Oh."

"Get the hell out of here. I'm too busy for this shit. You owe me some brilliance, got it? I'm starting a tab."

"So what does that mean?" Dean says.

"It means that I'm glad you didn't sign a contract just yet. That little stunt on *Nightbeat* made you untouchable… in public at least. Do you know we have professionals who eliminate bad publicity like you? It makes holding someone off a bridge look like gym class. But I'm just saying. Anyhow, do what you do best. Keep your head low and we'll keep signing the paychecks for now."

That evening Deshler sits at a corner table of the Beef Club. The room is nowhere as empty as his drink. Lifting eyes from a fourth Rusty Knife, he catches many stares. Their meaty looks dig deep, their gossip crams his ears. He doesn't feel drunk. He never does when he's stressed. But Deshler wants the room to start spinning as fast as possible. Gibby probably would want that. A comfort and familiarity find the Cliff Drinker. He's sorry for ever thinking about selling those Butthole Surfers bootlegs.

The Beef Club is a swarm. People from both camps tell stories. Bust-A-Gut employees say they knew Dean was working for the other guy. Winters employees say they've heard he's a spy from Bust-A-Gut. One woman claims she heard in the ladies toilet, from someone who read a blog, that he's actually a Health Watch employee. Someone else heard that he's Roland Winters' long-lost son and that's why he's moved up the old ladder so fast.

However, none of these people want to be seen actually talking to Deshler.

Drinking is the only thing that will push away all these pressures. It always works. It's what makes the Cliff Drinker the Cliff Drinker. The crush of two bosses squeezes a fist around Dean's head. The Rusty Knife jangles that force loose.

Double Harry was not fun during their phone conversation this morning:

"So where does this leave me?"

"Weeeeeell," Double Harry said, real easy.

"Harry, come on. I love this company. It's my calling in life."

"Oh, we've got some work for you to do, don't worry."

After lunch some guys in janitor uniforms boxed Dean's belongings up while he worked. They said his office is being moved and that's all they knew.

FORTY-FIVE

"Get them while they are still lasting," Dimitri sputters into a microphone. His hearty cheeks redden under California sunshine. The crowd of hundreds cheers so loud it reminds one cook of a Metallica concert. The mob fans throughout the Olde-Tyme playland.

So far, the Moscow Five and Juan Pandemic's first public appearance together is going just like Delia scripted. The Space Burger team took a few days off after the television special to travel and give phone interviews. But today, beef-crazed maniacs are gathered under the smoggy Los Angeles sky for a glimpse of history.

A flimsy stage sags with the weight of the Olde-Tyme Space Burger team, the restaurant's manager and the mayor. "You have heard me speak correctly, gentlemen and ladies." Dimitri is Yakov Smirnoff warming-up a Vegas crowd. All smiles and exaggerated accents. "Winters Olde-Tyme Hamburgers is retiring the Space Burger in honor of Moscow Five!"

The crowd divides in cheers and boos. Three of the five astronauts—the happy ones—lift a hand and wave to the liquid horde. Yuri and Pavel's swing in dramatic parade marshal arcs while Keith and Sonja gently step behind.

Secretly, Sonja hopes fans aren't traumatized by what happens next. She likes people, she really does.

Half an hour before this insanity, Pandemic shoved himself in a corner of the tour bus. The gleaming new ride is painted green and says *Space Burger* in letters that can be read at seventy-five miles-an-hour.

"Finally," Pandemic's drugless voice said into the phone. It was loud and clear and proud. "I've been trying to get a hold of you for a couple days, Dad."

"Sorry, I'm busy. But I'm here now."

"Did you see me on TV? I nailed it!"

"Yep, yes," Dad sounded distracted. "The hair looked good."

"I'm really working hard. I've been studying the company. I've been nice to all my interviewers. I think I'm really doing a great job. I'm sorry I was so mean, pop. You were right. Thanks." He breathed deep, realizing he'd never before been within a mile of sincerity with his father. "Thanks for giving me this chance. I want to make you proud."

"Tim."

There was a long pause.

"Yeah?"

"Tim, I have some bad news."

"What?"

Roland Winters, taking several little breaks, explained the situation to Timothy. The whole thing lasted less than a minute, but took hours on Pandemic's end.

Tears leaked down and soaked into his nylon mustache. Salt water loosened the adhesive and it slipped a bit.

"But Dad," he blubbered.

Roland Winters sat in his office sniffing a glass of scotch. It burned.

"We had a deal, we…" Pandemic's lightweight frame tightened. His words, gummy with mucus. "I'm your *son*. How can you do this?"

"Mmmhhhh," he oozed. "We never had a *deal*, Tim. I discussed your proposition with the Board of Directors and they denied it. It's not really even my call. They think you're too much of a liability to work with in any capacity. I really fought for you, I did."

"I saved your ass," young Winters whined, throat sprained sore from sobbing. "You needed me to do this and I did it. I'm going to be part of the company. It's my legacy."

"Tim, I do need you to do this. Grandpa needs you to do this. You are doing an important job and we'll compensate you for it. The problem is the Board…"

"Bullshit, bullshit," he screamed. "Grandpa wouldn't let some board push him around."

"Timothy, I'm not your grandpa. God knows I try. I'll say this once, the best way for you to get involved with the company is to do your job now. Show everyone you can be trusted, that you're a responsible businessman. That's the kind of thing these guys pay attention to. Okay?"

Pandemic dropped the phone. He staggered to his bunk.

Across the bus, Henry, Sonja and Keith chatted at the table. Henry filled them in on his life, ignoring the last six months embarrassing himself as Lothario Speedwagon's bassist.

The scrawny Russians are the first brother and sister in space, they claimed. They grew up outside of Moscow and joined the military prior to the space program. Sonja was on a submarine and Keith actually flew MiGs, but never saw combat.

The topic quickly changed.

(No, be serious.) Keith's eyes were full of wonder. (Nobody actually *eats* Space Burgers for pleasure.)

(I have,) Henry said, proud. (They're good. Better than the Monte Cristo.)

(Even starving,) Sonja said. (I thought they were disgusting.)

(Space Burgers are not disgusting. Borscht is disgusting.

Cabbage soup is disgusting.)

Keith's laugh filled the bus. His fellow flyers stared and rolled eyes. (Cabbage soup! I will be eating the cabbage soup until I live for one hundred years.)

Sonja nodded. (Those hamburgers will be eating you, Henry. In the heart, yes?)

(Look at me,) he began smiling, realizing the two were toying around. (I am healthy enough to be a cosmonaut, yes?)

(You do not want to know the space life, my little Henry,) Sonja's eyes went serious and small.

(What was space station like?) Hamler asked in shattered Russian.

(It was not what you do think. Not in the smallest percentage,) Sonja said, eating an apple. Henry couldn't picture her wearing a big furry hat and pounding around in the Moscow snow. In the right light she could be from California or Arizona, he thought. Except for those teeth—those are a hundred percent Bolshevik. (It was a dark time and we are fortunate to be breathing the air now.)

(Yes,) her brother added, staring at the other three spacemen playing cards. (Everything here is not as it was up in space. This is not the scene we saw. They can try to kill us, but—)

Sonja snapped a spring-loaded squeeze on Keith's shoulder, hushing him. She bit more apple.

(So how will you protect us from more insane Americans?) Keith said, speaking slow enough for Hamler to follow. Henry could never picture when people were supposed to look like brother and sister. Especially these two: he had brown eyes, she had blue. He had a flat, boxer's nose, she had a long, straight machete for a vodka-sniffer. (You cannot clothesline everyone. You all carry guns, yes?)

(Every American must own gun, is law,) Sonja said with glittering eyes.

(I am giving a gun, but most Americans do not,) Hamler said and flipped open his jacket, revealing the holster and dark butt of a semiautomatic pistol. Lately, his opinion of the gun had shifted from fear to pride. (I have never owned one before. I am telling of my boss to *bang bang* Americans who *bang bang* at Russians, yes?)

The siblings nodded and Sonja said: (Let me see this weapon. This gun that will save my life.)

(I think not to.) He closed the jacket curtain on the gun.

(It will not be a problem. I have handled many guns from my time in the Navy.)

(Yes, I have, as well,) her brother said. (We have great respect for weapons.)

(This is not an option for today's.)

(Henry, we are friends. Do not be afraid.)

Henry thought long. (I am not afraid. Nothing brings the fear to my heart. Except maybe for tall heights. But I am a charge-taking gentleman of the Earth.)

Sonja giggled. (This is not the first gun we have known, Little Henry. It will be a trust we share.)

Hamler shrugged, it spread his face wide. (The other cosmonauts will be seeing none gun, please.)

The Russian siblings nodded and pointed near Hamler's breast pocket.

Hamler slipped the gun out with a fabric whoosh and passed it across the Formica table. Its black metal sucked in the light, every divot and crease outlined perfectly. The cosmonauts made approving noises in no language.

(Is it loaded?) Keith said.

(It is a beautiful machine. I am sure it feels beautiful to shoot. To *bang-bang*, yes?)

Hamler eyed the room, ensuring nobody noticed the firearm. (Yes, its power is more than my human soul.)

Keith glanced up from the gun: (May I hold it? It has been many years for me.)

(Quickly. Please be careful.)

Keith lifted the gun like its barrel was sculpted granite. He twisted it sideways and shucked out the clip. (Mmmm, this feels natural. Feels comforting.) A relaxed smile, the first Henry had seen, formed on the spaceman's face—teeth just as rotten as hers.

LA in the winter was so much hotter than home. The air conditioner was blowing on Henry's face. Outside the window, people were wiping sweaty brows and wearing tank tops. It was a weird, peaceful balance. Weirder still when factoring in the loaded firearm. But Henry was calm—everything seemed to be in its correct place. He was getting close to the people he was protecting. And that was good. The more he knew about Sonja and Keith and Dimitri and the rest, the more acute his senses grew. Their budding friendship made Henry want to protect everyone so much more. This job was becoming fun. And that was something Hamler hadn't experienced since lifeguarding the summer between freshman and sophomore year.

Suddenly, Delia Ellery stormed through the motor home. "Hello! Does anyone have a watch? We need to be outside signing autographs. We need to shake hands. We need to sell *hamburgers.*"

She was sweaty and out of breath. Her suit jacket sleeve rolled into a nub. "Scoot, scoot. Dimitri, please get everyone moving."

The cosmonaut leader stood and barked a few commands until the others rose and slid out the door, muttering Russian curses.

Hamler walked back to Juan Pandemic's bunk. The contest winner was wrapped into a knot, sobbing. "Dude, come on. You've got to get out there."

"I can't believe him. What kind of father does this? God."
His mustache was wet fur, matted and sticky. His toupee had a
serious cowlick, eyes cracked raspberry-red.

"Juan, man, I'm sorry. We need to get through this today.
Tomorrow's a day off. It'll be okay."

"I can't do this, I can't…" He rolled over and his back
convulsed with sobs.

Delia stomped up and pulled Pandemic's leg. She convinced
the heir to go and stand on the flimsy stage with the other five,
then come back and be a bawl baby later.

The crowd goes nuts. A line spills out the restaurant doors.
People whisper about hoping there are enough Space Burgers
to go around. American hero Juan Pandemic looks confused.
He looks like he's wearing a disguise.

At the core of the mayhem, near the back of the stage, Sonja
slinks behind Yuri and wraps his body in a Russian military
submission hold. The unsuspecting cosmonaut's limbs twist at
bizarre angles, his face burns fluorescent tones.

The audience waves banners: "Cosmonaut Fever," "From
Russia with Love," "I Heart Space Burgers." There is a flurry of
excitement, jumpy and electric in the air. The noise speaks in
tongues.

Keith reaches into the cargo pocket of his jumpsuit. He
slips behind Pavel before Yuri drops. In a kung-fu quick move,
Keith's foot buckles the backside of Pavel's knee. Keith floats
behind the now-kneeling spaceman and shoves the barrel of a
black handgun shallow in the plump cosmonaut's ear. He pulls
the trigger.

The crowd noise strangles the huge gun crack quiet, down
to a finger-snap. But every television crew in the greater Los

Angeles area captures the murder as a fire hose of blood and chunks spray loose.

Dimitri drops his waving hand. On the nightly news footage, he smiles along, like missing a prank. He turns back to Delia for direction. Her clipboard clatters to the ground.

Skinny little Keith, his blue jumpsuit covered with a wet flash of red, turns and stuffs the gun in Yuri's mouth and pulls the trigger with similar results.

On the shaky video flashing across eleven o'clock televisions tonight, contest winner Juan Pandemic flops his hands at the crowd, oblivious to the carnage and splatter around him. His mind on another planet.

Like choreography, Sonja grabs Dimitri's limp arm, tugs it and trips their leader to the ground. The now silent crowd blocks all but Keith's upper body in every camera shot. The beef-crazed mob stands motionless as the struggle tumbles across their view. The gun is clearly pointed toward the body of the chief cosmonaut. With the crowd noise at zero, three shots pop.

By the final bullet, Juan Pandemic is now in a headlock. He's so weak he might crumble into sand under Sonja's surprisingly muscular arms. Keith, standing lean and edgy, motions for Hamler to leap onstage.

Hamler recalls the violently ill feelings from murdering Christopher Winters. That disgusting stomach and chest seem like a game of double dutch standing at the edge of the stage, a mist of blood nesting in his beard.

A tiny voice, stop-drop-and-rolling in the back of his brain, whispers crucial spy training: "*Grab your gun. Save the day. They are not your friends.*" Henry tightens his spine and goes for the holster. Suddenly, the firearm in Keith's hand looks familiar. Suddenly, the sting of failure is all his body knows.

Hamler lets out a defeated sigh.

The bloody cosmonaut whispers in Little Henry's ear.

Defenseless, Hamler steps to the microphone and speaks in a shaky voice. "The Moscow Two want the world to know the truth. Do not attempt to stop them," he says, nodding while Keith whispers more, jerking and angry. "Or they will begin ending civilian lives, as well. These three were not innocent. Do not attempt to stop the Moscow Two. They wish for all police to…" his voice echoes through the parking lot and dissolves into Los Angeles smog.

A whirlwind mob grows from the center of the crowd. News cameras capture a stampede of burger-loving, death-fearing Americans. This is the point most cameramen are trampled— their feed whipping into a thrashing blur and growl of static.

One camera's sound rolls amongst the retreating avalanche. When it plays on *Nightbeat*, Hamler's voice booms over the PA: "Please, these two say they only want justice." There is a lot of static and the meaty slap of skin slamming skin. "These two say you do not know the real truth about outer space and Winters hamburgers."

FORTY-SIX

Each heartbeat stomps into Deshler's brain, swelling it larger—larger—larger. He pokes open an eye and recognizes all the posters. His bedroom smells moist, forest moist.

Coiled into a ball on the bed, Dean is still tightly wrapped in clean office clothes. A necktie chokes across his Adam's apple. He's fifty percent sure he'll find no bloodstains.

The napalm power of *Broken Piano for President* shakes through Dean's memory, jiggling the jelly of his eyeballs.

He checks the nightstand and finds both wallet and keys in sight. This is looking like another Hall of Fame morning. Already, it's one hundred percent better than yesterday at work.

Though Deshler's insides attempt a somersault, his lips burst open a large grin, thinking maybe he's finally getting the hang of Cliff Drinking. Thinking maybe he can be a responsible drunk.

Deshler reaches for the wallet to see how much money was blown last night, but instead picks up a folded sheet of white paper beneath it. A murky splotch of stale beer has spidered toward the edge and dried:

Moral Compass Records
2613 SE Pine St
Portland, OR 97214
503-234-6990

This contract hereby employs the musical services of **Lothario Speedwagon** to **Moral Compass Records**. Upon signing, the artist(s) will receive a monetary advance of $**500,000** against all future record sales. All profits from said recordings shall proceed directly to **Moral Compass Records** until the advanced sum is balanced. All profits after this point will be divided fifty percent (50%) to **Moral Compass Records**, twenty-five percent (25%) to Artists and Repertoire representative **Antonio McComb** and the remaining twenty-five percent (25%) to the artist(s) **Lothario Speedwagon**.

This contract represents a legal commitment on behalf of the artist(s) **Lothario Speedwagon** to render all master recordings and copyrights for **three (3)** albums and/or **eight (8)** years of service to **Moral Compass Records**. In return, **Moral Compass Records** will handle all manufacturing, marketing and distribution costs for said recordings.

Deshler Dean	**11-29-11**
(Signature of Artist #1)	(Date)
(Signature of Artist #2)	(Date)
(Signature of Artist #3)	(Date)
Antonio McComb	**11-29-11**
(A&R Representative)	(Date)
Malinta Redding	**11-29-11**
(Witness)	(Date)

"This is so fake," Dean's diesel engine rattles. He recalls other bizarre things he's written with help from his muse, whiskey. His band's keynote song, for one.

He reads the letter three times before rubbing fingers over the Braille-like notary seal and second guesses.

"Could I have?" he growls and grabs a sip of warm High-Life by the bed. Dean coughs and swallows the old ale. "This, this is…a record deal," he says, a little more lubricated.

He turns on the clock radio and slips in a cigarette. John Cougar Mellencamp sings about R-O-C-K in the USA. The cigarette tastes like blood.

This takes the cake as the strangest note Deshler has ever woken up with. However, it is a close race:

NOTES

- **Three Months Ago:** "Sir, your leotard is back from the dry cleaner."

- **Twelve Months Ago:** "Call me. Franklin Delano Roosevelt – 416-278-1233"

- **Forty-eight Months Ago:** A medical bill for the birth of twin girls. $13,755.

- **Six Months Ago:** "Healthy Wally's: 4442 S. Elm Street. 2:00 PM -**DO not miss**."

- **Twenty-two Months Ago:** "Dean, give me back the keys to the Wiener Mobile."

"Well, I guess you're still alive," Malinta says from the doorway, looking like she tripped a landmine. Her hair is what friends call *frizzy* and hairdressers classify as *beyond repair*. The wound on her blonde head is naked and opened back up. It is pink and meaty in the dim light.

"Hello, Miss *Witness*," Dean says, feeling usual embarrassment disappear. "Can you maybe tell me what happened last night?" Deshler flaps the contract at her.

"I can't believe you never told me you are in a mother F-ing band, Dean. How long have we been *working* together?"

"God, I don't know." The truth sounds lonesome.

"What other mysteries are you keeping? Where's the pile of skulls in your closet? Where's the string of illegitimate kids? How many other secret jobs do you have?"

"Beats me." More lonesome still.

"It's like every time I get anywhere near you, you shove me away."

"I know. I wish I didn't."

"So just don't."

"My head," he holds said throbber with two hands, "doesn't work that easily."

"That is nowhere near funny, babe. You've got too much riding on this to screw up now." Her voice fizzles into a sleepy hum.

"Well, I'm not sure how much I have riding on anything. I might be fired at Winters…maybe the other guys, too. Everyone's pissed."

"Just stay focused, okay?"

"Did you crash here?"

"*Yes.*" She rubs swollen eyes. "I couldn't take your snoring so I slept on the couch." She flops down at the foot of Dean's bed and kicks a pile of pants across the room. "Our kids wouldn't get a minute of sleep, if we had some. What with Daddy sawing away—"

"Please don't talk like that. Just remind me again where this contract came from," he says, carefully holding the white paper like it was blood-soaked.

"Dean, Jesus," she hisses and spikes eyes in his direction. Deshler watches the tight, angry lines in her face melt as she warms. It looks like sympathy. "I went to the Beef Club and…" She rubs at the gash. "Aren't you tired of this? Don't you think we can find an easier way?"

"I'm sorry."

"Why is it always like this?"

"I wish I knew," he says, knowing exactly why.

"So, everyone at the club said you were shitty drunk, spilling people's drinks, crying. I've never seen the entire room so mad at one person. They were all talking about your *television appearance*. You're lucky nobody kicked your ass again. I mean, come on, Dean. You've got a dod gamned job to do."

"Very ladylike."

"*Jobs* to do, I should say. You know?" Her eyes try to hammer something home. He doesn't get it.

"Like I said, those jobs aren't necessarily mine anymore. Plus, I don't remember that TV thing."

"Well, forget about it. I'll take care of loose ends. We need you to focus."

Malinta leans her long giraffe frame across the bed and sinks her head into Deshler's lap. Her legs curl together. Dean eyes over the contract, then her face. Malinta's wound is hot and wet against his stomach. He dives in and kisses her. She clips Deshler's lip with teeth.

"Oh, God, you taste terrible," she says with a bitter face. "I think you got sick last night, hon."

Deshler gives a relief pitcher's nod. "That's not out of the question." He lights another cigarette and shares with Malinta. Things are silent and musty in the bedroom. This moment is good, wholesome and rare in Dean's life. If the rest of the day were this calm, it'd be beautiful. But something inside the Cliff Drinker can't help but kick it in the ribs. "Seriously, what's with the contract?"

"What's with the *band*? Lothario Speedwagon?"

"I, well, sorry. I guess I should have said something."

"So many." She gnaws her cheek for a bit. "Secrets."

"I'm sorry."

"Yeah, I mean, you're an artist? Come on, I'm supposed to know everything about you. And according to that creepy Antonio guy, you're a really brilliant one. You and I, we're more than all this. Seriously, what else are you hiding?"

"So, wait, when did we meet last night?"

"Down the street…at a bar, that nasty dive, the Purple Bottle, you know? And you were sitting at a booth with this nerdy little guy and he's pointing at *that*," she finger flicks the paper.

"Who?"

"This guy, the record company guy, um," she snatches the contract and runs a French manicured nail down it. "*McComb*, Antonio McComb. He looked like a troll, a science geek troll. And you guys were really deep in conversation." She hands back the paper. "I had to practically scream to get your attention. But you were *really* stupid drunk."

"So is this an honest-to-God record contract?"

"Beats me. He had me sign as witness. I don't know a contract from a dinner menu. I can't believe you're in a band. You are such a little shit."

Dean's eyes go big and silly.

"Shut up. I'm talking about *trust*, are you familiar?"

"Look, it's not. It's…" He hisses the cigarette stub into the beer bottle. "Jesus, I don't think the band is even together anymore. I don't know if there *is* a Lothario Speedwagon." This cranks the distortion pedal in his heart to MAX.

"Who's talking about your band?"

"We…I…" Dean's muscles go tight. "Fine."

He doesn't realize how helpless he looks. It forces Malinta to take a long breath. It forces her to rub her hands together, hoping nerves disappear. "Well, if it makes you feel any better, there's only ever been one obese president."

"Merci."

"What?"

"*Thank you.*"

"Seriously. I'm talking stuck-in-a-bathtub-fat. Not Bill-Clinton-Chubby." Her lips pucker and whistle a sweet note. "Seems pretty good, one out of forty-four."

"Huh?"

"That son of a bitch loved beef. All the obese presidents do. Roosevelt, Clinton, Taft."

"That's a big help." He smiles and looks down at Malinta. Dean is getting used to having her in his life. A little surprised, he realizes how much he's enjoying being with her. While, yes, booze is probably partially to blame, it's tough recalling life before Malinta Redding.

And that's a good thing.

FORTY-SEVEN

Winters' and Bust-A-Gut's corporate offices are one mile apart. Many years ago, when Bust-A-Gut was drawing blueprints for its headquarters, Winters' skyscraper stretched seventy stories tall. The Globo-Goodness Corporation Family of Corporations sunk a *seventy-one* story tower in the ground as close as they could to their rival.

The Winters family has been trying to find a way to add two more stories ever since.

The city below these behemoths is freckled with parking garages, shoe stores, homeless people, taverns and the Beef Club. One storefront is under construction on the tight road connecting the two buildings. The fresh awning is striped white and red. It says—"Healthy Wally's: A Division of Health Watch International."

Inside, construction workers install an enormous rice cooker, three grills and a walk-in tofu refrigerator.

At thirty other locations around this country, the exact same plans are used to hammer together replicas. Each one is boxy and plain and clean enough for surgery. Every building has an enormous, cross-eyed Wally the Moose statue greeting customers.

The failure rate for a new business in America is higher than the divorce rate. The failure rate for a restaurant is even worse. But the proprietor of these establishments has an edge. She knows success in the restaurant business relies heavily on killer marketing and word of mouth. Actual food is a distant third.

She's ready to strike, and almost has everything in place. She just needs the word of mouth.

FORTY-EIGHT

Little Delia Ellery splashes thick drops of sweat on the tour bus floor. She calculates an escape route as the engine roars and the passengers jerk unbalanced. The bald cameraman nearly drops all that expensive equipment.

Delia retreats to a bunk after she realizes the only exit is guarded by one of the Russians—the girl with the gun. The Space Burger tour manager can't focus with all this Kremlin talk.

Keith stomps up the cramped bus unzipping the bloody jumpsuit. He turns back to his sister as she leans against the door and rattles off a cayenne stream of Russian.

Keith slips out of the suit and past Delia's bunk. The one-armed woman's concentration hemorrhages from the realization that fresh human blood smells sweet and unlike anything from the butcher shop in her hometown.

Where are the police? she thinks.

Minutes earlier, Keith and Sonja took a deep breath when the tidal wave of frightened hamburger fanatics flushed away from the stage. Sonja grabbed Dimitri and Delia's frightened bodies by the collars, leading them back to the green bus. Lathered shiny and red, Dimitri apparently survived the gunfire. Sonja yelled at Hamler and walked the pack through the Children's Playland toward the bus.

Keith fired his pistol in the air once and hollered some scrambled letters back to his bodyguard, then pointed the pistol at a fiberglass statue of Christopher Winters. "Dude, uh sir," Hamler said in a loud, distracted tone. "You. Mister cameraman hiding behind the statue," he said as a young bald guy with a black video camera popped his skull from behind the glossy ketchup red suit. "The guy with the gun says, unless you want to die, you are coming with us. Cool?" Hamler paused before the final word, shuffling the puzzle pieces together, realizing what a slaughter he just witnessed. One he should have stopped. Way to be a take-charge guy.

The man's squeaky voice probably didn't sound American to the Cosmonaut terrorists. It came out tiny, like a flute—a flute that just shit its pants. "Whatever you say comrades, I'm not the enemy. I don't want to die. Tell them, tell them I don't want to die. I'm a journalist."

Slightly dizzy and surprisingly calm, Henry said, "Yeah, I think wanting to live is implied. Come on."

The pack easily strolled to the idling tour bus where the driver, an older woman with red hair and bad skin, napped in a bunk. No police firefight. No outraged fans. Just the quiet scatter of a hundred carloads fleeing for their lives.

Juan Pandemic/Timothy Winters pulls off his mustache the way oil painters make clouds. His delicate stroke leaves a tattoo of inflamed skin under the nose. He slaps the lip fur on the window, breathes fog across the glass and draws two eyes as the Los Angeles cityscape zips past the bus.

The bald cameraman sobs like asphyxiation, peppered with squeaky mumbles.

Keith, stripped to tight white underwear, yells from the

bedroom at the rear of the bus. Sonja hollers over to Hamler.

Henry keeps an eye on both ends of the cabin. "Sir," he tells the weeping newsman. "*Dude,* knock that crying shit off right now." Hamler hardly remembers letting the Russians check out his gun. It makes his palms wet and salty. A few days ago, Pandemic called Henry the world's best bodyguard. Now two people are dead, and maybe more to come, thanks to him. Hamler needs to think of a plan. It's his responsibility.

His head drops. *I'll just screw things up even worse if I try something. Innocent people die. Just sit tight and this thing'll work out. Don't get involved.*

"I've just never—" the shiny-skulled cameraman peeps. "Guns are so scary…I don't want to die, man."

"Yeah, I know." Henry hardly has the energy to speak, bobbing around in such a soup of dread, drowning. "None of us do. Look, the one in the back is getting dressed. They say they want you to film them. They just want to make a movie. They wouldn't kill the only person who can operate the camera, would they?" Henry bites his cheek for being so nice. Babysitting this guy is not part of the job description. Though, he's pretty sure his daily duties just swirled down the toilet.

"I guess not." The man's face is gooey and dark.

"Just pull your shit together and stop crying. Don't give anyone reason to start shooting."

Keith finds a clean blue jumper and wanders back into the main compartment. The two Russians stand like old comrades discussing the rising value of the ruble. The temper in their voices unwinds. Both whisper and look at their interpreter. (Tell the cameraman we're ready,) Sonja says, showing off those horribly twisted teeth. (We will film exactly where you are sitting.)

Hamler relays the message.

Outside, the city moves fast, a shuffle of blurred buildings.

The sweaty cameraman breathes heavy, lungs groaning like tight rubber. Pandemic stands and lets him take a seat.

(No, no, we want Mister Juan in shot too. Up, up, up, please.)

Hamler relays the message.

"You know, I'm, *ahhhh*, not feeling it." Pandemic sounds spaced, digging fingernails under his wig. "I don't think this is for me. Tell the, the space guys, you know, *thanks for not killing me*, but I'm going to go put my head in an oven or something."

After some intense discussion and gun cocking, Juan Pandemic reconsiders. Delia is ripped from her bunk and plopped next to them.

Finally, the cosmonauts remember Dimitri on the floor, full of messy holes. Two shoulder shots and one through the hand, it appears. White towels and blankets sponge up the blood in a peppermint candy swirl. His large, scared eyes watch the girl with the gun.

Henry overhears them address their victim: (Sit up here, Dimitri,) Keith says, giving the space commander a hand. (Are you feeling well? Do you need water or more bandages? We want you to look your most handsome when you *spill your guts,* yes?)

In a sitcom-perfect American drawl—the kind owned by countless southern farmboys—Dimitri's Russian vocal chords scurry off and disappear like the Los Angeles crowd. "No, dude. Christ, *owwwwww*. Y'all win. Put the gun away. You guys win."

"Whoa," Pandemic whispers.

Jaw shaking and voice full of anger, Dimitri speaks more: "Surprise! I ain't Russian, asshole."

"Dimitri…you're…wait," Hamler says. The self-proclaimed spy master can't believe he missed that one. "Shit."

"I know what they want. Jesus, you bastards didn't have to shoot me. I was gonna quit soon anyhow. I was going back to help Daddy with the chickens." He rattles the same off in Russian. The cosmonauts stare at him with bored, skinny faces.

Like a family portrait—Pandemic, Dimitri and Delia sit between Keith and Sonja. Hamler stands a shade off camera relaying translations. "Uhm, okay, I've got enough battery for, like, five minutes," the cameraman whispers.

Hamler relays this message.

"Okay, we're rolling."

Keith speaks slowly and professionally, looking into the camera. Sonja digs the firearm into Dimitri's temple.

"Ladies and gentlemen, we understand our actions today at the Winters Olde-Tyme Hamburgers restaurant must have seemed," Hamler waits to find the right translation.

The cameraman points to the ceiling, mouthing the words: "Speak louder."

Hamler clears his throat. "Must have seemed *irrational.* Clearly, these are acts of rebellion and uncivil disobedience. I, Second Lieutenant Keith Kassabova and Captain Sonja Kassabova, wish to inform the American people and the citizens of the world, that the Space Burger drama you have witnessed was a lie." Hamler pauses as Keith holds for dramatic effect.

Delia quietly sobs. Her cheeks are burning hot coals.

Sonja tells Dimitri to read a statement or receive a fourth bullet. She passes a note card full of Russian scribbles. In a sharecropper's Alabama mumble, he says: "The men you know as Lieutenant Pavel Telingrad, Lieutenant Yuri Kassirimov and Captain Dimitri Nimov, *who is me,* were paid actors. We was never in space like Sonja and Keith." He winces and wobbles, nearly ready to pass out. "The truth is, the original three spacemen died from starvation. Their seventeen days spent without food due to the negligent Winters Hamburger Company proved overwhelming. In the interest of the public, Keith and Sonja, *the only survivors*, were silenced and the three of us took the deceased's places back on Earth." Dimitri slumps his head. "My real name is Carl Janomi, I'm a double major in drama and Russian language studies at Mississippi State."

Sonja's speech swells again. Henry translates it for the camera: "Our actions today were the only conceivable way to relay this message past the corporate censors who murdered our fellow space travelers. Forgive us."

There is another pause. Pandemic gawks with the wet, plastic eyes of an orphan meeting his real father.

"Please also forgive our future actions. We understand we have broken many of your American laws today. Do not attempt to send the police. We have several hostages and will not hesitate to execute them…" Hamler trails off. Sonja gives him two evil eyes. "Execute them if an attempt to capture us is made. We only require safe passage back to Russia in order for the hostages' lives to be spared. However, we will take any violent steps necessary to ensure our security."

"Oh lord, please save me," Delia squeals. Her head slumps against the fold-out table and glosses it in tears.

"That's it, that's all the battery strength I have. I'll need a new one if they want to record more," the cameraman squeaks.

Hamler translates the message. The interpreter notices the city buildings are whipping by the windows. There is a glassy rattle coming from the cupboards as speed builds.

Keith responds.

"They say that's cool, they said what they need to."

A gray film of annoyance covers Sonja's face. She clutches Delia's bony neck and yanks it back. In thick, wet syllables she growls to Hamler. "Sonja says, Delia, that if you don't, you know, shut up, she'll kill you. She says that, oh Jeez, she says they should kill you anyhow for getting them into this situation."

"Why me?" She butchers the word *me* into six syllables. Delia's eyes are a wiry, ruby mess of veins. "I'm just the tour manager. I didn't come up with any of this."

Pandemic leans in close to Keith. "Dude, I, *hey*, Keith, *comrade*…" Practically wrestling their hands together, Pandemic manages to give him a hearty handshake.

The bus slows and the bodies jerk forward. Fingers randomly clutch tabletops and walls.

Hamler translates for Delia.

"Yo, Henry, hey, tell Keith that I know what he's talking about," Pandemic says with a bounce. His face is more alive than in the three years he and Hamler have been friends.

"Timothy…*Juan*, I don't have time for this."

"No, man, please, tell the cosmonauts I'm on their side. Tell them I'll do whatever needs to be done to get back at my dad. Tell them that…that…that I can be a *big* help," he says, stretching arms wide.

Hamler, eyes rolled, translates Pandemic's wish.

The translator shifts focus back to the women. "Delia, Sonja says, 'if you're not responsible for this ordeal, then who is?' She says, 'if you're not the one they should kill, then who?'"

Keith waves at Hamler and rattles off some words.

"Dude, just a sec."

Delia's mouth drops. Keith's voice drowns out the one-armed tour manager.

"Ugh, fine. Pandemic, Keith says he likes you and appreciates what you just said. He certainly has much work for you to do. And basically, what translates into, *welcome aboard*."

"Hell yeah," Pandemic says, rubbing tender lip flesh.

"Hen…Henry," Delia says, politely raising a hand. "Can you tell them…" Hamler gets a headache, his eyes burn and his blood pressure rages to Astrodome proportions. The urge for caramel and nuts and milk chocolate swells inside him. "Tell the cosmonauts if they want someone to blame…um, you know, someone to *kill*," she says the final word in a hush. "That they should find a man named Deshler Dean."

"You're kidding?" Pandemic says.

"Wh…what did you say?"

"Deshler Dean. He's the reason their friends died. He's the reason for this tour. He's such a little shit. He's the one they should be mad at, not me."

Juan Pandemic and Henry Hamler lose all breath. Their heads grow fuzzy. The police sirens behind the bus fade away with all other noise. Hamler knows all the Snickers on earth won't fix him this time.

FORTY-NINE

Walking into Winters Corporate Headquarters, Vice President of Hamburger Development, Deshler Dean half expects his keycard swipe to glow red and security to shoo him away. Probably crack him in the ear with a baton.

Deshler catches a breath opening the office door. He pictures a Deshler Dean mimic making calls from his desk. If he's not fired yet, the cramps in Dean's stomach say he will be soon. His assistant, a guy a few years older named Austin, says, "Hey Skipper, did you see the Browns game last night?" Austin has a brushy goatee that makes baby-faced Deshler jealous.

"Missed it…I was…" Deshler tries to think of something to say other than wasted. "Working."

"Gotcha, bossman," the beardy assistant says with a *rock-on* fist. "Have a killer day."

Dean stands over his desk for a few minutes without breathing. All his belongings are returned to their original location. His stapler, his snowglobe, each pen is back in order. There is, however, a new addition.

The newcomer on Deshler's shiny maple desk *looks* like a hamburger. But under sterilizing white office lights, he's not convinced. "Is that." He pauses to stoop down and twist his neck. "Toothpaste?"

A cold lump of meat coated in neon blue gel peeks from between sesame seed buns. Dean is convinced this is the equivalent of a severed horse head under his quilt or a salmon wrapped in newspaper. *I'm as good as dead*, he decides.

"Whatever you do," his shadowy lungs rumble through the silent morning office. "You are not eating that."

Dean yawns and takes a closer inspection. *This hamburger-type-thing is something Henry would snap down in a second.* The blue slime looks like candy—some sugary paste his former bassist would suck through a straw. Deshler wonders if Hamler and Pandemic got his voice mails. *The least I can do,* Dean figures, is let those guys know the band has a contract. *If there still is a band. That is, if the contract is even legitimate.*

Deshler's desk phone rings with a flickering red light atop.

He swears the blue goo just slithered toward him. Dean takes a breath, knowing any second this globby monster might begin gnawing a knee.

Still ringing, the phone reminds Dean he still hasn't called the number on the record contract. He hasn't confirmed there is an Antonio McComb or even a Moral Compass Records. After checking his bank account, he's positive there is no five hundred grand. Dean wants to wait for his bandmates before moving forward.

Deshler walks around the desk. The Caller ID says it's the CEO. With one eye on the mutant hamburger and a boulder of anxiety in his throat, Dean lifts the receiver.

"Surprised?" Roland says.

"Many times over."

"Come on up to my office, buddy. We're knee-deep in it today."

"*It?*"

The CEO gurgles a laugh. "Don't worry. We'll talk about the Flu Burger prototype, too. It's just the whole cosmonaut mess is really…" the CEO sighs. "It's, *you know.*"

"What mess, Roland? What prototype? I thought I was fired."

His boss slashes in: "Don't you watch TV? What mess?

Deshler, I really need a chuckle today, but not now, not about our poor Cosmonauts. Get your ass up here."

Deshler kicks around the possibility of a trap. Corporate espionage. He bites his lip, waiting for the poorly disguised hamburger to blow up like the plastic explosive it really is.

There is no big boom, so Dean hangs up and concludes he simply imagined everything from that disastrous Friday. It's entirely possible he hallucinated that morning: the furniture movers, Lepsic's threats, the *Nightbeat* program and Moral Compass Records.

Deshler calculates his odds at about fifty percent.

Dean rests his elbows on the desk. The surface has been freshly waxed with a piney smelling something. A gag slithers up the back of his neck after inhaling medicinal stink from the sandwich mixed with wood polish.

His phone rings again. The Caller ID says Bust-A-Gut.

"Hello?"

"Brilliant," a grumbly low voice says. "This thing is going better than we could have hoped. You, son, are a homerun, three-pointer and a touchdown wrapped into one."

"Hello?"

"Dean...Dean? It's Clifford Findlay, *your boss.*" The final two words sizzle. "This Space Burger crisis, wow. Talk about guerrilla marketing. Jesus shit, man."

"Seems like it's all anyone can talk about." *So this is Findlay?* Dean thinks, half-disappointed the voice isn't more...exotic.

"You shouldn't be talking about it on this phone, I understand. I do. We'll be brief."

Deshler runs his tongue over aching gums. Findlay's voice sounds familiar. It sounds like Lepsic holding a handkerchief over the phone.

"Back to business. I mean, wow. Cosmonaut Terrorists. Diarrhea-publicity for old Winters. Two dead..."

Dean's brain is break dancing. He needs to sit. He needs more lies. Suddenly, too many people are listening to him. *There's only one place to turn*, he thinks, and summons his inner-Gibby. "What is…public opinion looking like, exactly?" He hopes this leads to clues.

The man on the phone runs through what the news has told the nation thanks to exclusive and bloody footage. Focus groups say to run the Tribute to Christopher Winters spots nonstop. This, Mister Findlay's voice explains, will remind customers what innocence Olde-Tyme burger lost. It's no longer the same company loyal diners remember. A ground rule double, a free throw, just an extra point. You know, nothing too impressive.

"Also," the man says casually. "We're going ahead with the mozzarella campaign. The climate is right, thanks to you."

"The climate, yes," he says.

"Wow, compadre," Findlay's hefty voice gropes for air, sounding more familiar, and less impressive, by the minute. "We had no idea this was up your sleeve. Look, I don't want to know how you ruined Winters by setting this up. I don't want to hear another word about it, okay?"

"Uh." Stress splinters Deshler's vision into a thousand needles. "Yes, I think that's best."

"All is forgiven, let's have a meeting tonight. Lay low, Desh."

"Wait, wait…have we met? Mister Findlay, you and I haven't *physically* met, right? Shaken hands, grabbed a drink, that kind of thing."

"Goodbye, son. If you can't reach me, call Lepsic, that guy's a genius. And funny, too."

Dean hangs up and chews on that last line.

One thing Deshler isn't chewing is the bun soaking up blue cold syrup sauce. Five crippled strips of bacon droop and fade into blueberry taffy. Lettuce spoils brown at the edges. He plucks the wax paper under the burger and slides it across the desk toward the trash. It wiggles like a gelatin mold.

The burger is a few skids from the empty morning garbage can when the phone buzzes alive again.

There's a neck cramp as he lifts the receiver.

"I know I'm not supposed to do this," a woman's smoky voice says. "Not supposed to contact you. I know we agreed on *total radio silence.*"

"Malinta?" he asks, knowing that's not her tender whisper.

"I don't have long, the others will be back. I just want you to know the train is on the tracks."

Dean's patience broils, burns and blackens to ash. "Oh Jesus Christ," he howls, voice rising a panicky few registers. "What is with everyone knowing my business but me?"

"Listen. I assume you're taking care of that business."

"Tell me, please tell me, *Mysterious Voice*, what am I doing? What do you know that I don't seem to have figured out?"

The voice breathes into the phone, her lips smack together. "I hope Malinta wasn't wrong about you. Just focus," the last word explodes.

Dean tugs his tie, his face hot with frustration. "Au revoir, Miss *Mystery Voice.*" He hangs up.

Dean yanks the Flu Burger into the trash with a papery thump.

FIFTY

It's ten at night and the familiar theme music for *Nightbeat* begins. Our anchorwoman, Sharon Smalley, layers her voice atop the images. "Tonight, exclusively on *Nightbeat*: the Moscow Two speak. We have the first and only footage of the Russian terrorists after their frightening reign. Hear what former hostage and *Nightbeat* cameraman, Donald Dumford, has to say about his ordeal." A quick headshot of the squirrely bald hostage pops up.

"Then," Smalley says, "a super volcano brewing under one of America's largest cities? When will it erupt and where?" The theme music flows for a few notes. "And finally, part two of Leah Pullem's investigation into the hazardous effects of hamburger consumption." Bloody text superimposes over a golden shot of a burger with a crusty-looking bun: *Death Burger...Part Two*.

Commercials begin: Cholesterol medication. Luxurious cars at frighteningly low prices. Prescription drugs for blood pressure. Sunday night movie preview. Medication for anxiety. And one more before the show kicks in:

The commercial focuses on a cocksure teenage fry cook in a Bust-A-Gut uniform dunking a batch of cheese sticks in oil. It cuts to a sexy young waitress carrying a stack of hamburgers through the kitchen. The boy whips a hot batch of mozzarella around and slams into the girl. At slow motion speed their food flips through the air together.

Cartoon voices pipe in: "*Hey, mozzarella stick, lookin' gooooood.*"

"Burger, my man, we should get together sometime."

"Oh, yeah, I've been dreaming of working with you guys forever!"

The scene cuts to the boy and girl, knocked to the floor, rubbing their heads and smiling. A hefty Mozza-Burger lands, fully evolved, in each of their laps.

A remake of the Village People's *Macho Man* thunders in. This version is called *Mozza Man.*

A warm, trustworthy voice thunders overhead: "Bust-A-Gut is proud to serve you a Mozza-Burger tonight. It's the only sandwich combining the world famous flavor of a Bust-A-Gut burger with the ooey-gooey yum of mozzarella sticks. Mmmmmmmmmmm."

The commercial finishes on the boy as he pulls out of a hearty bite. "Hey," he says with a smile and a dollop of marinara on his nose. "This bun is made of *cheese!*"

With all the horrible Winters publicity from the nightly news magazine, Bust-A-Gut strategically launched this new campaign tonight. However, the blue and yellow dome-lovers didn't research what topics are covered in this evening's *Nightbeat* episode. Our producers happily cashed their check, knowing it would probably be the last they'd see from the restaurant.

"You may remember Leah Pullem's report on the dangers in Winters Olde-Tyme Hamburgers," Sharon says. "Tonight, she takes a look at the other side of the coin in the next chapter of her series, *Death Burger.*"

Standing with an Olde-Tyme Victorian restaurant to her right and a Bust-A-Gut dome to her left, Leah says, "While America's oldest burger chain is clearly cutting its caloric brake lines, Winters Olde-Tyme Hamburgers is not alone. Rival Bust-A-Gut appears to be nipping at our ever-growing waistlines with equal recklessness."

This half of the story focuses on the Monte Cristo Burger's

rise to rock star status. Statistics suggest the calories in one deep-fried sandwich is equal to the weekly dietary needs of an entire pygmy tribe. Leah shifts focus. She has obtained top-secret documents about Bust-A-Gut's plans to counter the runaway success of the Space Burger. In a dramatically lit shot, she holds a basket of crispy brown mozzarella sticks in one hand and a hamburger in the other. She waterfalls cheese rods over the burger. "By stacking America's two most fattening dinner foods on top of each other," she says. "Bust-A-Gut plans to finish the burger wars."

Sadly, *Nightbeat* producers didn't view the Mozza-Burger commercial before cashing Bust-A-Gut's check and this moment falls a little flat.

The remainder of the piece wanders the same path as the Winters episode. People died with their hearts waving white flags, fingers greasy with ground beef. "Truly," she concludes, "there is no safe haven from bypass surgery.

"Or is there?

"Stay tuned."

Quick commercials for anxiety meds and cars cut the segment into easily digested fifteen minute bites.

"Did you know," Leah says with a library as background. "That America has only elected one obese president?

"And if you're like millions of Americans, you've probably asked yourself if there is a connection between calorie counting and success. Well, the answer might surprise you. Certainly, America has featured several overweight leaders, but only William Howard Taft got stuck in a bathtub. An embarrassing feat, which never happened to the svelte Abraham Lincoln. Remind yourself this: Abe freed the slaves, but what did Taft ever do?" The screen pans to a tight shot of meat. "To top it all off, it's rumored Taft was eating a juicy hamburger when the bath-time boondoggle occurred."

A stock shot of a claw foot tub gets a camera flyover.

"One woman," she says. "Wants to prove being healthy is unquestionably the path to success—whether you are aiming for the presidency or just to shed a few pounds. She is Willamena 'Wally' Dayton."

Footage of a teen girl in a fast food uniform, braces and a name tag that says **Summer**, cuts in: "Welcome to Healthy Wally's, can I interest you in our baked polenta cakes? Only seventy-five calories!" She flashes a shiny grill of teeth across the screen.

According to the show, Ms. Dayton wants to fix America's hearts by way of its stomach. She is reversing how this country eats. Her small empire is expanding and charging into a town near you. Healthy Wally's fast food restaurants offer revolutionary items like grilled portabella burgers and teriyaki tofu fries while her competition still serves red meat and milkshakes.

Run-Thru Windows, Leah says, put Healthy Wally's on the map a few years back. Wally thinks with a little exercise and proper diet, we can turn this country back into a success. To encourage fitness, anyone who jogs through her restaurant while grabbing a bite receives an instant ten percent discount.

Leah claims Wally is expanding in a major way. Leah claims this woman wants to teach everyone a healthy lesson. Leah claims they are in an alliance with Health Watch International. Leah *claims* all this because Dayton is shy and wants her food to do the talking. She doesn't appear on camera. Never grants interviews.

The shot fades and it's commercial time again.

The same teenage girl from the newsmagazine, Summer, shows off her brace-face behind a clean red and white countertop. "Is this your first visit to Healthy Wally's?" she says. There is an enormous red HW over her shoulder. "Well come on, silly," she giggles. "Don't be afraid to be healthy!"

The dining room is a tight pickle jar of smiling faces eating tofu dogs. "Here at Healthy Wally's, we use all-natural foods to fill you up the healthy way," Summer giggles again. "You know, the Wally way."

Acres of salad. Mile-long coops of boneless, skinless grilled chicken. Woodstock proportions of tofu. These are the corners of Wally's food pyramid. "So put down that fatty heart attack burger," she says with a *come-on-in* wave. "And live a little—at Healthy Wally's."

Commercials for allergy medicine follow. Before they cut back to *Nightbeat,* there is another poorly planned Bust-A-Gut ad featuring a stressed out family finding togetherness through hamburgers.

Nightbeat rolls ahead and talks about the possibility of a super volcano: an ocean of molten rock waiting to zit-pop America and bring another Dark Age. The city standing on this biblically large grenade is, oddly, the same city that houses the headquarters for Winters and Bust-A-Gut. But experts tell us it doesn't matter which city it's under, everyone in America will be dead. This new Dark Age is hanging out around the corner, smoking a cigarette, waiting to have a word with us.

In the last segment Sharon reviews the testimony of the Moscow Two. Clips are shown. Dimitri/Carl Janomi's statement scrutinized. Experts weigh in with theories. Can this really be true? Winters Olde-Tyme Hamburgers calls these claims "deranged." Why haven't the murderers been captured? Nobody knows. Some experts think the Russians have fled the country. Some think the space terrorists are on their way to Winters' corporate headquarters to get revenge. Some think it's all a publicity stunt.

FIFTY-ONE

Okay, so everyone's got problems.

This story is getting crowded with them. But hey, you and I are busy, too. So here's a public service. Instead of rattling on for pages and pages of plot and feelings and blah blah, we'll chop out the gristle and bone until all we have left is a meaty fillet. You guessed it: time for a montage.

Every montage needs a soundtrack, so here's the musical setup—in Deshler's, the Salvation Army band kicks into a shaky, booze-stinking march. The tuba player, breath piney with gin, nearly falls backwards.

MONTAGE #1

Walking the stairs to Winters' office, Deshler can't decide if he is lucky to have a signed record contract or cursed. *This is my one chance to be an artist*, he thinks. He's tired of waiting to hear from Hamler or Pandemic, so he pens a note on the back of his hand to phone Moral Compass Records.

The montage trumpets are woozy, the drums stomp.

Inside Winters' humidor of an office, the entire upper crust stands, smiling. One executive fixes Dean a scotch, neat, without asking. "Deshler," Double Harry says, forcing a rare grin. His teeth are coffee-stained under thin lips. "Can you forgive me? We," he looks at the boss. "We know the truth now…your *girlfriend* told us."

Sitting in a comfy chair, teeth grinding tight enough to shoot sparks, Dean waits for the deathblow. The catch.

"Dean," Winters says with a mustache-faced smile. "Malinta told us the whole scoop. She explained that trick Bust-A-Gut pulled. And yeah," his face grows serious, the folds in his neck shift. "It's underhanded, having an imposter Deshler Dean appear on the news spreading lies. I mean, Harry and I've seen some slimeball maneuvers, but that about takes the bun. I was ready to cut you loose after that first *Nightbeat*. We were referring to you as *Eggs*."

"Eggs?"

"As in, eggs Benedict," Harry says.

"You know, Benedict Arnold. We were moving your office into the cafeteria. Gonna have you start making copies!" Winters erupts in a laugh that looks painful.

The march music is low now, rising slightly, getting more inspired with the *ooom-pa-pa* beat.

The room follows with similar laughs.

The soundtrack's trombones pull a long slide.

"We just want to have a face-to-face," Double Harry says, taking off his hat. Things are bald up there. "Just to straighten all the kinks. Make sure the exec team is on the same page. Bust-A-Gut'll never admit it, but Malinta said she couldn't see this happen to you. Said she wanted to be a good person. Sweet girl."

"Yeah," he gasps. She is a sweet girl, Dean realizes. Though he's realized it for a long while, he's just been trying to shove it beyond his thoughts. Deshler hasn't wanted to admit how strongly he's come to depend on Malinta.

Is it love? Dean wouldn't know. But a solid guess would say—maybe.

"We're not going public with this info, either. Winters Olde-Tyme Hamburgers is taking the high road."

Roland pipes in: "That's what Dad would have wanted, God rest his soul."

Electric blanket warmth wraps around Dean. He feels safe now. This is, at the very least, a Get Out of Jail Free card.

"A wise man once said, *enough of this bologna, let's get down to the fried chicken.* Did you see the Flu Burger prototype? Delicious, huh?" Winters chuckles.

"We have it in fifteen test markets right now. It's fast-tracked. I've got our people wining and dining the FDA. Those assholes'll approve everything, no problem," says Harry. "We know that Bust-A-Gut launched its new mozzarella sandwich this week, too. We shouldn't have much lag time. If there's one thing we learned from the Christopher Winters commercial mess it's that we have to strike while the iron's hot. We're shooting the ads right now. Rush job."

The background music pulls in the reins and whispers over our hero's voice.

"It's blue," Deshler says. The room is staring, watching, listening. Everyone wants to know what he has to say.

"You're welcome."

"It's blue."

"Great, huh? That came from a hundred hours of focus groups. People believe blue represents purity and royalty. Makes us the king, I guess. We tried red, green, and even gray. But no dice."

"We also learned." Winters adjusts his seat and tightens his back. "This Healthy Wally's place is the real deal, too. They're partnering with those assholes at Health Watch. Nobody has any confirmations, but we're thinking they might have a lot to do with our other publicity snafus. Those guys have a hard-on for hamburgers."

The room and soundtrack both drop to morgue silent. The ice in someone's glass grows warm and cracks—*tink.*

"Speaking of bad publicity." Winters bangs his hand solid on the desk. "Let's get down to big business. Obviously, the Space Burger campaign is a cold duck. God…" His top lip sucks in and his knuckles pop. "If you would have told me three weeks ago, when those pinkos landed, that *this* would happen. Heh…I would have retired."

Deshler hasn't had time to watch the news. He sips a thimbleful of scotch and waits for people to stop eyeballing him.

The montage band is apparently back from a smoke break or something. They're getting rowdy and loud. Cymbals and snares and saxes rev engines.

"Our chief intelligence officer, Tony Archibold, is personally heading a team that will," Winters clears his throat, "*eliminate* this publicity. Until that point, we deny everything." Ordering the death of his son brings back a familiar tumor in Winters' throat.

The band leader starts swinging his baton a little harder and the Salvation Army brass section sways again.

A no-name exec from the back of the room pipes in her two cents: "We can deny, sir. But is this true and how much did we really know?"

"That's a good question, Tammy," Winters says, shuffling through the papers at his desk. "We," the CEO snorts and clears his throat once more and adjusts the flower in a ketchup-red lapel. "We don't know anything, right Harry? This is a shock to the company…and we'll be taking the high road on it, as well."

"There's nothing we can do now, what's happened has happened," Double Harry assures. "Let's just focus on a successful public relations recovery." With that, the meeting adjourns.

Dean, with his neck safely out of another noose, starts to

hustle. Not only did he keep his job, he gets to play the victim. Our hero seems to be even more important than before. People want his thoughts. It's nice to be wanted. Once again, being an artist fades further from his brain until it's a speck on the horizon.

Now that all the talking is over, the Salvation Army band really rips into it. They're out of tune and full of horn honking. It's the perfect soundtrack for a Cliff Drinker.

MONTAGE HIGHLIGHTS

• Dean sucks at the business end of a red wine bottle while hurling himself into data from the test markets.

• He slowly dips his finger in the cough medicine ketchup with a sour face.

• He drinks more.

• Malinta comes in and out with smiles and kissing and shared meals. They hold hands, they whisper.

• Here, he tastes the blue jelly again with less horrible results.

• There's a scene with Deshler and a man talking over Indian food. Some would say he looks like a science geek troll. The man holds up the *Broken Piano for President* cassette and kisses it. They shake hands.

• The sloshing band stomps into New Orleans funeral march. A hazy calendar flaps through our vision. About seven days flutter across the air.

• There is a fuzzy shot: bottle after bottle of cheap red wine emptying. A shot of Deshler sleeping at his desk fades into a quick upper-body shot of him dipping a long finger into the goo and licking his lips.

At this point in the montage the band peters out, the drum kicks randomly, the trombone slides as far as it can and the trumpets clear their spit valves.

The last shot has Deshler opening the mail. There's a letter with no return address. Postmarked from his zip code, as usual. It's a card congratulating him on the birth of his new daughter:

Roses are red, Violets are blue, I know where Clifford Findlay is, but do you?

FIFTY-TWO

Okay, right, I know, that last montage wasn't very montagey. The ending, yes, but before that? Not so much. Agreed. Here's another attempt. It'll be better, I promise.

The next montage opens with primal electro-spy music thumping in the background. It's cold as science.

MONTAGE #2

"Dude," Pandemic says, stabbing out a cigarette in a forest of crumpled butts. The highway melts across the window. "Tell her, tell Sonja that…that I'll kill for them. I'm a soldier. I'll do whatever needs to be done. Remind them who my dad is again and shit. That's gold."

"I am not," Hamler looks over his shoulder and starts whispering, like the cosmonauts understand. "I am not telling them. You're out of your mind. You're not yourself. I'm sorry I got us in this mess. I'm really sorry. But we're just going to have to sit tight."

The drummer scoots closer with a face of breaking bad news. "Henry, I don't think I need a bodyguard anymore."

"What?"

"I'm not in danger."

"Fine. At the rate I'm going that's not a bad idea." Henry's head drops.

Juan Pandemic scratches his puffy pink mustache mark

and digs under his eyes. "I'm sorry I've been an asshole. I… haven't, you know…had a taste in a long while. It's getting to me. Withdrawals, I think. But this shit's serious, I'm not freaking here. I really want to help these space dudes. My old man ruined their lives, he ruined mine. If you think about it, he ruined yours, too. You know?"

Bleep-ba-bleeep-beep-beep-deedledeedledee the soundtrack goes. Somewhere, a German lords over a turntable, nodding sad to the beat.

"But what about Deshler?"

"I don't buy that shit. Stumpy pulled that name out of a hat."

"Pandem…*Timothy*?" Hamler lifts a shaking head. "That's not a name you make up at random. That's impossible. Don't you see what's happening?"

"Dude, so she heard us mention him, whatever. Or well, okay, what if Dean does have this secret life? We're not any better." Pandemic waves a finger around the bus and points at the Russians. Sonja is asleep in the passenger seat. Keith cleans the handgun—it's dislocated into a dozen little chunks. "Look at what we're into here, man."

"Dean always said you're not yourself until you're someone else."

"That's the first thing to come from your mouth that sounds right."

"So…?"

"So, forget Dean." The drummer is standing, near shouting, a geyser of energy. "We can't even talk to him like a human lately. When's the last time he *wasn't* an asshole to you or me? We quit the stupid band. And you can quit being his roommate if that's what's bugging you. You can move into my place."

Nodding, soaking up Juan's words: "Maybe when all this

junk is over, we can start a new band."

"A pop band."

Henry's heart gets a spicy zing. The same electric charge it leapt with from love and candy, or rare applause, zips around the body. "A really catchy band. Like, lots of hooks and harmonies."

"With a piano."

"A guitar."

"Tambourines."

"Xylophone."

"The Juan Pandemic band!"

Henry's face goes crooked and Juan even shakes his head, laughing.

"The Hamler-Pandemic Experience."

"How about Ham-demic?"

"When this is all over, dude, Hamdemic is on." With this pleasant thought, the ghost of Henry's misery and failure whisks away. Amusement has been in short supply since Los Angeles. Just as Hamler realizes he's actually a little happy, his crushing depression sinks deeper.

Slinky disco beats and digital pulses fill the unusual silence between their conversation. It doesn't fit the scene at first, but, then, oddly, it does.

"Just forget it, man. What are we going to do? This is all my fault. I'm a total failure."

"Easy, Henry."

"No, it's true. I know that. Plus, I think it's my job to, you know, stop them." The bouncing bus ripples Henry's flesh. "But, I don't think that's a good idea, do you? I'll just get someone else killed. Probably me. Not that that's a bad thing."

"Let's…" Pandemic pauses while highway rumble fills the space between them. "Let's just be patient and see what happens. I like our odds."

"Juan, no. We need to do something. I need to take action."

"Just relax."

"No."

The soundtrack speeds up, but still sounds mysterious. The music bloops forward as Lothario Speedwagon's former rhythm section blazes down the highway.

MONTAGE HIGHLIGHTS

• Pandemic checks his phone, which reads: *30 New Messages.* He presses a button and listens. It's Dean rambling, something about "possibly signing a record contract," something about "not sure what's going on," something about "I know you probably don't care, but I'd love to talk to you about it."

• Hamler and Pandemic argue so hard the cosmonauts pull them apart.

• There's a tender scene of Pandemic trying to communicate with Keith. It's not clear whether young Mister Winters' hand-signals translate into: "I want to help decapitate my dad."

• The backside of a sniper takes center stage of this montage. He glares into the scope, sitting atop a billboard overlooking the highway. A silver flicker appears on the horizon. The sniper lifts his head and talks into a radio. It's Hamler's boss, Tony. He peeks through the scope again and yanks the trigger.

• Inside the bus, the chunky red-headed driver jerks the wheel and falls to the floor. Sonja leaps over the spurting corpse and grabs the controls.

•　Finally, the bus pulls back onto the highway with a bloody lump wrapped in a blanket and an angry one-armed woman by the side of the road. Delia shakes a fist as dust clouds above her.

FIFTY-THREE

See, better, right?

Oh, not by much, huh?

Okay. Here's a tight montage. You're the boss. Stop getting grumpy, I said I knew you were busy.

The corporate montage is hardest to pull off. Best to simply plug your nose and dive right into the clichés, starting with the 1960s Motown classic, *Money (That's What I Want)*.

MONTAGE #3 HIGHLIGHTS

- The first scene shows a young guy, decked out in blue and yellow, in Bust-A-Gut's kitchen working his ass off to deep fry enough buns for the Mozza-Burger. Orders stack up like dollar bills at the US Mint. People can't stuff enough deep-fried cheese in their stomachs.

- There is a bridge between scenes—a montage within a montage: bar charts and paper money exchanging hands, newspaper clippings tear like a tornado through a trailer park. "**Burger Wars Heat Up**," one reads. "**Food Fight**," another says. "**Burger Giants Unfazed by Bad Publicity, Sales Up 23%**," another reads.

- There's a long line of puffy-eyed zombies inside a neon Winters mansion. One man *a-choos* into a ten-dollar bill and hands it over in exchange for three Flu-Burgers. This guy's miserable and no amount of chicken soup cures his pale, sweaty face. In flashing shots, we see he can't focus at work, can't play with his kids…doesn't even want to make love to his wife. Greasy blue cold syrup soaks through wax paper and leaks out in a halo before he severs off a hearty bite. The man is instantly cured. This renewed gent plays with the kids, knocks 'em dead in the boardroom and in the bedroom. He drives past a Winters billboard, it reads: "Don't starve your cold or flu. Feed them both with Winters' new Flu Burger." The man gives the billboard a thumbs up.

• The cosmonauts are a hot topic on talk radio and news-centric cable stations. People nowhere near associated with Winters Olde-Tyme Hamburgers end up in huge screaming matches—always a ratings grabber. One faction says that since Yuri and Pavel were essentially lying to the American people, we should forget them and not give this matter any more attention. Otherwise we're just supporting murderers. The opposite faction says not to forget the fallen actors. Yes, they were lying, or so Dimitri claims (Winters Olde-Tyme Public Relations has denied comment, saying the allegations are "fictional.") This faction wants people to remember that two innocent men died and there are crazed murderers with a bus out there. They call for a boycott of the burger giant and anything Russian, which basically comes down to top-shelf vodka and furry winter hats.

• The final scene in the collage is a kaleidoscope of sunshine, vegetables and tofu burgers. The pristine white and red awning over a local Healthy Wally's opens to the inside of the restaurant. There are a few dreadlocked customers ordering Flaxseed Soy Shakes and Broiled Spinach Tots. An older man holds the door for a young, professionally-dressed woman. The restaurant is nearly empty. Business isn't as good as the restaurant hoped. The skinny teller yawns. The finely dressed lady walks up, she is tall and looks like a giraffe. She mouths the words, "Salad Burger," over our money-themed music.

She turns and we see Malinta Redding.

FIFTY-FOUR

Deshler punches digits into a phone halfway through another Beef Club night. After a few Rusty Knives there's a familiar magnetic tug in his pelvis. "Bon soir!"

"Son of a bitch."

"That's no way for a lady to talk."

"This is the call I get?" Malinta says. Her voice is dense and Antarctic.

"Hey, c'mon, what are you doing tonight?"

"I'm going to drink some tea, watch *Nightbeat*, put on my pajamas and go to bed...alone. There is a very important meeting tomorrow."

Deshler clamps both eyes shut until the right words emerge, the ones that will change her mind. "Well that's too bad. *Nightbeat* is really boring."

"Is this all you have for me, Dean?"

"Malinta, hey," the rest of his plea thrashes against voices at the Club. Yes, okay, she sees right through his call. It's about sex. Big surprise. But a tender side of Dean—a side Gibby Haynes would have used as a urinal cake—knows what else sex means and he craves it. With sex comes that closeness, that calm. Malinta, by just being herself, pushes out all the unwanted anxiety from Dean's life.

He's come to depend on it more heavily than he realizes.

Malinta's voice is knife-edged: "Sounds like things are picking up there. You'd better let me go now."

"Hey, whoa, hey. Are you mad? We've been getting along so great."

"Deshler…there's too much going on to keep catching you up."

"I just wanted to see if you and I could hang out…you know."

There is no patience in her voice: "How much longer do you think I can do this? In case you haven't noticed, alcohol is starting to destroy certain plans—"

"Catch me up? Baby, I'm winning this biathlon. I'm on top of my shit. I'm busting my balls doing—" He turns to the corner out of earshot. "Doing *two* jobs right now. Don't you think I deserve a little slack? I sure as hell think so."

Dean is balanced against a corner, pressed as far as possible from the joyous Beef Club sounds. An inside urge tells him to continue, to wear her down. The silent treatment will work, this urge says.

That quiet holds and holds and holds.

"Today's six months."

That quiet holds and holds and holds, and it scratches at Dean—it draws blood.

"Six months until what?" Deshler's throat braids tight during the silent hum. He whispers, "Six months until *what*?"

She sighs.

"…'till what?"

The dead air opens raw: "I'm saying it's our six month anniversary. I'm saying we've been dating, me and you, boyfriend and girlfriend, for *six* months now. And it feels like one random hookup after another. Does that sound like a healthy relationship to you?"

Six months? The Cliff Drinker is shocked. He'd have guessed a month at most.

He answers truthfully. "I don't think so." Dean's never

minded the blackouts, mystery bruises and brutal hangovers. He can live with drunkenly landing a job and signing a record contract. But he finds it disappointing the Cliff Drinking style blocks out regular love and affection from a beautiful woman. Not to mention the bedroom stuff.

"No, you don't. Well, I'm not going to sit around while you forget another half year. I'm a good person. You might not think so, but I am. And I don't deserve to be treated like this. What if I got pregnant? What kind of world would we be bringing a kid into?"

"You're not, right?"

"Good luck with your mission and all."

"My what?"

"I'm not falling for this. I know you better, Dean. You're not going to push me away by being a…a dick. And then pull this clueless, cutesy shit with me."

"Easy."

"You are not going to make me feel guilty again, because those days are long gone."

"Okay," he says. Dean's redwood baritone grinds into sawdust.

"All I've wanted the last six months is to improve myself. To maybe have you make that trip with me."

"That sounds nice."

"But all I get in return is a big pile of shit—crap."

"I didn't mean—"

"Goodbye."

There is nothing on the phone. The roomful of revelry sounds far off, though he could grab a Beef Clubber he's so near.

Suddenly, Dean has no control over the way his neck sways or his eyes cross. He sips at a Rusty Knife and thinks, *Why the hell did she talk to Harry and Winters if she's been holding this anger inside?* Deshler briefly chalks it up to women being a mystery, but he knows that's not the whole deal. He hopes there isn't a pea-sized deal brewing in her, either.

Our hero doesn't get a chance to let this phone call sink in before he is interrupted. "Mister Dean," his young assistant says, running to the distant corner. Austin has never been allowed in the Club and jerks his head like a pigeon. "Mister Dean, there's something serious going on with the Cosmonaut Campaign."

That old urge for control wants to snap at Austin, but Dean instead rubs both eyes and counts for several seconds. When he reaches five or ten, stress has eased.

"I know, it's screwed. It's dead. Take the high road, go home, man."

"It's not that. Mister Winters wants to see you in his office now."

"It's, like, ten."

"Sir, I don't want to scare you. But I heard some guys talking today." Dean's assistant looks around for eavesdroppers. "The cosmonauts are coming back to town."

"What, do they want their paychecks before scurrying off to Russia?"

"No, sir."

"Okay?"

"They're coming back to kill you."

"*Fan*tastic," Dean says.

FIFTY-FIVE

"Wait, what does that mean," Timothy Winters says, wearing the toupee backward as a joke, eyes covered in hair, trying to get a cosmonaut to laugh. "Mission *objectives?*"

The bullet hole in the tour bus windshield spreads like tree roots. A constant white noise crinkles the cabin air, leaving moist highway scents and confusion. Keith has been at the wheel for the better part of the day. The sun sputters its final rays across the horizon. Luckily, the bus has been bullet-free since he inherited driving duties.

Dimitri could very well be dead. No one has checked for a pulse in hours.

"I think he just means they need a plan A, a plan B, and so on," Henry says. His stomach suffers in empty pain. The bus ran out of food hundreds of miles back and no one's mentioned stopping at a candy store. "It doesn't exactly translate perfectly."

(We need more gasoline before entering the city,) Keith yells back from the driver's seat. (The bus will not travel much further.)

Keith enjoys piloting the monstrous machine. (Very similar to steering rocket from launch pad to space station,) he told Hamler earlier. (That is, if I was ever given chance to steer rocket. Real Dimitri always at control panel. Mister Big-Shot.)

"What did Keith say?" Pandemic asks. "He's with me, isn't he? He's knows I'm black metal. I'm hardcore, baby."

"No, dude, he was talking about fuel." The undersides of Henry's eyes build fatty lumps, his shoulders twist thick. The stress of interpretation and guns and buses and guilt erase his brainwaves down to pocket change. More than once he's thought about curling up and crying. Exactly once, however, he's thought about leaping out the bus window at eighty miles-an-hour.

Sonja, dark hair strung tight into a ponytail, turns to her brother. (Well, just stop at the next petrol station. Are you listening to the plan?) She stands and looks out the movie widescreen windshield. The road is a limitless dead stretch of uptilled farmland and naked trees on both sides. (Keith, are you paying attention to the mission objectives?)

(Sister, we are no longer in military. We have no mission objectives,) Henry deciphers him say. (We are…I do not know what we are. I no longer know who we are. We are not ourselves. Will any mission make us feel better?) Keith's bony shoulders slump forward, like he's hunched over a typewriter.

The cosmonauts stop and glance in Henry's direction until he begins paying attention to what they are saying. They pick back up.

(The drive is making you weak. I will relieve your shift at the filling station. Your mind must be sharp for our mission. And, yes, we need a mission. We need a goal. Without one, our lives are wasted like comrades on space station.)

The bus plows on, heavy and shaky as a motel massage bed.

Timothy Winters' voice quickly distills to a grainy hush. His hands cover his belly. "Henry, tell them I'll be right back. Don't go over the mission without me. I need to know." Pandemic's face wilts, nearly sucking down his tongue. "I'm gonna be sick, man."

The wannabe Russian terrorist pushes his bandmate out

of the booth. Hamler catches a full glimpse of his friend, a whisper of his old self. "Is it, you know, because of the *drugs?*"

"Yeah, man, you don't have to whisper," he says, wobbling to the bathroom. "It's not some secret. This is what happens when you stop smoking *the drugs.*" Veins in Pandemic's arms and neck are deep blue tattoos. His scalp has a brushy growth of fresh hair, revealing a receding line.

Without warning, the bus jerks under the canopy of a quiet gas station. Around the pumps, dull neon yellow fills the bus. There's nothing for miles except horizon, farmland and the faint purple sky of the city.

"About time," Pandemic manages to spit up as the wheels chug to a stop and he bursts from the restroom. He gains balance by latching onto a countertop. "I need some fresh air." His throat gurgles with evil, messy possibilities.

Juicy gasoline stink floats into the cabin as the drummer exits. Sonja and Keith motion for Henry to fill the tank. "Hey, Mister Pandemic," Henry hollers, noticing the place is empty and silent. "Can we borrow your credit card again? Preferably the Timothy Winters one, since I'm guessing it's the only card that wasn't canceled years ago."

Juan Pandemic hovers above the grimy plastic trash barrel between gas pumps. Breathing heavy, Hamler swears Pandemic's ribs poke through his thin shirt. Henry pickpockets the drummer as a throaty voice splits the air from behind him.

"Pardon me, young fella," it sings familiar in Hamler's ear. The bodyguard is wrist-deep in another man's back pocket. "How about I buy this tank?" it says, smooth, husky and sexy. The kind of voice attached to dark skin and a neatly manicured goatee.

Hamler spins on his heel, chest all jumbled.

"What are the odds, huh, Henry?" says Martin, wearing a smaller white bandage over his nose bridge.

A wild jerk of time whips through Henry Hamler. This, he assumes, is what it's like getting a money-shot from resuscitation paddles. His body seemingly expands to zeppelin-size, then shrinks to a shirt button. Back and forth, repeat—repeat—repeat.

Slowing down significantly, the simple pitter-patter of the heart plucks Hamler out of the ditch he's been hiding in since leaving Martin. Guilt washes off like summer mud, fear disappears like steam. Paranoia, however, plants a flag in his brain and claims the land for its own.

According to Hamler's corporate espionage training manual, when a Winters Olde-Tyme Hamburgers agent encounters a possible hostile adversary—such as an ex-boss from the company you spied on—the agent is supposed to perform one of four defenses in the first moments of the conflict:

• Use **Sweep Kick #5**, rendering the opponent helpless and obtaining higher ground.

• Use **Submission Hold #17** by twisting the left wrist of the hostile agent until you feel that distinct *pop*. This should put the opposition in a state of shock long enough to further assess the situation.

• If the enemy appears immediately aggressive, use the heel of your palm to break the enemy's nose, hopefully jamming the cartilage into the brain, thus ensuring death: Also known as **Hostility Defense #1**.

• Run.

The enemy has been in contact with Henry for a dozen seconds. The young agent hasn't employed any of the four recommended defenses. Rather, he stares and smiles into Martin's perfect, chocolaty eyes—praying his hair isn't a mess.

Hamler reminds himself to relax. Hamler reminds himself this is a coincidence. Hamler reminds himself not to stir Martin's brain with the bone of his once-beautiful nose. "Wha...Mart...I...Oh, shit."

"You're surprised, huh? That's okay. I don't normally hang out at gas stations." *God, that smile.* "But I'm here on good terms."

Hamler's temples pool wetness. He remembers watching a training video with Tony. In that flick, a bad guy secret agent tells the good guy this same line. There are five key words that signal deceit. Martin just said all five.

"Martin, you shouldn't be here."

"It's okay, Mister Findlay sent me."

"Findlay?"

"Henry, you're not the only one around here who knows how to spy."

"No, this is just another temp job. The pizza delivery thing didn't pan out...sorry I didn't call you."

Between the gas pumps, Pandemic's dry heaves sound like gears grinding on a manual transmission.

"Henry, cut it out. I know you're a spy. I knew all along. I was supposed to spy on *you*. Pretty stupid, huh?"

"But the cheese."

"I'm a man of many talents. Dairy acquisitions is simply one of them. I just happen to be a little better at espionage." Martin leans against the bus's side, arms folded, radioactive charm just dancing from his body.

Hamler inches closer, debating the merits of Sweep Kick #5. Martin's soul patch is a perfect rectangle below his lip. Henry is hypnotized.

"So the thing between you and I...it was just an act?"

"I didn't say anything about that."

"So?"

"Me? I had a good time."

"M—me too."

"I like you, honestly, I like you." His tough hands swallow Henry's softies.

The Russians yell out the door. They keep faces hidden. Their voices are eager, demanding to know why gas isn't pumping.

"Tell them Clifford Findlay's called the cavalry," Martin says with a smile. His dimple nearly sucks in the entire goatee. "Does that translate?"

"Martin."

"Listen, you've got to trust me here." Martin puts his manly-strong hand on Hamler's doughy shoulder. "Bust-A-Gut sent me to help get you back to the city in one piece. In case you didn't notice, the police aren't trying very hard to stop you guys, but Winters is."

"No." Henry's skin is overcome with the cold air. He's not wearing a jacket and pinpricks form along his flesh.

"Who do you think shot out your window and your driver?"

"What are you saying?" Hamler doesn't really care what Martin says as long as he keeps grasping that shoulder. A heart-shaped sonic boom passes through Henry's body.

"This is why I like you so much. You're so damn innocent. It's really cute."

"Innocent?" *Cute?* The thought gives his heart more fizz.

"Henry, you four are *bad* publicity. Horrible. Every second this fiasco is on the news, Winters loses money and market share. There are a lot of people trying to stop this bus. I'm here to help."

"That doesn't make sense."

"Sure it does. Bad press for Winters is good news for Bust-A-Gut. Get it?"

Martin uncaps the tank and starts filling. The fuel pumps slow like pudding.

"I don't think this is a good idea, Martin. No offense." Hamler sucks on his cheek. It gives him a stomachache to say. "But I don't think you should be here. With us. It's my responsibility to protect—"

"Okay," Martin's voice trails off.

Pandemic crawls between them. Oil stains soak into his jeans. Martin grins like a proud papa watching baby's first scoot across the carpet.

"Look, I'll lay it out for you," he continues. "If you guys don't let me help, you'll probably be dead. Not just the Russians, all of you."

"How can I trust you?"

"Trust your gut."

Hamler's gut is a sprinkler system.

"Come on little guy," Martin says to the crawling bug of a hamburger heir. He lifts Pandemic the way he does milk jugs. "In you go." Playful swat on the ass. "You're going to be the worst publicity of all."

Propping frail Timothy Winters on the bus step, Martin digs in a coat pocket. Hamler tenses. If this man wasn't adorable, he tells himself, Submission Hold #17 would be in order. That pocket could house a gun or a knife or a bomb.

Instead, Martin pulls out a plastic baggie, knotted into a tight egg of white dust.

"I know you're hurting, man. Listen up, this is some serious shit. Hey, hey—" Martin shakes Pandemic until his pained eye slits zero in. "It's produced from *very* pure sources," Martin says, palming the lump into Juan Pandemic's fist. "Careful with this, I don't want your heart blowing out."

Some color leaks back into Pandemic's rice paper cheeks. Eye slits widen. A meth-tooth smile zigzags across his face.

Henry watches this drug deal go down without swallowing a breath. His stomach problems aren't getting better. Empty cold breeze flaps his clothes.

Henry and Martin let the numbers on the gas pump rise and watch one another carefully. Something bright and starlit and beautiful glows inside Henry's chest. He knows he shouldn't trust what Martin says, but is powerless. *Kiss him, kiss him, kiss him* repeats in his mind, but he holds still. The pump clicks off and Martin steps close to Hamler, maybe aiming to connect lips. *Kiss him.*

Hamler doesn't fully fall in love with Martin until around the fourth bullet rips through the gas station air. Martin, mouth puckered and ready, takes note when two dime-sized holes magically appear on the shell of the bus. Martin yanks back, tosses Henry inside, and leaves a stack of twenty-dollar bills for the gas. The perfect gentleman.

Inside, Martin shoves Sonja into the driver's seat as bullets shatter the side mirror and the head of a gas pump. That's when Hamler discovers a jawbreaker in his pocket. That's when Henry's heart starts purring for Martin again. Louder than ever before.

FIFTY-SIX

Let's take another quick break. We'll catch you up if anything noteworthy happens to Juan or Deshler or Hamler in the next few minutes. Cool?

So, let's pretend you and I just met for coffee and are making small talk. Yes, my wife's fine. She says hi. How's the job treating you these days? Oh, I say with a pouty face, hang in there, things'll get better.

But, let's not waste time, okay? Let's slice directly into the turkey breast of this talk. "So, what's the deal with this crystal meth?" you say. "I watch the reports and read investigative newspaper articles. I know American teenagers ingest it like termites in a Louisville Slugger warehouse. But what *is it*?" you ask.

Other questions include: "Is it *bad* for you?" "What's it made from?" and "Where can *I* get some?"

Whoa, easy. One question at a time. Anxious, aren't we?

Let me tell you what I know. Methamphetamine is classified as a psychostimulant by the FDA. This drug is once-in-a-great-while prescribed to narcoleptics and overactive tots with ADHD. It was originally seen as a medical breakthrough and extremely useful by doctors everywhere. But, like most useful medical breakthroughs, some industrious American learned how to steal it, boil it down into nuggets and smoke it.

Crystal meth is a colorless rock version of the above. And in case you don't watch the news or read investigative reports, it is very popular. And the vast majority of users, unlike medicinal Methamphetamine fans, aren't concerned with curing their narcolepsy. These adventurous boys and girls are more interested in staying awake for days at a time and screwing like their genitals are carved from marble.

"Wait, hold on," you say. "What are *Psychostimulants*?"

Let me break it down for you. Remember when you used to pop a Yellowjacket during finals week to stay up until dawn and study? Yeah, that's right: Speed. Well, crystal meth and speed are practically kissing cousins. Just think of your little study-buddy as a Roman candle and Crystal as the booster rocket that propels cosmonauts into orbit.

Former users claim the drug is one hundred times more addictive than heroin or cocaine, which could explain meth's popularity since the beginning ticks of the twenty-first century. Another no-brainer is directly related to its cheap production costs. Unlike more exotic narcotics—your heroins, your cocaines, which must be imported—crystal meth is as American as baseball and obesity. Armchair chemists from Portland, Maine to Portland, Oregon set out to decode this prescription drug's contents and were happy to discover whipping up a batch was as easy as a drive to the nearest Wal-Mart.

The drug can be produced cheaply by combining household cleaners and over-the-counter medicine. The battery that powers this amphetamine juggernaut is called pseudoephedrine. Go look in your medicine cabinet right now, chances are some tiny plastic bottles with this magic drug are right in front of you. So, with pseudoephedrine, a coffee pot, some lye and a little American elbow grease, you could be cooking your first batch of meth instead of reading this book.

Also of note: these little shards are usually smoked through a pipe. Although, people with a taste for a stiffer cocktail prefer it snorted or injected—much the same way cocaine and heroin slide into home plate.

So, right, you had some questions.

Is it bad for you? Well, I'm not here to tell you how to live. What's bad for you may be my idea of a honeymoon. Besides a vampire-like lust for tiny white rocks, some side effects include severe tooth decay and intense skin welts caused by constant scratching. Also, staying awake for weeks on end has been known to twist biological clocks into a blackberry thicket. But hey, chances are, nature being the way it is, stuff like that was bound to happen anyway. Right?

Where can I get some? Good question. Unlike hard street drugs of the past, there is no need to adventure downtown through dark alleyways and rat-nest crack houses. Meth has taken on a rural flavor in America. Don't get me wrong, inner-city folks love this stuff, too—it just seems that you can't drive down a dirt road or date your cousin without tripping over a meth lab. I've heard pseudoephedrine practically pours out of the faucets in the sticks. My suggestion would be to find the nearest trailer park or high school and ask around. I'd question the first person who looks like Pandemic.

Which reminds me, we should get back and see how Juan's pal Deshler Dean is making out.

FIFTY-SEVEN

Waking up drunk is a totally different problem than waking up hungover. Deshler Dean will talk your ear raw regarding the finer points of both.

The Cliff Drinker has been quoted saying: "Basically, one's like waking up with your car dangling over a cliff—that's coming-to still drunk as shit. But a hangover is more like waking up crushed in the passenger seat at the bottom of the ravine."

Deshler wakes up with the brain tingling. Still a tiny bit drunk, the Cliff Drinker's front tires dangle over a Grand Canyon-size hole.

Never in his alcohol ingesting career has Dean worried about dying. He's never considered waking up staked out on a fluffy cloud and plucking a harp as a possibility. However, peeling his face off a leather couch in the corner of a boardroom, he's seriously considering the reality of purgatory.

"Johansson," a man's cheery, Sunday school voice says. "Whaddya have for us on your end?"

The room is trimmed in candy cane white and red. There's a mural of a cartoon moose and some jitterbugging vegetables on the opposite wall. The space is long and hollow. Deshler is ninety-seven percent positive he's never been here before.

Someone stumbles through a PowerPoint presentation. The lights are dim and nobody notices Deshler's heap rise. His first thought is: *I'm a ghost. Maybe I'm haunting this boardroom.* He barks out a phlegmy cough to check. No one at the packed table flinches.

The graphics on the wall have the heading: **Healthy Wally's Market Share**. There's a three-color pie chart—the remainder being yellow and green.

The ghost is forty-five percent sure he's a ghost…possibly a poltergeist.

The ghost rolls its head from shoulder to shoulder. Its vision is dishwater clear at best. Here's the kicker: no headache. No nausea. No bloodstains, even though the ghost vaguely remembers burning through several glasses of Rusty Knife.

Deshler considers lifting these phantom limbs off the couch, sprouting angel wings and flapping away. He briefly wonders what the difference between a phantom and a ghost is. *Not now,* he thinks.

"That's great, Johansson, that sounds very solid. Tell your people keep fighting, we've got our big bullets in the gun," the happy voice says. The tail end of each sentence bounces around the room. It's Dexter Toledo. But Dean wouldn't know that, not being an avid *Nightbeat* watcher.

Deshler sits up and discovers he's surfing last night's booze wave. His mouth tastes the way used floss smells.

"So, let's review some numbers quickly. Bust-A-Gut is steady, the Logistics Department says the dome's popularity is growing with the Mozza-Burger. Winters, oh boy, folks," the man's voice dissolves like sugar in water. "This Flu Burger whaddya-callit is shooting through the roof. I mean, the numbers are huge. They are kicking tail feathers. This makes the Monte Cristo look like a bologna sandwich. Everything else is history. Long story short, people are gaga for those hamburgers. What a surprise and what a gift. These new findings make the heart attack angle we were using look doggone silly."

The group grumbles, upbeat and pleased. Deshler hears one guy grunt, "Yesssss."

"I know, I know, we're all excited about the Flu Burger, but you all must keep a lid on Healthy Wally's plan to fight it. We're almost there. That being said, *Nightbeat* is on tonight. I trust everyone will watch. This episode should be interesting to say the least."

A squirrelly bald guy lifts his voice above the rest: "The Flu Burger is really taking off in rural areas, too. *Big time.* The Northwest, Oregon, of course. The Midwest is picking up steam. It's going better than planned."

"That's fantastic. I know it was a bear, switching the campaign focus at the last minute. But we couldn't have asked for such a gift. I'll pass this information on to Miss Dayton when I speak with her."

"Dexter, sir, where is Wally? Not to sound skeptical, but we're all sort of worried. I haven't seen her in weeks."

"That's understandable. The boss is traveling. Don't forget, there are dozens of new stores opening around the country. She's personally inspecting them all. Bottom line, Wally Dayton would love to be here, and she will be soon, but we'll have to soldier on alone for a while."

The crowd mumbles to each other.

"Ron, can you get the lights, please," Toledo calls. "Ah, what a treat, folks. The Man of the Hour is up and at 'em! Welcome, Mister Dean."

Golf course whispers flood around the boardroom table. "Welcome back," one woman says.

Deshler is only twenty-five percent sure he's never been inside this room and zero percent sure he's a ghost. He stands and his legs sway off balance.

A short black guy rises at the other end of the room and locks eyes. "Well, Deano, you think you're still up to giving us a few words? Or do you need to freshen up a bit?" This guy owns the happy voice. Toledo wears the same straw golf hat he sported during the *Nightbeat* interview.

Dean wants to run fast. His voice is a rusty tuba, low and out of tune. "Well, now, I...eh, perhaps I could tidy up?" He notices pink speckles of vomit on the left pant leg. His fingers buzz electric, cycling through his memory bank, trying to figure out what *few words* this man is referring to.

Toledo chuckles, the room follows quietly. The guy actually holds his sides.

"Oh, come on, Mister Dean. You're working double shifts for Winters and Bust-A-Gut, but you can't find time for us?" This cracks the boardroom up.

Dean jumbles across the floor. He wants water. He wants aspirin. He's heard Pedialyte is great for this type of sickness. He wants that, too.

"I really need to find a restroom, excuse me, please, uh... Mister..." he rumbles the words slow. "M-mister?"

Dean takes a haunted house leap when he spots Malinta. Her towering blonde head sits at the end of the table to the right hand of the happy guy. Dean smiles. Malinta makes eye contact, then drops focus to a stack of paper, then back up to Dean. "Mister Toledo," she says. "Gee, I think I can fill in while our...while Mister Dean powders his nose. I have a report about my interview."

"That'd be great, Ms. Redding," Toledo says. "Take as much time as you need, Dean. We're bunkered down here for the rest of the day, as you know."

Dean's vision jiggles a little. If drunkenness were measured like a keg of beer, he'd be sputtering foam. Hangover city is just around the corner. And that city is a collapsing son of a bitch.

Deshler's one hundred percent positive he's been to this boardroom now. He's just not sure why. But, he is reminded, *I've imagined things before. What did the doctor call them? Alcohol Induced Hallucinations.*

ALCOHOL INDUCED HALLUCINATIONS

- Ernie the Keebler Elf discussed his vote for Governor.
- He and Abraham Lincoln played a game of RISK. Abe won.
- His band signed a $500,000 record contract. (Still possibly not a hallucination)
- Pepsi beat Coke in a blind taste test.

A poster of a goo-goo eyed moose with a red sweater greets Deshler as he avalanches into the hallway. The antlered beast snacks on Healthy Wally's Carrot Stick Poppers. The hall lighting is blunt white. Tall, palmy plants line the wall.

"Nope, nope, nope," says his bullfrog throat. "This is not the real thing. Hallucinations."

Deshler swears under his breath, doing his best not to act like a fresh escapee from the padded cells. Just like in the boardroom, everyone in the office stares as if he is their embarrassing child. He waits for the elevator. Two other women inspect the Cliff Drinker up and down, smile and bite their lips.

The elevator is wrapped in mirrors. Deshler checks his hair and notices he isn't wearing a shirt or shoes. His creamy skin is sleep-creased from the couch. He decides the best bet is to go home and pass out. Whoever this boardroom is, they can wait.

On the street, Dean is relieved to find a wallet, keys and cell phone in his pants. The frosted pavement pin-pricks his bare feet as winter air jacks up the hangover's intensity. His muscles are cold and glassy. He's ready to shatter apart any second.

"Mister Dean, Mister Dean," a young guy says, jogging

down the street. "Dexter says to call him later. He wishes you could have stayed longer. He apologizes for Ms. Dayton's absence, she's traveling."

The guy's smooth face has intern written all over it. The young man drops his jaw and takes in the full shirtless package of Dean. "Whoa, dude. Can I call you a cab?"

"No, I'm perfectly fine. I love frostbite," Deshler rumbles.

"Sir, Mister Dean. Here, take this," the intern says, slipping off a puffy green ski parka. "You need it."

"No, man, no, please," he tries to shrug off the coat.

"You can just return it to me tomorrow, you know?"

"Tomorrow?"

"Oh God, your feet. Here, borrow my shoes, too. Sir, wow, is there anything else? Wow."

"I really don't think you want to be doing this…" He waits for the name.

"Mikey, I'm Mikey Medved."

"Just go back in and stay warm. I'm okay, Mikey."

"It's my honor." Mikey shrinks back, looks embarrassed. "You're…you're *the man*."

Gibby would wear the coat, Dean thinks. "Great point, I'll take it."

The intern scoots off to the office. The jacket is a size too large and drafty. The shoes flap on and off. He hums the first few lines to *Broken Piano for President* to take his mind from this tangled place.

When the atomic bomb detonated in Hiroshima, it ignited with a tiny trigger. A device no bigger than a fist. In an instant, this small switch erupted into a ball of hell. There is a similar switch in Dean's skull. It just clicked on, ushering a Hall of Fame headache.

Standing, measuring this pain, Dean soaks up each awful ache. *You deserve this*, he thinks, *you had this coming*.

The vibratory blasts are so dense, Dean hardly notices his pants pocket buzzing. He ducks into a bus shelter to answer.

"Dean…McComb here." The voice is tight and belongs to his new science geek troll friend at the record company. "How goes it? You talked to the other Lotharios?"

"Huh?" His hangover is dialed to black hole proportions. Matter disappears at algebraic rates.

"Dean, we talked about this one. The Suits, the big wigs at Moral Compass, get a little nervous simply handing over five hundred grand, my man. You know, they kind of like to catch their new acts live. Very hands-on management. The Purple Bottle is booked for tomorrow night. Tell all your friends. We can use a receptive crowd for the Lothario Speedwagon showcase. Trust me, the Suits have never seen anything like your band. They'll flip."

The wind hums through the tiny phone. "Excuse me?"

"Hello, Dean? This is Deshler Dean, right? Lead singer for Lothario Speedwagon. Signee to Moral Compass Records. Soon-to-be rich bastard. Does any of this fit the description, man?"

"What showcase? Lothario Speedwagon…the guys aren't even in town. The band broke up."

Husky silence.

His head slumps against the Plexiglas bus stop. A stiff drink sounds perfect. *My mind*, he thinks, *works so much better that way.*

"Do *not* pull my leg today, buddy," the exec says with a car salesman's tongue. "I'm fit to pop, I'm so *excited* for you guys. No pressure, but this is the deal breaker. But don't sweat it. The day before I signed the Butthole Surfers to Capitol, they were way tighter wound than you."

"Gibby?"

"Of course, they didn't try to convince me that their band broke up, either."

"*The* Butthole Surfers. Gibby Haynes?"

"Dean, hello? God, you are nervous. Remember going over the papers, you said those were the magic words. Anyone who signed the Surfers is good enough for you. We just talked about this *again* the other night, remember? At the Indian joint? I'm not a big fan of repeating myself."

"I did?" Deshler says, crossing the record contract off the list of things he hallucinated.

"I'm sorry, I didn't catch that."

"I *did!*"

"So, anyhow, I hope you have something knockout planned for the show. But remember, these guys aren't as—" A bus pulls up and roars next to Dean.

"What? I…I'm on the street, I missed that."

"Not as hip. The Suits aren't as hip as you and I. So, you know, tone it down a few notches. I think it'd be best for your career. You know, for the band."

Dean thinks about his hero. Dean remembers reading a story about how Gibby was an honors student and captain of the basketball team in college. Haynes even landed a prestigious job at an accounting firm after graduation. The man's life was set—success and money and a house on a cul-de-sac were easily within reach. Gibby, though, gave it up for the puke and sweat and scum of being a touring musician.

People needed to listen. Haynes sacrificed stability for art. He poured the piss wand all over it.

Dean thinks about the boardroom full of happy people he just left. He thinks about the boardrooms full of unhappy people at Winters and Bust-A-Gut—people who never seem to be satisfied with him, even though they say, "Good work." People who want more from him, people who say, "Yesterday is history, what have you done for me lately?" People who say, "How's your workload? Well, too bad, here's more."

Man, he thinks. *I never want to step inside an office again. That shit isn't for me. That shit isn't for artists.*

"Yeah, totally, we'll knock 'em out. We'll, you know, blow that place away." His head is a single pinprick from exploding. Lying thins Dean's skin to slime. *But am I lying?* he wonders. "Yeah, man, we'll be there at nine."

"Dean, we discussed this, sound check is at eight. You guys need to play your best."

What would Gibby do? Dean thinks.

With no idea where his bandmates are, or if they will ever speak to him again, or who the guy on the other end of the phone is, Dean summons the shit-faced gospel preacher voice he uses at concerts—the one that makes people's heads jerk back and pay attention: "Lothario Speedwagon will be there and ready, count on it."

FIFTY-EIGHT

Nightbeat begins the same way it does every episode. Sharon Smalley's voice is cool and professional. A very popular anxiety drug over two-million Americans rely on may deliver explosive seizures. Which one? Stay tuned to *Nightbeat*. She says geologists think there may be a way to prevent a catastrophic volcano blast, but maybe not. Find out in our second half.

"But first," our host says, "The drug epidemic sweeping our drive-through windows. Which drug and what drive-through? Find out after our commercial break."

No sign of ads for Winters' Flu Burger or Bust-A-Gut's mozzarella madness. Plenty of airtime for department store clearance sales, anxiety medication that may or may not be linked to seizure and laptops.

"Methamphetamine in powder form, better known as crystal meth, is a serious problem," Sharon tells us from behind the desk. "The government and pharmacists across the country have made it harder and harder to obtain over-the-counter cold-and-flu-medicines containing pseudoephedrine, the main ingredient in the drug's production. However, America's top hamburger chain recently made it much simpler."

She reviews the same basic ideas covered a few pages back on meth's production, popularity and effects. She sounds much more professional than that chapter, though.

"It's cold and flu season in America and this year over three-million sniffly noses have turned to Winters Olde-Tyme Hamburgers for the cure. The chain's *Flu Burger* is a hamburger laced with symptom-fighting medicine. However, the sauce's major ingredient is the aforementioned pseudoephedrine."

A greasy stack of meat and cheese, frosted in blue cough medicine, gets a pornographic close-up.

A man with a scatter of teeth and a complexion of purple-red scabs is interviewed. His caption reads: *Ryan Miller, Chattanooga, TN – Age 18 – Meth Addict.* "Yeah, we used tuh have trouble getting the cold medicine fer our lab. But then we got the idea tah use the Flu Sauce from Winters. It takes uz some werk, but we gidit jus right for crystal. After a while, we jus paid off the night manager for gallon buckets of it, so we did'n have to scrape it off the meat n'more."

Sharon is back on screen. "And that is how a *methademic* begins. No one we interviewed saw the beginning. And nobody sees an end in sight. An unnamed source from the FDA claims the green light for this product was a snafu, a one-in-a-million glitch that should have never occurred. The FDA denied further comment to *Nightbeat.*

"This, of course, begs the question: 'Didn't Winters Olde-Tyme Hamburgers foresee this problem?' A spokesperson claims that, no, they felt that was the FDA's territory. The spokesperson, who appeared on our program last week and still wishes to remain anonymous, claims, and I quote, 'Winters' only interest is providing great taste and flu relief to hungry sickness sufferers, you ignorant *expletive deleted, expletive deleted, expletive deleted.*'

"However, recently, while preparing this piece, one Winters employee did step forward. She, too, requests anonymity."

The woman's voice is a scrambled bomb threat, electronically slowed down and gutted into a distorted grunt. It's hard to understand the first few words. "—yeah, heck yes, we knew. Me? I was working on the development. I asked my supervisor if this was wrong and he assured me what's good for the company is good for me. I even mentioned the possibility of this sauce being used for drugs, but they…they silenced me. How? Well, let's just say I no longer work for dod gamned Winters Olde-Tyme Hamburgers." The woman's face is hidden under a shadow, it makes her look like a giraffe. Just above the eyes, when the dim light hits her just right, there is a thick scar, a healing wound on her left temple.

"When given this evidence, an official Winters Olde-Tyme Hamburger representative denied *Nightbeat* a comment, claiming they are taking the high road."

The shot turns to a Winters restaurant with the caption: **Gresham, OR**. There is a line of thin, jittery men and women waiting under green and gray Victorian gables. They claw at crusty faces and welty arms.

"When we return, what can be done to stop this epidemic and who is to blame? On *Nightbeat*."

The two minute and thirty-second break is filled with an entire Healthy Wally's commercial. Its slogan says: "At Healthy Wally's, the only thing you'll get addicted to is better health."

FIFTY-NINE

Dean comes home and a birthday card is slid under the apartment door. It's four months before his actual birthday. The card has a religious theme. The paper is baby blue. The handwriting is tiny, geometrically perfect angles.

Lothario Speedwagon, Live @ the Purple Bottle.
-See you there, Deshler.

SIXTY

"Whough!" Pandemic wheezes from the back of the bus. Loud, sinus-cleansing snorts briefly capture Henry's attention. "Whough!" But Henry's focus stays on the floor.

With his spine against the carpet, the rumble of the road spreads through Martin's body. Martin was not greeted with the warm hellos he secretly hoped for when the bus bailed out of the gas station. After dodging stray bullets, Martin's situation fell straight down a rusty chute to Hell. Currently, Keith is screaming with one foot on Martin's neck, harsh interior lights flooding the bus. The gun is a fraction of a second from exploding into that small, black goatee.

"No, no, he's not a bad guy," Hamler says with all his lungs, then repeats in Russian.

(You are lying, I have seen him before. I know his kind. This is clearly a trap, Little Henry.)

"Whough!" Pandemic snorts from the rear.

(Shoot him, Keith. He will destroy us,) Sonja screams from the driver's seat, foot deep on the accelerator.

(Henry, Henry,) Keith says. (Ask what he planned to do with us. Ask who sends this *Martin* here to murder us.)

Hamler asks, trying to sort out the translation with his heart smashing into his chest.

"Okay, okay, easy man," Martin says with arms stretched above his head, knuckles dug into the carpet. "Henry, does this guy understand that I could break his leg in three places right now?"

"Martin, come on. What…" Hamler's face is the color of Christopher Winters' suits. "What am I supposed to tell them?"

"Just explain that you know me, I'm not a threat." Martin coughs from the boot crushing his Adam's apple. "I'm the good guy, *you* know that. Tell them my bosses sent me to help. I'm an Intelligence Officer at Bust-A-Gut. I have some explosives, some guns, candy, water…I'm here to help." His head twists for breathing room. "I need you to vouch for me here, Henry."

Keith steadies the gun sight. Martin studies the Russian's quiver-lipped stare and jerky movements. The gunman is clearly uncomfortable with the prospect of killing.

Henry sweats and worries about never feeling Martin's scruffy beard again. About never wrapping their fingers together again. The tension is beyond any panic he's known before.

Another snort rips from the back room and stabs the silence.

Suddenly, the bus jerks like a wooden roller coaster hitting an embankment. Everyone pushes into the wall. Keith's handgun shatters eardrums when the trigger trips.

For a snap of time the cabin is construction site loud.

They're the family dog and some kid is blowing a tiny silver whistle.

Gray smoke lifts and Martin sits up, gooey blood leaking across his sideburns. "MARTIN! Martin!" Hamler drops to the floor, scooping the bloody man in his arms.

"Owwwwww. God…shit…owwwww," Martin howls, groping his ear. "I'm fine, it just grazed, *shit*, it just grazed me."

Henry digs his nose into Martin's hair—that smell and his warm body make Henry happy. Panic is still dashing all around, though.

(What was that, Sonja? I…I, oh Jesus, I nearly killed the prisoner.)

Sonja cranks the wheel hard and the bus rocks the opposite

way with a violent, stomach-flipping thud.

(Pull together, Brother. We are being attacked.)

Out the window, a black van steams to the side of the bus. Pandemic walks from the bathroom, clearing nasal wreckage. "What is everyone looking at?" His voice is electric as a birthday clown's. His nostrils are spackled white.

Hamler pulls back from the window. "Get down, dude." He notices Timothy's lips aren't green anymore. His scabs have faded into healthier tones. *Shit, meth addiction suits him.*

"Some of us," the man also known as Juan Pandemic says. "Are trying to get some work done here. I can't…you know, *do my thing*…oh, forget it."

Martin zips open his duffel and metallic clanging fills the bus. Keith holds the handgun close to his chest. The barrel soaks heat through the blue jumpsuit and warms the skin.

"Whooo, that van looks pissed. Henry, tell the cosmonauts I said that," Pandemic says, hardly taking a space between words. The white rocks he crushed and snorted race wild through his brain. His fingers beat a manic drum solo against the window. His breaths are short jets. "Whooo shit, that's a big gun, dude."

Martin's blood soaks into his shirt collar, leaving a sticky trail from the ear. He shatters the window behind Hamler with the ass end of an assault rifle.

Henry's chest fills with champagne bubbles. He falls in love all over.

The gun sputters and flames spit out the end. It shocks Henry how graceful and silent it is. Bullets move faster than Pandemic's eye blinks.

Keith aims the pistol out the window and pops a shot, gives a yelp and drops the gun on the nighttime highway. It's hard to see out the window with the interior lights on. The cabin smells like bottle rockets.

For a handful of seconds the bus is peaceful, the only sound is the road and the wind whipping through broken windows. Then, Martin pings and donks around that long duffel bag. Everyone monitors his moves.

The electric tingle of a ringing phone jitters Juan Pandemic and wildly flashes his skull around. "That...uh, whuh, that's mine."

From the workout bag, Martin yanks a dark metal lump the size of a Bonzo Breakfast Sandwich.

"Hey, Deshler, man, hey!" Pandemic says into his cell, plugging one ear with a finger. "Yeah, dude, things are great. No, it's not too late to call, you know me. I'm having a blast! Um...the funeral is really cool, how've you been, bro?"

Henry peeks out the shattered window as the black van pulls next to the bus. Hamler catches eye contact with his boss, Tony, in the passenger seat. The bus window spreads enough exterior light to see the senior spy's receding hair flutter in the wind. Tony holds a gun that needs both hands. Henry falls to the floor and covers his ears.

Martin and Keith drop quick. A dozen metal puncture noises—like popping open beer cans—rip through the cabin. The dome light shatters and things go black. Henry can't tell the difference between eyes open and eyes clenched shut. During a quiet spread, lasers of moonlight crisscross through the bus, outlining bullet paths.

Before Hamler catches his breath, Tony's firing squad gives an encore.

More peace and white noise from the broken window bully through the bus. Then more bullets shred the walls into an aluminum web. Another beat of silence before a scatter of bullets chop the bus interior to chunks.

Hamler's stomach tickles like it did after murdering Christopher Winters. He reminds himself how simple it was to stuff that syringe into the governor's neck and how close he came to strangling Malinta. He wonders how easy it would be to fire a gun at Tony. A defensive fire grows where the tickle used to live—Hamler imagines delivering a bullet to Tony's skull so the man will stop attacking Martin.

Henry opens his eyes and sees his love yanking a metal pin from the grenade and counting. "One Mississippi. Two Mississippi. Three Mississippi." Martin leans out the busted window. The wind whips loose blood from Martin's ear back into the cabin.

"Oh, wow, no shit," Timothy Winters says via phone. "Dude, yeah, water under the bridge. Man, I love Lothario Speedwagon. I've really been missing it." He doesn't mention Hamdemic's plans for world pop domination. There is no talk of xylophones or saxophones.

Martin throws the bomb softball-style. It bounces under the engine and shreds the black van into a seventy-mile-an-hour scrap yard. Fiery orange lightning fills the bus and quickly fades.

Pandemic speaks louder: "Oh, that? Car trouble. Backfire. No sweat…So, yeah, let's do this. Tomorrow night, huh? Yeah, Lothario rides again! Okay, yeah, no I'll call Henry. Don't sweat it."

The busload stares at one another. Henry frisks himself for holes. The wheels spin ahead. A strong arm moves around his neck. Martin pulls himself tight against Hamler and whispers sweet into his ear.

(Who was that?) Keith asks.

Henry relays the message.

"Tell Keith that was his home office paying a visit," Martin says. "Roland Winters saying hello."

"Whoa, what was that?" Pandemic says. His body jerks like it was under a strobe light. "It was all *boom* and kak-kak-

kak-kak around here. I was trying to make a phone call, you know?"

There are muscles within Hamler that want to grab the phone and smash it under his shoe. Quickly, Henry realizes how lucky he is to be alive and in love. He takes in a sweet, full breath and asks the first happy thought that comes to mind. "Did you ask Dean about the cosmonaut campaign?"

"Oh, no, it slipped my mind. Besides we're both supposed to be at funerals, you know?"

"Just about had my own," Hamler says.

"What?"

"Forget it."

"Did I miss something?"

Still marveling at having a beating heart and relieved he didn't need to shoot Tony, Hamler decides some disclosure is in order. "Okay, uh, I've gotta tell you guys something," he says in a stiff voice. Henry repeats it in Russian. "I'm a spy for Winters Hamburgers and that guy was my boss." He repeats his side of the story: Killing Christopher Winters, stealing secrets from Bust-A-Gut as a temp and nearly murdering Malinta. This does wonders for Hamler's guilt—tense muscles thaw, wrinkles of stomachache smooth, red-hot asthmatic lungs go icebox.

Martin admits his role in this mess, too. He was supposed to monitor Henry's spying tactics for Bust-A-Gut. This isn't the first time he's murdered for the hamburger giant. Frankly, it happens all the time. Orders from the top.

The black smoke hanging in Pandemic's brain takes in Hamler's confession. Grandpa is dead because of his best friend. His heart fires like Martin's assault rifle. Pandemic can't lock together the pieces of that story, but saves them for later. In a slobbery crumple of words, Juan manages to tell the others he's actually the son of Roland Winters. Grandson, obviously, of the murdered Christopher Winters. Caught up in the moment he also says obvious things like: "I think I might have a drug problem," and "I haven't seen a dentist in ten years."

Sonja and Keith trade serious squints. The wounded cosmonaut Dimitri huddles in the corner shivering and watching every word.

SIXTY-ONE

Dean stumbles into the Club. The bartender is just shutting off the lights, but lets his best customer grab a stool. Deshler slugs a drink and listens to phone messages.

Cigarette smoke soon fills his tired vision.

The Beef Club is cold and lonely this time of night or morning—whatever. Dean likes the quiet—mind humming numb with rare focus. There is some delicate, yet weighty, quality to the world in this silent moment. The entire city has finished making its rattles and thumps, and time moves slow. From the blackest corner of his memory, Dean is shocked by a thought.

Finally, Deshler understands why Dad needed silence so badly.

Dean's voice was just starting to crack and his brother's driver's license was fresh the last time the whole family was together, enjoying Bust-A-Gut's new Teriyaki Jerky Burger. In the dining room of their cramped house, surrounded by paintings of pine trees, the legs of Dean's life began their wobble.

The commercials encouraged folks to eat teriyaki jerky sandwiches using chopsticks. Unfortunately, Dean's mom didn't see the future burger genius give Dad a set of sticks. Doubly unfortunate, because Dean didn't know about Dad's problem back then. The young boy knew Dad wasn't allowed to hold anything more dangerous than a spoon after returning from another trip to the hospital. Young Dean knew knives, forks and screwdrivers were off limits. But the little wooden sticks just slipped his mind that meal.

Like most dinners, it didn't take long for the two teenage sons to start moaning for Father's attention. Dad always demanded silence, hardly recognizing the boys, choosing to crawl into a cocoon of internal focus. Muttering about percentages—a holdover from days vanished. Days as a professor.

That internal focus that won him so much praise in the Statistics Department eventually cost Dad his job. Mom was supporting the group pulling double shifts at the restaurant, developing shaking hands and twitchy eyes in the process.

"Dad, did you hear about that?" "Dad, check this out." "Dad, Dad, hey Dad." It was nothing special, but it was the last spark before Father's wick blew out. All young Dean wanted was a taste of Father's time. Just a moment where the man would listen. The boys yelled louder and louder until Daddy Dean's circuits popped.

Sitting over his burger, a perfume of soy in the air, Dean's father grabbed a chopstick and lanced both eardrums so fast nobody knew why the man was shrieking until blood rained onto his shoulders.

That was the last time Dean saw his father. Later that day, his older brother fed the young Cliff Drinker schnapps and introduced Gibby.

Dean knows he doesn't need the silence as bad as Dad. But now there is a brief appreciation for that quiet desire. There is such a pleasant electricity running through the world when you don't want to be heard and nobody is listening, anyhow.

At this hour, most executives are passed out and home. Dean's eyes wander around and the ice shuffles in his Rusty Knife. The Cliff Drinker's never noticed the far corner of the Club before. The room is so empty he now sees that end is clearly taller by a foot.

Dean remembers flipping through that pictorial history of the hotel sold in the lobby. The place was once a landmark of elegance. The Club used to be a small ballroom with chandeliers and tall murals and swing bands.

Looking up at the hacksaw patch job on the ceiling, it's pretty clear where the chandelier hung. Deshler assumes the other end of the Club is the tiny stage where bands jazzed it up.

He takes a quiet, pleasant sip and checks a phone message. "Dean, Thurman Lepsic here. Call us immediately. Mister Findlay wants to strike while the iron's smoking. I'm sure you've heard, but we had to fire Malinta for her participation in that stupid show. Impersonating a Winters employee…well, technically I'm supposed to call the show stupid and careless and disavow any approval. But wow, what a woman. She sacrificed herself for Bust-A-Gut. You're a lucky bastard. We'll have to make a statement, of course, but, as you know, people never listen to apologies. Damage's been done. Anyhow, every news outlet in the country is picking up on this Winters crystal meth story. Their head is through the guillotine. We just need…need to pull the rope, I guess. *Chop.* This is beyond urgent. We have to come up with something hardcore. Or something classy. Which do you think? Call me."

Next message: "Deshler, it's Double Harry, holy shit, we're everywhere. How did we miss this? Jesus, the news is saying that little kids, *eleven-year-olds*, are smoking this stuff. I don't even know what crystal meth is, let alone that it could've been made from hamburgers. Dean, Mister Winters is bouncing off the walls. We haven't heard from Tony, which means the bus is still in play. I repeat, the *bus* is still in *play*. You need to get here immediately. Jesus H., I don't know what's going on. We've got PR and Marketing thinking it over. This is DEFCON One stuff. Yes, I said, *one*. Did you know most people misuse that term? Five is the least serious, one actually means *nuclear war imminent*.

"Regardless, get down here immediately, got it?"

Next message is a whisper, barely more than static. Dean strains to listen: "Deshler, old buddy, hey man, hey hey hey, this is Pandemic. I'm making this quick. Everyone else is sleeping except for Sonja. Funny, I can't get a wink of shuteye, myself," he sniffles. "Man, I'm totally down with signing a contract and playing a gig. But, um, we're kind of underground here. I didn't tell you this before, but I'm the Space Burger winner. Henry and I have been going around the country with some Russian dudes. He's my bodyguard. It's a long story. Anyway, I don't know if the Purple Bottle is the best place for us to be seen. I'm pretty sure we're wanted by the police. Call me. Oh, we're back in town now, so let's get a move on. One more thing, shot in the dark here, but you don't happen to work for Olde-Tyme Hamburgers or know some one-armed chick named Delia by any chance?" An endless, grainy pause fills the message. "Oh yeah, and Hamler killed my grandpa…he's a douche bag. Long, long story."

"Who is *Sonja*," Dean asks the Rusty Knife. Whiskey soaks into his stomach as he stares around the room. "Right, the cosmonaut chick…the one that's supposed to come back to the city to kill me." A weight of fear thunders down his throat and nests in his lap. *Well shit, this complicates things.*

The bartender went home a long time ago. Dean is alone, but the silence isn't so pure now. It's full of audible hiss, like Lothario's tape.

He needs something to remind him he's human. He needs someone to push away all the stress and anxiety of life. He thinks, a bit dreamily, that someone might need him to do likewise, what with losing her job and all. Dean dials the number.

"Hello?"

"Malinta, don't hang up, okay?"

"Dean, do you have any clue how early it is? I can't believe you even remembered my phone number. What a huge step."

Dean works up courage and decides he doesn't care if this sounds stupid. "I saw you, you know, at that boardroom."

"*That* boardroom? Sweetie, don't you think I noticed you, too? The whole place saw you. You looked like an idiot. Thank God they don't know we're together."

"Who were they?" he nearly asks, but figures it'll just piss her off more. So he keeps quiet and takes a sip. Melting cubes clink.

"Jesus, Dean, you're drinking?"

"Well, yeah, so?"

"Look, I know you must be stressed with everything finally splattering against the fan. But, I can't. I can't put up with this. I really can't have you calling me. I have to worry about all my responsibilities, too. We need stop seeing each other, I think."

"Wait." A nausea plagues his stomach. A sorry sickness worse than a morning after abusing Night Train. His lungs work double.

"We're not going through this again. I told you, no more guilt trips."

"I was just wondering." Deshler takes a deep breath, surprised Malinta hasn't hung up. "Look, I'm sorry I forgot our anniversary. I'm sorry I forgot us. Things have been…well, really abnormal lately. I'm usually pretty reliable."

"I know you've got a lot on the books. I just have too much

going on right now to deal with this, too."

"Really? I heard you lost your job."

"Well, yeah, that's a pretty big piece of our goal. Frankly, I should have done it sooner. Now I can focus on the important stuff."

He knows Malinta is one wrong word from hanging up, so Dean stores this confusion and gets down to business. "All that doesn't matter. I don't want to talk about work. The reason I called is I need you to see the real me, listen to the real me. Well, part of the real me. Something fantastic is happening in my life right now. Apparently, that record contract was real. We're playing this incredibly important show tonight and I was hoping you'd come to cheer me on."

Her voice wilts, "Dean…that's…that's really sweet. But…"

Without thinking, a defense spits out. "I can't do this alone. I can't be a good person, can't be *myself.* I can't make this leap without you." Dean pauses, realizing it's true.

She breathes long into the phone, matching Dean's cigarette exhale. "Alright, when and where? You know I can't miss something like this."

"Um, well it was supposed to be at the Purple Bottle, but…"

Dean looks at the end of the Beef Club. He paints a picture of what this ballroom was like in full swing. In its glory. Dean invents an idea so good he wonders if he's drunk already. He scans the far end where jazz once wailed. He imagines men and women dressed fancy, hot music filling the air, elegant dancing—the high-water mark of class and sophistication in town. *The perfect place*, he thinks, *to puke all over the stage.*

"It's at the club. The Beef Club."

"Really?" she sounds fairly impressed. Her voice rises, more wowed with each syllable, "I think I see what you're getting at. Tonight is Friday. God, that's good."

"Yep, that's the place. Crazy huh? But that'll be convenient for you. You can't miss it now."

"This sounds like trouble. Do you think you can pull it off?"

"Of course. Our concerts are very civilized. They're practically yoga classes."

"Okay, I'll," her voice dissolves into confusion. "I'll get the ball rolling and tell our friends about it."

"Great, oh wow, great. I'll see you then. Take care."

"Focus, babe. *Focus.*"

Wrecking ball weight comes down on his shoulders. He sweats and uncontrollably taps toes. After enjoying the return of calming silence, he phones Moral Compass Records to leave a message for Antonio McComb.

SIXTY-TWO

Dimitri/Carl Janomi is on a bunk, flesh pale and a soaking red blanket cloaking slumped shoulders.

The bus is behind a truck stop on the city limits. Frosty air leaks through hundreds of bullet holes. It smells like powerful chemical cleaners. From the right angle you can see the lonely city skyscrapers outlined in the darkness—one for each hamburger giant—poking up like dismembered fingers. The gas pumps and chicken fried steak place and gift shop are dark for the night. The only light is a phone booth waffled with cracked windows.

Sonja drags Dimitri to the front of the bus. Helpless, his head swings limp from side to side.

"Is he dead?" Martin whispers.

"I thought so for a while, but now I'm not sure," Hamler says, shivering. "We haven't seen him talk or move since Los Angeles."

Sonja grumbles into Janomi's ear. Henry can't make out the words. The dying actor is a shadow in the dim light—his breath visible. Keith comes out with a backpack and slings it around Janomi's bloody shoulder. They kick open the door and lower him.

Snooorrrrrrrrrrrrrrrrrrrt.

"Whough…shit," Pandemic says. His right palm is cupped to his face amongst shadowed light. White powder grains cling to his hand. He gags out wet throat noises. He hacks a few coughs, licks the palm and turns to the pair. "Martin, thanks for this."

"Don't mention it." He leans back, gently rubbing Henry's thigh. Inscribing little designs with his fingertip.

"What happened to quitting?" Henry says.

"Man," Pandemic dazes for a minute, face twitchy. He looks at Henry and his voice gets mean. "Like you'd care. My dad wanted me to quit. My grandpa wanted me to quit. But they never figured it out."

"It?" Henry says.

"I've got reasons."

"That doesn't make sense."

"Yeah, it does," Pandemic snarls.

"Yeah," Martin nods, a surprisingly sympathetic pucker to his lips. "It does."

"You need to listen to my man, here," Juan says, offering Martin a fist to bump. "He's not nearly as big a prick as *some* people."

"I'll do that," Henry says. "It still doesn't explain—"

"Long story short, dick, is I'll quit when I say. Not them. What'll that fix?"

"You're the boss."

"Got that right." He's still waiting for the fist bump. "I needed this bad, Martin. It's top shelf. Who do you buy from? Can I have his beeper number?"

Martin finally trades knuckle taps and says: "You don't want to know."

Henry watches Martin speak—so casual, so laid back. There is tons to learn from his love.

"Yes, I do."

"You don't."

"I do."

He gives Henry a look. "Bust-A-Gut."

"What?"

"Our lab made it from Winters hamburgers, actually."

"Dude, did you poison me?"

"I said you didn't want to know."

"Dude."

"Relax, it's pure. It's just from the Flu Burger syrup."

"Oh, right on, I'll buy that." Pandemic's eyes poke from his face like a couple of fishbowls. They are trapped in Hamler's apologetic stare. "I forgot, you and I are not talking, dude."

"Juan, I'm sorry, man. I can explain," Henry says. He stands, hands shaky. "I didn't know it was your grandpa."

Pandemic concentrates on Lothario Speedwagon as a tornado of nerve endings build behind his nose, meth soaking into the gooey tissue near the brain. "I am going to gouge out your eyes. See these fingers? They're pupil-bound. So, until I blind you, we are not speaking."

"Dude, Juan, come on. I…" He steps close, but Juan shoves him hard. Henry stumbles back, but Martin steadies him.

There's a crash outside the bus. The Russians leave Dimitri against the inside of the phone booth. His blanket stains the cracked windows with sticky blood.

(Ask your friend, does he have any handcuff?) Sonja says, shutting the door.

The van rumbles to life with Keith behind the wheel.

"Martin, do you have any handcuffs in your bag, they want to know."

"I don't."

The bus lurches forward and Sonja fumbles with Martin's wrists and a bungee cord. She yells at the spy.

"Martin, she says to loosen up. Not to struggle or you'll be killed. Listen to her, please. I need you."

"Henry, we're going to be okay."

"Just, please, for me. For us."

"These guys don't speak English, right?"

Henry shakes his head.

"*These* guys aren't Russian military. They're too clumsy. They're too—"

Sonja elbows Martin in the skull. It makes a dull, meaty thump. He leans back on the bench, tongue resting funny.

"Hey!" Henry yells.

In a flash, Martin's hands are a nest of rubbery bungee cords. He's led, pings of light bursting in his eyesight, to the bedroom at the rear of the bus.

(What are you doing? He's not a threat,) Henry yells to the cosmonauts. (He's *helping* us. You are getting the stupid?)

Sonja's voice is so heavy, Henry's skin tingles with a thousand needles: (You are our prisoner, I am thinking you are forgetting. We are needing no help. Your boyfriend has outstayed his welcome. He is fortunate we have not put bullet through his eye.)

(Bullshit, I'm knowing you weren't even a Russian soldier,) he says. (Or a cosmonaut. You're too stupid. Too dumb.) Henry stands and says the final two words eye-to-eye with the spacewoman.

Henry Hamler has never been pistol whipped. In all honesty, he's never really been in a fight. His older sister knocked him around some as a kid, but for the most part his skull has always been blunt-force-free. That is, until the hind end of a cosmonaut terrorist's 9mm digs into his forehead.

For a moment all he can grasp is that sharp chemical smell in the air.

It takes a few blinks to figure out what just happened. It doesn't hurt at first: He is fly before swatter. Matador before bull. Baseball before bat. Suddenly, a spotlight burns behind his eyes. His neck snaps back and up. When Hamler's vision fizzles, root-canal pain pours through his skull.

Henry flops back onto the bench and goes to sleep as a bubble of skin grows around the pistol's point of impact.

SIXTY-THREE

Bright and early, the Public Relations Director for Bust-A-Gut claims this is a once-in-a-lifetime stumble from the competition. The sun is just rising orange through skyscraper windows. "First the cosmonaut *thing*," she says. "Now this crystal meth fiasco. We look like chocolate bunny rabbits. Let's get Mister Findlay's approval ASAP."

"Gosh," a woman says. "Where's the old man been? I haven't seen him in forever."

The Marketing Director claims they can position a new ad campaign during prime time as early as next Wednesday. "As long as we get a plan established by the close of business today. It being Friday—expect to work all weekend."

The team clears out and a few minutes later, Lepsic and Dean sit alone in the boardroom. Every surface shines with freshly waxed wood and morning light. The room is warm and soap-scented.

The veins in the VP's normally creamy face are a ball of yarn. "Deshler, I'm worried" Lepsic says. His eyes are wet and ready to pop. His unshaven jaw is a bristle broom.

"About what?"

"Ethically, you know. I don't know what move to make here."

"Really, worried about ethics? Well, I guess, what does the boss think, Thurman?"

"That's just it."

"What's just it?"

"You may have noticed I've been calling all the shots for a few weeks. You have to promise your silence on this one." Lepsic's mouth is wrapped tight, clinching his teeth.

Dean's never seen him so vulnerable, so strung-out. If there was ever a time to hang Thurman from his ankles over the bridge, it's right now. Dean exercises control, though. "Okay."

Lepsic pulls apart his tie until it makes a scarf. The skin around his nose and eyes is cracked and peeling. He runs an unsteady hand through once-perfect hair. "He's...Mister Findlay is in a coma. Doctors don't think he'll ever recover. We've just been keeping things under wraps. I've been, well, I guess *pretending* to be him since then."

"Thurman, what are you saying, what happened?"

"Don't know. We just found him lying in the street near the Club a while back. His car was stolen. It's a miracle the news has been suffocated this well. *Nighbeat* would flip its wig."

"Whoa."

Lepsic's confession reminds Dean of spending the rest of his teenage years pretending Gibby was a parent. It helped while he and his brother cried themselves to sleep, thinking they caused their real father's breakdown. It didn't help that Dean's mother would remind the pair every time she lost patience.

However, around sixteen, Dean learned a valuable lesson: *No matter how screwed up things get, there's always a logical explanation.* "Truth is," a relative told him at Christmas that year. "Your dad had mental problems, didn't you know? Had them since before you were even born. When he'd forget to take his medicine the poor guy always stuffed things into his ears. Started with fingers and pens, then graduated to raisins and your toys, and then...I'm sorry...that chopstick. Said he heard voices chattering, telling knock-knocks, but mostly numbers. Said he heard *endless streams of statistics.* Numbers, numbers, numbers. You boys had nothing to do with it." By the time

Dean learned this tidbit, Mom refused to leave her room and her sons were sent to foster care. Gibby was Dad.

"That's not the problem, though," Lepsic continues. "The trouble is I don't know what to do. I don't know what Findlay would do. This is a great opportunity, but God, we've really been straying from our mission statement lately. This is uncharted water for me. Where does it end? When I stepped in, I was hoping I could clean this company up a little, you know? Make us honest. But, Christ, is that what Findlay would do?"

A fog crowds between Dean's ears—he's not shocked, just disappointed he didn't figure it out sooner. "Wow, Thurman. You'll make the right choice. I trust you."

"What would you do?"

Deshler realizes he's late for a meeting at Winters. Then something cracks open and surges through him like smelling salts. A crunchy clarity, more perfect than last night's silence. A blood-and-guts kind of thinking. Dean smashes his career to pieces with a gap-toothed grin. "Go for the throat, that's my advice. Destroy them—put your boot between their teeth. Which reminds me, I've got a dentist appointment. I'll be back later. We'll solve this, okay?"

SIXTY-FOUR

Hamler's fingers are balled up cold and tight when his eyes open again. He has no idea what time it is, but the sun is up. His shoulders shake with shivers. The cosmonauts stand on Pandemic's porch as the home's owner jabs at the lock with unsteady fingers. Keith props Henry up, leaning him against the house numbers.

Sonja lugs the duffel bag over one shoulder. She scans down the street for cars. The rising sun snuggles neighborhood rooftops.

The key clicks, the door opens. Inside, the cosmonauts moan and breathe heavy through their mouths. The stale urine belch of meth cookery hangs in a thick, permanent cloud.

(Put ice on your head and go to sleep, Little Henry. We are nearly complete with the mission objectives,) says Sonja, holding an elbow over her nose.

(What are you talking about? *What* is this mission? You haven't told us,) Henry says, regaining some vision through his foggy mind.

The two Russians plug their eyes together across the room. Keith takes quick breaths through his mouth, careful not to use his nasal passage. (Your friend knows, he is helping soon. You have no worries. Just translate.)

(Pandemic?) Suddenly, his mind is clear and his heart asks its first question. (Wait, what did you do with Martin?)

(He is no longer part of the mission,) Keith says. (We have parted ways.)

Entering from the kitchen, Pandemic brings a glass of water for both cosmonauts. "Don't murder anyone before you go to bed, dick."

(Go to sleep, Little Henry. We have very few hours until Mission is complete. You must rest. We will rest also.)

SIXTY-FIVE

Recalls, refunds and rehab are the orders of the day. Olde-Tyme PR says: claim ignorance, offer sympathy and, for God's sake, stop serving the Flu Burger! Call the FDA and help with their investigation. "We are *not,*" they emphasize during a meeting Dean is thirty minutes late for. "Going to look good no matter what happens."

"Our finances," the accounting guy says. "Are drilling a hole to China." According to his team's predictions, the company could be bankrupt in a year. Maybe less. "This," he says with a sour mouth. "Is an Enron-sized nosedive. Possibly worse."

On top of everything, marketing informs the group that the cosmonauts are still loose. They still have Juan Pandemic captive, as well as the translator. Most of Tony, the undercover agent, was found in a barbecued wreck early this morning, fifty miles outside of town. "What is the *high road* if these Russian psychopaths return to the office with machine guns?" they ask.

A file folder containing photos of all those on board the bus is passed around. Two look surprisingly familiar. *Funerals my ass*, Dean thinks.

The Marketing Director says, looking directly at the CEO, "It's time to go to Plan B if we want to salvage this and put a tight lid on the situation."

Roland Winters nods, "We have a Plan B?"

Winters' office is clear now. Double Harry and Deshler are facing the boss in creampuff leather chairs. Harry crosses and uncrosses and recrosses his legs—unable to find comfort.

"Well boys, what do you think?" Winters says, rotating skin folds with a temple massage. A mix of sweat and aftershave clouds over the desk to Dean's nose.

Deshler wants to speak, but there is a tension in the air that says shut up. His bridge-burning exit at Bust-A-Gut heaps confidence atop his frizzy-headed soul. Why not go two-for-two?

"This isn't really our area, Roland," Harry says, removing his hat, planting both feet on the ground.

"No, I think it is. You guys are *idea* men, thinkers, troubleshooters." He removes his ketchup jacket and reveals Dijon sweat stains. "Just shift from ground beef to ground control. I need you."

Those eyes, Dean thinks. *Yikes.*

The men fold their hands like prayer group. They sit silent. Dean is loving every second of this mess.

"There's another problem, gentlemen. Have you ever heard of the Purple Bottle? Dean, you're a young guy, maybe you're familiar."

"Uh, yeah, chief," Dean says, lungs lifting heavy for air, half-shocked. "I know it."

"I heard through the grapevine that my son's *band* is performing there tonight. Lothario-something-or-other. This is pretty hard to swallow with the hot water he's paddling around in, but who can tell with that kid? Harry, you know Tim. Anything harebrained is possible with him. I mean, Christ, with the drugs, who knows?" Winters' face hangs in a way that says he's genuinely concerned.

Keep quiet. Shut up. Shut up, Dean tells himself. *They think the show's at the Bottle, you are okay. Keep quiet.*

"Should I get a team? To…" Harry holds, then whispers the same as when suggesting Christopher Winters' murder, "*Take care of things?*"

Dean twists in the slick leather chair like someone just finished frying hamburgers on it. *Chill out. You are okay. They think it's at the Bottle.*

"Well, here's the funny part, Harry," he says with a dash of optimism. "I had our people dig into it. This Purple Bottle's manager says the concert has been moved."

"Get an address?" Harry whips out a pad of paper.

"You won't need that. The guy says the show is moved to the *ballroom* at the hotel."

"Ballroom, what ballroom?"

"Think about it."

"The Beef Club?"

Deshler's hair grows hot and itchy. His necktie is a rope of lava.

"That's what I want to find out."

SIXTY-SIX

(You have rock and roll concert tonight, yes?) Sonja says, kneeling next to Henry, half-asleep atop naked floorboard slats.

Rubbing yellow crust from eyes, Hamler butchers another translation: (No. Mister Pandemic is a sausage stuffed with excrement and lies.)

(He is saying it is quite important. You will play.)

(That is a canyon of trouble, Sonja.)

(No, little one, this is my offer. It is very significant to young Mister Winters. He has been a good comrade to Keith and I. You have been a more than excellent translator. You are free to go.)

(Again, don't you police think want talk to me?)

(Perhaps, but police not wanting you for wrongdoing. You will not know our location. You are innocent.)

(Have you been smoking Pandemic's pipe?)

A wrecked smile appears: (No my friend, our mission is nearly over. You are no use to us. We are setting you free on the condition that you play your music. It is great opportunity.)

Do not trust her, his mind says. *They killed Martin. These people are evil. Do not trust her.*

Sitting up, Hamler's voice rises: (Wait, Pandemic doesn't speak Russian. How did you talk to him?)

Sonja's lips part and her tongue rests against the back of teeth to speak when Keith stomps up from Lothario Speedwagon's practice space and into the living room. (Let us go, sister. It is time to be on our way. The mission needs us.)

(So long, Little Henry. You have been a great friend. Perhaps we will meet again,) Sonja says, rubbing Hamler's hair like a stray dog.

"Where the hell is Martin?" he screams, but in a whistle of freezing wind through the front door, the Russian pair disappears.

Henry stares at the closed door for a long minute. Gaps around the frame welcome in white light. Things are cold and lonesome. His head thumps.

Henry turns toward Pandemic's room, but stops. For a flicker, he thinks about what it would mean if someone murdered his own grandpa. He thinks about Martin…dead? The guilt grinds deeper into Hamler's muscles and he realizes there is only one way to make it up to Pandemic. Hamler walks into the dungeon of a bedroom. It's chalkboard-dark. Henry can't see the mattress, even with the daylight coming through the open bedroom door.

"Dude?"

Some blankets turn over and springs creak.

"Yo, Juan," he whispers into the void.

A low moan ripples through Hamler's body. It reminds him of Deshler's singing. Kind of like Lothario's song *One Foot in the Womb*.

"Pandemic, I'm in. Let's play this show tonight." Hamler stands with toes hanging in the darkness and heels in the light. "Who cares about making people happy?" he says. "I want to make art. I want to be part of this. Any idiot can get a crowd to cheer. It takes guts to piss people off. I get it now."

"Seriously?" Juan's chest runs through a lumber mill. The band is sitting in his palm. "Tell me what you are saying, for real."

"Yeah, man. Let's make Lothario work. I'm in. I'm in."

Hamler enters the room. It's as bottomless as guilt and cold as loneliness.

"I might not jab out your eyeballs after all," Pandemic rasps.

"Thanks." Surrounded by nothingness—pupils still pinpoints, unable to make out shapes in the room—Hamler says, "The Russians left."

"I figured."

Henry's foot lands on something soft. Wet and squishy. Hamler does not want to know what it is. "How did you guys communicate?" He takes a backward step.

"Huh?"

"How did you tell them about the show tonight?"

"I didn't."

SIXTY-SEVEN

Deshler says good morning to his assistant, Austin, and tells him only to forward calls from Harry and Roland. "Oh, here's your mail," the secretary says with a three-coffee grin and a small stack of envelopes. On top is a card featuring a Thanksgiving turkey.

Change of venue noted. See you tonight. Malinta's head looks pretty good these days.

SIXTY-EIGHT

This morning there's a bicycle messenger zipping through traffic. He wheels between choked streets and across sidewalks. People grunt and call him an asshole.

The cyclist was paid twice the usual fee by a guy who looks like one of the Moscow Five—the one that got shot—to deliver a DVD to the television station that produces *Nightbeat*. The disc is snug and dry inside a black shoulder bag.

SIXTY-NINE

The enormity of tonight's concert finally sinks in, and nerves thrash at his belly. Dean can't focus—he starts writing emails and forgets to whom, walks down halls and forgets to where. So, when our hero leaves work it's no shock he can't find that key to the hotel's back door. He must use the main entrance and parks the car down the street in order to skip valet. He vaguely remembers Friday being Napoleon's night off. *Maybe I'll luck out*, he thinks.

The sun is setting earlier every day and the last gray-blue flecks of sky are nearly gone. Deshler sucks in a milkshake-smooth breath of frigid air and walks toward the front doors.

In Dean's perfect world, Pandemic and Henry are setting the gear up right now. According to his drummer, Henry is totally excited about the gig. Deshler, though, wants to die.

Napoleon's never met the band without their masks on. He's only heard me talk about those guys, Deshler thinks. *Thank God he won't recognize them when they load in, if he's here, that is.*

Deshler's insides twist tight and his toes shrink into fists after turning the corner, staring his old coworker in the face. Their steamy winter breaths mold into one cloud. "Hey buddy, been a while."

"You could say that," Napoleon says.

The air under the awning is colder than Dean remembers. It burrows through jacket lining and makes him shiver.

"Look man, I'm really sorry I ditched you and haven't

been around, there's just been…" he tries not to sound like an asshole. "Some *things*."

Impatient, Napoleon looks over Dean's shoulder like a car is coming. "What do you want?"

"I'm just going upstairs."

"Why don't you use the back door like usual?"

"How'd you know that?"

"People talk, Dean. People are always watching."

"Man, I feel like shit. Can I buy you a beer soon and hang out? Make it up to you somehow."

"How about tonight?"

"I've got some *things* going on tonight. Upstairs. I really, really wish I could. But this can't be ignored."

Dean, happily, doesn't feel like an asshole.

There's a bulge of cars waiting for Napoleon to trade their keys for a valet ticket. One guy in back, with a blue SUV, honks a little hiccup.

"Maybe…listen, unless you're gonna park cars, I'll catch you later. I have *things* to do."

Dean is an asshole.

"Sorry man, I'll make it up to you. I promise."

Napoleon's face puckers into a knot and the tension in his voice softens. "Yeah, forget it. Maybe I'll see you later. I really have been wanting to talk. I still have one of my films to show you, okay? Only a couple minutes of your time."

"Yeah, you bet. That'd be really great. I can't wait to see it."

"Great! Okay, when? Deshler? Hey, when?"

Dean is gone.

SEVENTY

"God, I'm a pussy," Pandemic says. "It's been, what, a couple weeks since we've played?"

The Beef Club is empty and everything echoes. "Yeah," Henry says, huffing, pushing a tall bass amp on the stage. "I know. This shit feels way heavier. The road'll do that, I guess. Makes you soft."

"I never said soft." The last-night fragrance of stale beer is in the air.

"You said pussy. That's worse."

"No thanks. You can be soft, asshole. I'll be a pussy."

"Okay."

"You might think you're off the hook by playing this show."

"I never said that."

"Good, because you're not."

Minutes pass, Pandemic adjusts his Konkers until they are in perfect chaos. Under the tall windows, gashes and hammer slashes shine through the oil drum's black paint. He whomps it a few times. "Damn, can a barrel be out of tune? It sounds like crap." He smacks the floor tom a few times. "Man, this too. I think that gunshot screwed my hearing up. My ears're ringing bad. Does this sound right?" He hits the floor tom a dozen times.

"Yeah, maybe. I don't know, man. I can hardly tell if I sound okay."

Hamler's bass goes: *Blomp-Blomp-Buh-BlompBlomp.* He

steps on the distortion pedal, a tiny red light shines to life and his amp explodes with the same noise as their ringing ears.

Hamler cuts the squealing and watches his bandmate. He's been fighting it—trying to play nice—but Henry can't hold back. "So you didn't see *anything*?"

"Man, we've been over this." Pandemic works hard to ignore him.

"Just, come on, play along. Did you see what they did to him?"

"No, man. I told you. I was in my own head pretty deep. Like deeper than I've ever really been. It was so intense I was cleaning the little cracks between stereo buttons on the dashboard. I couldn't stop. I had to."

"And you didn't see what they did with Martin?"

"No."

"Did you hear a scream or a gunshot or a stab?"

"Who hears a stab?"

"Juan."

"No, man. I spaced it. I don't know."

"Just focus…"

"Leave me alone."

Several more minutes pass. Silent.

"We should set up the black lights," Pandemic says.

"That's Deshler's job, forget it," Hamler says, picturing bitter thoughts about their last meeting in the practice space.

"Go easy on Dean. We'll deal with lights later. Let's just put on the masks before anyone—"

A motherly woman in a wide skirt walks through the door of the silent club. "Excuse me, gentlemen. Just what do you think you're doing here?"

The sun powers through the windows in wide yellow blocks, bordered by shadow, outlined on the floor. She is standing inside a sunny rectangle.

Pandemic sounds surprised, "Setting up."

"We're playing a gig tonight," Henry says.

"Well, young man, I don't recall scheduling any *entertainment* for this evening." She marches toward the stage, in and out of the light.

"Somebody did. We're going on in a couple hours."

"We've received a few complaints from guests. I'm going to have to ask you both to leave," she props up a smile. "Immediately."

Henry and Juan freeze and look at each other, hoping one will make a move and speak up.

"Immediately," she repeats.

There is nothing but the sound of her toe tapping hardwood. This continues long enough for the bandmates to trade looks and urging eyes, begging the other to speak.

A voice booms through the club, so gritty and huge it could only be one man: "Doris, I can answer all your questions."

The three turn as Deshler Dean walks to the stage in a suit and tie, that normally wild hair brushed back. He does not look like himself.

"Doris, I hired these fellas. It's Ed from Accounting's fortieth anniversary party." At this point, lies squeeze out of Dean the way cheese oozes from Mozza-Burger buns. "This is the jazz combo I found. Didn't the night manager tell you any of this?"

"Mister Dean, everything must be okayed through me. Not Randy."

"Oh, gosh, I'm so sorry. This is my first big party for the company and, well, gee, Mister Winters will be so disappointed if it doesn't go off without a hitch."

"Mmmm-hmmmm."

"Could you let this slide, just as a favor to an old coworker?" Some amazing, charming look overcomes Dean's features. It's confidence. He wears it well.

She holds a breath and looks at the ceiling. The folds of her neck tighten smooth and milky. "Alright, Deshler. But you're still a valet in my book. Just keep the volume down and finish before eleven, please."

"Consider it done, Doris. You won't regret it. You're making the most powerful man in the city *very* happy."

The singer watches her leave and spins around. "Hello boys!" Dean bellows. "How were your so-called funerals?"

SEVENTY-ONE

A few hours later, employees from both hamburger chains nearly spill their drinks at the sight of the young fast-track executive, Deshler Dean, standing on stage with a fat guy and a skinny guy wearing neon pink masks.

If Deshler chopped off every confused corporate face that says: "*Dean*? Is that *Dean* up there?" he could fill the bed of a pickup truck.

The Club seems extra packed this Friday. Men and women are lined along the walls, sitting on laps, clustered in clots around the room. There is a ton of space near the stage—everyone leery about getting too close.

A nerdy guy in glasses and a suit, hair greased to a part, walks up. An Asian couple follows, better dressed than any executive at the club.

"Snazzy venue, guys," he says. "I don't know if I've introduced myself to the rest of the band. Antonio McComb, I've been working with our man, Deshler, to get you guys signed to Moral Compass."

"Hey," says Henry with a warm smile, lifting his mask.

"Right on, bro," Pandemic yells and taps on a cymbal. His eyeballs roll around at odd angles through the mask's holes. Martin's Flu Burger meth is picking up steam. Getting stronger and stronger, pushing harder. Pandemic likes that.

"This is Toji and Yung-Yung, *The Suits* as we call them at Moral Compass."

Toji is a paper doll. Henry imagines his bass vibrations

blowing the woman across the room. The man is a sharp blade with a deep black mustache.

Hellos are exchanged. The pair walk away and take a brave seat by the stage.

"Okay, it's up to you guys now," McComb says to Deshler, resting a wingtip on the edge of the riser. Dean looks deeply at McComb. Big open pores, nervous eye ticks, clipped fingernails—the Cliff Drinker has absolutely no recollection of ever meeting. None. "Impress these two and there's a sack of cash with your name on it."

"Okay. Sure."

"Literally."

"Literally?"

"The suits deal in cash, because, supposedly, they're mobbed-up. Maybe. Who knows?"

"Okay."

"So, literally, a sack of cash. Well, not *literally*, literally. They're too classy to lug around a sack. But who's being picky, right?"

Pandemic twists the drum's tuning peg. He hits it with a hollow thump and scratches his scalp.

"Yeah, well, we'll just do our thing and see what happens," Dean says. He catches a glimpse of hundreds of the semifamiliar faces filling the Club. Double Harry, by the window, peers up through wiry bifocals. Thurman Lepsic walks over and shakes Harry's hand, they grin, chat like old roommates and motion toward the stage. Deshler tries to swallow but his throat is a desert.

Dean realizes he is choosing between work and art, security and happiness. *Actually, the choice is easy. After my bosses see the band, I'm probably fired anyway.*

Hamler gobbles a handful of jawbreakers and crackles open a beer can. "Oh shit, beer," Deshler says to nobody specific.

"I'm sober." A watusi of nerves dance through his chest and stomach. He's never performed bone-dry before. For the first time in dozens of concerts he wonders if people will get, or possibly hate, Lothario Speedwagon. The nervousness erodes that usual pre-show swagger down to a limp.

Holding a heavy microphone to his lips, Dean gurgles: "Check…test, test, test, mic one, is anybody listening?" It flash-floods against the windows. Cheap drinks shake toward the edge of tables. The entire crowd plugs a finger in its collective ear. Deshler twists the level down a hint.

Pulling off that tie and ruffling his hair back into a mushroom cloud, Dean looks up and sees Winters and Napoleon roll in together like a couple of bowling balls. Malinta trails behind as the ten pin.

Winters makes eye contact, sends a shimmering smile and flicks a rapid wave in the air. *You've picked art, you've picked art*, Dean reminds himself. *You've picked art.*

"What would Gibby do?" Deshler accidentally mutters into the microphone. It broadcasts over the heads of anyone who's anyone in the burger business.

SEVENTY-TWO

Making his way around the stage, Roland Winters reaches up and grabs the shooting star executive by the shirt. A soap bubble of anxiety expands inside Dean. "You and I are having a nice talk later. A nice long talk about him," the ketchup red and mustard yellow walrus points to his son. "About this," he spreads a hand across the entire stage. "And about your future at Winters Olde-Tyme Hamburgers. But right now, I have bigger potatoes to French fry."

Dean reminds himself where art needs to rank in life. The soap bubble pops into a shiny spray. "I quit," slips out Dean's mouth. The feeling is electric. "Listen, I choose art," he screams, but the boss has already gone and started yelling at Juan Pandemic. Dean doesn't mind. A sturdiness builds inside him—he doesn't need people to listen.

"Just what do you think you're pulling, champ?" CEO Winters says, kneeling behind his son's drum kit. "There are a *lot* of people who want to have a word with you. I didn't even know whether you were alive and I find you *here*."

"How did you know it was me," he asks behind a wall of hot pink papier-mâché.

"A father can smell his numbskull son from a mile away."

Juan's fingers spin a drumstick with nervous energy. "Well, to answer your question, since you sent some thugs to kill us, I didn't think it made much difference to you."

"*Thugs*? What do you mean, thugs?"

The stick-spinning stops when the drummer makes a tight fist. He breathes to slow his mind and focus. "I mean, the guys you had shooting at the bus. The guys Martin thankfully blew up. Those guys on *your* payroll."

"Oh, you're an accountant now? You know my payroll?"

"Not to mention having my bandmate murder Grandpa," Pandemic digs fingernails deep and hard into his scalp. "I don't want anything to do with this scummy company."

"Listen, Tim, the police are on their way. Those cosmonauts are dangerous killers. Psychopaths. I understand you're confused. I'm told it's called Stockholm Syndrome. It's when people feel empathy for their kidnappers. It's perfectly natural." He places a meaty paw on Pandemic's shoulder. "Little kids locked in sex dungeons for years can often claim they love their rapists. It's a messed up world, Tim."

"Dad, there is some important stuff going on tonight. Not that you care, but I'm a good drummer. Much better than at anything else I do. And if I play my ass off, my band is getting signed to a record label. I can make money playing music. I won't be your problem anymore. Everyone wins. You can ignore me for the rest of my life and I'll do the same."

"Well." The elder Winters scratches a scatter of chubby chin dimples. "I'm just so glad you and Mister Hamler are alright."

"I bet." Juan shuts his eyes and speaks into the darkness. "You know what? I don't need a dad. I never did. I'm all the dad I need."

"Super. One more thing, kiddo. There's a press conference scheduled for tomorrow morning. We need some positive spin from this whole situation. I mean, some uplifting story about how you guys survived would be really helpful."

"I'm touched you're so concerned about my wellbeing."

A SHORT LIST OF THE TIMES IN PANDEMIC'S LIFE HIS FATHER TRULY CARED ABOUT HIS SON'S WELLBEING:

• **1979** With the birth of his only son, Roland Winters learns of the monstrous tax breaks from combining wealth and fatherhood.

• **1990** Needing to prove some dominance at the company picnic, he drags Timothy to victory at the Three-Legged Race.

• **1992** Roland wins custody of Timothy after a messy divorce. "This," he tells a colleague, "is just the thing to teach that bitch a lesson."

SEVENTY-THREE

"Malinta, you came. That is so awesome."

"Well, I kind of had to, it is Friday after all. Tonight's the most important night for, well, so many reasons." It seems impossible, but Dean swears a blush forms on her cheeks. The urge to kiss it away is strong. "Do you have a second? We need to talk before things start."

"Totally, tell me at the bar. I really want a drink." Dean hops from the stage and grabs Malinta's hand. A gossipy murmur snakes around the club. "Actually, I could use about six."

"Sweetie, come on," her voice lifts and bites like needles. "Not tonight, it's too important."

"Come on?" Dean glares at his woman and is reminded she doesn't know about Lothario Speedwagon's secret ingredient. "Shit, okay, well, let me say something."

She stares, waiting. The blush has died.

"After tonight, I want to start fresh. I think things are finally getting in order for me. I think I can be a good boyfriend. I just need tonight," he says and a surrogate Night Train warmth builds inside.

"I know how important all this is to you…and us."

"I like being around you." He is careful not to slip with the other L-word. "I need to be around you."

Her eyes half-close and a soft finger runs up Dean's side. It wouldn't feel weird right now, he decides, to plant that kiss.

With all eyes on him, Dean hesitates kissing. Dean's never hesitated when a crowd is watching, but assumes alcohol had something to do with that. *God, a drink sounds good.*

Napoleon pops up before them as Malinta moves in gently closer. "Do you two have a spare second?" the chubby valet says, digging through a backpack. The fleshy smell of sweat comes into clearer focus.

"Um, no dude, I've got to sing in a few minutes. Plus, people are starting to look a little worried," Deshler says, wondering whether he should take off his shirt for the concert. He wonders if the Cliff Drinker would rub peanut butter on his bare chest. He's not even sure of its symbolism at this point. Though, Deshler's pretty certain Iggy Pop did it once. "Shit, where's my mask?"

Malinta says, all nervy: "Does anyone know what time it is?"

"Way after nine-thirty," Dean says. "We were supposed to start at, like, nine."

"That all can wait. Come sit with me for a sec," Napoleon says. His gritty fingers pull out a laptop. "I've got a little film you both need to watch. Indie flick. Low budget, but good."

Deshler and Malinta search the yolks of each other's eyes. "Look, buddy," Dean says soft. "I promise I'll watch them with you, but right now isn't—"

"Sit, sit, sit, it'll all be over in a flash. About a minute-thirty to be exact."

"I really," Dean is simultaneously unhooking shirt buttons and slinking toward the bar. "Have some things…" He is consumed with intense guilt—equally consumed with Malinta thoughts. The shirt opens and bare chest meets steamy Beef Club air.

"Malinta," Napoleon says. "Talk to him for me. Pretty please."

Her green eyes grow more than a little confused.

"You two know each other?" Dean says.

Both look at him like the answer is "yes," and "yes" is obvious.

Dean stops himself from asking more. "Quick, okay, man."

The three huddle around the computer in the corner.

"What am I doing? I don't have time for this, buddy. I'll check this out after our set, I swear." Deshler lifts from the seat as Napoleon hits PLAY and the empty screen zaps to life. "I need to find some gin."

"Hey," Napoleon uses a commanding voice.

"Or beer…"

"*Hey.*"

"…mouthwash even—"

"You know that touching Arbor Day card, that new baby card, that birthday card, that Thanksgiving card?" Napoleon says, breathing through asthma heavy lungs. "Those are from me. Is that enough to calm you down? Now, I want you to stand still and watch."

Onscreen, the camera's focus is hazy. Dean's baritone rattles through rickety laptop speakers: "F-F-F-Findlay doesn't know. *That's* why I have to use the screwdriver, babe."

The focus clears up and the lighting adjusts. The video shoots from the back seat of a parked red car. The upholstery is smooth white leather. The dash is wood-grained like antique tables.

"Wouldn't you have the keys if Mister Findlay said it was alright to borrow his car?" Malinta says. The camera nauseatingly swings to her blonde head. Thin shoulders pop through a floaty black outfit.

"Napoleon saw him," Deshler says, full of Cliff Drinking

stutters and slurs. The camera focuses on the driver's seat again. Dean's skull wobbles back and forth. He hacks at the steering column with a screwdriver, stabbing it to death. "Tell her, tell Malinta that the lovely Mister Clifford Findlay," Deshler's voice slurs and chops in a way that says *too many dollar beers tonight.* "With his fat ass and birthmarked face, said, 'Yes, you can borrow my shitty German car that only starts with a screwdriver.'" He lifts the tool—"A blunt object," newscasters and reporters could call it.

In the heat of the Beef Club, Deshler squints at the screen where his body is broken into a thousand pellets of light. Onscreen, a golden hamburger swings from a thin chain around the rearview and captures Dean's attention. So familiar. It locks his eyes for a few moments—he's seen it before. His head trembles, he doesn't remember this happening. The Cliff Drinker forgets about gin and beer and mouthwash.

Back onscreen, the camera jumps around. Napoleon's voice comes from behind the lens, "Well, is it a birthmark? I always thought it was, like, a skin disease. You know how it's all red and pink around his left eye? I just assumed Clifford Findlay had psoriasis or something, not a birthmark."

"Dude," the driver stutters, taking a break with the screwdriver. "Just tell Malinta what the bossman said, please."

"Oh, yeah, Mister Findlay said to borrow the car. He said he'd do anything for Deshler. But Findlay never gave any of us keys, I don't think. Can you believe that? Isn't that cool? I've parked this car a million times."

"Good enough," Malinta says, making a pouty face. "Let's just go. I want to score some—" She looks back at the camera and whispers like a little girl stealing candy. "D-R-U-G-S."

There's a heavy plastic *crack*. The camera jerks to Deshler's wavy head. "Ahhh Haaa!" The engine kicks to a meaty sports car start. "I knew I had the key somewhere." The shot zooms to the screwdriver's blue plastic handle sticking out from the ignition like a broken arm in a cast. Dean chugs the rest of a beer bottle and tosses it out the window with a shatter.

At the Beef Club, Deshler's throat hurts: "Napoleon...turn-this-off."

Cannonball words drop from Malinta's mouth. "What are you trying to do here? This is stupid, just, just..." Napoleon flashes a quick glance at her. Malinta's green eyes balloon with tears.

"What is this, dude?" Deshler asks, their hands lovingly clasped in fright. "I don't remember ever—"

"Just watch, it's getting good," Napoleon says.

Henry's bass cuts through everyone's concentration: *Blomp-Blomp-b-blomp-SCREEEEEEEEEEEEE.*

"Let's go, let's go, I'm so bored," Malinta says in Napoleon's directorial debut.

"Dude, put that thing away, I don't..." Deshler's voice trails as he slams the gearshift into reverse. "Want to be on camera."

The video drives through a parking garage and out the wide mouth of an exit.

"After this," Malinta says. "I'm done."

"Yeah, right," Dean chuckles.

"I'm serious. Good people don't use drugs."

"You, a good person?" Napoleon says, laughing.

"Shut up. Do you want me to call my guy?" Malinta says. "Or, Napoleon, honey, should we use yours?"

Deshler plunges the gas pedal completely down. The engine opens and sprays horsepower.

"Whoa, easy, easy," Napoleon says, steadying the shot. The screen looks out between the two front seats as the stolen car screeches onto the street.

Pandemic slams the kick drum. He hammers a roll on the car hood. The thick metallic punches rattle Napoleon's laptop. Someone cuts the lights. The room is dark and everyone hushes. The computer screen blossoms with intense clarity. A purple black light glow springs up around the stage. Two neon masks float in the darkness.

Staring between Dean and Napoleon, Malinta clutches a hand over her heart, bunching her shirt in a fist. The other hand goes cold and moist within Dean's palm. "Oh...my... God."

"Hey Napoleon," Deshler says, turning around, looking into the camera, still driving. "Remember that time you and I skipped work—"

The screen jerks out of control in a flash. The soundtrack for this intense lurch is an empty aluminum thud, much like Pandemic beating a car hood—hollow metal gongs. Then, thick weighty slaps—like raw brisket dropping on the sidewalk.

Hot burning rubber noises distort the cheap speaker into fuzz before the camera goes black.

The screen is darkness for only a beat.

The video starts up again. Napoleon jumps out of the back seat and pans around the empty downtown lit with streetlamps. The shot bobbles to the open passenger side window. He steadies the camera on Malinta's bloody head. "Whoa, shit," the cameraman barely utters. She has a deep cut on the left side of her head. Her blonde hair sponges the extra blood. She's unconscious.

Napoleon runs and the camera bounces with the sound of sneakers across wet pavement.

The backside of Deshler's head, hair all tangled, is clearly lit under an orange streetlamp. He looks down at the limp body stretched across the cement. The one he just smashed with Findlay's car.

SEVENTY-FOUR

The Japanese record moguls huddle shoulder-to-shoulder in a booth. They speak about Lothario Speedwagon in an airy native tongue. The online rumors of the band's breakup are obviously false, they say with a teenage thrill.

(Can you feel it?) the man says. (That excitement when we're on the verge of something great. I can't believe some valet left Lothario Speedwagon's CD in my car last time I was visiting. This feels like destiny.)

(They're still a cult band back home, but with the right advertising,) the woman grins. (They will be huge.)

(Marketing says *Broken Piano for President* is so hot the tape fetches sixty dollars at record stores in Tokyo.)

(A&R told me bootleg MP3s eclipsed twenty thousand downloads last week.)

(This is an easy sale. I almost don't want to hear the band,) the man says confidently. (I think the idea in my head will be impossible to live up to. It's happened so many times before.) The man's frown has a gravity—a hungry, swallowing sadness.

They playfully eye one another. She reaches under the table and pulls out a black leather bag.

SEVENTY-FIVE

Napoleon's camerawork slows. Huffing lungs stretch behind the lens. Deshler staggers like marching on two broken ankles, then crumbles into the cement.

Near Dean is a bloody body lying inside a halo of orange lamplight.

Napoleon flashes the shot up and down the street. All is empty and black.

"Get back in the car," Deshler says, his voice hollow and scared. "Dude, just turn around and get…"

The Cliff Drinker lifts up and drags himself out of the scene.

Napoleon zooms on the motionless body in the middle of the street. The shot starts at the leg and works a close-up around the bulged stomach and to the chest. He's in shirt and tie. There's a dark sticky pool gathering under the man's armpit and around his skull. With the streetlamp, the face is lit like a Hollywood glamour shot. The eyes are open and pushing out shocked. The skin is mayo white except for the dark pink and red splotch on the other side of his face, the same glob Napoleon was convinced is psoriasis.

"Napoleon," Deshler's distant voice echoes. "We can't wait here. Get in the car."

Napoleon holds the tight shot around the CEO's face. Findlay's dead teeth pause below purple lips. If Findlay is in a coma, like Lepsic claims, then the atom bomb was just a fancy firecracker.

There's an engine rumble and Napoleon swings the camera around. The ruby red sports car squeals and Deshler is a set of taillights weaving across traffic lanes without Napoleon. The film dissolves into an empty screen.

SEVENTY-SIX

Pandemic sits behind the drum kit wondering why Deshler chose this club of all places. *Not exactly a friendly crowd,* he thinks. *Maybe I should've stuck with the Russians.* A few light knocks on the oil drum clear those thoughts. *Nah, then I wouldn't get to play this gig.* An icy slither commands attention in his throat. *Would the Russians be proud if I stabbed Dad right now? Is there a terrorist cosmonaut code of honor?*

They would kill Henry. They'd rip his chubby skull apart.

Is that what the mission objectives were all about?

No. It was probably just a smokescreen, some horseshit line they fed me to keep quiet. His eyes adjust to the dark and he spots Dad back by the bar. *I was going through withdrawals, not thinking straight,* he decides. *Maybe there was no mission objective. People hallucinate their balls off when kicking. Maybe there was no Space Burger Contest, no cosmonaut terrorists.* His heart slows to a normal thump while he fingers a plastic baggie of white shards hidden under sock elastic.

"Dude, Juan, what's taking Dean so long?" Henry asks, leaning his guitar against the amp. "We need to get out of sight. This is a huge mistake. I think we should bail."

"I don't know," Pandemic says, realizing the last few days weren't hallucinations. "Wait, no, no. This is our big chance. This is our opportunity to do something with our lives. I don't know about you, but I've been thinking a lot about responsibility."

"You've what?"

A sudden bath of calm fills its water around Pandemic. *It's not Henry's fault Grandpa is dead. It's Dad's. I need Henry, because I need the band, because I need a family. These guys—unlike Dad and Grandpa—never asked me to be anyone else.* "I'm tired of being lazy, I want to put my mind to this and make it happen. Even if we don't get signed, this is what I want. I'll do anything for it. I'm not a hamburger guy. I don't want to be my dad or even my grandpa."

"Yeah," Hamler sighs and thinks about the last time he saw Pandemic's grandpa. He doesn't want to make a living doing that, either. He wants to spend the rest of his life with Martin. "I'm really sorry. I mean that."

"I know."

"I would take it back if I could."

"It's okay, man. I forgive you. Don't feel bad. I shouldn't have been treating you like this."

"Thanks," he says, locking eyes, understanding fully what a kind person Juan is. "Maybe you're right. We should split. I'll give Dean ten more minutes."

Pandemic lightly taps his stick to the floor tom skin. Its snap isn't as deep as normal. He still can't understand how the drum's tuning got ruined during its short trip from the practice space to the club.

Timothy Winters/Juan Pandemic lifts the mask and watches Hamler silently mouth, "Oh shit." He focuses on the entrance, still well lit, where two guys in buzz cuts and cheap ties flash shiny badges to Roland Winters.

SEVENTY-SEVEN

Dean swallows a deep breath, fingertips bubbling with numbness—the same guilty pang he used to feel when Mom blamed him for Dad's behavior. "So, what does this mean?" he manages to spit up before pushing that long breath through his nose.

"How could you?" Malinta's voice washes away into the chit-chatter of the dark club.

Napoleon folds up the computer. "I'll give you the original VHS and this, the only copy, for…well…" He tucks the white laptop under a sweaty, tapioca arm. "I haven't figured that part out yet."

Their eyes adjust to the darkness and each body becomes clearer and more carved out. They spend a few silent seconds watching each other's face.

"Hey, hey, big guy," McComb says, wedging his body against Deshler's. "A thousand sorrys. I wouldn't interrupt if it wasn't important, but our friends Toji and Yung-Yung are on their way back to the hotel."

In Deshler's skull, he's already muttered: "Look, man, I need a few minutes here." But his mouth hasn't unwound yet. He bites the tip of his tongue as neck muscles tighten. "Wh-what? What does *that* mean?"

"Not trying to scare you, bud, honestly. It's a good thing. They're convinced you guys are great." McComb's face is close, seeking the singer's eyes in the dark. "They didn't want to spoil anything by judging your performance. Must be some Japanese custom-thing, like taking off your shoes. *Anyhow,* don't let me ramble. Lothario Speedwagon is in. Congratulations. Consider the band signed." His lips pull tight and a whisper forms just loud enough for the entire group to hear: "And here's a little taste of your advance." He presses a small leather satchel into Deshler's stomach.

Malinta looks at the clock on the wall. She has five minutes to escape. She nearly forgot.

McComb leans behind Dean's ear. Cold eyeglass frames dig into Deshler's steaming skin. "A hundred grand up front," he pokes Deshler's arm. "Four hundred more when you guys decide which producer to record your debut with." He pulls back and leaves the bag in Deshler's arms. "Told you it wouldn't be in a sack."

"I don't—"

"As you were, gang." McComb disappears into the dark.

Compared to the previous evening Dean spent at the Beef Club, things couldn't be more different. Silence is replaced with hundreds of rowdy, confused voices. The overhead lights are replaced by dull purplish glow from the stage. Yesterday's peace and sense of purpose are replaced by some chaotic mess brewing inside.

Everything still smells like stale beer, though.

Napoleon blubbers out a wet, throaty laugh. "That'll," he slides into giggles. "That'll be *just* about right!" The laughs continue, loud and oblong, like some choking animal.

Malinta's green eyes lock on the tiny bag. "Just let it go, hon," she says, flicking eyes back at the wall clock. "It's not the end of the world. But if that tape landed in the wrong hands."

"Not to scare you," Napoleon says in a low blubber. "But it *will* if you don't…you know." Napoleon's hairy knuckles slip on the top of the bag. He gives a forceful jerk.

"*Fine,*" Dean says in a tone barely registering as a chirp. He is reminded there is a lot more coming from Moral Compass. He's reminded he's not in it for the money. "When, ugh, when'll I get the tapes?"

The new thousandaire presses a button on the side of the computer. A shiny silver disc pops out and he hands it over. Napoleon reaches into his back pocket and pulls out a black plastic VHS tape. A huge grin hangs between his cheeks.

"Well, I guess," Deshler says, mustering back his usual growl, his chest full of heat. "I guess this is goodbye forever. *Later.*"

The chunky valet spreads open the leather bag and sees it stacked with green bills. His lips crack a smile. "You bet your ass this is goodbye. All I ever wanted was your attention, man. To be friends on the same level—not Deshler Dean and Sidekick Number One. The way all this came together, it just felt like a good opportunity to prove my point. You know, you're not the only guy who wants people to listen to him. You just shove away anyone with another voice."

SEVENTY-EIGHT

Eyes finally adjust to the light. Everyone has a hazy red quality about them.

"Boys," CEO Winters says in his most professional voice. "These gentlemen are from the police department." He flashes a smile to Lothario's drummer and bassist.

Guy #1 with a buzzcut says, "I'm Detective Hogan." He points to Buzzcut #2. "And this is Detective Ireland."

The meth Pandemic inhaled before setting up still farts around his skull. Pure shit like this owns a momentum independent of anything else. "*Ah, Ireland,*" he slurs in a leprechaun voice. "*That's a fine Irish name.*"

Roland Winters jabs quick fingers at the rhythm section. "Boys! Take off those stupid masks. This is important."

"Relax, pop."

Winters' shoulders get broad and tense. He leans into his son.

"Why don't you," Juan says, "go into the corner and try to pretend you're grandpa some more?"

"Timothy!"

"Forget it," Juan leans back, loose. "You don't understand."

One detective butts in. Pandemic can't tell the difference between the two cops. "If we could, we'd like to ask you a few questions about the past couple days."

The police wait at the foot of the stage. Hogan is close enough to kiss the oil drum. Ireland smells the burning hot vacuum tubes in the back of the bass cabinet.

"We're busy, can't you see?" Henry says—wondering what Martin would do in this situation. Martin would've stuck up for himself. *Good job.*

"Henry," Roland Winters says with a stern, fatherly tongue. "This takes top priority, understand?"

"Whose priorities?"

"Yeah," Juan says with a cymbal tap.

"Oh no," Ireland or Hogan says, whichever is closest to the CEO. "We have lots of time. We'll gladly wait until after the... *performance*. Right partner?"

His partner agrees.

"Well, alright then, let's get some drinks, sound good?" Winters says, putting a hand on each detective's back. "Ever drank merlot from a box? Delicious. My father loved it."

Henry and Pandemic gawk with foreign confusion.

"Oh, and one last thing," the buzzcut says. "We have orders to use force if necessary. You know, just in case you get any wild ideas."

SEVENTY-NINE

Malinta Redding pushes her on-again/off-again boyfriend down the emergency exit stairwell. His sober senses are scrambled from the recent financial loss. A Hundred. Thousand. Dollars. *Poof.* His feet don't even stop shuffling until they realize Malinta's cattle-prodding him down gray cement steps two at a time.

"Wait, whoa, easy," he says, as the fog in his brain burns off like San Francisco around lunchtime. The stairs smell like basement. Walls are wet and cold against fingertips. "I need to get back up there. We still have a gig."

"Just move, it's almost ten. Go, sweetie, run," she says, shoving the back of his head, descending a spiral of blocky steps.

His voice echoes from the stairwell basement to the rooftop: "Malinta, are you out of your mind? If we don't play that show my career is over."

"Deshler, if you play that show you'll be *dead.*"

EIGHTY

"Psssst, Henry," a whisper forms in the dark behind the stage. "Henry, quick, back here."

Hamler flips off the mask and sharpens his espionage reflexes. The handbook doesn't specifically reference what to do when a strange voice calls your name from the dark. Henry thinks for a second that the book should, though—what could be more spy-like than creepy voices and shadows?

"Hello?" Henry says, stiffening fists, inching toward the black wall of the Beef Club.

For the second time in a day, Henry Hamler nearly jams his boyfriend's nose cartilage through his brain. Hostility Defense #01, some call it.

"Martin!" The clutch of his heart finds an extra gear and stomps the gas. Henry swoops low, out of breath, arms going tight around his man. Squeezing, squeezing, squeezing. Martin's hair smells, as expected, great. Henry never thought he'd smell it again—it's a comfort, a thrill. Kisses follow so fast Henry doesn't even examine them, he just repeats.

"Grab Juan, those two guys aren't cops." Martin says, wiggling from the hug. "If you two are left alone with them for five seconds they'll pry your spine out through your throat."

"Thank God you're okay. I thought for sure they killed you." He stops and takes a deep breath. The moment he's been dreaming about pauses when he thinks about the band. The urge for another kiss is tough to fight, but he manages. Martin looks so dead serious about this. "I'm sorry, but we have to play a show, I promised Juan. It's *the* biggest gig of our lives. I'm sorry, I can't. I have combat training. I can handle these guys."

"Henry, it's me. Why would I tell you something if it wasn't important?"

Hamler leans closer, crouching down to lip-level. Thinking about another round. "Where have you been? What happened?"

Martin comes into the light, so handsome and pure. "Not sure, I woke up in a highway underpass. Didn't Pandemic see?"

"Don't ask him."

"The radio was *really* dirty," he says from behind the drums.

"Look, I have a hunch. Nobody at headquarters seems to agree, but I can't see something happen to you. You mean too much to me."

EIGHTY-ONE

"Dean, if you play that show you'll be *dead*."

The second Malinta's lips close, the stairs jerk back and forth. There's a crashing, squealing explosion from the eighteenth floor. Lumps of concrete jar loose and twirl down the stairwell. The noise is so violent it could be a Lothario Speedwagon jam session pumped through nightmare-loud speakers.

Dean smells fireworks. Burnt hair. Bonfires.

The explosion barrel-rolls Malinta and Deshler across the stairs and smashes them against walls. A string of *kabooms* lob the pair further down the concrete.

Lights flicker off in a hellish strobe effect that reminds Deshler of that Butthole Surfers concert so many years ago, but with a higher chance of concussion.

An alien fear finds Dean: *Save Malinta. Is she okay?*

How's that alien? you're probably saying. It is a foreign jolt when you've never, ever, not once since being shipped off to foster care, worried about another person but yourself.

It's a shock.

EIGHTY-TWO

"Tonight on a very special *Nightbeat*," Sharon Smalley says.

It's ten at night and our show begins. After the bike messenger delivered a DVD with a handwritten note, the producer canned tonight's initial episode about volcano-proofing your home.

"Shocking footage of the Moscow Two and their captives. Hostage Carl Janomi, better known as imposter cosmonaut, Dimitri Nimov, and his daring undercover surveillance footage." The theme music rises to its climax. "The mystery of the cosmonaut reign of terror will finally be answered on *Nightbeat*."

Commercials start.

EIGHTY-THREE

Malinta is fine. She's actually the one dragging Dean. She swings open the exit door at the bottom of the crumbling stairs. Bright sunshine ignites above them. The dead Friday night street is lit up like noon as another apocalyptic bomb rattles through the building. The smell of charcoal and tire fires sweep over the city. Dean begins sweating.

Deshler coughs ash and noxious gases outside his old valet post. Black slime drools to the cement.

A rush of relief pillows Malinta's brain as the Beef Club windows explode like laughter in church. Pellets of flaming concrete and mahogany and body parts rain across the street. The mission is a success.

Things fell behind schedule tonight. Lothario Speedwagon was actually supposed to perform. But rock concerts rarely start on time—too many unscripted moments with voyeuristic valets and buzzcut detectives. Malinta honestly wanted Dean to have that last gig with his friends.

But, she thinks, marveling at their luck when Dean switched venues. *This works out for the best. More birds, less stones.*

Henry's bass amp was plugged tight as a tube of cookie dough with thirty pounds of plastic explosives. The speaker system shredded apart in a fiery pop that melted the club's windows at exactly ten o'clock. This triggered Pandemic's floor tom and the oil drum—both weighed down heavy with an explosive fertilizer compound. At least that's how Malinta was told it would happen.

She hates not being more hands-on. But Wally is supposed to be an expert at demolition. Her assistant is also said to be pretty slick. Rumor has it Wally spent time in the CIA. The explosives team supposedly had plenty of time to set up the trap. Plus, Malinta reminds herself, she's been trying not to be such a control freak. It's no way for a respectable lady to behave.

EIGHTY-FOUR

Nightbeat grabs our viewers by the throat the instant teeth whitening gel commercials end. Grainy home video footage ignites across the screen like Pandemic's drum kit. It's not a great shot, it wouldn't even fly at Sundance, but it's pretty simple to make out Henry Hamler and that scrubby beard standing in a bus full of bullet holes. He waves his doughy hands around explaining to his boyfriend, drummer and two terrorist cosmonauts everything we already know: there's a spy network amongst the two burger giants, he murdered Christopher Winters under orders from Roland and he was told to execute the VP of Bust-A-Gut's Marketing. Juan Pandemic confesses his sins: he's actually Timothy Winters—hardcore meth addict, son of Roland and contest winner. Martin explains his role, as well as how commonly he kills with orders from Findlay and Lepsic—he lists off Winters employees, foreign diplomats, rogue fry cooks, and the original Bonzo the Burger Clown as victims.

Henry never realized the blood pooling from Dimitri's blanket was corn syrup and dye—nobody ever actually saw any bullet-chopped flesh. Carl/Dimitri played possum for thousands of miles, hiding a fiber optic spycam and praying for this dramatic monologue. After getting dumped in a phone booth, he shed that wet blanket and walked to the safe house a few miles away. He quickly dubbed a DVD and called a bike messenger.

"Shocking footage," Sharon says. She interviews a professor

of economics from a nearby university. Our anchor asks what this video means to consumers. "Sharon, I'm afraid this is the Big One. A culinary Mount Vesuvius. Who do you trust when it comes to eating now? This footage proves both corporations are filthy, backstabbing liars. Add this to the already harsh publicity Winters Olde-Tyme Hamburgers and Bust-A-Gut have shouldered and you get two ruined American institutions. You get the consumer saying, 'Good riddance.'

"Sharon, the people will take their empty stomachs and their hearty wallets somewhere else. Personally, I don't see this as the death of two restaurant chains…which it is. Rather, this is an amazing opportunity to diversify American palettes. There's room for more than two fast food restaurants. Mark my words, someone will step up and fill this gulch, Sharon."

"Fascinating, professor. This has been a head-spinning day. Stay tuned for a recap before your eleven o'clock news."

Our commercial break is nothing but Healthy Wally's ads. Each one is tailored to be clean and innocent. Tailored to fill a gulch left by two major burger houses.

EIGHTY-FIVE

Deshler swallows his vomit in one fiery chug while Malinta opens a van door. He remembers being half-drunk a few nights ago, listening to his assistant explain, "Word on the street is, the cosmonauts are coming to chop off your head, sir. Maybe your testicles, too. Corey, in the mailroom, heard they only want one, though."

High above the street, thick tongues of fire lick against the outer wall of the hotel, thirsty for second helpings. A ketchup-colored blazer smolders in a lump by Dean's feet. It slowly fizzles into ash. The neck of a bass guitar hits the street and klonks around like a baseball bat. Snowflakes of bright pink papier-mâché nest in Dean's hair. The street is a warzone.

Deshler is fairly certain he's never met Sonja and Keith, though he recognizes them from the *Cosmonaut Watch* file Winters gave him. Wiping ashy goo from his chin, Deshler squints a few moments into the dark van. *They look skinnier on television,* he first thinks. Followed closely by: *Wait, does this mean I'm being neutered?*

Dean quickly scans the rest of the van—two slabs of beef who look like the dead cosmonauts, Yuri and Pavel, ride in the back and wave. Another guy, who strongly resembles Dean himself, sits shotgun with a gap tooth and scarred chin.

Dead bodies sprout up like random burning weeds across the street. Concrete, tables, chairs and greedy valets dissolve and crackle into charcoal eighteen stories up. Emergency sirens blast in the distance.

"Hop in, comrade," the man America knows as Cosmonaut Keith says in a perfect Midwestern accent. Keith's dialogue is so effortless, he and Dean could have grown up down the street from one another.

Sonja waves a friendly arm and pats the empty seat next to her with an inviting smile. Teeth still yucky.

"What are my options here?" Dean squeezes out, assuming any one of these people will shoot or stab or uniball him. His rib cage rattles at each heartbeat.

"Relax," Malinta purrs and swats his ass. "I said you'd die if you played that show. Trust us. Your blood's still pumping, isn't it?"

His chest says she's right, but his eyes dart all over. The van is clean, probably rented. "Are you going to," his throat stiffens like swallowing a handful of sand. "Hurt me…somewhere special?"

"No."

"Are you going to kill me?"

"The exact opposite, actually," Sonja says with no Russian accent, smiling even bigger. "We'd like to offer you a job."

"What would Gibby do?" he mutters, sensing a trap.

"He'd get in this stupid car before a body lands on him," Keith says. "That's what he'd do."

Deshler burns like he was a bass amp full of plastic charges. Malinta pushes, Keith pulls, and Dean stumbles into the van just before another spine-rumbling explosion detonates upstairs.

Dean catches a breath long enough to see Malinta behind the wheel. They are already pulling away from the bombing. She swerves to avoid the mess.

"You okay?" Keith asks. "Need any ice water or some Fat-Free Ahi Tuna Poppers?"

"Easy," Sonja says with English so perfect she could easily

anchor a show like *Nightbeat*. "I'm sure our friend has some questions."

"Yes," our hero's voice trickles. "Questions."

The town is rolling past the windows, all of it unfamiliar to Dean. Streetlamps showcasing another mysterious chunk of the town he thought he knew so well.

"So, like I was saying, we at Healthy Wally's have a great offer for you. A real leap up the ladder," Sonja says. "But I'm getting ahead of myself."

"Way ahead," Keith chimes.

"Wait," Dean's mouth hangs open, confused. "Healthy Wally's?"

"I hope you're comfortable with the explosions and all that jazz."

Dean's fear liquefies and leaks out his pores, disappearing into the van's air. "I heard you don't speak English. Aren't you guys Russian?"

"Well, it's time someone told you the truth...*again*. Malinta, darling, didn't you already have this chat with Deshler?" Sonja sighs. "Anyhow, the Russians, they're all dead."

"So you're a ghost?"

"Let me clarify. All five original cosmonauts starved to death up in that floating garbage can because *you* had them send their food out in a ridiculous space suit."

"Wait, whoa. Me?" His muscles tighten in defense, his brain cycles through odd scraps of memory. Burning hot adrenaline splashes through him. His fingertips dig into the seat—a rush like playing a great show with Lothario Speedwagon.

He feels like someone completely different. Not himself. He disagrees with his rant to Hamler: *you aren't really living until you are someone else.*

It all sounds like such bullshit now.

"I'm trying to kiss up to you, here. Relax. Healthy Wally's

got word of the new Space Burger Campaign, so our moles at Winters pulled some strings and next thing you know our team is at a casting call for the new Moscow Five. I'm pretty proud of myself. I think it's rare for a company's president to be so hands-on, don't you?"

Deshler sucks his tongue in disbelief.

"Not to toot my own horn, but look at the grunt work I've been doing the last few weeks. Whew. I'd like to see those two idiots." She points back at the flaming Beef Club. "Winters and that vegan hypocrite Lepsic, carry out an act like this on their own. Christ, I deserve a daytime Emmy."

"You said it, Miss Dayton," Keith pipes in. "The rest is history, Dean. We owe you everything. Heck, I mean, sacrificing your band so you could destroy Winters and Bust-A-Gut, what a plan. You're like a chess master. You see ten steps ahead."

"Easy, we're not hanging his portrait in the Louvre."

"Sorry, Wally."

"Look, let's cut the tofu here. You're not perfect, pal. Your work in the last six months has plugged more arteries than adding lard to the water supply," the woman who is not really Sonja says. "Relax, sit still, I'm not mad. But, I mean, a *deep-fried* hamburger?"

Words barely deserve to be called a mumble: "What would Gibby do?"

"He'd shut the bleep up and listen to *the* Wally Dayton," Malinta snaps from up front.

"Not very ladylike, Ms. Redding," Wally says. "I am not a broken record," her voice becomes stern and motherly. "If you want to be taken seriously and move up in the company, you need to be a...what?"

"*Lady.*"

"Pardon?"

"Lady. I need to be more ladylike. I need to watch my

language. It's in the handbook, I know I just—"

"Exactly," she nods, satisfied. "You are forgiven." She turns back to Dean, "Now, once Malinta told us about you and what you do, it seemed like a natural pair—like rice cakes and soy cheese. I knew we would work together and change the world."

Dean's panicked mind always reverts to the band. He imagines himself onstage with a blasting speaker system to his back. He's a foot taller than everyone, throwing bags of God-knows-what at the audience. Confidence fills his body and explodes through all muscles. "When were you planning on telling me?"

"Dean," Malinta says. "We've had this conversation about five times. This exact same one. Remember the paperwork you signed? You more or less planned this whole thing." She pauses a beat. "I mean, this drunk amnesiac routine is just part of your cover, right? An act?"

Dean reminds himself he could easily be at the Beef Club in a dancing pile of firewood right now. He's alive and he tells himself not to listen to this woman's stories.

"What about us?" He is near tears, throat some new kind of achy.

"Ughhhhh." Malinta's eyes are on the road. Her voice could go either way and it sends Deshler's heart loose.

"This doesn't sound ladylike, either," the guy in the passenger seat says. Dean can't get over the resemblance to himself.

"Shut up," Malinta snaps.

"Quit it, both of you," Sonja says.

"It's fine, Wally," she says. "Sweetie, jusqu'à hier. Okay?"

Her eyes are bold and green in the rearview. Speaking French is a rusty nail into his neck. "That means *until yesterday*," Dean says.

"Oh, I meant until tomorrow."

He senses her tone. It's one that isn't that far off from so many others—others that used him for no good.

His throat hurts. Something says not to reply, but Dean can't stop himself. "Jusqu'à demain." His stomach goes sick.

"Thanks for the lesson. Now, on to bigger and better." The face known around the world as Sonja Kassabova, the cosmonaut, leans in close—her breath smells wholesome, like a farmer's market. "Deshler, we are home free. Thanks to your concert and our explosives, all of Bust-A-Gut and Olde-Tyme Hamburgers' management are now deep-fried. I mean, sure, we have to confirm each casualty. But once that is done, our people—Healthy Wally's people," she says with a nudge to Dean's elbow. "Are embedded in both companies and they'll take over running these cholesterol factories into the ground." Her eyes glow shiny and wet. "It's the dawn of a new day for American calorie counts. Doesn't it feel terrific?"

She sucks in a long breath and whips her hair back and forth with glee.

"We want you on board for the whole thing. I personally chose you as our President of Development. But we need the photo negatives of all your inventions. You know, black replaced by white, hamburger patties replaced by polenta cakes, that's the gist. Use those same brain muscles, but for good instead of bad. You're lucky. Not every evil genius gets to pay for his sins. Most times they just get hung in a courtyard."

"So." Dean drawls out breath, pretending his lungs are full of cigarette smoke. He pushes thoughts of Malinta from under the light in his heart and out into the cold dark. It's tougher than you'd think. "You killed all those people? What about my band? What about the record company dude? What about Napoleon?" His chest is a particle smasher. Tiny explosions vaporize inhibitions, his chains.

"Look, pal," she says lovingly. "In order to make an omelet

you have to break some soy-based vegan egg substitute." She pauses. "Oooh, that's good. Write that down. We should whip up a breakfast menu."

"Soy-based, vegan. Got it, Wally," the man America thinks is Keith Kassabova says.

"Do you see what I'm saying? Those guys, I'm sorry, but they were a necessary sacrifice. They were witnesses to Keith and Sonja. That record company man, well, *whoops*. And I did you a favor by vaporizing Napoleon—we've seen your *video*. Listen, we'll compensate you the money you were going to get advanced from Moral Compass, no sweat. And we have the lawyers to make your drunken hit-and-run accident disappear, too."

A string of sour notes play through Dean's head, similar to the guilty urges that ripped him apart as a teenager. These burn hotter, though, knowing he is actually to blame this time.

The cosmonaut/terrorist/restaurateur peps up: "Not only did we save your can, but we're giving you the career of a lifetime. Penance through health food. You're the best in the biz and we need you."

He doesn't have a hangover, but Dean's head is a nuclear test site. Black gas clogs his mind. "But you can't offer me a record contract, can you? You can't offer me a career as an artist. All my work with Lothario Speedwagon is ruined if I take this job." Dean smashes the seat in front of him. His knuckles are skinned back and bloody.

"It's still ruined if you don't. Sorry," Wally says.

"Soy-based vegan egg substitute, dude," Keith says.

"Just relax. We'll talk about that once we're back at headquarters and you're in a new, comfy office."

"Won't people wonder about me? Why I'm working for you guys now?"

"That won't be a problem, buddy," fake-Keith says, putting

a gun to the Deshler Dean lookalike in the front seat. "Meet the solution to your hit-and-run issues. Sorry, Rodrigo, but these aren't the fake Hollywood bullets some people get."

In the back seat, Yuri and Pavel high-five each other and whisper: "That was awesome, dude."

Wally Dayton speaks lovingly: "See, we had Rodrigo impersonate you on *Nightbeat* a while back. Pretty good likeness, huh? I mean, yes, he took some artistic license with the script, but we were happy."

"Clear your calendars and your colons," the imitation Dean says, sheepishly.

"Yes, Rodrigo, you're a wonderful improviser."

Dean takes in a breath and tries to calm down. "Thank God. I didn't remember doing that show. I thought I was crazy." He blows across rapidly bleeding knuckles.

"Not crazy, but if you turn down this offer, you might be. See, we'll plant *somebody's* body back at the Club." She nods toward Rodrigo. "Make it look like Deshler Dean expired in the flames. And you're a free man."

"Goodbye jail time," Keith says. "Can't convict a dead man for running over Clifford Findlay."

The guilt crushes Dean's temples, but he is interrupted by the fake Deshler. Rodrigo stiffens. "So wait, we're not going to the tofu factory?"

"The tofu factory in the sky." Keith wallops the back of his skull with a karate chop and the Deshler Dean imposter dangles limp into his seatbelt.

"It's a no-brainer, hon," Malinta says, pulling the van around the block and back in front of the club.

Dean can't concentrate. *Hon. Hon? HON?*

"I need some time to think about this." Bits of Beef Club rain on the metal rooftop, sounding like a drum roll on Pandemic's Konkers.

"Sorry. Not a luxury I can afford. The Moscow Four and I have some massive cosmetic surgery to be removed. I need to get out of the underground and run a successful restaurant. Good gosh, I will *not* miss these silly teeth." She flicks a gross incisor.

The other fake cosmonauts mumble, griping about bad haircuts, awful dentures, uncomfortable contacts. Something wet splatters the van roof.

"So, Dean," Dayton says, confident and pleased. "You're either in…or you're in. I'll toss in some free plastic surgery if it helps. God knows your nose will thank you."

Dean leans forward and rubs his eyes. When vision shines back, he glances at the hotel. The front doors burst open in a cloud of soot and three men crawl out. Hamler and his boyfriend lead the pack, while a skeleton-thin Pandemic follows close behind.

Dean realizes for the first time in a long time that he is in control. People are listening. His knees punch together realizing who has been at the wheel all along. "What would Deshler do?"

ACKNOWLEDGMENTS

Several people helped keep this book going for many years. None more so than:

- Cameron Pierce.

- James Greer.

Thank you.

ABOUT THE AUTHOR

• Patrick Wensink is the author of the novel *Black Hole Blues* and the story collection *Sex Dungeon for Sale!*

• His humor writing has appeared in Groupon. His music journalism has appeared in Willamette Week, Skyscraper, Smalldoggies, and others.

• He is the recipient of the Patrick Wensink Foundation's 2011 Nobel Prize for Good Looks.

• He lives in Louisville, KY with his wife and son.

• Discover all things Wentastic: www.patrickwensink.com.

A NOTE FROM LAZY FASCIST

Thank you for purchasing this Lazy Fascist original. Without your continued support, independent publishers like us would cease to exist. I hope you enjoyed *Broken Piano for President* and have an opportunity to discover some of the other wonderful titles in our ever-growing catalog.

If you're just now joining us, we want to welcome you aboard and offer a brief explanation of what we do: Lazy Fascist publishes authors who, through careful exploration of unique linguistic landscapes, create monstrous, unclassifiable fictions. We value explosive language over explosive weapons, but we think it's best when we can have our Bruce Willis with our Borges.

We've published everything from minimalist dark comedies to meta-fictional SF, along with historical fiction, fairy tales for adults, and hybrid plays. We seek out books that are emotionally hard-hitting, critically engaging, and exhibit crisp, original prose. These books tend to be difficult to pigeonhole under any one banner, but together they form a complex mosaic of the disenfranchised, the poor, and others who are struggling to survive—and make an impact—in an increasingly bleak world. However, we're not all about doom and gloom. We like to laugh, demand the absurd, and love great storytelling above all else.

We also love zombies.

If you've been following us for a while, then you know how exciting 2012 will be. Several of last year's releases—

The No Hellos Diet by Sam Pink, *Of Thimble and Threat: The Life of a Ripper Victim* by Alan M. Clark, and *A Plague of Wolves and Women* by Riley Michael Parker—appeared on prominent year's best lists and this year, we'll be publishing even more of today's top authors. Here are a few of the Lazy Fascist titles you can look forward to in 2012:

Anatomy Courses by Blake Butler and Sean Kilpatrick

The Obese by Nick Antosca

Zombie Bake-Off by Stephen Graham Jones

The Devil in Kansas: Three Stories for the Screen
by David Ohle

Colony Collapse by J.A. Tyler

A Pretty Mouth by Molly Tanzer

No One Can Do Anything Worse to You Than You Can
by Sam Pink

I Am Going to Clone Myself Then Kill the Clone and Eat
It by Sam Pink

The Collected Works of Scott McClanahan Vol. I
by Scott McClanahan

Dodgeball High by Bradley Sands

FOR MORE DRUNKEN ANTICS
WITH DESHLER DEAN, VISIT
BROKENPIANOFORPRESIDENT.COM.

CPSIA information can be obtained at www.ICGtesting.com
Printed in the USA
LVOW101037240712

291241LV00004B/1/P